TWELFTH KNIGHT

TWELFTH KNIGHT

ALEXENE FAROL FOLLMUTH

TOR
TEEN

TOR PUBLISHING GROUP
NEW YORK

TWELFTH KNIGHT

Copyright © 2024 by Alexene Farol Follmuth

All rights reserved.

Endpaper art by Little Chmura

A Tor Teen Book
Published by Tom Doherty Associates / Tor Publishing Group
120 Broadway
New York, NY 10271

www.torpublishinggroup.com

Tor® is a registered trademark of Macmillan Publishing Group, LLC.

The Library of Congress Cataloging-in-Publication Data
is available upon request.

ISBN 978-1-250-88489-3 (hardcover)
ISBN 978-1-250-88490-9 (ebook)

Our books may be purchased in bulk for promotional,
educational, or business use. Please contact your local bookseller
or the Macmillan Corporate and Premium Sales Department
at 1-800-221-7945, extension 5442, or by email at
MacmillanSpecialMarkets@macmillan.com.

First Edition: 2024

Printed in the United States of America

0 9 8 7 6 5 4 3 2 1

To David, for twenty years of little talks,
and to the women of fandom,
who first made me feel there was space for my voice.

DRAMATIS PERSONAE

VIOLA REYES: A young woman of seventeen years and one of our main protagonists, Viola, often called Vi, is headstrong and self-assured, with an occasionally shrew-like temperament.

JACK ORSINO: A popular and exceptionally talented athlete, our other protagonist, Jack, is often referred to as "Duke" after his place in his family's football legacy.

SEBASTIAN REYES: Often called Bash, Vi's twin brother is a cheerful thespian as well as a convenient source of personal inspiration.

OLIVIA HADID: Wealthy, beautiful, and popular, Olivia is the estranged girlfriend of Jack Orsino and classmate of Vi Reyes who is harboring a mysterious secret.

ANTONIA VALENTINE: Vi's best friend and closest confidante, who is also very entrenched in the masculine worlds of fandom and gaming.

CESARIO: Named after Vi Reyes's favorite character on her favorite TV show, *War of Thorns*, Cesario is Vi's masculine alter ego in the game *Twelfth Knight*.

TWELFTH KNIGHT

BATTLE THEME MUSIC

Jack

When I was a kid, everyone naturally assumed that because I was the son of Sam Orsino, I was an All-American quarterback in the making.

They were . . . *half* right.

I mean, I can see the logic. My dad, the only son of a janitor and a waitress, famously set the Northern California record for passing yards when he was at Messaline High in the '90s, only to be surpassed four years ago by my older brother—so yeah, I have some idea of what people expect from me. The family arm! Practically my birthright. People assume I'll be no different from my father and brother: a playmaker, a leader. Someone who can command the field, and in a lot of ways, they're not wrong.

I do see the game differently than other people. I think the commentators usually call it vision, or clarity, even though to me it's something more innate. When Illyria was recruiting me last fall, they said I saw the field like a chess prodigy, which feels closest to the truth. I know where people are going to be, how they'll move. I feel it somewhere, like the tensing of a muscle. I can sense it like a change in the wind.

Like, for example, right now.

Messaline Hills, California, isn't exactly Odessa, Texas, but for an affluent San Francisco suburb, we know how to pull off your classic Friday-night lights. The late-August heat burns away as the sun molts into stadium brights, transforming the familiarity of our home turf to the singular mythos of game day. The stands are packed; whoops and chatter buzz from the crowd, all alight with Messaline green and gold. There's a snap from a drumline snare, sharp like the edge of a knife. From the field, the tang of sweat and salt mixes with the charred scent of barbeque, the storied hallmark of our home opener's Pigskin Roast.

Tonight, standing on this field for my final year feels like the start of an era. Destiny, fate, whatever you want to call it—it's here on the field with us; I can sense it from the moment our next play is called, my team collectively suspending in time for the same fleeting breath.

"HUT!"

There's immediate pressure on Curio, our quarterback, so I force some space and quickly change directions, shaking off a linebacker to reach Curio's left for the handoff. We've run this exact play hundreds of times; it worked last week in our season opener, an away game against Verona High, and it's going to work again now. I take the ball from him and spot an oncoming defender, shouting for a blocker to take my right. Naturally he misses, so I pivot again to drop a right-side defender. He can't hang. Too bad, so sad.

Now it's just a forty-yard run with the entire Padua defense at my heels.

You know how I said everyone was half right about me following in my dad's footsteps? That's because I'm an All-American *running back*. It's who I am, what I love. After watching me take off with the ball every chance I got during my first peewee season, my coach had the foresight to start me at running back instead. My dad supposedly threw a fit—once prophesied to be the rare Black quarterback who could rival Elway or Young, *his* career had ended abruptly, with an injury cutting his pro dreams short. Naturally, he saw in his two sons the mirror-slivers of his own glory, craving for us the greatness foretold for himself.

But when I took off for the full length of the field, even King Orsino couldn't argue with that. They say every great football player's got some supernatural spark, and mine—the thing that makes me the best player on the field—is that when I catch even a *glimpse* of an opening, I can outrun anyone who tries to stop me. What I've got absolute faith in is the pulse in my chest, the sanctity of my own two feet. The knowledge that I will fight my way back up from every hard fall. Most people don't know what their purpose in life is, or why they exist, or what they were meant for, but I do. In the end, it's a very short story.

In this case, only forty yards.

By the time I'm across the goal line the band is blasting our school fight song, the whole town going wild in the stands. As far as home openers go, I'm definitely giving them a show, and they return the favor with their usual chant—"Duke Orsino," a variation on my father the king and my brother the prince.

This year, nobody uses the phrase *if* we win State, but *when*.

I toss the ball over to the ref while glancing at the too-late Padua cornerback, who looks less than pleased about me scoring on his watch yet again. He's probably the fastest person on his team, which must seem like a hell of an accolade if you haven't met me. Some people really take issue with coming in second—just ask Viola Reyes, the student body VP to my president. (She demanded a recount after the results had us coming in within twenty votes, ranting something about election protocols while staring me down like my popularity was somehow both malicious and personal.) Unfortunately for the Padua cornerback—and Vi Reyes—I really am that good. The speed and agility that secured my spot at Illyria next fall isn't something to sneeze at, and neither is the fact that I spend every minute of every day being likable enough for ESPN.

With . . . *minor* exceptions. "A little more steam next time," I advise the cornerback, because what's a game without a little smack talk? "Few more sprints and you'll have it."

He scowls and flips me off.

"ORSINO!"

Coach motions me over to the sideline as we swap with special teams, rolling his eyes when I saunter over with what he calls my "eat shit" grin.

"Let your runs do the talking, Duke," he grunts to me, not for the first time.

Humility's easy to preach when you're not the one being lauded by the crowd. "Who says I'm doing any talking?" I ask innocently.

He glances at me sideways, then gestures to the bench. "Sit."

"Sir, yes, sir." I wink at him and he rolls his eyes.

Did I mention that Coach occasionally goes by Dad? Yep, that's right—King Orsino became Coach Orsino, and thanks to his work in the community as varsity football coach, he's still the local boy made good. He won Man of the Year last year from the Bay Area Black Business Association, plus he's been honored at almost every school function in the last decade. Together, our wins while proudly wearing Messaline emerald and gold afford us a rare place in this town's predominantly white history.

When it comes to the Orsino skill on the field, some call it luck. We call it a legacy. Still, compared to my father and brother, I've got a lot more to prove. At my age, they were both All-Americans and top-recruited NCAA prospects, too—but *unlike* me, they had State Champion titles under their belts by the start of their senior season. I may be the best running back in California, arguably the country, but I'm still fighting my way out from under a shadow that goes for miles. As far as nicknames go, Duke Orsino is a great one until you consider what that actually means in terms of lineage. Every year is a vicious new experiment in *close, but no cigar.*

Still, it's a good thing I've got such a powerful motivator, because while I'm having the game of my life tonight—I've already run for two hard touchdowns so far, bringing me within a single good run of the Messaline record for career yards gained—Padua's got a battalion of big defenders putting in work to keep our offensive line at bay. Our defense is holding their own against Padua's sleeve of trick plays, but Curio, our senior QB who's finally risen through the ranks, isn't nearly the player Nick Valentine was in his senior season. It'll be up to me to make sure we're getting that ball to the end zone come hell or high water, which means my all-time record is definitely getting broken tonight.

I shake myself at the sound of the Padua crowd's cheers; their receiver makes an incredible catch that leaves our side of the stands groaning. This will be a tough one, definitely. But these stakes, however crucial, are no different from any other game. It's always about the play right in front of me, and the moment it passes, we're on to the next one.

Ever forward. Ever onward.

I roll out my neck and exhale, rising to my feet at the exact moment that a perfect spiral gets Padua to first and goal. If they score here, it's our turn next. It's *my* turn. My moment. Everyone I know is out there in the stands holding their breaths, and I won't let them down. Before I walk off the field tonight, they're all going to bear witness to my destiny: a winning season.

A state championship.

Immortality itself.

Am I being dramatic? Yes, definitely, but it's hard not to be romantic about football. And I don't think it's unreasonable to say there's always been something waiting for me. Something big, and this is my chance to take it.

So right now, it's time to run.

𝔙𝔦

Things in the game are definitely getting heated. We've lost some of our best players from last year, and with a pace this arduous, focus is everything, so getting this team to a win is going to take . . . well, a miracle.

But miracles have been known to happen.

"They're coming" is all Murph says. Instantly, I feel a shiver. This is the exciting part, but also the time when most mistakes are made. I lean forward, anxious but not concerned. We can do this.

(We *have* to do this. If we don't, there's no way I get my shot, and that's just not an acceptable alternative.)

On my left, Rob Kato's the first to respond. "How many are there?"

Murphy, or Murph (whose real name is Tom, though nobody calls him that—honestly, don't bother learning anyone's names, they're really not important), says from across the table, "Ten."

"Some people will have to take two." That's Danny Kim. He's new—not just to the group, but to the game itself. Which is exactly as helpful as you'd expect, and he's just as unworthy of committing to memory. (I'd happily number them instead for ease of consumption, but I've been in all the same AP classes with them for the last, oh, four hundred years, so for purposes of atmosphere, let's pretend like I care they exist.)

"I will," volunteers Leon Boseman, on Rob's left. The boys call him Bose or Bose Man, a brotastic endowment of reverence with no meaningful effect on his personal appeal.

"And me," I say quickly.

"What?" That's Marco Klein, on Murph's left. He's a huge bitch. But I'm used to him, so better the devil you know, I guess.

"Check my character sheet, Klein," I growl. "I've got a black belt in—"

From outside Antonia's kitchen window there's a sudden, deafening roar, followed by the blast of a marching band.

"Ugh, sorry." Antonia rises to her feet and closes the window. "Gets so loud on game days."

The distant sounds of high school football are successfully muffled, leaving us to return to our kitchen table game of ConQuest. Yes, *that* ConQuest, the role-playing game for nerds, ha-ha, we know. The thing is that 1) we *are* nerds, by which I mean we collectively make up the top 1 percent of our graduating class and are probably going to rule the world someday even if it loses us some popularity contests (don't get me started on the idiotic grift that is student body elections, I *will* throw up), and 2) it's not just for antisocial weirdos in basements. Did you know that tabletop role-playing games like ConQuest are the forerunners to massive multiplayer online RPGs like *World of Warcraft* and *Twelfth Knight*? Most people don't, which drives me crazy. I hate when people dismiss revolutionary forms of media just because they don't understand them.

Though, don't get me wrong—I get where the misconception comes from. Murph's floppy ash-blond hair is currently swept forward to cover an Orion's belt of cystic acne. Danny Kim has anime-style black hair that still doesn't take him past my shoulder. Leon is best known for his hyena cackle; Rob Kato's prone to uncontrollable stress sweats; Antonia—the only person here I actually like or respect, by the way—is wearing a hand-knitted vest-thing that's more lumpy than trendy; and hey, even on a good day I still look like I might be twelve, so current company might not be the perfect sell. Still, this game *is* a revolution, regardless of whether a bunch of high-achieving teens have settled into their post-pubescent forms or not.

"You were saying?" Antonia prompts me, though I'm still annoyed with Marco. (He once begged me to make Murph invite him, as if Murph has ever been in charge.)

"I've got a black belt in Tawazun," I finish irritably. It's Arabic for balance, and one of the five major fighting disciplines from the original ConQuest game. They say that *War of Thorns*—my favorite TV show, a medieval fantasy adaptation about warring kingdoms—originated from a massive homebrewed ConQuest campaign that the book series' author, Jeremy Xavier, played QuestMaster for when he was a student at Yale. (He's kind of my hero. Every year I cross my fingers that I'll run into him at MagiCon, but no luck yet.)

"Isn't Tawazun like, ceremonial fan fighting or something?" says Danny Kim, who, once again, doesn't know anything. Yes, there are hand fans in Tawazun, but the use of a fan as a weapon is not uncommon in martial arts. And anyway, the point is that it's all about using your opponent's momentum against them, which makes it a super practical choice for a smaller female character like Astrea. (That's me: Astrea Starscream. I've been role-playing as her for two years now, refining her story a little more each campaign. Basically, she was orphaned and trained in secret as an assassin for hire, but then she found out her parents were murdered by the people who trained her and now she wants revenge. A tale as old as time!)

Before I can correct yet another of Danny Kim's annoying misconceptions, Matt Das answers. "Tawazun is basically jiu jitsu."

"And either way, I said I could do it," I add, "which is all you need to know." There hasn't been much combat yet; we got into a little skirmish earlier with some bandits, leaving us with a small onyx arrowhead that none of us know what to do with. Still, I shouldn't have to prove anything to him.

"Why don't you just, like, seduce him?"

Okay, I kind of hate Danny Kim. "Do you see 'seduction powers' listed anywhere on my Quest Sheet?" I demand, this time not very patiently. Danny exchanges a glance with Leon, who brought him here, and suddenly I want to smack both their heads together like a pair of coconuts. But I don't, of course. Because apparently I'm supposed to be nicer if I want people to agree with me. (Big ups to my grandma for that sage advice.)

"Believe it or not, Danny," I say with a pointed smile, "I'm just as capable of imaginary martial arts as you are." More so, actually, since I've done Muay Thai with my twin brother Bash for the last four years. (Bash does it for stage combat, but I do it for moments like this.)

Danny Kim doesn't smile back, so at least he's not a complete idiot.

"I can try something," Antonia cuts in, ever the peacemaker of the group. "I've got a love potion that might work. Feminine wiles or whatever, right?"

She did *not* just say feminine wiles. I love her dearly, but come on.

"Is that your official move?" Murph asks her, reaching for the dice.

I smack a hand out to stop him because for the love of god, ugh. "Larissa Highbrow is a *healer*," I remind the rest of the table, because every campaign, *without fail*, leaves at least one of us in need of Antonia's healing powers in order to keep going. She's basically the most crucial character here, which naturally the boys are unable (or unwilling) to recognize. "You should stay back and tend to the wounded."

"She's right," says Matt Das, who's surprisingly helpful despite being new to our group. (Matt is tan and wavy-haired and seems well acquainted with deodorant, so if I cared what anyone here looked like, I'd say his appearance was reasonably good.) "The rest of us can handle combat amongst ourselves."

"Or—" I begin to say, only to be interrupted.

"Can we stop talking about this and actually fight?" whines Marco.

"*Or*," I repeat loudly, ignoring him, "maybe we should try diplomacy first."

In unison, the boys groan. Except Matt Das.

"Uh, they're coming at us with axes," says Rob.

"Murph didn't say shit about axes," I remind him, since as Quest-

Master, Murphy's the one who narrates the game and gives us the information we need. And likewise, he *doesn't* give us information that's not applicable. "Do they have weapons, Murph?"

"You can't see from this distance," Murphy answers, briefly skimming the page in the QuestMaster's Bible (it has a stupid name and I covet it). "But they're getting closer by the minute," he adds, reaching blithely for a pizza roll.

"They're getting closer by the minute!" Rob informs me urgently, as if I cannot also hear what Murph just said.

"I get that, but it might be a mistake to just *assume* they're armed. Remember what happened to us in the Gomorra raid last year?" I prompt, arching a brow as they all nod, minus Danny Kim, who still knows nothing. "We don't even know if these guys are with the rest of the army."

Luckily for me, I'm being blatantly ignored.

"I say we shoot first, ask questions later," says Leon, blowing off the invisible barrel of an imaginary pistol even though his character, Tarrigan Skullweed, specifically uses a bow and arrow.

I glance witheringly at him. He winks at me.

"How far away are they?" Antonia asks Murph. "Is there a way that someone can get closer to see whether they're armed?"

"Try it and see," invites Murph, shrugging.

"Oh sure, does anyone volunteer to fall on *that* grenade?" demands Marco.

Okay, this is exhausting. "Fine. Combat it is," I say, "and let the die be cast."

"Is that from *War of Thorns*?" asks—who else—Danny Kim. Yes, it is, and it's also from a scene right before Rodrigo, the main protagonist who is honestly kind of a dud compared to the other characters, leads his army into a losing battle.

"Whose turn is it?" I ask loudly.

"Mine." Rob sits up. "I take my sword and throw it directly at the heart of the biggest warrior."

Well, that's typical, but at least Rob's character, Bedwyr Killa (I know, eye roll, but it's actually not the worst of the bunch), is massive and strong in addition to being impractically reckless.

Murph rolls. "It's a successful hit. The leader of the group falls to the ground, but just as he does, his arm comes up, and—"

Oh my god. I swear, if he's holding a white flag . . .

"—the white piece of cloth in his hand flutters to the ground," Murph concludes, and I groan. Of course. "The rest of the horde falls around their leader in anguish."

"Great work, boys," I sarcastically applaud them.

"Shut up, Vi," says Marco half-heartedly.

"So what now?" asks Matt Das.

If I were in charge? We'd use Antonia's character's magic to heal him and resolve the conflict, possibly trading with the horde for supplies or extracting information about the missing gems that make up the whole purpose of this campaign. But I already know there's no point bringing that up—if I'm going to successfully parlay the group's good graces by the end of the night, then I need to win this game *their* way.

If the boys crave violence, then violence they shall have.

"We've obviously got to fight now, don't we? I'm next," I remind them, turning to Murph. "I approach the horde's lieutenant and offer safe passage in exchange for surrender."

Murphy rolls. "No go," he says with a shake of his head. "The lieutenant demands blood and lunges, aiming a knife at your chest."

We do the usual contested strength check, but I know my skills. "I wait until the last possible moment, then slip the knife, twisting his arm around and directing it into his kidney."

Murphy rolls again. "It's a critical hit. The lieutenant is down."

I sit up straighter, pleased. The boys look impressed, which reminds me that even if they're the portrait of incompetence, I do actually want them to believe I can handle this.

"I take the next biggest one," says Marco. "With my mace."

"I shoot an arrow," adds Leon.

"At what?" I ask, but he waves me away.

"Arrow lands in the blade of a horde member's shoulder, but it's not fatal. Mace is a swing and a miss," says Murph.

"Another swing," says Marco.

"I use my lasso," says Matt Das, whose character is kind of weirdly Western—a vestige from an old campaign, I suspect.

"Lasso holds, but not for long. Mace lands, but now they've got you surrounded."

The others are excited about the possibility of battle, but what everyone always forgets about ConQuest is that it's a *story*. As in, there are good guys and bad guys, and all the characters have motives. Why would the horde come over with a white flag? We must have something they want. They're built into the quest regardless of who our characters are, so it has to be something we've picked up within the game. That weird arrowhead . . . ?

Oh my god, I'm an idiot. The quest is literally called *The Amulet of Qatara*.

"I remove the Amulet of Qatara from my holster and hold it aloft," I blurt out, shooting to my feet, and everyone turns to stare at me. Blankly. (This is why I hate playing with people who don't pay attention. It actively makes me dumber.)

Murph, however, gives me a noncommittal thumbs-up. "The fighting stops," he says, "and the horde requests a personal parlay with Astrea Starscream."

Finally. It's time to get this done.

PLAYER VS. PLAYER

Jack

My girlfriend Olivia's cheerleader-sanctioned curls fall into her eyes, so she doesn't see me wink when I make my way back onto the field for our next possession. Her friends do; they giggle and nudge her, but by the time she looks up I'm already manifesting myself in the Padua end zone. *You gotta see it,* Coach says. *See it, make it happen. Success is not an accident.* I've got scrolls of his wisdom in my head that play out like flashes on a neon marquee. *Champions are half intention, half work.*

"Just get the ball to Duke" was Coach's last instruction to Curio.

This'll be a draw, meant to look like a passing play. A bit of misdirection, just in case Padua's figured out a thing or two about the way I play this game—not that I expect them to stop me. It's one thing to read the field and another thing to control it. I line up directly behind Curio, with junior hotshot Malcolm Volio on my left and sophomore receiver Andrews on my right.

Curio drops back, scanning the field as Andrews positions himself for what looks like an intended catch, and then Curio turns and delivers the ball to me. I make it through the blockade of guards, centers, and tackles, and boom. The field is wide open.

The same cornerback from earlier realizes he's fallen for the trap. He changes directions, so I veer toward the visitors' sideline, narrowly missing an oncoming tackle. It pushes me farther out than I'd like, nearly running me off the field, but I meticulously tightrope the sideline. It's funny how you can know a field after so many times running it, reading it reflexively beneath your feet. I know in my bones when I cross that first-down mark; ten yards, then twenty, then thirty. By now the crowd is screaming, the visiting side booing loudly from my left to mix with the chants of my name to my right, and I can't help a smile.

The end zone is in sight by the time the cornerback finally reaches me like an arrow, shouldering me out of my narrow strip of safety. He shoves into me once, leaving me struggling for a few more yards, then a second time, ramming into my torso. I nearly crash into one of Padua's cheerleaders, catching myself just before I pitch headfirst into their entire offensive line.

I'm forced out of bounds before I can reach the end zone, which leaves the cornerback looking smug as hell. Doesn't matter; I still got us within ten yards of a touchdown, meaning at worst we'll get a field goal, breaking the tie. I just hope we do it quickly—there's still time to put more points on the board, and I want to be the one to do it.

It only occurs to me as I'm jogging back for the next play that I just ran about eighty yards. Impressive on its own, but better yet: record-breaking. I hear a few of the Messaline alums cheering and glance over, spotting Nick Valentine, our former QB and my best friend. He's holding up a poster that says "DUKE ORSINO" and a picture of a goat, as in GOAT: Greatest of All Time. Most career yards in Messaline history.

Not a big deal, I tell myself, but then I spot my dad on the sideline, chewing his usual stick of Big Red and typing something quickly into his phone. He gives me a thumbs-up, stoic as ever, even though I know for a fact he just texted my brother Cam.

Yeah, okay. I won't lie, this feels pretty good.

"Hell of a run," says Curio when I take my spot for the slant. "Feel like going again?"

"And take all the glory? You try for once," I say. He rolls his eyes and calls for a passing play, so this one isn't intended for me.

Curio's throw isn't perfect, not that I get a full glimpse of what happens. The Padua cornerback is covering me now, probably instructed to do whatever it takes to keep me out of the end zone. Understandable, but he's starting to piss me off. He shoves me, pointlessly, and I shove back.

His response, unpleasant by the looks of it, is inaudible over the sound of our band playing the Messaline "charge" chant. I line up near Volio again, buzzing with annoyance, and catch his sidelong glance at me.

"You good, Duke?"

"Peachy keen, Mal. This one's mine. Curio!" I call, and our quarterback looks at me, the two of us exchanging a glance that says this'll be a blast, literally. I'm gonna take the ball and run it into the Padua end zone where it belongs.

The play starts and the ball is mine, tucked safely into my torso while I lower my head and shove myself forward by sheer force of will. My mom hates to watch this; she covers her eyes, but for me, this is when the game feels most like war—there's something undeniably primal about it, and dangerous, too. I grit my teeth around my mouthguard and pummel as far forward as I can, the usual necessary evil of gambling my body based on four years of weight training, a dash of good karma, and a whole lot of blind faith.

Almost immediately I'm wrestled sideways from my right and left, wrenched in two separate directions. Something smacks into the front of my helmet; I tuck my chin in time to prevent my head snapping back, but elsewhere there's an impact to my right knee. It's a blow from a weird angle, a hard, forced contortion—

(Shit.)

—and in a blinding splice of pain I find myself at the bottom of a dogpile, the ball forced into my gut just a yard shy of a touchdown.

For a second I'm too dazed to get up, blinking away stars.

Does anything hurt?

No, nothing hurts. (This happens every time I get hit. A flash of something; nerves or whatever.) I'm slow to get up, though, letting Curio pull me to my feet while I try to recover my equilibrium. Once I'm upright, I'm fine.

I think.

I bend the knee back and forth, testing.

"Everything okay?" Curio asks in a low voice.

"Yeah." I would know if something was wrong, right? "Yeah, fine."

Beneath his helmet, he's expressionless. "Looked bad."

For a second I wonder, but then Coach calls for a time-out from the sideline. There's a buzz around the stadium, bracing, and it's the insidious kind. The kind of tension reserved for a loss.

Curio frowns, waiting for my response, and I shake my head. We still need a win, and I'm the only one who can get us there.

"Just in shock, sorry," I call, jogging over to the huddle. "Everything's fine."

Our offensive coach, Frank, pulls up next to me. "That was a bad hit, Orsino," he says in his low rumble.

"Nope." I put on my sunniest face, knowing Coach is watching. "It's fine. Bruised, that's all."

He cocks a brow doubtfully. "You're sure?"

"With one yard left to go? Of course I'm sure." I feel weird, a little unsteady, but I can definitely move. Besides, losing this early in the season means no state championship. Poof, there goes the season, my whole legacy up in smoke. "I'm fine," I say again. "Nothing to worry about."

Frank's eyes narrow to slits, then dart to my dad. "Risky," he murmurs. "Might be better to pull him now."

"No way," I cut in instantly. "We're *one yard* from the win, Coach!"

If anyone's going to be as hungry for the win as I am, it's Coach Orsino. He nods once, stiffly, and my relief nearly knocks the wind out of me. "Run a counter. Volio," Coach adds, "stay close."

We break and head back to the field, Curio still eyeing me while I test my stance. "Sure you're good?"

I shove in my mouthpiece, shrugging, and Curio nods with understanding. Sure or not, this is happening. As far as I can tell, my knee is tender, but fine.

Ever forward, ever onward. I happen to catch the eye of the cornerback, who's watching me as we set up for the snap. Not watching—*staring*, creepily. I blow him a kiss and get settled at the line of scrimmage, shaking off my misgivings as the end zone comes into focus.

Third down. It's do or die now, so Volio and I set up for the counter—another well-practiced misdirection play.

"On one," shouts Curio. "HUT!"

I drop backfield and Curio does a beautiful, Oscar-worthy fake to Volio, which works on everyone but my BFF the Padua cornerback, who can't take his eyes off me. Not that it matters; Curio tosses me the ball and I'm off like a shot, veering away for a clear opening. I know without a doubt that this touchdown has my name all over it, and the crowd knows it, too.

"DUKE, DUKE, DUKE—"

From my periphery the Padua cornerback drops, aiming for my legs—for my *knees*—and I swear I see it in flashes, like it happens in slow motion.

His red uniform from the corner of my eye.

The yellow of the goalpost.

The green of the turf.

The bright white of panic when I feel something go wrong—

No, that's not it; I don't feel it. I *hear* it, loud as a gunshot this time, like cracking a knuckle but indescribably worse. The sound rings harsher than the impact, though I don't register it until after I get dragged down. Instead I think, *Is the ball still in my hands?* And then I think, *This isn't right.*

Something is really, really not right.

"Enjoy the view," snarls the Padua cornerback, who gets called for a late hit. Or something. I can't fully understand what the ref is saying because I'm busy telling myself *Get up, come on, Jack, get up,* but something's misfiring. It's like my brain and my body got disconnected somehow, unplugged from each other.

"Jack? Jack, can you move?" That's Frank.

"Duke." Coach's face appears, all morphed and unrecognizable.

The ref is talking to me now, I think. "Son, you okay? You need help?"

I hear my dad call for a medic.

"Oh my god, Jack!"

That's Olivia, her green-and-gold glitter blurring when I try to look at her and realize I can't quite focus. An ache is settling in, like a cramp or a wave. It rises somehow, tightening my chest.

"Jack, are you okay?"

"*Messaline all-star running back Jack 'The Duke' Orsino is down in the Padua end zone!*" calls the announcer over the speakers. I can hardly hear him over the sound of what I now realize is the fight song, meaning we did it. We got the touchdown. And the win.

Which is good. Great, even. I'd be pissed if we hadn't.

And anyway, I'm fine, right?

"Coach, this ain't good," Frank murmurs to my father, who says nothing.

I close my eyes, exhaling out.

Champions are half intention, half work. I can will myself to the end zone. *See it, make it happen.* I can will myself off the ground.

Only this time, I don't think I can.

𝔙𝔦

"The head," Murph soliloquys, "now severed from the body—"

"Lovely," I mutter to myself. (Well, to him. But if anyone asks, it was under my breath.)

"—looks up at you, eyes aloft, and whispers one word—"

"Toni!" shouts Antonia's mother, Mrs. Valentine. "Are you in here?"

"Yes, Mom, in the kitchen!" Antonia shouts directly into my ear, and then flushes. "Oops, sorry, Vi."

"I'm used to this sort of mistreatment," I assure her.

Antonia's mom walks in, so we all sing "*Hiiiiii, Mrs. Valentiiiiine*" at her like a Greek chorus. Antonia's older brother Nick, home for the weekend, enters with a kind of "FYI I used to be king of this place" strut while her younger brother, Jandro, shuffles in behind him.

"How was the game?" Antonia asks Nick on the group's behalf, just to be polite. (She once had to explain to Leon how football worked, and he immediately said it was too complicated. "It's not any more complicated than a quest," she insisted at the time, because it's very important to Antonia that everyone feels comfortable and informed. "Every player has a Quest Sheet, basically, with plays they're allowed to do or not do—"

"—and the ultimate goal is tossing a toy around from one over-stuffed jock to another," Leon scoffed in reply. This from a boy who thinks he could probably shoot lethal arrows if he was just "given a fair shot.")

"Well, the game was great," Mrs. Valentine answers her daughter cheerfully. "The new QB's got nothing on Nicky, of course—"

"Mom," grumbles Nick.

"But he'll learn—he'll get there!" she assures him.

"Mom, Curio was fine. Can I go?" Nick asks, looking jittery. "I want to get to the hospital."

"Hospital?" echoes Danny Kim, who I forgot about for a second.

"Is it that bad?" Mrs. Valentine asks Nick, who shrugs, riffling a hand through his hair.

"His mom was trying to talk him into it, so I'm guessing he's there now. Cool if I take your car?"

"Yes, that's fine—"

"You can just take yours," Antonia offers him quickly. "I won't use it tonight. If we go anywhere, Vi can drive me."

Nick looks at me briefly, dismissing me in nearly the same moment. "Thanks, Ant."

Then he's gone, leaving the rest of the room to glance quizzically at Mrs. Valentine.

"What happened?" asks Matt Das.

"Oh, someone got hurt. One of Nicky's friends."

"Who?" asks Leon, perking up. Football may not interest him, but knowing things about other people's personal lives always does.

"Jack Orsino," Mrs. Valentine tells him.

"Jack?" echoes Antonia, shocked, at the same moment I reflexively grumble, "Ugh, Jack."

Antonia's eyes cut to mine with a swift, silencing glance. This is partially the result of Antonia being a Nice Person, but more significantly it's the fact that Jack Orsino's cheekbones and chest measurements regularly motivate her goodwill.

Basically, it's no real shock that Jack Orsino won Associate Student Body president, given that the whole thing is a farce. First of all, his friends on the football team were responsible for counting the votes, so you can see why I demanded a recount. After nearly a month of hard-core negotiating with all the biggest and most underrepresented clubs on campus, I felt a margin of eighteen votes was pretty freaking negligible, so I invoked the election guidelines that require a more statistically significant victory to win. But, of course, instead of choosing an *objective third party* like the guidebook specifies, they just let the same apathetic jocks count them again.

Not that the official results were ultimately that surprising. Jack, bronzed like an Olympian god with the preternatural confidence of someone born with perfect skin and a six-pack, has all the necessary prerequisites to win at high school, whatever that turns out to mean ten years from now. (I got vice president as runner-up, so it wasn't a wasted effort, but still.) The point is, you can never overestimate the voters, who see dimples and a varsity letter and decide that counts as budget competency or even the slightest attempt at effort. From my perspective, aka the lowest possible degree of interest, Jack is like if the smirky rebel captain from *Empire Lost* were darker, taller, and more difficult to work with. Think your classic cinematic rogue, but unlikely to show up in time to save you because . . . Wait, hang on, you needed something? Huh, weird, it totally slipped his mind.

In Jack Orsino's case, I wholeheartedly agree with Leon that football is just a matter of tossing a toy around. Jack's one of the ones who runs around with the toy, which as far as I'm concerned takes very little skill. At least as quarterback, Nick had to be tactical. Jack just . . . runs. (Unsurprisingly, he acted like I kicked his puppy when I asked for the election recount, which is *literally* a school requirement. I assume he finds it hard to believe that rules were ever meant to apply to him.)

"What happened to Jack?" asks Antonia, who looks concerned, because of course she does.

"Well, a rather unsportsmanlike play, I'd say," says Mrs. Valentine, glancing over the table to see our various dice, guides, and Quest Sheets. "What's the adventure today?"

"*The Amulet of Qatara*," I answer, hoping that will be enough to get us all back to the game. "It's one of the more classic quests."

"Oh, that's nice," says Mrs. Valentine.

Behind her, Antonia's brother Jandro snorts quietly.

"Someone was just beheaded," I inform him, as Antonia blanches and Mrs. Valentine nudges him out of the room.

"Let them play, Jandro. You guys have fun," she tells us warmly. "Need anything? Snacks, soda?"

"We've got plenty, Mrs. Valentine," I tell her, because my mother didn't raise me to be impolite. "Thanks so much for offering."

"Okay, I'll stay out of your hair." She smiles at us and gives Jandro another small shove into the living room while we turn back to Murph.

"Damn, wonder what happened to Orsino," he says vacantly.

"Who cares?" I drum my nails on the table. "Can we wrap this up?"

"Yeesh, you're in a hurry," says Marco.

"Um, don't you want to win? We just took out the last of the Cretacious horde."

"Well, she's in the middle of saying something," says Murph.

"Okay, what's she saying?"

"*Staaaaaaahp*," Murph conjures up in a low, creepy ghoul voice.

I roll my eyes. "Okay, great. Famous last words."

The rest of the quest is fairly straightforward. Now that the last enemy horde has been wiped out, the caves have been explored, and the bad guys have all been successfully dismembered, there's not much more to say. Antonia's character, Larissa, heals us in preparation for the next stage of our quest, and then we reach the moment I've been waiting for. This is the point where, as a group, we would decide which ConQuest expansion book to do next, and I am . . . somewhat invested in the outcome.

"Now that we've arrived at the end of this quest," I say, clearing my throat, "I have a proposition for the group."

"Aye, aye," says Leon in a bawdy sailor's voice.

"I'm not done," says Murph.

"Yeah, I know? That's the point," I say impatiently. "Before we finish—"

"Whoa. This is so small," says Marco, who appears to be staring at a misshapen pretzel.

"That's what she said," snickers Leon, followed by laughter from Danny Kim.

"Um?" I say, exasperated. "Hello?"

"Guys," Matt Das cuts in. "Just hear her out, okay?"

God, at least not everyone here is an idiot.

"Yeah. My house, my rules," adds Antonia, bowing theatrically to me. "Astrea Starscream, the floor is yours."

"Actually, this is more of a Vi thing," I tell them, giving Antonia a small but grateful glance. "About what quest we do next."

Leon unhelpfully contributes, "I thought we were doing *The Cliffs of Ramadra* next?"

"What's that?" asks Danny Kim, because of course he does.

"It's supposedly the game that inspired *War of Thorns*," says Murph.

"Ooh," says Danny Kim instantly. "That sounds cool."

"It's a battle game," says Rob Kato. "Like, a hundred percent combat, supposedly."

"A shit ton of gore," adds Leon with palpable glee. "Like the show."

"The show's not *that* gory," Antonia says, making a face.

"Whatever. You only watch it for Cesario," says Leon snidely, which irks me.

Cesario's one of the main characters on *War of Thorns*, a fallen prince from the rival kingdom who used to be the main villain. His redemption arc is the most interesting plot in the show, but every boy in the world thinks girls are only watching the show for his abs.

"We hadn't actually agreed on doing *Cliffs of Ramadra* next," I point out.

"Yes we h—"

"Look, the point is I wrote a new quest over the summer," I say, cutting to the chase. "And I just think—"

"You wrote a quest?" asks Matt Das.

"Yeah." I'm very excited about it, though I'm trying to temper that for now. They'll smell my hope like blood in the water and mock it to death just for being my idea before I get the chance to make it sound like their thing. "So, it's kind of like a political thriller," I tell them. My brother Bash and I dreamed it up after we watched some super-old mobster movies at our grandma's house. "The game opens in a bazaar-like setting—"

"Bizarre like weird?" asks Murph.

"Bazaar," I correct. "Sort of like an underground fae market, but—"

"Fairies?" echoes Danny Kim, with an expression that I would love to personally remove from his face.

"In the quest," I continue loudly, "we'd be in a world with a corrupt capitalist system that enables the tyrannical rule of a shadow king—" I can tell I'm talking too fast, based on how everyone's eyes briefly glaze over, so I move on. "The point is, to successfully make it through this world, we'd have to fall in with a gang of underground smugglers who coexist alongside the shadow king's assassins. But since this is a world where magic can bind you to your word, that means everything we do in the world of this quest has long-term consequences—"

"Sounds complicated," says Murph, frowning.

"Plus you always want to take too long on the tactical parts," Marco adds.

"Well, no, not really," I say, answering Murph, since Marco is obviously just whining and therefore not important. "I mean, so long as I were QuestMaster—"

"You want to be QM?" asks Marco.

"I mean, I wrote the quest, so—"

Leon and Murph exchange a look just before Marco cuts in again. "So basically we'd never do any fighting, then."

"Guys." Again, I actually *do* a combat sport, but if I hear them refer to it as kickboxing one more time I will definitely snap. "Obviously combat is still essential to the story, it's just—"

"I feel like the battle games are more engaging for the group," says Rob with obnoxious faux pensiveness.

"Okay, that's *literally* false—"

"I think it could be fun," Antonia says. "Could we maybe do a single quest first, to try it out?"

"Well." I know Antonia's trying to help, but she . . . isn't. "Like I said, there would be long-term consequences to every action, so—"

"I don't understand. We're fighting fairies?" says Leon.

"No," I grind out, trying not to lose my temper. "I said it's *like* a fae market, as in it's a magical black market dealing in contraband, where we would have access t—"

"Let's just take a vote," suggests Murph, as I grit my teeth, bracing for an outcome I was *sure* I wouldn't have to deal with. I mean, come on, right? I played their choice of quest. I won *several* rounds of combat when they were all dumb enough to fall into the same trap of hypermasculinity. I've proven that I know what I'm doing.

Haven't I?

"All in favor of Vi's fairy quest?" asks Murph.

"Oh my god," I say as I raise my hand, "it's not *fairies*—"

But it doesn't matter. Antonia's hand goes up, and then, gradually—after a long period of time glancing around—Matt Das's does, too.

That's it.

"You're joking," I say.

"All in favor of *Cliffs of Ramadra*?" prompts Murph.

Danny Kim's hand shoots in the air and whatever happens after that, I don't care. I rise to my feet, grabbing my dice and my notes and shoving them into my bag.

"Geez, sore loser," says Leon, but I don't care anymore. Isn't it bad enough to have to go to a school where people only care about looks and clothes and football without having to *also* contend with a band of group-think dudebros who never give me the benefit of the doubt? I swear, there's no winning. Not even among massive ConQuest dorks who spend their free time speculating about Antonia's boobs.

I worked *all summer* on this quest. I designed it specifically to appeal to everyone: battle scenes, cool enviro, interesting and unique plot. But no. I'm a girl, so obviously it's a *girl* quest.

"Hey" I hear coming after me. "Vi, wait!"

Matt Das follows me out the Valentines' front door, stopping me before I reach my car.

"Vi, come on, I'm sorry—"

"I worked on this for two months," I tell him bitterly, not wanting to look at him. All I need is to start crying right now. "Like, you have no idea how much work went into this, and how much research and planning and—"

"Look, I'm sorry." And he looks it. "Those guys are idiots."

"I know." I turn away, and then, taking a breath, look up. "Sorry. I didn't mean to just rush out of there."

"Hey, I would've, too. They're being completely ridiculous."

"Yeah." I chew my lip. "Look, thanks for that. For voting for my quest and stuff."

"Yeah, no problem. Leon's a dumbass."

"Ha. Yeah."

"And Danny Kim? Like, do you even know *anything*, dude?"

"I know." I roll my eyes and exhale. "Ugh."

"Hey, I know it sucks, but it's their loss. Just come back and kick all their asses next week."

"Yeah . . . yeah, I guess." I look up at him, sighing. "Thanks."

"No problem. Wanna get out of here?" he offers. "Go get some froyo and talk about it?"

Talk about it? Yeah, no thanks. All I want to do is get online and lay waste to some fictional characters until the urge to throw darts at real people safely evacuates my system.

"Oh, thanks for the offer, Matt, but—" I shrug. "I'm tired. Kinda just want to go home." I turn to my car, but apparently Matt's not finished.

"What about tomorrow?" he asks, stepping between me and my car door.

"What?"

"Wanna catch a movie or something?"

"Oh . . . maybe." This suddenly feels very weird. "I don't know, Matt—"

"Seriously?"

I blink at him. "Matt, I just want to go home, okay? If I'm up for a movie tomorrow, I'll text you."

"But you won't, obviously." He folds his arms over his chest.

"Okay, what is this?" I ask him with a sigh, gesturing to his posture. "I've got RenFaire all day and then I hang out with my mom and my brother. If they've got something else going on, I'll let you know."

"Oh, how convenient."

"Um, yeah, sure." I reach for my car door and Matt shifts, blocking me again. "What the hell?"

"If you're trying to blow me off, just say so," he tells me snidely. "I mean, what more do you expect me to do, Vi? I took your side. What else do you want?"

Tension climbs all the way up my vertebrae. "Whoa, what's going on?"

"I get that you think I'm not cool enough to go out with or whatever—"

"What?" He's got to be joking. As if I've ever not gone out with someone because they weren't *cool enough*. I'm currently wearing a shirt with a math joke on it.

"—but I'm actually nice to you, Vi," he rants, "and I just don't think it's fair for you to act like I don't exist."

"Matt," I say sharply, "I didn't know you were trying to ask me out, okay? I was just telling you my plans."

"Well, now you know," he says stubbornly. "So are you going to call me or not?"

"Um, not?" I tell him, because duh, he's standing between me and my car, and even if he is a nearsighted nerd who wouldn't pose a threat under any other circumstances, he's still making me feel like I don't want to be anywhere near him, tomorrow or any other time.

"Great. Really cool of you, Vi," Matt says, dripping with sarcasm.

God. "Can I get into my car, please?"

He waves me toward it, bowing derisively as he goes. "Just so you know," he says with his hand still on my open door, "I'm the only guy in that room who doesn't call you a bitch behind your back. Even Antonia looks like she wants to half the time."

I bristle at the mention of Antonia. Nice guys, I swear. "And let me guess, you think you're so brave for letting them do it?"

"You *are* a bitch, Vi," he snaps at me. "I thought there was more to you. But apparently there isn't."

It really shouldn't sting. It shouldn't.

"You actually thought I'd go out with you?" I force a laugh, coldly. "Not in a million years."

Then I get in my car, locking the doors and driving away well before my hands stop shaking on the wheel.

CRITICAL EXISTENCE FAILURE

𝔙i

Antonia's calling before I pull into my house's driveway. I consider not answering—I'm still furious, especially after Matt Das decided I *owed* him a date—but then I think better of it. It's not Antonia's fault that acknowledging my ideas is such a Sisyphean task.

"Hello?" I sigh.

"Look, you just have to let them warm up to it, that's all," she says in her soothing, pacifist middle-child voice. "It's not personal. They just like what they like, that's all."

"It's just such a boys' club," I mutter. "I hate it."

"Can you blame them? You always take my side over theirs, too. Maybe they think *we're* the ones who exclude *them*. Two sides to every story, right?"

Oh, Antonia. Innocent little Antonia. "I take your side because you're actually capable of intelligent thought."

"Well, whatever. I think your quest sounds cool," she assures me. "And they'll come around eventually."

I exhale, leaning back as I shut the car off. "How long is eventually?"

"Not long. A couple of months, maybe."

"God." I shut my eyes. "I just don't get what their issue is. I mean . . . I played their game, I did what they wanted—hell, I'm better at it than basically all of them—"

"Well, that's kind of the problem, don't you think?" Antonia says patiently. "You have to let them win sometimes, Vi. It's a matter of keeping the peace."

"Um, no it's not," I say, a little annoyed now. It's not like she's new to RPGs or fandom. It's not this *one specific* group of boys that I'm bitchily terrorizing. It's completely systemic. "Why should I have to shrink myself down so they can feel big? Doesn't make sense."

"It's not ideal, but it works," she points out. "You catch more flies with honey."

"I have absolutely no use for flies."

"You know what I mean."

I still don't agree, but whatever. No point arguing with her when it's definitely not her fault.

"Also," she adds, "Matt was kind of upset when he came back in."

I snort in response. "So?"

"So, what'd you say to him? He was only trying to be nice."

I can feel my hackles rising. "Did he tell you what he said to *me*?"

"No. He didn't say anything."

"Good." At least he had the decency to not be a dick about me in front of other people, though that seems like a very small mercy at the moment.

"So what happened?" she presses.

"Ugh. Nothing. He asked me out."

"And you said . . . ?"

"No, obviously."

"Vi!" Antonia sounds scandalized.

"What?"

"Come on, Matt's nice. And he obviously likes you."

"So?"

"So what?"

"So that's a reason to go out with someone?"

"I mean, yeah, why not? You obviously have things in common."

"By that logic, I should date *you*."

"We'd be very cute and weird together," Antonia blithely agrees, "but stop dodging the point. You can't be so picky."

"I'm not picky. I just don't want to pick *him*."

"Well, whatever. Matt or no Matt, you can't be surprised when the guys are dicks to you."

I bristle again. "So you're saying I deserved this?"

"Of course not. I'm just saying you're kind of unnecessarily hostile with everyone. Like, did you have to death-stare Danny Kim every time he asked a question?"

Uhh yes, definitely. "I'm considerably less hostile than I could be, actually." God, imagine if I actually *said* everything that went through my mind. "And they *were* stupid questions."

"There's no such thing as a stupid question," she recites. (Her mom is a teacher.)

"Any question you could answer with five seconds of deductive thought is a stupid question, but okay," I reply.

"Clearly my point is sinking in beautifully," Antonia sighs, and best friend or no best friend, it becomes extremely apparent that I need a break from this conversation. I need a break from this whole night, honestly, because thinking about it only makes me angrier.

"Also, apparently Jack Orsino might have torn his ACL," Antonia adds, but I definitely don't care about Jack Orsino. I get enough of him in my daily life without unnecessary medical reports from the cult of self-enamored jocks, plus he owes me a signed budget report. And at least 10 percent of my sanity back.

"Look, I'm tired," I tell Antonia. "I'm just gonna go to bed."

"What? It's, like, barely ten—"

"Long week, I guess. And we've got an early day tomorrow." Antonia, Bash, and I all volunteer at our local Renaissance Faire and to no one's surprise, I'm the driver.

"Sure." She sighs. "Just . . . promise you'll give it some time, Vi? Don't give up on them yet, just . . . give them a little while to see that they're wrong. Okay?"

"Okay." Yeah right. There's no way I'm showing up at another ConQuest Friday after the hellscape I just sat through, but she doesn't need to know that. I'll just make excuses for a few weeks until she finally takes the hint or gives up.

"Okay. You sure you're okay?"

"I'm good. See you tomorrow."

"Okay, bye." We hang up and I take another breath, throwing the car door open and dragging myself to the front door.

Our neighborhood is one of those painfully homogenous

suburbs—you know, the kind in movies about middle-aged men who cheat on their wives. We live in a duplex that's so close to the house next door that I can look over and see the neighbor's Yorkie yapping at me from where he's perched on top of the couch.

"Nice to see you, too," I inform him, unlocking the door and letting myself inside to find that someone's home, although it's not my mom, since her spot in the driveway is vacant. This is not very surprising, as Mom's never home on Friday nights.

Do you ever think about how fortunate you are to be born in a time of indoor plumbing and polio vaccines? Well, my mother is fortunate to live in a time of online dating. She is very, very good at dating, with specific mastery over the realm of casual relationships. She is not very good at marriage; I don't have firsthand proof of this, since apparently she and my father did not reach that stage before she got pregnant with Bash and me, but seeing as she's never been with anyone long enough for us to know them, I pretty much take her word for it.

You're probably thinking oh, sad, your mother must have some terrible flaw that keeps the men away, HOW TRAGIC. Everyone's worst fear is ending up alone (unless you're my grandmother, Lola, whose worst fear is my mother never knowing the joy of being one man's personal hype crew for the rest of her life) but what's the actual sense in that? As far as I can tell, most marriages are just a man purchasing his own housekeeper, cook, nanny, and life coach, all for the low, low price of two months' salary toward a diamond ring.

The truth is my mother's gotten plenty of offers. She's been proposed to so many times I've genuinely stopped keeping track. I do think my mother would make a fantastic husband—going to work all day and coming home to a home-cooked meal and a clean house does seem like a wonderful daydream, so I can totally see why The Men are so very cross about feminism—but the role of *wife* is not her speed. She and I don't really do submission; we're tough and critical, and that's not everybody's cup of tea.

But like I said, my mom is very good at dating, which is technically part of her job. She's a freelance writer who found some success a couple of years ago with an online magazine called *The Doe*, a feminist e-publication that produces a mix of overhyped clickbait, listicles, and political think-pieces. Mom, hilariously enough, writes a popular dating advice column, so normally she spends her evenings using The Apps to "find love," or something close enough to write about it.

Since it's not my mom that's home, that leaves my twin brother Sebastian, who bounds down the stairs the moment I toe my shoes off. "Finally," he says, gesturing frantically for the keys to the car, which he swore he didn't need tonight. "Last-minute change of plans," he explains when I toss them to him. "We're doing a brass thing at IHOP."

Bash is a drama kid *and* a band kid, which are both extremely insular ecosystems that mean I have no idea what he's talking about 90 percent of the time, but he's useful to have around if you're trying to brainstorm a ConQuest character. We also both enjoy hand-to-hand combat, though he won't spar with me anymore. He claims I gave him a nosebleed; I think the air was just dry.

"Have fun," I offer wearily, shouldering my way past him, and he stops me.

"They didn't go for it, huh?" he says, sympathizing with a grimace. He and I are both olive-skinned and dark-eyed with the same heart-shaped faces and almost-black hair, leading people to comment how alike we are until they get to know us. He has Mom's temperament, I have her view of the world, and somehow that makes us polar opposites. Most people guess that one of us takes after our dad, but that's pretty much unknowable. We've never seen much of him outside of spare visits when he's in town.

"Nope," I say.

"Idiots." Bash has this way of tilting his head while smiling that's very soothing. (He was allegedly a very easy baby while I was . . . not.) "You'll get 'em next time."

"In, like, a hit-man way?" I ask optimistically.

"If you want. I believe in you." He grins.

"They are actually idiots, though," I grumble.

"I mean, obviously. I cowrote it, so, you know." He shrugs. "I know this."

"Cowrote is a stretch." Bash isn't much of a writer. He's more of a "let's do something else now, I'm bored" kind of person. He's not happy unless he's making people laugh, which is why even though my mom thinks being an actor is a maniacal career choice, she can't really blame him. His personality leaves very little room for alternate pursuits, and for what it's worth, he is wildly talented.

"Well, whatever. They suck."

"Thanks," I exhale. I appreciate the simplicity of Bash's approach. "Have fun."

"Want to come?" He jingles the keys at me.

"Nah." I have plans with my ideal company: myself. "See you later."

"Don't burn the house down," he calls after me as I make my way up the stairs, flipping on the lights in my bedroom. It's a little messy, like usual. Clothes on the floor, which I kick aside. The *War of Thorns* poster from last year's MagiCon is on the wall next to my shelves with the complete *War of Thorns* paperback collection (I have the UK special edition hardcovers, too—the covers are to die for). Not that I'm obsessed with one fandom, of course. I've got plenty of science fiction and fantasy books littering my room, plus my graphic novels, ConQuest guides, RenFaire memorabilia . . . I'm kind of a functional hoarder, I guess. My prized possession sits above my desk: the *Empire Lost* poster signed by the director himself, for which I waited in line for nearly fourteen hours (I'm a sucker for a space opera). And then of course there's my laptop, which is essentially a treasure trove of everything that matters to me.

I sit down, open the screen, and pull out my noise-canceling headphones. I'm going to do exactly what I've done most nights since the school year started. I don't know if it's just because it's senior year or something, but I swear, I'm more stressed out than ever. School's a lot, but it's not just that. It's something, I don't know, existential. An itch, like maybe the people and things going on around me don't feel right. Or that it's me who doesn't fit.

The sound of *Twelfth Knight* starting up is so soothing that I might as well be one of Pavlov's dogs.

The lore for the game is that after King Arthur dies, his relics get scattered around eleven realms. The remaining knights have to prevent the world from descending into eldritch chaos as Camelot comes under siege by a corrupt aspiring tyrant: the mysterious Black Knight. You can choose to play as a sorcerer, enchantress, barbarian, creature, Arthurian knight, assassin for the Black Knight . . . you name it. I pick Arthurian knight, because duh. Swords, mostly.

I select my character and queue up for combat mode. Boys seriously think that girls only want romance and ballgowns and puppies, which is proof they don't understand the first thing about actually *being* a girl. I play this game because in the real world, I'm stressed. Or angry—and don't I have good reason to be?

When I first started playing MMORPGs, I used to use a headset. I don't anymore. You know why? Because when boys hear a girl's voice, they either come for you unnecessarily, thinking you'll be easy prey, or they think everything you say is flirting. Being nice to a geek while being visibly female is the kiss of death. Do you know how many times I've gotten vulgar messages or explicit pictures? And if I say no, do you know how many times I've been called a bitch?

Not that all guys are awful, but the awful ones are impossible to escape. And certainly impossible to tell at first glance. Which is why I play under the username Cesario—and my character? You guessed it: modeled after Cesario on *War of Thorns*. Tough, capable. Muscular, sharp. The best blade in any given arena and the most tactical person in the field. Quads the size of pillars. A man with everything the boys want to be and have and do, and guess what? Everything *I* want, too, because believe it or not, not every girl wants to be a princess or a healer or some big-chested daydream who only plays to lose. I may like girly things on occasion, but I'm not just here for people to look at. I don't want to be considered beautiful without being seen as capable, too.

It's not that I don't feel at home in my body. Periods and awkward growth spurts aside, I don't have a problem with the form I take. But if I looked like Cesario in real life, I'd have no reason not to be QuestMaster for the game I designed. Nobody would question my competency. No one would think they deserved a date with me just because they did one nice thing. Jack Orsino wouldn't be able to waltz around school like he owns it just because everyone forgives his every personality flaw whenever he smiles or catches a ball. And most of all, Antonia wouldn't be able to say things like "it's not personal" whenever the boys gang up on me. I wish it *were* personal! I wish they could hate me for normal reasons, like my personality, instead of just looking at me and seeing long hair and boobs and deciding that's enough to validate all of their presumptions.

So of course I'm angry. I'm angry *all the time*. From the betrayals of my government to the hypocrisies of my peers, it seems like the awfulness never rests and neither can I. No matter how many combat advantages I give Astrea Starscream, she'll never be taken seriously. No matter how smart I am or how hard I work, my acceptance is always conditional. And it's not just me—I don't know how any girl can exist in the world without being perpetually furious.

But once I sign on as *Cesario*, my chat is instantly filled with dudes who want me to queue up for their battle campaigns, so in at least one place, I'm valuable. In at least one world, I'm safe.

> yo, finally. u down to clown on gm0n33
> bro shut up I called cesario for morholt

> I beat that like two months ago, I type back.

> UHH YA hence calling u for morholt

See? When I'm Cesario I'm trusted. Admired, even. I'm still me, but without any harassment in the chat or attempts to mansplain the things I care about. They don't have to know who I am. They just know I'm a dude, and that's enough for them.

> u can't just call him I need a partner
> nd that's my problem y???

Boys, honestly.

> hey losers, I type back, rolling my eyes. who says I can't do it all?

Jack

"I told you this would happen," my mom says from the kitchen, talking to my father in a voice I'm not meant to hear from where I'm currently couchbound in the living room. "I told you, nobody's body is meant for this. This was bound to happen to one of the boys eventually."

I stare at the ceiling. I'm not surprised she's here, exactly. She no longer lives here, but they've embraced that celebrity "co-parenting" strategy that means my brother and I come first. I guess having 50 percent of your children down for the count is reason enough to stay the weekend.

"You know what Dr. Barnes used to say about Jack." Mom's voice continues. "He's too fast for his body, it can't keep up with him. He's been lucky so far, but—"

"What do you want me to do? He'll rest. He'll heal." My dad sounds certain, though he always sounds certain. He's a "fake it 'til you make it" kind of guy.

"I looked it up, Sam, it could be over a year of recovering from surgery, plus rehab—"

I flinch. *Do your thing, ibuprofen. Come through.*

"Are you kidding me?" My mom's voice is sharp in response to whatever my dad just said. "Sam. This is your son. You saw how hard he went down!"

"Duke knows how to take care of himself—"

"Don't call him that," she snaps. "And you want him in a wheel-chair by the time he's forty? How many of your old teammates are suffering now? How many have had their personalities completely rewritten by head trauma, or *worse*—"

My mom is not a football fan, as she tells us constantly. She's a fan of my dad and his program, but she harbors not-so-secret hopes that the NFL will eventually fall apart. There's something insidious about it, she says, all those white owners and Black players. *Dance for us, entertain us,* but without the social activism of the NBA.

That she herself is white is not really a matter of relevance— "It's the optics," she says. Mom is a doctor of optics, being a school board administrator whose job is to make what's untenable about public school education look like diversity and progress. She works for the next county over, which includes the school my father would have played for if he hadn't had such a killer arm. It has some economic discrepancies, unlike here, which is predominantly middle class and white.

"This is his life, Ellen," my dad says, his voice rising. "I never forced him. He's the one who chose to play, he's the one who signed with Illyria—"

"And what choice does he have, Sam? It was either be like you and love what you love, or never get a minute of your time!"

I reach for my phone, tuning them out. There's a couple of new messages from Nick, saying he'll be back to hang out next weekend after my surgery. One from my brother Cam, complaining about school and telling me I'll be fine. One from Curio, with a link to a local news article about how the Padua cornerback is suspended from their next game—not that it makes a difference to me or my knee. One from Olivia, though when I open it, I realize she just "loved" my last message saying goodnight. No actual response. Hm.

Olivia's been weird lately. More than just lately, come to think of it. She went to New York with her cousins for a month in July, and I haven't seen much of her since school started a couple of weeks ago. Probably my fault; even without the two-a-days for football, I haven't had much free time.

Guess I've got plenty of it now.

I ignore the blip in my chest, tapping her name in my favorites list.

"Jack?"

She answers, light streaming in from where she's sunbathing in her backyard. I miss her viscerally, out of the blue, like a strike of lightning. The way she smells like vanilla and salty air; like the bonfire last summer where I first talked to her. "Hey. You busy?"

"Kinda. Girls' day." She shows me her younger sisters, both still in elementary school. Then she gives me a weird smile, like maybe she's worried or something, or distracted. "How are you feeling?"

I'll just say it: Olivia is absolutely gorgeous. That dark hair that fades in places to gold, tan skin, eyes to match . . . she's like a day-dream brought to life. It's pretty cliché, the football star with the cheerleader, but nobody looking at her could possibly blame me. She's not the vamped-up prom queen archetype, you know? She's different. Interesting, funny, sweet.

"I'm fine," I tell her. "Don't worry about me."

"Yeah, I know. You're going to be fine." She does the same thing again, that wobbly, elsewhere smile just as my parents' voices get louder from the kitchen.

"Want me to come over?" I offer, suddenly desperate to leave my house. "I could bring you guys some lemonade. Or whatever's suitable for girls' day." Admittedly, I have no idea. My mom isn't the pampered type compared to Olivia's mom, who always smells like the lobby of an expensive hotel.

"Shouldn't you be resting?" she says absently.

"I can rest anywhere," I assure her.

"Mm." She glances over her shoulder. "Well, my parents aren't home. They're at brunch with Teita." Her grandmother, who's like her mother, only fancier.

"Oh." Olivia's family has fairly strict rules. "Well, that's fine. I just haven't seen you in a while."

"Mm," she says again, shading her eyes.

Is she mad at me? Maybe.

"I know things have been weird between us lately," I say, and she exhales like she took a swift hit.

"You do?"

"Come on, Liv. I'm not totally oblivious." She gets up, probably to move out of her sisters' earshot. "Everything okay?"

"Yeah. Well . . ." She grimaces. "I mean, yeah, mostly."

"Okay," I laugh. "Super convincing, go on."

"Well, I just—"

She hesitates again, and I realize she's probably waiting for an apology.

"Maybe I should talk first," I tell her. "Because I do feel like it's my fault."

"You do?"

"I mean, of course. I'm never here for you." This was the primary complaint between my mom and my dad: the lack of time. "Maybe me being injured is a good thing for us." Silver lining, right? "I'll be a lot more available now," I remind her, feeling slightly better about that prospect, "so maybe we can—"

"I think we should take a break," Olivia blurts out.

"—get back on track," I finish, and pause. "Wait, what? Because I got hurt?"

"What? *Jack*," she says, aghast. "Of course not!"

"But—" I blink, and then my entire world shifts.

Again.

"It's just . . . my parents, you know, they've never liked the thought of me dating," Olivia says with a wince, which isn't new information, exactly. Her parents are very conservative and strict in a way I've never understood, but I never got the feeling it was a problem.

"You want to go on a break because your parents don't like me?" That doesn't make sense. Everyone likes me. Even people who don't like me kind of like me. The Hadids certainly seemed to, so at what point did this start to matter to her? Am I supposed to win *them* over now, too?

Because I could do that. "What if I came over later? I could bring your mom flowers or something, or pretend I understand doctor stuff—"

"No, no," she says quickly. "It's just . . . never mind. It was just a thought. You know what I mean? Just . . . it doesn't matter." She shakes her head. "Forget it."

"Olivia." She can't be serious. "I can't just *forget* this—"

"I'm just stressed," she says quickly. "School's been really overwhelming, and you know, my family, college stuff . . ." She trails off. "But obviously I still care about you—"

"You *care about* me?" I echo. I told her I loved her almost nine months ago and she said it back, though it suddenly occurs to me that she hasn't said it lately. "Loving" a text message isn't the same thing as "I love you."

Whoa. How much have I missed, exactly?

"No, Jack, I'm—" She exhales, frustrated. "I love you, of course I do. And I always will, I swear, I just . . . it's just a bit weird, you know, with everything—"

Just then, my phone buzzes, nearly dropping from my hand. "Olivia, I don't—" It buzzes again as I fumble to clear the message from the screen. "Sorry, hang on, I just—"

"Look, I'll let you go, okay? I'm sorry. I know you've got a lot going on, plus Leya needs my help with something. We'll talk later, promise," Olivia assures me, and then, before I can stop her, she's gone.

I stare at the blank screen, cursing it in silence. Particularly once I see who the texts are from.

we really need to touch base on the plans for the aloha dance, says Vi Reyes. *the social committee needs to know their budget*

Nobody gives a shit about this dance, but try telling that to Vi Reyes. She's kind of like the character in a movie who takes off her glasses and shakes out her hair to reveal she's been—gasp!—pretty the whole time, only she doesn't wear glasses and I've seen her hair down. Her overall vibe is the headmistress of a Victorian school for misbehaving orphans.

But arguing with her won't solve anything, so I take a breath. Several breaths.

good morning sunshine, I reply. *perhaps you might have heard I'm somewhat heroically debilitated at the moment? still waiting on the flowers btw*

why, she replies, *are you dead*

Before I can answer, she messages me again.

do you need your knees in order to sign off on a budget

I roll my eyes.

please do not injure yourself with concern for me, I say. *I don't know how I could live with the guilt*

also, I add, *just get ryan to be the second signature*

The checking account for ASB (meaning Associate Student Body—something about Vi makes everything devolve into high-powered acronyms, like I'm suddenly some kind of Wall Street drone) requires two signatures from three possible people: the president, vice president, or treasurer. Vi could easily bother someone who isn't me about this, but I honestly think she does it to annoy me. I'm one of her relaxing hobbies, like needlepoint or listening to smooth jazz.

ryan, she replies, *is an idiot*

interesting, I reply, unable to stop myself from adding, *so does this mean I'm not an idiot?*

She starts typing and I instantly regret saying anything.

you're PRESIDENT jack honestly if you're not going to take this seriously I don't even know why you're here

all I'm asking for is ONE SIGNATURE

pretend it's an autograph

presumably you love that

Oh my god. Nobody can win a fight with Vi Reyes. I'm about to toss my phone away and give up on the day altogether when I get a text from Olivia.

I'm sorry, Jack, but I think I just need some time

Ironic, I think with a grimace, considering time is just about the only thing I have left.

DEATH CRY ECHO

Vi

On Saturday, I wake up and perform my latest ritual of checking my social media for any news about this season of *War of Thorns*. There's an interview with Jeremy Xavier, plus a few loglines ambiguously promising a "big twist," though who knows what that means. Character death? Probably. It'd better not be Cesario. Which reminds me, I just wrote a thread the other day about how male villains always get the most complex redemption arcs compared to women. (Which isn't to say they don't still get killed off.)

I tagged Monstress Mag, my favorite female-run pop culture blog, but alas, no likes or retweets from them. Not that I need the attention, but it'd be nice to be taken seriously. Fantasy fiction is already dominated by the opinions of nostalgic fanboys who would rather stan their problematic faves than apply any critical thinking, and while playing *Twelfth Knight* as Cesario works for that world, *my* world is a little different. I mean . . . out in the wilds of social media, wearing my actual face? I need all the intersectional feminism I can get.

I notice that Antonia didn't like or agree with my tweet, which is . . . I mean, it's fine. I don't need performative likes. I keep scrolling through my timeline, though, and notice that she *did* like something else.

is it just me or is WoT twt full of people who are wayyyyy too invested? like just watch a different show lol it's not that hard

Did she . . . did she just subtweet me?

No, probably not. She wouldn't do that; plus, all she did was like it, and I should know better than anyone that every *War of Thorns* post winds up attracting the attention of some Cesario hater or some dude who insists that the female lead, Liliana, is a Mary Sue, which is basically just code for "I don't like or respect women." So what if a female character is "unrealistic"? How else do you explain every single male comic book hero? Every "Chosen One" archetype? Honestly, it's a mystery. That's probably what Antonia was mad about.

Probably.

In any case, as much as I'd love to stab some pixels in the *Twelfth Knight*–verse, I have to get up, because it's almost time to go. The weekends tend to be exhausting right at the start of the year, because the Renaissance Faire is just wrapping up in our region. We have shorter days since we're minors, but Bash is an early riser. He likes to think of his day as a race with the sun.

"VI," he bellows with a predictable smack against my bedroom door. "YOU HAVE TEN MINUTES."

The rest of the morning is lost to the struggle to shove things into my mouth and grab my stuff—boots, belt, handy leather pouch, metal cup for hydrating with peak authenticity, socks, "bloomers" (cough: leggings), chemise, bodice, underskirt, overskirt, hood . . . oh, and sunscreen, because not everything can be historically accurate—before getting herded into the car by a hysterical Bash.

"Would you relax?" I grumble to him, but he nudges me inside and then nods to Antonia, barking at her to get in the back seat as she comes hurrying up the drive.

Good. That saves me having to acknowledge her. Bash chatters on about play rehearsals and bickers amicably with Antonia over set pieces while I let my brain wash away in a wave of '80s-inspired alt-rock.

Normally my sense of the real world vanishes the moment I set foot into the world of the Faire, which is a sprawling public park in the middle of nowhere that gets magically transformed into a reproduction of Elizabethan England. Not the aristocratic courts of London or the ill-fated gloom of the Tower, but a joyful imagining of the northern countryside, complete with costumed actors, elaborate painted gables, and decorative thatched roofs on wooden market stalls that stretch as far as the eye can see. It's like time-traveling to a lost era of bucolic simplicity, but a version where people who look like us actually get to take part rather than being, you know. Colonized.

From the elaborate castle-looking gate, the Faire is a winding labyrinth of whimsy: food stands serving up mead and turkey legs, booths selling fairy wings and elfin ears, tarot readings beside henna tents, a functioning blacksmith, enchanted gardens, Globe-style stages, and endless alleys of artisan stalls. Where else but the tournament of horses can you cheer on two pretend knights in a fake joust without worrying about your precious teen ennui? The Faire is vibrant, colorful, and alive, and most of all, it's fearless and unapologetic. It's like a theme park for people who love history and swords.

Bash is the youngest member of the improv cast that performs something called Fakespeare, and he almost always plays an absurdly funny version of a villain. I'm not an actor, but I carry non-alcoholic beverages, chat with guests, sit in on performances (like Bash's), and cheer when the audience is supposed to cheer. I also have a reputation for being responsible, so if anyone needs someone to handle cash or take tickets, they often turn to me. Whatever I get to do on a Faire day is perfectly fine by me, and for a glorious, sweat-sheened series of late summer weekends, I spend my time playing make-believe and snapping the occasional picture of fantasy costumes for cosplay ideas when it's time for MagiCon later in the fall.

Today, though, I'm in a definite funk, and for the first time it feels like some of the Faire's usual magic isn't working. I can't alleviate the feeling that something is off, which doesn't help when I encounter people who aren't exactly my favorites.

"Anon, Viola!" calls one of the oncoming guild members cheerily. He's somewhere in his late twenties and his Faire name is Perkin, which is odd considering his actual name is an era-appropriate George. (Another person not worth committing to memory, of which there are many in my thriving social calendar.) "'Tis a lovely morning, is it not?"

"It's three P.M.," I mutter in an undertone, positioning a shoulder between his smiling face and my distracted one. He's always standing just a little bit closer than he needs to be.

"In another beauteous mood, I see. Save a smile for me," he says with a wink, and thankfully disappears. He's like that, usually. Just around to taunt me for a couple of minutes before he finally registers that I'd like him to go away.

Later, though, when I'm bringing water for the crossbows, axe-throws, and javelin guilds who are out in the sun without cover (trust me, there's no point putting a roof over amateurs with javelins) he's on my case again. "Where's that smile, Viola?"

I give him one for the express purpose of showing my teeth, and he laughs.

"One of these days someone will have to tame you," he informs me.

He's still using that joking tone, but I bristle. The implication feels insidious, particularly when you think about what that kind of language might actually mean. "*Tame* me?"

Two of the guild members around him snigger, reminding me I'm alone and outnumbered. Suddenly, I feel very aware that nobody I trust is around, so I quickly turn to walk away.

"Whoa, what's the hurry?"

George reaches out, touches me lightly, and I flinch.

"Frightened of your feelings, Viola?" he teases.

"Let go of me." I jerk my arm to shove him away, maybe a little too hard. He shrugs, laughs again, and exchanges a glance with the other two, like *I'm* the one who's being unreasonable.

"You know we're just playing, lass." This time George is using a Scottish accent. He is very good at that, and I have to say, most of the cast does love him. *Playful* is a good word for him, and I guess other people don't take issue with his "jokes."

Like Antonia, for example, who appears from around the corner. I know I should be relieved, but the way she instantly lights up at the sight of George only makes me feel worse. "Oh, hey George," Antonia says, and he bows.

"M'lady," he offers with a flourish.

"M'lord," she replies with the same smile she uses to get extra sriracha from the Thai delivery guy, and then she glances at me. "Everything okay?"

I open my mouth, but George cuts me off. "The lady wounds me, as usual," he says with a wink. "But we're all friends here, aren't we?"

He and Antonia share a laugh, which I experience in jeering slow motion. I can't really explain what's boiling over in my chest, but something inside me peels away, like a drop of cold sweat in a bucket I'll never be able to set down.

The anger rises up again, sharp and acid.

"We're not friends," I tell him. "And unless you want me to file a report, you'll leave me alone."

"Whoa, Vi," says Antonia, frowning at me like I've maliciously spoiled her fun. "Did something happen, or . . . ?"

"No." George's smile is locked in place. "Understood, Vi. My fault. Never know who can take a joke."

The uneasiness in my chest takes root, blooms, and rots. I turn away quickly, making some excuse about having to go get something for Bash.

"Sorry about her," Antonia says quietly in my absence. "She's just like that."

I'm out of sight by then, but I stop like I just punctured a lung.

"Not a problem, lass," George replies. "Viola is much famed for her . . . intemperance."

"Yeah, you could call it that." Antonia laughs, and my gut lurches.

"Lucky she has you for a friend," replies George.

"Oh, stop." I don't have to look to know Antonia's smiling her sriracha smile again. "So, how've you guys enjoyed the Faire?"

They continue chatting behind me and I hurry away, pain catching up to me after shock, followed by a sudden queasiness.

She *apologized* for me?

I'm just *like that*?

The end of RenFaire season is supposed to be fun. There's a parade! We toast our success with turkey legs! We pretend to fight each other with swords! We take pictures together and promise to keep in touch, even though after a week it'll just be dumb memes posted to our Facebook group by an adult man named Kevin! But instead of enjoying myself, I feel numb for the rest of the day, and kind of nauseated. Like I've been stabbed in the back, only I have a feeling it wouldn't sound like that if I tried to explain it out loud. Just like with Matt Das and the rest of our ConQuest group, I'm the troublemaker, and it's Antonia who knows how to be likable. How to be liked.

Except . . . why? *Why* does she do that? It's not like she hasn't had guys make the same inappropriate jokes they make to me or call her the same horrible names on the internet. She and I are in the exact same trenches, so why doesn't she understand that it's not okay for people to act like I'm something they have a right to control? *Smile, Vi, you need to be tamed . . .*

"You okay?" asks Bash when we pile back into my car.

"Yeah." I swallow and start driving. Antonia doesn't act like there's anything wrong. Instead she unplugs my phone and plugs hers in—something that wouldn't normally bother me, except right now it's more salt in the wound.

"Cool, sure, go ahead," I mutter sarcastically.

"What?"

"Nothing."

Eventually we make it home and Bash jumps out, because as always, his social calendar demands that he be somewhere in ten minutes or less. "You can drive me, yeah?" he yells over his shoulder.

"Don't take too long," I bellow after him. I need to get out of these bloomers, stat.

"Do you mind taking me home after?" asks Antonia from the back seat. "I don't feel like walking."

Oh, cool. "Thrilled to be your chauffeur," I mutter.

She catches my eye in the rearview mirror. "Okay, what was that?"

"What?"

"My house is, like, a few blocks that way, Vi. If it's an inconvenience I can walk."

"So I'm a bitch if I make you walk, is that it?" I ask, feeling my skin prickle with frustration. "Even though I've had a super long day and just want to go home and change?"

"Um, you're not the only one who had a long day." She frowns.

"Oh, of course, how could I forget." I can feel my anger slipping out from my control. "You *also* had the very hard job of soothing all the people I tormented."

"Wow." She sits up and opens the car door, shaking her head. "Clearly you're in a mood today."

"Wonder why," I grumble to myself.

She shifts like she's going to walk away, but then changes her mind, pausing next to my window. "I'm not your enemy, Vi."

You're not my ally, either, I think bitterly. The anger flickers again, then sags into something worse.

"I'm just tired," I tell her. "Frustrated. Stressed."

"You could try being a little nicer," she suggests in a playful tone, but all I can hear is the passive-aggressive reminder that she's *sorry.* Not to me, of course, but *for* me. She's sorry that I'm such an awful person. She's sorry she can't change me. She's sorry that she's friends with me. "Might take away some of your stress, you know," she adds, "if you just let people be themselves without threatening to tell on them."

I open my mouth to say it wasn't a threat, but then I remember that even if I *did* tell on George, nothing would happen. He didn't *do* anything—that's the whole point. What did he call it? A joke. Right. The real joke is that it's not a crime to stand too close or refuse to hear the word *no.* It's just . . . boys being boys. I don't think I could explain "he makes me uncomfortable" beyond just saying that.

But I'd kind of hoped my best friend wouldn't require an explanation.

"See you tomorrow?" she says, smiling.

But before I can answer, Bash comes barreling out, shouting to me like I'm the getaway car. "Drive!" he instructs me, giving me an unnecessary shove.

"Sorry, Antonia, I have t—"

"No worries. See you!" she calls to both of us.

I pull out of the driveway and she waves. Apparently everything is fine.

(Everything *is* fine, isn't it?)

Jack

"So, the knee," Dr. Barnes says. "It's a very aggressive tear. ACL, PCL, meniscus, the works. I did my best with what I could repair, but it's going to take some time before we can really start rehabilitating it."

I zone out while he says things like six weeks on crutches before I can put weight on it again, eight months typically but more likely twelve for a full recovery, regaining full range of motion may be difficult given the state of the knee when we went in, the good news is I'm young I'm healthy we have the best physical therapy available and there's no reason the graft shouldn't take, it's important to remain optimistic but recovery cannot be rushed, not if I want to regain full use of my knee, not just for football but for normal activities, walking running any form of vigorous exercise, cannot predict what the future will bring but if you put in the work you'll reap the rewards, Jack are you listening, Jack, I know it's a lot to take in, your mom and dad are completely behind you we've already discussed your PT schedule with Eric and honestly, don't stress about this, kiddo. Life has a way of working out.

I blink and look from Dr. Barnes to my father.

"Can I still go to practice with the team?" I ask.

Dr. Barnes seems to understand that I'm not asking for a miracle; I'm just asking my coach for my right as captain. As a senior. I'm asking, please, do not take everything away from me, not yet. Not like this, all in one fell swoop.

"Jack," my mom begins, her expression pained, but my dad shakes his head to stop her.

"Of course," he tells me, as Dr. Barnes looks at his hands. "Of course."

"Dude," says Nick, who comes to visit a few days after my surgery. "You look . . ."

He glances over the crumbs on my shirt, which are plentiful. I've been eating chips on the couch where I sleep and pretty much live, since it's too hard to get up the stairs to my bedroom on crutches.

"You don't look great, bro," he concludes with a charitable grimace.

"I'm fine." By which I mean a few things: I'm angry as shit, and bitter, too. I don't know what the hell kind of future I have now. My girlfriend only responds to one out of every three texts, which I think she's doing on purpose. Vi Reyes already texted me this morning about god even knows what. Homecoming? My one source of joy is that she seems as miserable as I feel. But no matter how much Vi's life mysteriously sucks, I've got my mom talking about possible majors like my football career is over while my dad sends me pages and pages of research about ACL tears like this is just a temporary thing.

Illyria will still give me my shot, he says, as long as I just show them I'm fine. If I want to come back from this, I can simply *come back*. See it, make it happen, exclamation point! Just visualize yourself as someone who isn't confined to the couch and hey, it's that easy! *Will* yourself upright, Jack, even if every spare motion costs you something! Even if everything you used to be is gone!

But what comes out of my mouth is "Dunno. I'm bored."

"Ah," says Nick with a nod, clearly relieved I haven't offered up something way darker, so I know I said the right thing. And anyway, it's true. It's barely been a week and I'm already sick of bingeing shows on Netflix, plus there's only so much homework a guy can do before he completely unravels. I should be on the field right now, but with football out of the question and Olivia still a mystery, that's most of my usual activities gone.

"I thought that might be the case," Nick says. "Where's your laptop?"

I rummage around for it, spotting it under the sofa. "Here. Better not be porn."

"No promises." He smirks at me, pulling up a new browser window and typing something into an unfamiliar log-in page.

"How's school?" I ask while I'm waiting, because I could at least make the visit worth his time instead of moping.

"It's okay. Classes are kind of boring," he says.

"Hard?"

"Sort of. It's all GEs, so." He shrugs. "Meh."

"Meet anyone interesting yet?"

"My roommate's okay. There's a few people in my dorm who seem cool. Okay, here we go." He pauses, hesitating. "Just so you know, it's—" He breaks off again. "Just don't tell anyone, okay?"

"It's porn, isn't it?" I theatrically sigh, and Nick gives me a look.

"Will you just promise, please?"

"Too late, I'm already live-blogging this conversation," I say, ham-handedly tapping the screen of my phone.

Nick rolls his eyes. "Right, forgot what a lovely mood you're in. Look, you remember the postseason I sat out with tendinitis?"

Viscerally. "Yeah."

"You were busy, and I couldn't move, obviously, so I found this." He flips the screen around.

"*Twelfth Knight*," I read from the landing page, frowning up at him. "What's this?"

"A game. Like *World of Warcraft* or *Final Fantasy*, but this one's way better."

"Uh," I say, fighting a laugh. "No wonder you don't want me to tell anyone. Since when are you a geek?"

"Was. *Was* a geek," he corrects me, "and only because I had hours of time to fill and nothing to fill it with, much like someone else we currently know." He pointedly sets the laptop on my lap. "Just trust me, okay? It's more fun than it sounds." He shifts to sit on the coffee table so we can both look at the screen. "First you have to create your character."

I look at him wordlessly. My intended meaning is, approximately: *Are you serious?*

He arches a brow in reply. This, clearly, means: *Like you have somewhere more pressing to be.*

Regrettably, he wins this round. I heave another sigh before relenting with "My . . . character?"

"Yes, your character. Here, click through here." He points to the screen and I scroll through a gallery of animated figures. "You can be a sorcerer, a mage, any sort of creature—"

I glance at him to see if he's joking, but he isn't. As much as I'd like to razz him a little more for this—I mean come on, a *creature*, seriously?—he's obviously just trying to make me feel better. The least I can do is take his efforts seriously. "What's the best?"

"Definitely a knight," he says quickly. He seems relieved, and I feel a little better already. "It means you have more skills in combat mode or in the different arenas."

If only I knew what he was talking about. "Arenas?"

"You can either do these crusade things where you try to find relics or win a series of challenges, or you can fight against other players. Kind of like on *War of Thorns*."

"You mean that weird TV show?" Vi's always wearing one of those shirts, so needless to say, I strongly doubt it's my thing.

"Dude." Nick glances at me. "You've never seen *War of Thorns*? Add that to the list. We're watching that next."

"Seriously?" I groan. With the sheer volume of embarrassing reveals so far, this is some hefty fraternal bonding.

"Seriously." Nick gives me another look. "Trust me on this."

Ugh. "Fine," I sigh, because as much as this show might suck, at least I won't have to sit alone with my thoughts while it's playing. "Is it actually good, though?"

"Bro. Yes." Nick nods vigorously. "I thought it was dumb at first, too, but then I got sucked in while my sister was watching. It's, like, weird at first, but really good. Here, finish setting up," he adds, pointing. "You'll need a username."

I type in my usual user ID, DUKEORSINO12, and pick Messaline colors for my armor. This feels stupid, but it's not like I've never played video games before. I get plenty of Madden in whenever a new version comes out. "Anything else?"

"Want to play a practice round first?"

"Nah." How hard can it be?

"My man." He claps me on the back. "Here, queue up for this arena. It doesn't have a huge waitlist."

I expected corny graphics given the old-timey font of the title page, but it's not so bad. I guess a castle is a castle. "Where are we in the game?"

"We're in Camelot for now," he says. "Everything starts here. The really cool battles and stuff are in other realms, like Gaunnes, or Camlann—you'll see."

A window pops up in the corner. "What's that?"

"Oh, someone trying to chat with you."

"Uhhh . . ." I'm not into that.

"A lot of the arenas work better if you have an alliance," he assures me quickly. "You play as a team and then eventually it's every man for himself."

"Oh." I type something back in the chat akin to *sure, whatever.* "So what happens in the arena?"

"You fight," he says with a shrug. "You strategize based on the other players. See how here you can tell how much life they have left, or where they have extra skills or relics? This one," he says, pointing, "has a ton of swordsmanship points, and that one"—he taps another figure with the back of a nail—"has extra brawling skills. You gain talents as you play."

"Does that one say they have . . . cooking skills?" I squint at the little plant symbol.

"Herbology. You need that for crusades. Quests, basically," he explains when I look at him blankly.

"Why?"

"Um, because you have to stay alive while you travel? And not poison yourself."

"Wait." That's wild. "I have to *eat* in the game?"

"You are your character," Nick says simply, and I give him yet another look. "It's weird, I know," he assures me with a laugh, "but hey, it passes the time. Plus if you play against someone who forgets to fuel up . . ." He shrugs. "It's just closer to a real game, that's all."

"Yeah, I guess." I can sort of see how this would feel similar to football. Find your position in the game, live or die by your skillset. Win by having more foresight than the others. Don't get killed. Don't do something stupid. Don't get hurt. Don't tear your ACL and lose your girlfriend in the same week. For a second, my knight avatar feels like the person I used to be.

Plus, I'll be honest—I have a tendency to get competitive regardless of circumstances. Doesn't technically matter the stakes. Our family Scrabble nights got so bad my mom gave all our board games to the babysitter.

"Okay, so how do I fight?" I ask Nick when the screen changes, letting me into the arena we've queued up for.

"Probably like shit at first," he says, "but it gets easier. Got your sword?"

"Uh . . ." There it is. "Okay."

"All right," he says, leaning forward. "Let's play."

"You look exhausted," my physical therapist Eric says, squinting at me. I'm sure I do, given how late I stayed up playing *Twelfth Knight* yesterday. "You sure you're okay?"

"Would I lie to you?" I offer sweetly.

"I mean, yeah, probably," Eric says, but thankfully doesn't push it. He's a fairly young guy, one of Dr. Barnes's former patients who got a degree in kinesiology after playing for Carolina. He's a few years out of school now, working as a PT assistant under one of Dr. Barnes's protégés while he completes his doctorate. "Just don't be stupid, okay? We'll be able to do more when the swelling goes down. For now, just focus on those stretches I showed you, and—"

"Ice and ibuprofen, I know."

"Good." He frowns. "You *sure* you're okay?"

"Sure, E. I'm fine." I'm not, obviously. I can barely stand, let alone walk, and worse than the pain is the guilt. Frank is switching the offense to a pass game while I'm out, putting the receivers to work in my place, but Curio's still shaky and I feel, I don't know, sick. Like this is my fault somehow. If I just hadn't messed with that cornerback, if I hadn't pissed him off, where would I be? I saw him coming. Why didn't I do something? I have dreams replaying the impact only bigger, more looming, like getting hit by a truck.

By the time I get back to school, I can barely meet anyone's eye.

"Hey, Duke," calls Curio, catching me as I walk through the school's gates. A banner for the Aloha Dance is draped across the entrance and I suddenly remember I'm going to that.

I think.

"Hey." I let Curio catch up as we traverse the school, turning the corner around the big gym. Messaline is one of those massive open campuses, so while Curio chatters about something, we pass the library, the freshmen and sophomore English and history departments, the upperclassmen electives hall. It's a long walk circumnavigating pristine, untouchable landscaping, which seems infinitely longer on crutches.

Luckily Curio's in no rush, though I don't really know what to make of him. He's always been fairly quiet, happy to be in Nick's shadow. I wonder if he's looking for some reassurance from me, since this is his last chance to win State, too. But he's not the one who already lost it.

"Is it true your brother's going pro at the end of this season?" Curio asks, blessedly interrupting my usual spiral of misery.

"Not sure." Almost definitely yes. It's always been Cam's goal, but that's between him and his publicist.

"Ah, cool. Bummer, though. I'd like to have seen your Illyria-Auburn showdown."

I don't know why, but the panic sinks in again, a little deeper every time. If Dad keeps me off the field all season, will Illyria think I'm not a solid investment? Will they change their minds? *Can* they change their minds? The terms of my LOI were about behavior, but what about injury? My spot on their roster might get revoked, and if it does, *then* what? Is there another school that would take me? What if I had to play D2? D3 even? I can't even process the possibility of not playing football at all.

"Hey," Curio says, catching the expression on my face. "Look, man, don't worry about it, I didn't mean to—"

At that precise moment, I spot Olivia. She's walking up the hill to the science quad alone, parting ways with one of her cheerleader friends, and before I really know what I'm doing I'm calling out to her, turning in her direction and accidentally driving a crutch into someone's foot.

"Jesus *Christ*, Orsino!" comes an unwelcome snarl to my left. "Do you not have eyes? Or is everyone else at this school some kind of inanimate prop to you?"

Oh, good. Vi Reyes.

"Not now, Vi," I tell her briskly, and she glares up at me from behind a curtain of long black hair. Up close it's jarring that she's got such an innocent-looking face, all soft brown eyes and rosy cheeks like a squeaky-clean TV starlet when she's so *clearly* cursing me out in her head. We've never had any reason to interact before this year, and if her coalition of nerds hadn't voted her in as my VP, I doubt we ever would have. Fortunately, now I have her in my life to inform me of the emails I didn't read (the ASB Gmail account gets a *lot* of spam—I think last year's president used it for their personal shopping addiction) and the various ways in which I have failed my fiduciary duty as an elected officer, a thing that cannot possibly apply to the concept of student government—and yet, try telling that to Vi.

"You're right, an apology would probably break your other knee," she says, glancing briefly at Curio before dismissing him and turning back to me. "Think you can summon the competence to sign off on the budget today?"

"Viola," I groan. This is the only conceivable way to say her name: as if you are slowly being drained of oxygen. "It's eight in the morning. Can't this wait?"

I scan the hill for Olivia, but I've lost sight of her now.

"Your devotion to this school is a real marvel," Vi informs me, before turning away to stalk in the direction Olivia just disappeared.

"She's . . . nice," observes Curio, frowning.

"Yeah," I mutter. "A real ray of sunshine."

"Anyway, listen," he offers, tentative again, "if you need anything—"

"Dude." I glance at him, wondering how to phrase this. "I'm not, like, dead. You know what I mean?"

He laughs, so mission accomplished. "Right, sorry. See you at practice?" he asks, turning in the direction of what I now realize is his class, but very much not mine.

"Yeah." The bell rings, and the rapidly vacating campus looms before me like a bad sci-fi shot.

Predictably, my day does not improve.

"Oh, come on. You again?" demands Vi two periods later, spotting me as we turn the corner at the same time outside the English building—which *would* be fine, if I hadn't already passed her outside Olivia's math class. "That's three times this morning. Are you stalking me?"

"Yes, Viola, I'm stalking you," I mutter, scanning over her head for a glimpse of Olivia from the interior hallway. "It's because you're so nice and friendly."

"Can you just sign off on the budget?" she snaps, shifting her backpack around and reaching into it. "It'll take five seconds, and since you're just *standing* here—"

At that moment, Olivia comes into view at the opposite end of the hall. "I can't, Vi, I told you, I'm busy—"

"With what?" she demands. To my complete frustration, she starts following me as I set off after Olivia. "You can talk to your girlfriend anytime, Jack. Like, literally anytime."

"Just—" I swear under my breath as Olivia slips into the classroom, either not noticing me or pretending not to. "Fine," I growl, snatching the binder from Vi's hands and gesturing for her to turn so I can use her shoulder to sign it. "Pen?"

She gives me an eye roll so pronounced I'm worried it's harming her medically. "Do you not own a *pen*?"

Losing my temper will not solve this. "You're right, let's just sign this later when I'm more prepared—"

"Wow." She hands me one over her shoulder, glaring at me.

"Great!" I shuffle my crutches, scribbling a signature, and shove it back to her just as she turns. Regrettably our hands touch by accident, forcing an awkward moment that she resolves by growling at me.

"Did you even read it?" she demands.

"Viola," I sigh, "you have the signature. I'm successfully unburdened of my will to live. What more do you want from me?"

Her eyes narrow. "Um, a *modicum* of responsibility, perhaps? Possibly an *iota* of dependability?"

"Great, measurable goals, I'll work on that for next time." I turn away, or try to, but she stomps in the opposite direction, reaching for the same door Olivia just walked through.

Hm. Interesting.

"Wait," I call after Vi, and she throws a glance at me so vicious I feel it like a water balloon to my skin. "Are you in Olivia's English class?"

"Don't tell me you want me to pass her a note." Vi folds her arms across her chest, a tacit suggestion that if I even bother asking, she'll take it as she's taken everything else so far today: extremely poorly.

"No, I just—" I fumble for an explanation that doesn't include *my girlfriend maybe wants to dump me.* "I thought you were in, like, all AP classes."

"Uh, I am?" She glares again for good measure. "So is Olivia."

"Oh." Right.

"She's in AP Physics with me. And AP Lit. And AP Calc." Vi frowns at me. "Did you somehow not know your girlfriend was smart?"

Yes, of course I knew that. Olivia's always been smart, but Vi's basically a mutant. The only thing I knew about her prior to elections was that she was deeply, obsessively into school, whereas Olivia has an actual social life. The chance of their academic schedules overlapping seems distinctly fake.

"No, I know, obviously," I manage to say, "I just—"

"Look, I really don't have time for this. Get your house in order and leave me out of it, Orsino," Vi snaps, shoving open the door and stepping into the classroom.

For the briefest instant I catch sight of Olivia, who's sitting at the desk nearest the door. She looks up, catches my eye, and looks away.

Okay, she's definitely avoiding me. But why? Is she angry about something I did? Pissed about something I didn't do? There's definitely *something* I don't know. And while I may not be able to do anything about my knee or my future at Illyria, I should be able to fix this.

See it, make it happen. I'm going to fix this, I promise myself firmly.

And a small voice in me answers: *Because I can't fix anything else.*

NO POINTS FOR NEUTRALITY

Vi

The moment the bell rings for sixth period, Kayla from the social committee accosts me. I've just sat down at one of the lab tables—Bowen, the leadership teacher, also teaches biology—not that she cares, and I only manage to wolf about three bites of peanut butter and jelly before she arrives on her usual cloud of smoke.

"Do you have the Aloha budget yet?" she demands.

There's peanut butter stuck to the roof of my mouth, which affords me time to displace my urge to suggest where she can stick the budget. (Kayla is very good at her job, but her energy is extreme. And let's just say we have very different priorities—for example, I've graciously left out the appropriative qualities of a welcome-back dance lined with tiki torches and empty references to indigenous Hawaii, because unselectively choosing my battles at this school can be a real drain on my peace.)

"You realize you could have been harassing someone else about this," I inform Kayla after a sip from my water bottle.

"Okay, but like, how hard can it be?" she retorts, which is a very good question that, as I recall, I was very recently asking someone else.

We went through this exact song and dance last week in advance of the Pigskin Roast, which I did not even attend. "Lucky for you, Kayla, I live to serve," I inform her drily, reaching into my bag. "Budget is now approved. Reimbursement check's ready to be handed over as soon as you give me all your receipts."

"Um, did I not say I'd need eight hundred dollars?" Kayla demands. Tragically she's now flanked by Mackenzie, a usually reasonable person unless there are garish decorations on the line.

"Once again," I reply with very little patience, "the administration requires receipts. You spend the money, I catalog the invoices and reimburse you. That's how it works."

"I could just get Ryan to do it," Kayla snaps, as Mackenzie nods vigorously. "He's the one who's actually in charge of the budget."

Oh yes, Ryan. The brilliantly uninvested point guard who ran for treasurer because . . . he lost a bet? Suffered a traumatic head wound? It's a mystery. "You know, Kayla, you're not the only one who wishes we lived in a world where treasurers did their jobs and people let you finish your sandwich," I inform her, tossing what remains of my lunch into the various bins for compost and trash. I hardly even touched it, because in addition to cleaning up one of the lunch activities for spirit week, I also promised my brother I'd listen to him rehearse his monologue for the fall play, and on top of *that* I agreed to do an interview for the journalism staff about the proposed changes to the student guidebook, which (surprise!) Jack Orsino could not be available for, according to his lack of reply. Fortunately, his daily itinerary of driving me to madness remains scheduled to perfection.

"No offense, Vi, but you're being, like, very bitchy," observes Mackenzie, a small crease forming between her brows.

"None taken," I assure her. "Get me the receipts and I'll reimburse you. Same day, I promise."

Kayla grumbles but seems to trust me on this. After all, I may be "like, very bitchy," but I'm also very reliable.

"So, we're good?" I ask them. "Because I have work to do."

Part of me wants to point out once again that they could have easily bothered someone else about this. Like, say, Jack Orsino, who's just now waltzing in from lunch. He sits clear across campus at the top of the quad with the other senior athletes and cheerleaders, though I did notice when I passed his table that Olivia Hadid was suspiciously absent.

Not that I normally care what Olivia Hadid does, much less Jack Orsino, but since I've been caught in the crossfire of Jack trying to hunt her down all day, I'm starting to think someone's finally lost their taste for whatever hallucinogenic Jack puts in his aftershave. I always thought they were sort of an odd pairing. Not because of

Olivia—she's smart and famously not an asshole. What I fail to understand is what she sees in *him*.

"I think Olivia Hadid broke up with Jack Orsino," I inform my brother that afternoon while we're driving home. (Correction: *I'm* driving, because Bash should not be handling any large machinery unless absolutely necessary.)

"What? No way." Bash sits up, delighted. "Before homecoming?"

"What?"

"They were basically a lock for king and queen."

"So?"

"So???" he barks back at me.

"What do you care?"

"Viola, I'm an artist," he sniffs. "The human condition is my muse."

"I don't think Jack and Olivia are prime examples of the human condition, Sebastian."

"*Aren't* they?" he barks again. "It's honestly very Greek."

"What?"

"His knee!"

"So?"

"He hurts his knee and she leaves him? It's like Delilah cutting Samson's hair and betraying him to the Philistines!"

"Delilah was essentially abducted by Samson," I point out, and am unable to prevent myself from adding, "which gets left out in pretty much every adaptation—"

Bash groans. "It's the *spirit* of the narrative—"

"The femme fatale myth is extremely misogynistic," I remind him, since apparently he doesn't read our mother's columns like I do, "and more importantly, *Olivia* did not take out Jack's knee."

"That would be exciting, though," Bash says enthusiastically. "Sort of like a Tonya Harding thing but in more of a vengeful, Tarantino-ed style?"

"The Tonya Harding thing's not vengeful enough as it is? That other skater's knee got bashed in with a steel baton. What were you hoping for, gunshots?"

"Well, fine," he concedes. "The point is you should add something like that into one of your quests."

"Oh." Normally I'd point out that gratuitous gun violence in this political climate is ethically untenable and aesthetically disruptive, but the energy's just not there when I reach for it. Instead, I vigorously tap the steering wheel. "Yeah, I'm not doing quests anymore."

"What? Why not?" I can tell there's a look of concern on his face, but for all intents and purposes, my eyes are on the road.

"I don't know, I'm busy."

We pull into the driveway and I know—I just *know*—he's going to talk to my mom about this. The two of them are always commiserating about my blood pressure, convinced I'm going to explode a vessel in my brain or something. Which, admittedly, I might. People are extremely irritating.

"What's wrong?" my mom asks immediately when we walk in. She writes for most of the day but makes a point to stop working and hover in the kitchen during the hours when everyone's floating around the house: before school, after school, dinnertime.

"Nothing's wrong," I say when Bash announces, "Vi fought with her nerd friends."

"Again?" my mom says.

Perfect. The ideal reaction.

"These are the ConQuest nerds," Bash clarifies, because last year I had an ideological divergence with my AP US History study group, who are also nerds but in a very distinctive way.

Bash slips onto the stool by the counter. "She says she's over it."

"I *am* over it," I say, though nobody's listening.

"Aw, honey." My mom turns to me with a longing sigh, going full Cinderella for a second. "They didn't like the story you wrote?"

"It's not a story, it's—" I break off, frustrated. "Never mind. And no, they didn't, but it's fine. I can't stand them anyway."

"You can't stand anyone," Bash says, so I backhand him in the gut. He coughs, then reaches up to tug my braid.

"Oh my god, *stop* it—"

"Hang on." Bash reaches into his pocket, his phone buzzing. "What?" he shouts cheerfully into the phone, walking away to take a call. "Oh yeah, hang on, I've got the scene pages right here—

though, brief sidebar?" he adds, thundering up the stairs. "*Jack Orsino* and *Olivia Hadid*—"

"BASH, I NEVER SAID THAT WAS—and he's gone," I conclude under my breath with a sigh, belatedly registering that I've been left alone with our mother's look of plaintive concern. "Stop," I tell her, groaning. She does this: worries. It's sweet but unnecessary. "I'm fine," I assure her, and add, "I don't want to talk about it."

She purses her lips, knowing better than to press me. After all, I take after her. When she and I don't want to be bothered, we do *not* want to be bothered, and there's no point pushing it. This is something a lot of her exes have learned the hard way.

"Fine. How was school?" she asks, pushing a plate of hummus and raw vegetables across the counter to me. I reach for a carrot, shrugging.

"Fine," I say, taking a bite.

"Just fine?"

I chew, very slowly, and swallow.

"How was your date?" I counter. "You never told us."

She does a mirror version of the slow-chew-for-deliberation.

"I'm seeing someone," she says.

"Duh."

"No, not . . . not for work." She tilts her head.

"For . . . pleasure?" I offer, like an airport customs officer.

"Let's just say it's going well." She plucks up another carrot, takes a bite. "Yes," she says mysteriously. "Very well."

"You're in an actual relationship," I realize, blinking. As I've hopefully made clear by now, my mom is *not* the relationship type.

"*Relationship* is a strong word," she says, predictably. She likes her own space, like I do. We are not the sort of women designed to pick a mate and settle down.

"Where'd you meet them?"

"Oh, you know."

"Of course I don't *know*, Mother, I'm seventeen. Are you trying to tell me you met your latest paramour on The Apps?" Normally she's not very withholding about these sorts of things. She prizes authenticity, as she says.

"No, actually." She tilts her head. "I met him at the grocery store."

"Your eyes locked over the deli counter or something?"

"Something like that."

I was *joking*. "Ew, Mom, are you dating the butcher?"

"No, no." She shakes her head. "He's . . . a community organizer," she says eventually, which sounds like a lie.

"So he's unemployed?"

"No." She rolls her eyes at me. "You're such a cynic."

"You raised me," I remind her.

"No way. You came out this way, fully formed." She reaches for a cucumber slice. "So," she says, which is obviously the start of a lecture. "About your friends."

I take a last swipe of hummus, sighing. "They're not my friends, okay? Friends would respect my ideas. Or, I don't know, care."

"Antonia does, doesn't she?"

I feel a little prickle of doubt. I may be avoiding Antonia, but she's not exactly rushing to talk to me, either. "Antonia's just one person."

"Sometimes I think you need to start seeing why that matters." Mom gives me a long look as Bash bounds down the stairs.

"I see it," I tell her, reaching for my bag. "I'm fine. And I've got homework."

"You ate all the hummus," Bash whines.

"You snooze, you lose," I tell him, poking him in the ribs and escaping the retaliatory swipe at the back of my head to make my way up the stairs.

I may have stayed up too late last night playing *Twelfth Knight*. In my defense, I got at least four hundred texts from Kayla after I told her that the invoices she sent me only added up to about seven hundred and fifteen dollars. *do you think I would lie????* she demanded. *do you honestly think I'm some kind of human ponzi scheme or something??????*

So yeah. I had to spend a couple of hours atop the arena leaderboards. Plus I watched a new concept trailer for *War of Thorns* season four and fell down a rabbit hole of fan-made videos. And fine, I *may* have logged on to my fan fiction account to read a few modern AUs, but that's between me and my emotional support villain, okay? It's called self-care. Anyway, I knew it was time to go to bed when I hallucinated the username DukeOrsino12, which I can only assume was my halfway comatose brain mixing up some other less annoying person with an email from Jack. (It was an impressively psychotic "lmao k" at three in the morning in response to my email about needing to actually go paperless if we plan to adhere to last year's ASB Student Carbon Footprint Initiative, which is now—mazel tov!—my problem.)

I settle in my desk before class, ready to zone out until the bell rings, but my temporary serenity is disturbed by the sound of whispers from the two dingalings behind me.

"—heard she dumped him. Isn't that wild?"

"Do you think he cheated on her or something?"

"Why else would she break up with him?"

"Wonder if she's looking for a rebound."

I blink when I realize they're talking about Olivia, who walked in and took her seat in silence as she always does. There aren't many girls in AP Calculus, so naturally she's a fixture of the disgusting nerdboi imagination.

"Good luck with that," I scoff to the guy behind me. It's Jason Lee, who'd have no shot with Olivia Hadid even if he magically produced Jack's facial features, a sense of humor, *and* a trust fund, and Murph, for whom I spare exactly none of my attention. Big as the school is, there are only about twenty of us who have almost every class together: the AP kids, as we unofficially call ourselves. Jason is one of them, as is Murph and also famed Nice Guy Matt Das, who is very pointedly not speaking to me. Olivia's technically an AP kid as well, though nobody includes her in that group. She spends most of the year in her cheer uniform and rarely talks in class, so her presence is more like a blinding anomaly that we've all collectively gotten used to.

Until now, that is, since apparently there's a rumor about her that I can't help but suspect I might have started.

I'm feeling plenty guilty about my comments to Bash by the time we get to AP Lit, because clearly people won't stop talking about Olivia and she either doesn't know it or is very successfully pretending not to hear. I don't really care if Jack's reputation loses a little shine over this, but Olivia's nice, she keeps to herself, and it sucks that people think they have a right to her personal life. I mean, how many times does the girl somehow get all the blame for a breakup? According to them, either Jack cheated and it's her fault for not keeping him interested, or she dumped him because she's evil and also probably stupid (depending on who you ask). Teenagers have no imagination.

"Okay, kids, it's that time of year again," says Mr. Meehan, a noted Shakespeare kook. "For our next assignment, we're all going to be performing scenes from the Bard's oeuvre."

Mr. Meehan is also the drama teacher, in case that wasn't immediately obvious.

"Let's see, for the *Romeo and Juliet* farewell—'Wilt thou be gone?' so on and so forth, as Romeo sets off a fugitive . . . Ah, Miss Hadid," he says, scanning the room and landing on Olivia, "I believe you enjoyed this one. How about you take Juliet?"

Olivia nods, and immediately five boys' heads swivel, exorcist style, to the front of the room.

"And for Romeo—"

Five hands shoot up.

"I'll do it," I say without thinking. Like, literally zero thought, which is unfortunate, because I've just agreed to do a love scene as performed by a horny idiot. (I'm not convinced by the Romeo and Juliet story, sorry.)

"Miss Reyes?" Mr. Meehan echoes, looking entirely too delighted. "You do know it's a male part."

No, Mr. Meehan, I had no idea. *Romeo,* you say? "Shakespeare routinely had men playing female parts," I point out.

"As per the conventions at the time." He's just being Socratic, which is tiresome.

"Mr. Meehan, unless you have an issue with me playing Romeo— *which*," I add, "I think we can both agree would be a problem given our *progressive* student body—"

"The part is yours, Miss Reyes," Mr. Meehan says immediately. "Moving on to the play that shall not be named—"

Thank you, Olivia mouths to me from across the room, which startles me. After all, it's my fault people are talking about her.

So in response I shrug, she half smiles, and we both turn back to our desks.

"Thanks again for doing this," says Olivia when the bell signifies the end of AP Lit later that week. Meehan gave us a few minutes to work on our scenes at the end of class, so we're vacating the same corner of the classroom at the same time.

"It's no big deal," I offer distractedly, still furious about at least four different things. High on the list? Kayla, who's already sent around an email about homecoming despite the Aloha Dance being tonight. Jack, who I'm just assuming did not read it. Antonia, who's now cheerily bombarding me via the ConQuest group chat like nothing's changed, meaning I may have to actually attend the Aloha Dance in order to avoid it. And Matt Das, because he's shuffling out behind us with the audacity to still exist.

"The last thing I need right now is to have to do a love scene with one of those idiots," clarifies Olivia in a low voice, which is a refreshing level of snark from her. "Not that they're *all* idiots," she adds in apparent penance.

"No, they absolutely are," I assure her, holding the door open as she follows me through it. "Though you could have just said no when Meehan offered you the scene."

"I know." It appears we'll both be walking down the corridor together, which is a first. "It's just . . . a really gorgeous scene, though," she says wistfully.

"Kind of corny, don't you think?"

"Oh, come on. 'My bounty is as boundless as the sea / my love as deep; the more I give to thee / the more I have, for both are infinite,'" Olivia recites to me, a little breathless.

"Is that One Direction?"

She groans. "Ohmygod."

"Personally I think Mercutio's in love with Romeo," I add, and she laughs.

"Maybe he is! The point is the sentiment. The words. The *meaning*—"

"That quote is from the balcony scene, not this one," I point out.

"Still," she sighs. "Don't tell me you're one of those people who thinks something can't be taken seriously if it's about love. I mean, what else is the point of being human, right? It's not just *romantic* love," she adds. "You know the Greeks had five? Platonic love, playful love . . ."

"I don't have a problem with love stories," I assure her, which is true. After all, I do fervently ship Liliana and Cesario on *War of Thorns*. "But the Greeks had *six* kinds of love, one of which is sex, and that's what *this*," I say with a nudge to her *Romeo and Juliet* script, "is about. It's like how *Titanic*'s not a love story so much as a cautionary tale about a dude who has sex with a rich girl on a boat and then immediately dies. If anything," I conclude, "it's about the dangers of capitalism."

"Wowwwww," Olivia says.

"I know. Huge con."

"So this is you having no problem with love stories?" she says, arching a brow. We've reached the corner where we'd typically part ways for lunch, though she seems in no hurry to leave.

"No problem whatsoever. This just isn't one."

"But what about the tragedy?" she prods me, still lingering despite the people pushing past us in the hall. "Fate? Star-crossed love?"

"Miscommunication is a classic comedy of errors trope. And didn't you notice the dick jokes?" I point out, and Olivia laughs.

"Comedy and tragedy both depend on disorder," Olivia agrees. "But the resolution? Pure tragedy."

"Okay, so does tragedy make a love story? Because if Romeo had just waited a few minutes before plunging a dagger into his chest, there'd be a laugh track and an off-screen divorce five years later."

"Oh, great," she groans, "you somehow managed to make *Romeo and Juliet* even *more* depressing."

I'm about to tell her it's one of my special talents when a sudden cacophony of crutches materializes on my left. It's Jack Orsino, of course, fruitlessly chasing Olivia as usual. He gets a few lingering looks that he apparently doesn't notice—this school, honestly. Pick a god who reads his emails, that's all I ask.

"Oh, hey," says Jack, sweating a little despite obviously pretending not to. "Olivia," he adds, turning to her after a sparse nod in my direction. "On your way to lunch?"

"Oh, um. Yeah, in a sec? But I'm kind of finishing my chat with Vi about our AP Lit scene," Olivia says, gesturing to me.

"Vi?" Jack says, shifting his furrowed glance to me like I'm a concept somebody recently invented. His eyes are a deep brown that's both intense and unnerving, because of course they are. Athletic abilities can't account for everything without conventional attraction as an added plus, though he looks . . . oddly exhausted?

Before I finish the thought, though, he looks away.

"You can go ahead without me," Olivia offers to him.

"Oh no, it's fine," Jack replies too quickly. "I can wait."

Good god, Jack. Even *I'm* cringing.

"Oh . . . um. Okay. Does tomorrow work?" Olivia asks, turning to me.

"Tomorrow?" I echo blankly, having gotten caught up in whatever this is.

"Yeah. To rehearse? After school," she says, Jack still staring between us like he's trying to solve a math equation. In fairness, I don't know what Olivia's talking about either, but if it causes Jack Orsino this much distress, so be it.

"Sure," I say. "That works. My house?"

"Great." Olivia beams. "I'll text you."

She doesn't have my number. Not that it wouldn't be easy to DM me on basically any platform, but still. Interesting enough to commit to the bit. "Sounds good! Bye, Jack," I add gratuitously, delighting in my opportunity to mess with him until I unintentionally meet his eye.

Yikes, he does look awful—like he hasn't slept in days. Something pricks in my chest, though thankfully it doesn't last.

"Bye," Jack says faintly, angling his crutches after Olivia with a crease of confusion still caught between his brows.

Jack

"Morning, sunshine," my mother jokingly singsongs when I stumble upright from the sofa. I nearly launch my teeth into the edge of the coffee table, tripping over my pile of textbooks on the floor. "You haven't been staying up too late, have you?"

She glances pointedly at my laptop, which is shoved into the sofa cushions. I put it there somewhere around three or four, or whenever it was that I couldn't keep my eyes open anymore.

Twelfth Knight is a weird game, complicated and a little bit like getting lost in some bizarro fantasy world that has its own language and rules, but I'm getting the hang of it. I've always seen the football field as a war zone in some way or another, and this really isn't that different. More important, I find myself thinking a lot about the game when I'm not playing it—new skills I've acquired and how to use them in combat, places in the realms I could go if I could beat certain levels or opponents, that sort of thing.

It's definitely not football. No crowd is ever going to applaud me for the things I achieve in this game, or anywhere off the field. But considering all the other things I could be thinking about—the way my teammates avoid looking at my knee, for example, or the way my dad no longer seems to know what to say to me at dinner—this is . . . pretty much ideal, even if it does keep me up most of the night.

"You know me, Mom. Bright-eyed and bushy-tailed, like always." I rub my eyes blearily, reaching for my crutches. "What are you doing here?"

She gives me a hurt look that I'm going to tell myself is only playful. "Can't a mother come by to visit her injured son?" she jokes, which is only further evidence I've upset her.

"I just meant—" I wave a hand. Doesn't matter what I meant. "Breakfast?"

"Already on the table."

"Great." I follow her into the kitchen, where she's set an enormous plate of eggs and bacon and enough slabs of toast to feed a small army. "Whoa."

"I figured you'd be hungry," she says, catching my eye. "I do happen to recall how you eat, Jack, even if I don't live here anymore."

I manage to drag out the stool and lift myself onto it, one of my crutches tumbling to the ground in the meantime. "At this rate there's about to be a permanent imprint of my ass in the couch cushions."

"You're healing," she says, "and don't say 'ass.'"

Seems poor form to argue with her first thing in the morning, so I don't. "Well, thanks, Mom." I lift a piece of toast to my mouth, listening to how she'll be doing breakfast with me every Sunday before physical therapy while my dad watches game film with the other coaches at school.

"I'm glad you're going to have a chance to rest," she comments idly. "Better you focus on other things besides football for now. Your college applications, for one thing."

My stomach drops. "I'm going to Illyria," I remind her.

She nods quickly. "Right, of course, but just in case—"

"And it's still my team," I add, the toast going dry in my mouth as I force a swallow. "I still need to be there."

"Oh, I know that, baby," she says, cooing at me a little too sympathetically. Like maybe she, too, feels sorry for me, clinging to an old dream even after all hope is gone. I heard her say that to my dad once, and even though I'm sure she regrets it now, it has a stain of truth to it.

Just like that, my appetite is gone.

"I should probably brush my teeth and get going," I tell her, nudging the unfinished plate in her direction. "Breakfast was great though, thanks."

She sort of half frowns at me. "You sure you're feeling okay?"

"Yeah, I'm fine." Not great. But at least I don't have to think about it while I'm sawing some computer avatar in half with a broadsword. "Everything's fine, Mom, I promise."

"Mm." She eyes me for a second. "How's Nick doing?"

After he left last weekend, he made me promise to finish binging *War of Thorns* so I can catch up with the new season, which he claims is going to be the best one so far. It's not a bad show—I assumed it would be, thanks to all the special effects and weird costumes and, again, the critically suspect endorsement of one Viola Reyes, but you do kind of get invested in the story, so I'll probably do that this weekend after the away game.

The one I won't be playing in.

"Nick's good," I say, clearing my throat.

"And how's Olivia?" Mom adds, picking up one of my pieces of bacon.

"Oh, uh." Honestly? I'd like to know the same thing. "She's a little stressed."

"Makes sense. She's got a difficult course load this year, doesn't she?"

"I guess." It feels a little bit like I don't know anything about Olivia anymore. Like I'm not that special to her, or maybe I never was. Sounds stupid, probably, but it seems like we've both talked more to Vi Reyes in the past week than to each other, which—

Hm. Vi Reyes again.

Very belatedly, something switches on like a light bulb. I've been thinking of Vi all morning, and it finally occurs to me why that might be.

Could *Vi* be the key to fixing things with Olivia?

Vi's little scowl materializes in my head, sudden and unavoidable and mildly less annoying than before. I wanted an answer, and conveniently, here she is.

"I really gotta get going," I remind my mom, shoveling a sudden, enthusiastic forkful of eggs into my mouth and beating her to my crutches. "Thanks again, though!"

"Hon? I figured I'd be driving you," my mom calls after me, gesturing to my knee.

"Oh." Right. "Yeah, thanks. Cool if we leave in five minutes?"

"Sure," she says, bemused, as I put aside thoughts of knights, away games, and mysterious sort-of girlfriends just long enough to start formulating a plan.

My first attempts at sorting out the best way to persuade Vi to help me are . . . not very fruitful.

"Vi? She's a bitch," says Tom Murphy. "Why do you ask?"

"Oh, total bitch" is Marco Klein's take. "Don't even bother."

"She's not a bitch," Rob Kato says hesitantly, looking startled that I've chosen to talk to him at all, "but like, she kind of has no soul, you know what I mean? So, like, yeah."

Even Nick's sister gives me a vague answer.

"Vi?" Antonia echoes, frowning at me. "I don't know, honestly. She's been . . . weird lately. What did you want to ask her?"

"It's more like I need a favor," I explain. "And I'm wondering if she's ever normal, you know what I mean?"

Antonia sighs, considering it. "Two weeks ago I'd have said Vi's not at all what people think she is," she tells me, slamming her locker shut. "Now?" She shrugs. "Good luck."

Oh good, great. Ideal. At this point I'll have to ask Olivia how she manages to have a civil conversation with Vi in order to get Vi to ask what the hell's going on with Olivia.

"Everything okay?" Antonia asks, frowning up at me.

"Huh? Yeah. Just a school thing," I lie quickly. "I need her to help me with something. Curricularly," I add, in case she suspects anything weird. Or worse, personal.

"Oh. Well that's not happening." Antonia gives a sharp laugh. "She already thinks you don't do any work. Not that that's true," she adds quickly. "I mean, you obviously know that. And I always tell her she just doesn't understand the pressure you're under. Or were under, but . . ." She, like everyone these days, glances briefly down at my knee, then looks hastily away. "I just meant—"

"It's fine. Sorry, gotta go," I say, realizing that lunch is over, which means I'm late for leadership class, which is not a good start.

By the time I make it to the classroom, Vi's already got a meeting going at her usual lab table.

"—*told* you that would look tacky," Kayla is saying, and Mackenzie, beside her, nods vigorously. "Don't you want homecoming to be, like, the best dance ever?"

"Like, no, I do not," answers Vi in a snotty voice.

"But this is our legacy," Mackenzie insists.

"I thought junior prom last year was your legacy?" Vi counters.

"That too!" Kayla snaps, while Mackenzie gives a vigorous nod. "It's about our *oeuvre*, okay?"

"First of all, I don't think a bunch of school dances qualifies as an oeuvre," Vi says with a low growl, "nor do I think there's any reason to spend that much money on chairs when we already own a full set of—"

"Hi," I cut in, as Vi groans and Kayla and Mackenzie whip around, instantly flushed.

"Jack," Mackenzie exhales. "We were just—"

"Chairs?" I prompt in my most charming voice.

"For the tables," Kayla informs me.

"For the tables," I agree. "Which we . . . need?"

"Well, people need a place to rest," Mackenzie says vigorously. "You know, when they're tired from dancing."

"Don't we have tables and chairs we usually use?" I'm not actually sure. By the look on Vi's face, though, the answer is yes, and whatever else is unquestionably wrong with Vi, she usually has the right answer.

"Well, *technically*, but—"

"The budget is pretty limited," I point out, which I assume is true, since I've never heard of a budget that was unlimited. "So maybe we could, you know, *table* this discussion?" I joke, nudging a slightly sour-faced Kayla. "If there's money left over then we can revisit it."

"You signed off on their budget," Vi reminds me under her breath, digging something out of her backpack.

Huh, okay then. "Well, listen, you're smart," I tell Kayla and Mackenzie. "I'm sure you can find some, uh, you know. Money that's like . . . stuff we don't need to spend?"

"Redundancies," Vi says, pretending to be looking over a page in a book that she definitely pulled out as a prop for this conversation.

"Those," I agree, with another smile in Kayla's direction. "The point is, it's not in the budget. Which isn't Vi's fault."

Vi looks up, half frowning at me.

"But I'm happy to help if I can," I conclude, and Kayla finally smiles back, relenting.

"Thanks, Jack. See that, Vi? There's a *nice* way to handle things," Kayla shoots over her shoulder at Vi, who gestures back in a way that Kayla thankfully misses before turning to me. "By the way, so sorry to hear about Olivia," Kayla murmurs, her hand lingering on my forearm.

"What about Olivia?" I say, as if I have no idea.

"Oh, just that you two were, *you know*—"

"We're fine," I assure her. "Better than ever, in fact."

"Oh." Kayla blinks, withdrawing her hand. "Well . . . great!" she says brightly, before wandering away with Mackenzie at her heels, the two of them launching into whispers the moment they're out of earshot.

"Liar," remarks Vi in a low voice.

"Beg your pardon?"

"You heard me." She flips another page in her book, which I slide away from her. She looks up with a glare, eyes narrowing. "What?"

"I'm not lying."

"About Olivia? You certainly are. Either that or you're even more oblivious than I thought."

As much as it pains me to have this particular conversation with Vi, it is clearly my opening. I glance around before shifting closer. "Did she say something to you?"

"She doesn't have to," Vi informs me in the most obnoxious way possible. "I have eyes."

"It's . . . complicated," I admit in an undertone.

"*Is* it?" she replies in a doubtful singsong, tugging her book back from me. "Seems simple to me."

"Well, it's not." *Not that you'd know anything about relationships,* I want to add, given how few of her own friends seem to like her, but antagonizing her right now seems like the wrong move. "Do you . . . ?" I clear my throat. "Do you think you could talk to her about it?"

"About what?"

"About—" I glance around again, but no one's listening. One of the rare benefits of Viola Reyes's personality: nobody wants to be within range of whatever's pissed her off today. "About me," I admit.

"Um. What?" She looks up, and to my complete dismay, she's . . . laughing. Or something that looks like laughter, which is definitely at my expense. "You want me to ask her about *you*? Out of curiosity," she begins, in a tone that I can already tell will take a hard turn for the mocking, "how many conversations about you do you think the average person has per day? I'm genuinely desperate to hear your answer."

God, she's unbearable. "Look," I grumble, "if you'd just do me this *one* favor, it could be mutually beneficial, all right? I could make sure it was."

Her dark eyes flick sideways to mine. "You'd have to be capable of something that actually benefits me," she points out, which is true.

Though, given the conversation I just interrupted, that's not entirely out of the question.

"I just did," I inform her.

"Did what?" She's barely listening.

"I helped you. Defended you." I gesture metaphorically to Kayla and Mackenzie.

"Did your job, you mean?"

I inhale, controlling the urge to snap. "Can you give me some credit here, Reyes? I'm trying to help you out."

She flips a page in her book. "By offering to do exactly what you were elected to do?"

"Uh, Viola," I inform her, leaning toward her in a move that never misses, "I think we both know that what I was *elected* to do was stand here and look pretty."

She snorts.

"Okay, hang on," I say, because I don't annoy that easily, but she's got the magic touch; she finds my buttons and pushes, even without a word. "In case it's escaped your attention, you're not exactly a walk in the park," I point out to her. "I don't know if you've noticed, but people really don't like you."

At first I kick myself for letting that slip when I'm supposed to be charming her—a task that may or may not be impossible—but she merely shrugs like she's heard it before.

"Nobody likes the person who does the shitty parts of the job," she says. "I don't expect to be liked."

"You don't *want* to be?" I challenge her.

She sets the book aside, twisting until she faces me.

"No," she says, and gets up to leave, only I nudge a crutch into her path to pause her.

"Come on. Everyone wants to be liked."

She shrugs me off. "Some people need it. I don't."

She probably means that, which is something I'll have to ponder another time. "Still. I could . . . make things easier for you."

"Oh yeah?" She looks up at me, skeptical, and about as annoyed with me as I am with her. "You'll smile my problems away?"

"I—" It's frustrating for a second, but then it occurs to me that just because Vi thinks that's a small thing doesn't mean it is. "Yes," I realize slowly. "Yes, that's exactly what I'll do."

She blinks. "Excuse me?"

Aside from being a great running back, I'm also extremely talented at having zero enemies. Minus the Padua cornerback—an offense for which retribution was painfully swift—I had to learn early on that when you look like me, it's best if you never lose your temper, ever. For better or worse, likability is kind of my jam.

"I'll deliver the bad news," I say. "I'll cut the budgets. With a smile," I add, just to taunt her a little. Just so she's as prickly as I currently feel. "All the so-called 'shitty parts' you hate."

She folds her arms over her chest. "So, again, your job."

She's exhausting. But I smile.

"The point is: if you help me with Olivia, I'll help you in return. Take it or leave it," I remind her, because she still seems determined to piss me off. "All I'm asking for is one little conversation. And either I can make things easier for you around here—"

"By doing your job," she supplies flatly.

"—or nothing changes," I finish. "Your call."

Another glare. Does she ever do anything else?

"This is the lamest form of blackmail I've ever seen," she mutters.

"It's mutual opportunism," I correct her. "A beneficial symbiosis, if you will."

"Uh, yeah. Don't think so," she tells me, trotting away.

Well, there goes that idea. I shift against the lab table, tired of standing on one leg.

Cool. Cool, cool, cool. God, I can't wait to go home and duel some bad guys. If Past Me heard me say that he'd probably check for a concussion, but today, it's never been more true. Wish I carried around a sword in real life. Not that it would solve my Olivia problem, but at least I'd have a sword. Before my injury, it was my reputation I carried around with me; the idea that I was the best at something, that I was popular and respected for what I could do. Without that, I feel naked. Unarmed.

Not that anyone is likely to uncover my depressing double life, but if they were to ask, I'd say I'm this invested in *Twelfth Knight* because I'm bored. Because I've got a one-track mind and I like to win. Because I'm the obsessive type, the kind who needs something to fixate on. My life used to be football, but now it's whatever form of competition I can give myself without leaving the couch.

But honestly, I think it might be more than that. I think I like the game because it's . . . an *escape*. Because it's somewhere that isn't my life or my problems. I can push buttons and kill monsters. I'm just as strong there as I used to be here, in real life. Without my speed, without my future at Illyria—without my future, period—I'm just—

"Homecoming," Vi says, doubling back, and I jump, lost in my thoughts.

"What?" Jesus, my heart is pounding. This girl is terrifying.

"You're in charge of homecoming," she says. "All the extra hours of setup. Wrangling all the volunteers. I don't want to do it. I'm tired of being in charge of everyone."

"Oh please, Viola. You love bossing people around," I mutter reflexively.

"Take it or leave it," Vi says, blandly echoing my words back to me. "You take over homecoming and I'll talk to Olivia for you. But that's it," she warns. "I'm not actually going to put the two of you back together or whatever. This isn't *The Parent Trap*. Got it?"

"I just want answers," I tell her, which is both mortifying and true, though thankfully she doesn't linger on it.

"Fine. Deal?"

She holds out a hand.

I'm not happy. I definitely still want to kill some bad guys when I get home. But at least there's something like progress on the horizon—so fine, Viola. You win.

"Deal," I agree, and take it.

BEAT THEM AT THEIR OWN GAME

Vi

"What's the deal with you and Orsino?" I ask Olivia when she comes over to my house for our monologue. (Instagram was her weapon of choice for getting in touch with me, no surprise there. Needless to say, her grid is *flawless*.) "Everything good there, or . . . ?"

"Whoa, Vi. Can't I take off my coat and stay awhile before we delve into my personal life?" she jokes, letting her bag fall to the floor. "Hey," she adds to Bash, who I didn't even notice was in the living room. He does this thing sometimes where he finds a sunny spot and lies there like a labradoodle.

"Hey," he replies, lifting a hand and closing his eyes.

"Sorry, I just . . . you know, all the rumors," I say. "So if you want to talk about it, I'm around." That, or Jack seemed genuinely pathetic and I really don't want to deal with the homecoming volunteers, which includes Antonia. Take your pick.

"There's really nothing to talk about," Olivia says, and looks at our dining table, which is covered in my mom's notes and two weeks' worth of unrolled Muay Thai hand wraps. "Can I set my stuff here, or . . . ?"

"Sorry, yeah." I kick out a chair. "Hungry? Thirsty?"

"I'm good." She glances over at Bash again. "Sebastian, right?"

"Or Bastian, or Bash. Whatever strikes your fancy." He cracks one eye. "And you are Olivia Hadid," he observes. Not a question.

She politely half laughs. "Yes—"

"And I, too, would like to know what's going on with Jack Orsino," Bash concludes. "But unlike my nosy sister, I can wait until you've been hydrated and fed."

"She *just said* she's not hungry or thirsty," I call back to him.

"Yet," he replies ominously, and to her credit, this time Olivia's laugh is real.

"We're just taking a break," she tells us. "No big deal. I need to focus on school and stuff."

Well, that's simple enough. Unsurprising that Jack can't understand it, given that he has never decided to focus on school or anything that wasn't football, but there we go. I've officially held up my end of the bargain and now homecoming is his problem.

He's right. This *has* been beneficial, so I waltz into the kitchen to fetch myself some congratulatory juice.

"Does 'stuff' include ritual séances? Demon summoning?" I hear Bash ask Olivia. "That's what I've always assumed the coven of cheerleaders does between episodes of sports attendance."

"No demons yet," Olivia assures him. "Just the usual blood sacrifice."

"I knew it." From the fridge I watch him stand up, wandering over to where Olivia's removing her books from her school bag. "Shakespeare, huh?"

"The Bard himself," I confirm, returning with my glass of orange juice.

"Solely the Bard of Avon at best," Bash corrects me. "Robert Burns is *the* Bard."

"Wonderful, Sebastian," I tell him. "Thank goodness you told us before we embarrassed ourselves."

"I should think so." He tips an imaginary hat at Olivia. "Farewell, then. I'll leave you to your recitations."

With that, he disappears up the stairs.

"He's funny," Olivia comments. "I like him."

"Bash has always been the likable one," I agree, and she glances quizzically at me.

"Yeah?"

"Well, it's a crucial part of his personality," I explain, shoving aside my bag of hand wraps. "He requires constant forgiveness. But you always forgive him, because how could you not?"

"Mm," she agrees, with a knowing half smile. "And which one are you, if he's the likable one?"

"The one who'll show up on time," I say, picking up my copy of the script. "Which is more than I can say for some people."

"Definitely." She's still looking at me funny, so I try to make conversation.

"Do you have siblings?"

"Two sisters. One's eight and the other's ten."

"Oh, wow. That young?"

She shrugs. "My parents decided they weren't done, I guess."

"Are you . . . close with them?"

"Well." Her lips twist thoughtfully. "I'm a bit more like the third parent than the third child, if I'm being honest," she says, and the furrow between her brows suggests that's not something she's proud of admitting.

"Oh." It feels personal, and I don't want to leave her hanging. "I guess sometimes I feel a bit like a parent myself. Or just generally older. Like, too old." Old enough to see things other people ignore. Old enough to be routinely disappointed.

"It's hard, isn't it?" Olivia says, drumming her fingers on the table. "Expectations."

Before she said that, I would have thought it was nice to be a beloved cheerleader like Olivia, which is what I sometimes think people want me to be. (Except my mom, who graciously allows me to live my life unencumbered by gender constraints.) But then I consider all the AP dudebros who only wanted to get into her pants, as if she only amounts to one thing.

"Well, look, I'm sorry I asked about Jack," I tell her honestly. "I just noticed you guys seemed weird with each other." I hesitate, and then, "Nothing's, like, *wrong*, is it? He didn't . . . *do* anything, or . . . ?"

"Oh gosh, no. No, never. Jack's a great guy," she assures me, and her insistence is so urgently fond that I'm starting to doubt what she told me earlier; how easily and emotionlessly she said it was "just" a break. "I know he's a lot sometimes," she adds. "You know, the whole Duke Orsino persona and stuff—"

"And stuff," I mutter in agreement.

"Right," she acknowledges with a thin smile. "But under the mask is a lot more, I guess."

"A lot more than 'a lot'?" I ask doubtfully, because my initial thought is: I've heard this before. You know, about boys. Boys who are jerks or clowns whose girlfriends think they're secretly deep. It's a classic story! People *love* giving boys the benefit of the doubt, or ascribing layers to them that don't actually exist. It's like when a girl says a guy is funny or smart when really, he's just . . . tall.

But Olivia only laughs. "Okay, okay, you're not a fan, I get it. I won't try to convince you. Shall we, Romeo?" she prompts instead, nudging the script in my hands as if she's more than happy to change the subject.

Maybe Jack's right to wonder what's going on here. There seem to be a lot of things Olivia isn't saying . . . but that's her business. And I have an answer.

My end of the deal? Fulfilled.

"'Let me be ta'en / let me be put to death,'" I reply, and she smiles at me.

"A *little* romantic, right?" she says. "'I am content, so thou wilt have it so.'"

"That's my line."

"I'm just trying to convince you. He's saying he's willing to die if that's what she wants."

"Exactly, it's a death wish. They're teenagers!"

"You're lying," she says, scrutinizing me for a second.

I roll my eyes. "Fine. They're pretty words. And it's a thoughtful offer."

"Meaning . . . ?" she prompts.

"Meaning I can appreciate a man who'll die if I tell him to."

She elbows me, rolling her eyes. "*Meaning* . . . ?"

"Meaning," I grit out with a sigh, "fine. You can have this one."

She grins at me.

"Thank you," she assures me, flipping her ponytail over one shoulder. "I'll take it."

*   *   *

After Olivia leaves, I bypass whatever new annoyance fills my inbox
and sign in to *Twelfth Knight*, ready (as usual) to stab someone in a
way that won't get me arrested or expelled. I figure combat's my
best bet and select the Camlann arena, which is by far the most
infamous one in the game. Legend has it that King Arthur falls in
the Battle of Camlann, so in the game's lore, only the best of the
best find themselves there. There's a short queue, but it's better than
wasting my time with amateurs in Gaunnes.

Like always, the list of people queuing up for the Camlann arena
is a mix of recognizable usernames (ahem, people I've beaten before) and totally meaningless letters and numbers. Only, tonight I
notice again that there's one that seems . . . a bit too familiar.

DUKEORSINO12.

Wait, so when I thought I imagined that—it was *real*?

"Absolutely not," I say aloud, slamming my laptop shut. My heart
is pounding, like I just got caught somehow. Like he's in the room
with me. Is it possible I somehow *summoned* him? I swear, it's like
every time I turn a corner, he's there. Even in my own head.

No. No way. Clearly I'm living some kind of chronic hallucina-
tion. I should go to sleep.

No, I can't possibly sleep, this is too weird.

Maybe I misread it?

I open my laptop again, taking a breath.

DUKEORSINO12.

Nope. I didn't imagine it. Still, I stare at the username, trying
to think how this could be wrong. I mean . . . it *has* to be, right? As
far as I know, Jack Orsino would rather drink poison than enter a
gaming world like this one. I don't keep tabs on what's cool with
Messaline's 1% given that, you know, I don't care, but this seems
pretty off-brand. That, and nobody uses their real identities in
RPGs. If that's actually Jack, he's clearly got some severe form of
narcissism and should very urgently seek help.

But that nickname. It's too specific. It can't be coincidence,
can it?

So I can't help it—I look. I *scour,* borderline stalk. His stats are interesting. He's lost a few battles but gained plenty of skills. A lot of skills, actually, like he's actively collecting them, though I guess I don't know what else he'd be doing in a MMORPG. I doubt he's out here trying to become an Arthurian tradesman or treat this like his own personal fantasy world.

I'm about to exit the realm when a notification pops up in the corner of my laptop screen, my phone buzzing at the same time. It's a text message from Antonia. She sent me something yesterday about the new quest the group is doing, which I liked, but didn't answer.

fyi, I don't think I'm going to MagiCon this year, she says.

My heart flips.

what?

oh, so now you respond. how convenient.

Oh good, we're about to fight. My hands shake a little, involuntarily, and I can feel a cool sweat start to break out under my arms. I hate fighting with Antonia. Other people don't matter—I can obviously hold my own in any argument—but there's something about Antonia. It's like over the years I've given her all my arrows—all my secrets and things I don't want the rest of the world to see—and now I'm terrified she'll shoot me with them.

i've answered all your messages, I say.

barely

i just needed time to cool off, okay?

from what????

I grit my teeth and change the subject. *why aren't you going to MagiCon?*

We volunteer together every year. It's the best way to ensure you get a ticket; conventions are expensive and they also fill up fast, especially since geek culture started going mainstream with franchise superhero films and stuff. You basically have to get on the list a year in advance.

seriously? she asks.

My laptop blinks in the corner, a notification from *Twelfth Knight,* and I hit Ignore.

seriously what?

You're not going to answer the question?

Before I can answer, she continues, *Just because you're pissed off with leon and murph you're going to take this out on me?*

How did this get so weird? Maybe I should have told her earlier that I was upset she didn't take my side when things happened with Matt Das. Or that it hurt my feelings that she stayed with the ConQuest group even after she saw how they treated me. Or maybe it was the thing with George, or the subtweet, or maybe it's everything, but when you break things down to their parts, they all seem too small. Like maybe she wouldn't get it even if I could explain it aloud.

the problem with you vi is that you're selfish, she says, and keeps typing. A series of messages:

I take your side all the time, and for what?

you know how many times I've had to defend you?

countless

believe it or not those guys aren't assholes to you for no reason

you're a bitch to them and then you wonder why they hate you

you can't exactly blame them for not wanting you to be in charge

I swallow, a familiar thump of pain quickly hardening to rage.

you think they like you because you're NICE? I type back to her, my hands still shaking. *they tolerate you because you do whatever they tell you. you're perfectly happy to let them step all over you*

yeah, I hear that's my problem, Antonia says. *apparently I love being stepped on. probably the same reason I'm friends with you.*

I stare at the screen.

That's what she thinks? About me? About our friendship? I tell Antonia the truth. *All* my truths. After seeing everything, my ins and outs, *this* is what she thinks I am?

I'm still staring at the screen when the *Twelfth Knight* notification becomes a flashing countdown in the corner.

10 . . . 9 . . . 8 . . .

"Shit," I say aloud, switching to the game, because apparently when I meant to hit Ignore, I hit Accept instead. As in *accept challenge.* As in I'm about to enter a match in . . . five seconds,

4 . . . 3 . . . 2 . . .

The screen flashes brightly and I'm inside the Camlann arena. Surrounding me are two mages, a sphinx, two fae, a demon, a page, and two other knights, one of which looks very familiar.

If I were in a different mood, I might find his character hilarious. He's used our green-and-gold school colors and the fleur-de-lis of our school crest. Even his avatar looks like him: dark-skinned and tall, dressed in armor and chain mail, and carrying my own signature weapon, a thick-hilted broadsword.

Antonia's message window flashes again, the start of a message appearing, but what can she possibly have left to say to me? Nothing I want to hear right now. I take out one of the fae easily, then one of the mages. Elsewhere in the match, "Duke Orsino" seems to be battling with surprising proficiency against the demon. The sphinx tries to use one of their trickery spells on me, but I have immunity; a truth spell from a relic, the Ring of Dispell, takes care of that, while the other mage seems to have dispatched the remaining fae.

Who's left? The page, one other knight, the last mage. Oh, and maybe—Jack Orsino, of course. He's out of sight and I take cover, waiting among the castle ruins. Anyone who wants to follow me in here will need illumination spells, which I have.

Before I can position myself to reach one of the towers, the chat flashes at the bottom of my screen.

DUKEORSINO12 would like to chat with you.

Of course he would, I think with a grumble—until I remember that he doesn't know it's me. As far as he knows, I'm Cesario, a stranger on the internet.

I click the window, which opens to a simple message. One word.

DUKEORSINO12: allies?

He's typing, and then:

DUKEORSINO12: just for this battle.

and then? I type back.

DUKEORSINO12: every man for himself

Fair enough. It's not an unusual request, minus the fact that if I accept, it'll be the second deal I've made with Jack Orsino in the same week. Unprecedented, frankly. If he knew he'd gotten me to agree to something twice in a row—

But he doesn't, I remind myself. He has no idea it's me. And considering that beating him right now would be exactly what my day needs . . .

"Okay, Orsino," I murmur to myself, typing back to him in the chat. "Let's see what you've got."

Jack

I'll say this for whatever nerd dreamt up *Twelfth Knight*, presumably in their parents' basement somewhere: it's thorough. There's not a detail left unattended; the castle ruins of the Camlann arena look convincingly real, and the trees in the wood even sway a little in the breeze. The font in the chat is a little too Medieval Times-y, like the Comic Sans of geekdom, but even that is only moderately distracting.

The other knight, some meaningless combination of numbers and letters, types back to me in the chat:

C354R10: I'll take the mage

I'm not usually the kind of guy who wants to chat with randos on the internet, given my knowledge of the internet, but what I *do* like is winning. If that means convincing some forty-five-year-old divorcé or twelve-year-old in Mozambique to take my side, so be it. It's not like we'll ever talk again, and however lame this knight might be in real life, he clearly knows what he's doing in the game. His avatar is practically draped in skills he's earned in the arena. A collection of relics appears above his head every time he pulls out a weapon, which is often. By comparison, I have a whole lot of nothing.

I expect the other knight to head for the mage, but instead he turns toward a set of stairs, removing one of his relics—a ring of some kind?—and holding it up until the stairs give way to a passage that extends to the other side of the castle. Somewhere in the middle is a jewel, green and obviously valuable, which the knight plucks up before taking the secret passageway to the outside, taking the mage by surprise.

whoa, what did you just do? I type in the chat.

The knight doesn't answer, being focused on the mage. Mages in this game have control over animals and this one has some kind of sidekick. I think Nick called them familiars, and I still don't understand the rules, but basically the familiars are like Pokémon: they evolve and change forms when the mage gains skills. This mage has a tiger, which I assume is pretty good.

The knight trades in one sword for some kind of glowing lance, another one of the relics—it has blood at the tip? That's totally metal—and pulls out a shield that's also glowing, so I'm guessing these are both things won in battle. Unfortunately I can't watch, because I have to take on someone else with my regular, non-glowing weapons.

My opponent is another knight, so this is your basic duel, like when I'm up against a cornerback to see which of us can knock the other out of position. Which reminds me of the Padua cornerback, whose suspension is up by now. Ironic, isn't it, that he still lost the game, but I lost my whole season? My entire future?

Nope, can't think about that now.

The knight lunges forward and I . . . whatever the word is for *get out of the way*, which flashes across the screen, but of course I haven't committed all seventy thousand random wizard words to memory. ("There are no wizards in the game" was Nick's response when I mentioned that, to which I reasonably pointed out, "Whatever.") Computer games just require focus, quick reflexes . . . all the stuff my body used to do. I strike, and the other knight throws up a little green glow-y thing that makes him look like he's suspended in Jell-O. I hit a button and my screen glows, too, waiting for the instant the knight's power runs out. The parameters of the game are simple—you can't just use your features forever. They cost you something, and this knight has less in his glowing health bar to spare than I do. He drops his guard and I get in a good hit, weakening him substantially. Now all I need to do is change positions.

Nick gave me a few tricks here and there, like using the alphanumeric keys to be closer to more commands instead of focusing on the arrow pads, but the most important thing he pointed out was that I had to think of combat in terms of the field. As a running back, you've got all kinds of advantages just by taking certain positions, or making it look like you might do something different from what you actually plan to do. In the game, you can move directly sideways, but from the right angle, it still considers you *behind* your opponent. As in, perfectly placed to deliver a hard blow while the other knight wastes precious time turning around.

I take the knight out with a backstab move he can't block ("parry," the screen says) and then I zoom back out, getting ready for whatever comes next. Looks like the mage conjured some kind of fire, because the castle's now engulfed in flames.

used the ring of dispell, shows up in my chat window.

what? I type back, zooming farther out until I see the knight coming toward me from where the battle with the mage must have taken to the burning tower.

C354R10: the ring of dispell shows passageways in the game
DUKEORSINO12: what is a ring of dispell

Before I get an answer, the knight comes at me with the bloody lance still drawn.

"Oh shit," I say aloud, then realize it's close to two in the morning. If my dad comes down here, I'll be in trouble for sure—he's not a fan of video games. Thinks they're ruining society, and he's probably right.

I manage to get out of the way of the lance, but the other knight is already positioned to do to me exactly what I did to the previous knight. It's down to the two of us now that the others have been taken out.

I turn, or try to, but the other knight moves faster. How is he doing that? I try to attack, but it doesn't work. He gets me with a hard shot that drains me of almost all my glowing yellow points. My . . . life. Or whatever is going on there. The bar that used to be green is red now, dangerously so.

Okay. Okay, I can do this. This is just like running it in on a fourth down. No room for failure? I can do that. I do it all the time.

(Used to.)

What do I know about this knight compared to the others I've faced since I started playing? He's not a bull. He doesn't just go for a kill shot every time. He's like me: he waits for an opening. So I'll give him one.

I get in position for one of the sweeping sword-moves and the other knight obviously sees it coming. He throws up his glowing shield—which, by the way, is glowing even *more* now, probably as a result of having recently defeated a mage with a tiger—and I pull back, then go for a more direct hit when he brings his sword back down. It's another type of trick play, where you pretend to go high and then aim low.

It works. I make contact in an attack that might take out another player, one with fewer glowing things, but for this knight it just causes their green bar to turn kind of orange. I have a feeling I won't be able to try that same trick again, so I turn for another backstab, but he beats me to it.

Boom, another hit from a solid angle: I'm out.

My screen goes black and then reopens to inform me I've lost, returning me to the landscape somewhere near Camelot that's basically a landing page.

Great.

I'm considering queuing up for another big combat arena to make up for some of the points I just lost when my chat window blinks open again.

C354R10: the ring of dispell was given to lancelot by the lady of the lake. in the game it means you can use it to see through enchantments
DUKEORSINO12: where'd you get it?
C354R10: I take it you're new at this

(What the hell is C354R10?)

DUKEORSINO12: where are you?
DUKEORSINO12: in the game
C354R10: why
DUKEORSINO12: paranoid much?
DUKEORSINO12: just want to see who I'm talking to
C354R10: didn't get a good enough look when I beat you?
DUKEORSINO12: okay, you barely beat me
C354R10: believe me, you got beat

He pauses and then types again.

C354R10: I'm in camelot square
DUKEORSINO12: the square? why?
C354R10: resources

Oh, right. This is where the tradesmen and stuff are. I maneuver through the capital, reaching the marketplace stall, and spot the other knight's avatar.

C354R10: trying to trade for something?
DUKEORSINO12: like what?
C354R10: that's what I was thinking. you don't have anything I want

This avatar looks *really* familiar. Not like someone I know, obviously. I don't know any seven-foot-tall knights. Linebackers, sure, but they don't have hair like that.

Oh wait—that *hair*. It's long and bright white and Fabio-esque, which is kind of unmistakable.

Are you supposed to be cesario from war of thorns????? I suddenly ask, piecing together the gamer-speak translation of his username.

> **C354R10:** you watch WoT?
> **DUKEORSINO12:** I started it recently. almost caught up
> **C354R10:** what season are you on?
> **DUKEORSINO12:** just finished 2
> **DUKEORSINO12:** cesario sucked at first but now he's really interesting
> **C354R10:** what did you think about the twist?

In the season two finale, Cesario basically switches sides. Well, not really. It's hard to explain, but basically Cesario spent season one as the primary villain, harassing the main character from the "lost" royal line and trying to kill him to get back in his father's good graces, but then—plot twist!—realizes his dad and his brother are pawns to some other mystery force. So instead of killing his main rival, he lets her go and sets off on his own.

Initially I thought this would be annoying or a setup for a dumb romance plot, but it's kind of interesting. It's like he's just waking up and having his own thoughts for the first time, so everyone in the show is predictable except for him.

> **DUKEORSINO12:** he's kind of the best storyline??
> **DUKEORSINO12:** he's the wild card
> **C354R10:** right? he's the most interesting one
> **DUKEORSINO12:** I didn't like him at first

I'm still typing when he responds.

> **C354R10:** of course not! you're not supposed to like him
> **DUKEORSINO12:** but then it's like he's the only one good at stuff and actually using his brain instead of just being blindly loyal

There's a flurry of typing from the other end, then a pause, like he deleted it.

C354R10: I assumed you were going to say something stupid
after that "but"
C354R10: but that's actually not a bad take
C354R10: so congrats

I stifle a laugh, and we reply at the same time:

DUKEORSINO12: means a lot coming from you, a total stranger
C354R10: you should really do more crusades

And again simultaneously:

DUKEORSINO12: what?
C354R10: lol tx

This time I pause to wait for his response.

C354R10: crusades are how you get relics like the ring of dispell
or the bleeding lance
DUKEORSINO12: is your bleeding lance literally called "the
bleeding lance"?
C354R10: I think it's technically the spear of longinus, the roman
spear that cuts jesus during the crucifixion, but the game kind
of shies away from . . .
DUKEORSINO12: angering christian parents?
C354R10: I was going to say directly religious icons but yeah,
that

I laugh a little.

DUKEORSINO12: the holy grail though???? crusades????
C354R10: I know right
C354R10: but that's arthurian drama for you

I feel like this is a way better conversation than I expected to have in my living room at two in the morning.

DUKEORSINO12: I guess that's fair. so how do the crusades work
C354R10: wow, you really are new at this
DUKEORSINO12: I kind of just started playing
DUKEORSINO12: my friend introduced me to all this
C354R10: you must have a really weird friend

I laugh again.

DUKEORSINO12: he hides it really well. on the outside you'd never know
C354R10: neurosurgeon? GQ model?
DUKEORSINO12: close
DUKEORSINO12: former quarterback
DUKEORSINO12: he graduated last year and handed off his account to me
C354R10: you cannot possibly mean nick valentine

I freeze for a second.

Suddenly I get really, weirdly paranoid, partially because I'm running on very little sleep and also because it's extremely weird to think this random dude guessed my best friend's name. That's not normal, right? Is there any way this person is looking into my house? I cover up my webcam just in case, then remember I'm being ridiculous. You couldn't know my best friend's name just by looking at my face, and anyway, it's not even on.

Unless I got hacked??

Oh my god. I'm totally going to get murdered.

C354R10: sorry, I should have mentioned earlier

He probably just realized that was a bit too creepy for comfort.

C354R10: your username . . . I kind of put two and two together

Oh, right. Duh. Even Nick thought I should have picked something less obviously me, so that's my bad, I guess. I didn't even think about the fact that anyone who goes to Messaline would know exactly who I am—probably because I didn't expect to find anyone from Messaline in the game.

DUKEORSINO12: it's cool

It's weird, but not *that* weird. I don't think I would have brought it up, either.

DUKEORSINO12: Does that mean you go to messaline too?

There's a long pause.

C354R10: yeah
DUKEORSINO12: no way. do we know each other?

Another pause.

C354R10: yes

And then,

C354R10: sort of
C354R10: not well
DUKEORSINO12: you obviously know who I am
C354R10: everyone knows who you are
DUKEORSINO12: true

I hate to say it, but the little bit of smugness in my chest is kind of a nice feeling.

DUKEORSINO12: still, it's not fair if you know me and I don't know you
DUKEORSINO12: who are you?

C354R10: nobody

DUKEORSINO12: you do know I'm on ASB right? it's pretty easy to find people

Not to be creepy, I hurry to add, because damn, this is a fine line to walk. Secret identities are really not my thing. But hey, he did it first, right?

C354R10: I'm still nobody special

I almost decide not to push it, but now the curiosity's getting to me. I'm assuming it's some weird, quiet freshman, but hey, could be worse, right? Could be a cybercriminal, or a mobster. Or some old dude trying to catfish me.

DUKEORSINO12: you're a lot better at this game than I am. and it'd be cooler to play with a real live human being than a stranger

DUKEORSINO12: come on, it's only fair

C354R10: fine

Nice.

C354R10: but don't tell anyone

I have to laugh at that.

DUKEORSINO12: uh, bro? believe me, I do NOT want anyone knowing this is what I do with my spare time

C354R10: lol. understandable

C354R10: this is deeply embarrassing for you

DUKEORSINO12: thanks captain obvious

DUKEORSINO12: so????

I wait and then, after a few seconds, Cesario finally reveals his true identity.

C354R10: bash
DUKEORSINO12: bash . . . ?
C354R10: reyes

As in *Vi* Reyes? Wow. It's a small world after all, though I don't think I even know what Bash Reyes looks like. I've never had a class with him. He definitely doesn't play sports. I think he does drama?

C354R10: but don't call me that

He says it just as I'm about to remark how weird it is to not only be playing against someone I know, but someone in my grade.

C354R10: it's just . . . the game's not real life, you know?
C354R10: I like that about it

Yeah, I get that.
He probably has no idea how much I get that.

DUKEORSINO12: no prob cesario, your secret's safe with me
DUKEORSINO12: now let's talk crusades

HEROES PREFER SWORDS

Vi

After DukeOrsino12 signs off, I remain locked in place, staring at the screen until it finally fades out and goes black.

Since it seems necessary to say: I really don't know what just happened. I have no idea why I brought up Nick Valentine. Stress? Temporary insanity? Probably my stupid fight with Antonia, actually, which is embarrassing *and* annoying. Or maybe my complete shock that *Jack Orsino* has a non-idiotic opinion about my favorite TV show. Admittedly, that never happens. The show's message boards are full of sci-fi dudebros who think girls only lust for villains because they're hot and we're dumb. God forbid you try to convince one of them that finding Cesario's storyline interesting isn't the same thing as siding with actual fascists! (Trust me, it won't work.)

Still, I can't believe I actually told Jack Orsino I was *Bash*. Did I get possessed by a demon or something? Normally I'm not this stupid—but in fairness to me, it's not like there was a better answer. There's no way I'm going to blow my cover, first of all. I'd never tell anyone in the game that I'm a girl. It's already the one place where a bunch of dudes don't try to "well, actually" me ten times a day. My character in the game is well known and respected. I can't risk throwing that away just because I was overtaken by a stroke of total derangement.

Besides, I *panicked*, okay? He's right that he could have just looked up whatever name I gave him on our ASB rosters (it would be the first time he ever looked at one, so how's that for irony?) which means that making up a name wasn't going to work. Plus, it's not like he and Bash are ever going to interact in real life. I know for a fact they have no classes together, and last I checked, Jack Orsino doesn't harbor any fantasies about performing in the spring musical. Nor would he want anyone knowing he plays fantasy RPGs in secret, right? Pretty sure that even if Nick Valentine *did* tell him that all this stuff existed, that kind of thing is strictly prohibited by the Jock Code of Oppressive Masculinity and Organized Sports.

So, fine. It's fine. I'll just . . . not sign on for a few days. No big deal.

It's fine.

I push my chair back, feeling that weird amalgam of things that only happens when you've stayed up way too late and the whole world feels kind of fake, like maybe nothing else exists outside of you and your thoughts. Normally I like this time of night for the solitude, but then I remember that Antonia's not my friend right now. Or maybe anymore.

An old, familiar rage flares up in my chest. The same anger I usually feel about people who aren't Antonia. Despite what Jack Orsino thinks, I don't actually need to be liked. What I want is to be respected, and the truth that Antonia doesn't want to face is that she very much *isn't*.

Which is of course an awful thing to think about someone who was, up until a few hours ago, my best friend.

Another familiar feeling beats against my chest, only this one is older, more tired: I know I'm not a nice person. Contrary to what Kayla or Jack Orsino or Antonia thinks, I really don't need anyone to tell me that. I already know there's something wrong with me; I know there's a reason people don't like me. Lots of reasons.

But secretly, I would like someone to see me for what I am and choose me anyway.

Or at the very least, not suddenly decide I'm no longer worth being friends with just because I wouldn't go on a pity date with Matt Das, or because I don't want to sit around a table with a bunch of arrogant, ignorant boys just to watch myself get buried under their opinions.

The anger comes back, sort of. A fizzling form of it, like flat soda. I feel tired, down to my bones, so I pull aside the covers and go to sleep, figuring I'll deal with DukeOrsino12 (and his more annoying alter ego) tomorrow.

I generally hope not to be accosted by people first thing in the morning, but of course sportsball superstar Jack Orsino doesn't let a little thing like human decency stand in the way of his personal needs.

"Well?" he demands, clopping after me on his crutches like a Clydesdale.

"Well what?" I mutter over my shoulder, fumbling to remind myself of one very important thing: *He doesn't know who you are. Your identity is safe. So keep it that way.*

It's weird to actually look someone in the face when you were just seeing them as a knight avatar a few hours ago. The pixelated version of him kind of summarizes the basics—he's tall, sort of leanly muscled, with a drop fade that's been growing back in over the last couple of weeks—but it misses, you know, the little stuff. The shape of his face. The patchy stubble below his cheeks that he really needs to shave. The lashes that look almost feminine, which currently frame a set of seriously bloodshot eyes.

God, he looks awful, which is honestly for the best. Nobody should look like him, it's indecent. Redistribution is necessary, like a wealth tax for bone structure.

"You look like shit," he remarks, inspecting me with a frown.

Oh good, a nice moment of synchronicity. "Sublime," I reply, resuming my path to class. "And with that, the day begins—"

"Hang on." He fumbles after me. "So did you talk to her?"

"Who?" I ask, just to torment him.

He rolls his eyes. "Come on. We had a deal."

"Fine." I pause long enough to face him. "She's trying to focus on school."

One brow shoots up. "Seriously?"

"She's got a tough course load."

"Yeah, I've *heard*, but—" He grits his teeth. "That's all you got?"

"What more do you want?" I counter irritably. "Is it really *that* shocking to you that someone might need a break from you? Maybe Olivia's tired of having to be your accessory all the time, or maybe she just—"

"She's not my accessory." To my surprise he looks . . . wounded. I expected him to play it off like he'd do under any other circumstances—*My job is to stand here and look pretty,* for instance, which was a total groan—but he flinches. "Is that really what she thinks?"

It's kind of unnerving how upset he looks.

"No, I just—" I break off, grimacing. "Actually, she only had nice things to say about you," I admit with a grumble. "Not that I agree with any of them."

He blinks. "She did?"

"Yeah. So don't worry about it. It's nothing you did wrong."

"Vi, come on." I turn to leave again and he lurches after me. "It can't just be that."

"Why not? She's got her own life. Maybe she just doesn't want to have to think about you right now."

Something about his tone changes. "Is that what you think relationships are? An obligation?"

Okay, this is turning into a weird lecture that I don't have time for. "Just . . . deal with your angst on your own time, Orsino. Okay? I talked to her. I held up my end of the bargain."

"*Did* you?" he asks, scrutinizing me beneath a furrowed brow.

Ugh. UGH. Other people are infuriating. If Jack and Olivia can't talk to each other, why is that *my* problem?

Only . . . I hate to admit it, but I guess he's right. Technically speaking, I *didn't* hold up my end, because even I was left wondering what her real reason was. She seems fundamentally weird around him from what I've seen, so I guess if he really cares about her, I can't blame him for wondering why she'd suddenly change.

"Fine," I exhale, "I'll ask her again. But you've gotta give me some time," I warn him, "because if I keep bringing it up, I'm just going to sound like a weird, obsessed stalker."

"Deal." He nods vigorously.

"And don't forget, the homecoming committee's your problem now," I add.

"Chill, Viola," he says, "I've got it."

He's unbearable. "You *do* know that telling girls to 'chill' is a famously bad call, right?"

"Don't sell yourself short, Vi," he says in one of his falsely cheerful voices. "You're not just any girl. You're a fun little tyrant."

"Oh good, now I'm *definitely* willing to help you," I grumble as I turn to leave. "Very convincing—"

"Dictatorship really works for you as a look," he calls after me.

"Walking away now," I shout back, shaking my head and almost bumping into Antonia, who barely looks at me.

Well. I guess that's that, then.

For the next couple of days I make a point not to sign in to *Twelfth Knight*, even though my fingers itch to play and the rest of me itches, too, I guess for something to think about that isn't the looming MagiCon weekend. Not that my not wanting to think about it has any effect on those around me.

"You haven't worked on your costume in a while," my mother remarks, startling me from where I'm reading one of the new Empire Lost novels on the couch.

"What?" I say, because I was busy being elsewhere in the cosmos.

"Your costume. I haven't seen you work on it in a bit."

"Oh." She means my cosplay for MagiCon. Last year I went as a character from a graphic novel I like (basically a haunted harlequin doll) but this year Antonia and I were going as our ConQuest original characters, Astrea Starscream and Larissa Highbrow.

Obviously I don't really see the point anymore. "Yeah, well. It's good enough."

"Good *enough*?" my mom echoes, arching a brow, because rabid perfectionism is another one of the areas where she and I have more overlap than Bash.

"It's not like anyone will recognize me anyway. It's an OC." Original characters are never recognizable for obvious reasons, though it'd be twice as cool to end up in one of the fan blogs while dressed as something that isn't part of a Disney-fied franchise. And if I got featured in the Monstress Mag blog . . . ?

But that probably wouldn't happen anyway.

"Hmm," my mother says, which is a terrible sign. A lecture is coming, so I swing myself upright and go full preemptive strike.

"You look nice," I point out with a note of suspicion, gesturing to her dress and heels. "Someone new?"

"Actually, no." Mom fusses with an earring, and I realize she's still lingering here for a reason.

"Mom, are you . . . early?"

"What? No. Yes," she says. "Barely. I don't know."

"What?" Did I mention this woman dates *for a living*? Babbling isn't something I usually see her do.

"Well, I just . . . I guess I started getting ready too early. A little early, I mean. Accidentally." She glances conspicuously away.

"Mom, I'm not judging you." She looks awkward, like she doesn't know where to put her hands, which is kind of hilarious. "This is the same guy?"

"Yes." She pauses. "Sort of a milestone, actually."

"Yeah?"

"Yeah. Six months."

"Whoa." That's a long time for her. Not that she hasn't had stretches of romance here and there, sometimes up to a year or so, but nothing recent. She smiles at me distractedly, glancing more next to me than anything else.

"Well, it's probably time to tell him you have kids," I say.

"He knows. I—" She stops. "I already used that one."

It's one of her "bye-byes," aka reasons to get out of relationships. Nearly always works on men, though it's kind of a panromantic buzzkill as far as I can tell. "When'd you use it?"

"Months ago. Right away."

"Is he one of those creeps who insists that you're meant for each other?" She gets a lot of weird emails. And even weirder things in her DMs, some of which are funny and others of which are gross.

"No. Not at all, actually." She glances at me. "But you're chang-ing the subject, anak."

"Me?" I protest innocently. "Never."

"You're fighting with Antonia," she says, sitting next to me. "You thought you could slip that by me?"

"It ran its course, Mom. That's all." My mother and I are alike in this. We're independent and tough-minded, firm on our principles, maybe sometimes to the point where we cut people out of our lives because they cost us more energy than they're worth. We don't need someone to talk to, or someone to hang out with. We like our own company just fine.

"Mm," says my mom. A neutral tone of disapproval, which is . . . unexpected.

"What's that supposed to mean?"

Mom's phone buzzes and she glances down at the screen, a faint but unmissable smile floating absently over her signature berry-red lips.

"Nothing." She clicks off the screen and rises to her feet, leaning forward to kiss my forehead. "Don't stay up too late, okay?"

"Okay."

"I mean it." She taps my book. "You have all day to read tomorrow."

"Uh, no I don't? I'm in like a hundred AP classes, Mom."

"Well, all the more reason to get your rest." She walks around the couch while I flop back onto it, returning my attention to the page. Then she pauses, falling to a halt with a little crease of thought between her brows. "Vi."

"Hm?"

"You don't have to be alone," she says, and part of me goes rigid.

"What?"

"It's nice that you're so independent. I love that you're so content by yourself. But Vi, maybe it's worth *not* burning bridges once in a while," she says, and I slowly lower the book to stare at her.

"Excuse me?"

"Would it be so bad?" she presses me. "Compromising sometimes? Letting other people win?"

"What?" Has she been smoking something? My mother would never, *ever* tell me to roll over and let someone else win. She's a champion grudge-holder, a master of having the last word. The first thing she taught me was how to clap back when someone comes for me—so yeah, to say this is coming out of nowhere is an understatement.

"I just think maybe you'll be missing out on some things, hija, if you never—"

"This from my 'never let anyone change you' mother?" I demand. "What happened to 'know what you stand for' and 'never let anyone make you feel small'? Suddenly I should just throw that out the window and worry about ending up alone?"

"I didn't say that." She bristles. "Of course I don't mean that, I'm just—"

"Maybe your new boyfriend's made you soft," I accuse her, and she takes a deep breath, which annoys me. It means I'm annoying *her*, which is the worst thing to feel, since it's not like I don't get plenty of that in all the other areas of my life.

"Maybe," she says slowly, "I've been so busy trying to make sure you didn't make any of my mistakes that I forgot to teach you something about what's important in life. Because it's not just about winning battles, Vi. It's not about being harder or softer than other people. It's not about being better, or being stronger, or being right. Certainly not if the cost is your chance to feel love and acceptance."

"God, are you dating a yoga instructor?" I scoff.

"I know that the fact that I write so casually about dating makes it look like I don't consider it important. But I only have that column because it matters so universally, and you know why? Because the only thing in this life that actually matters is how we're connected to each other," she says. "There's nothing else you get to keep or take with you except the relationships you have. The way you love, the love you give, that matters."

I open my book and pointedly focus on it.

"Think about it." She gives me a wistful look that I'm very focused on not seeing. "Okay. Night, anak. I love you."

I say nothing, not looking up from the same paragraph I'm pretending to read until she's gone.

Immediately, though, I get a rush of filial guilt: What if something happens to her and the last conversation we have is *that* one? God, I'd be revisited every night like Scrooge with his Christmas ghosts. I take out my cell phone and type *love you,* just to make sure there's no chance of paranormal haunting.

I know, she says, so I return my attention to my book.

And I have absolutely no idea what I'm reading.

Ugh. Now I'm all twitchy and worked up. I rise to my feet, prowling around the living room.

what are you doing? I text Bash.

No answer.

Two minutes. Four.

Ten.

Okay, screw this. I storm up the stairs and reach for my laptop, furious with myself.

The whole point is my convictions, right? That's what I'm fighting with Antonia about. Me! And my right to be myself! A self that *includes* my anger, which is spilling over at the moment into something else that makes me want to cry.

I log in to *Twelfth Knight* thinking he probably won't be there anyway.

Yeah, no, he definitely isn't here. It's Saturday night, he's probably—

DUKEORSINO12: where've you been???

I exhale sharply.

(Part of me, a very small part, feels a little nudge of reassurance at knowing someone was waiting for me. I squash it dead.)

C354R10: does it matter? if you want to play, let's play
C354R10: this isn't about real life, remember?
C354R10: we're not here to chat

There's no movement for a second, and then he starts typing.

DUKEORSINO12: good talk chief

God. Of course he's one of those.

DUKEORSINO12: so what's this about the camelot quest?

Ah. That, on the other hand, is interesting. I roll out my neck, ignoring my phone when Bash finally deigns to answer my message.

C354R10: k, so you know how the crusades are PvE
DUKEORSINO12: ?

Of course he doesn't.

C354R10: sry forgot you're a literal noob
DUKEORSINO12: do people really still say that
C354R10: only ironically. or when it applies
DUKEORSINO12: aye aye captain
C354R10: stop
C354R10: anyway the quests are player versus environment, PvE, meaning that if you want to go on one of the game's crusades, you play against computer-controlled enemies, NPCs. combat realms are PvP, or player versus player. you versus me for example
DUKEORSINO12: ok, and ???
C354R10: the camelot quest is both. which means that we play the crusade against NPCs, but we can also get attacked by other players who know we're trying to win
DUKEORSINO12: fair enough
DUKEORSINO12: and what are we questing for
C354R10: do you know the lore of the game?

Pause to roll my eyes at myself.

C354R10: nvm of course you don't
C354R10: the quest is to collect every relic from every realm. the holy grail and excalibur are the hardest—they're not on the map,

you have to find them. and the whole time other players can see
which relics you're carrying and try to steal them, so you have
to not die

DUKEORSINO12: sounds impossible

C354R10: it is

Famously so. Only a handful of people have ever beaten the
Camelot Quest and they're all pro gamers with sponsorships.

Man, I wish I could get paid to play video games. Unfortunately,
if you think gaming *casually* is bad, you should hear the way boys
talk about female players at tournaments—it really brings out the
ugly sides of some already questionable personalities.

DUKEORSINO12: cool. I can do impossible

Unsurprising that he'd think so. Equally unsurprising that he's
wrong; odds are he's arrogant enough to get himself killed in the
first quest realm, or the first time he got targeted by a competing
player. Unless, that is, he's smart enough to—

DUKEORSINO12: have you done it before?

DUKEORSINO12: /can you teach me how

Huh. *That* is a surprise.

I sit back in my chair, trying not to be impressed until I remember
that oh yeah, he thinks I'm Cesario. He thinks I'm a dude. This is
exactly the kind of thing that doesn't get said when people already
know you're a girl. Instead, people (boys) usually assume *they* can
teach *you* something.

One of many benefits to Jack Orsino not knowing who I really
am, since there's no way he'd ask me this in real life. About anything.

I consider it, chewing my lip, then shrug.

C354R10: I've never done it myself but yes

C354R10: I could help you

I've done most of the crusades that make up the Camelot Quest. After I stopped playing as myself, I played a lot of PvE alone until I figured out I could compete against other players as Cesario.

DUKEORSINO12: why haven't you done it yourself??

Cue grimace.

C354R10: you need a team

It's one of the most annoying things about this game. Some of the levels require another person just to pass. Even if you win combat rounds, someone else has to collect the relic. I'm not sure what the point is, but it's very ConQuest-y in that way, where it's almost impossible to do alone.

DUKEORSINO12: I get that

Of course he does. Mr. Team Sports himself.

DUKEORSINO12: so are we a team?

Not wanting to fall into the same trap as last time, I actually consider this before I answer. On the one hand, if Jack Orsino is incapable of anything, it's pulling his own weight. On the other, I *have* always wanted to try to win this quest. I already have a couple of the most valuable relics, and if you don't actively use them, you lose them.

Not to be a hoarder of digital weaponry, but anything that hard-won is something you want to keep.

C354R10: sure
C354R10: as long as you're not a total disaster
C354R10: /don't get us killed in the first realm
DUKEORSINO12: I learn fast

DUKEORSINO12: and how would I get us killed???

Poor sweet summer child.
Don't worry about it, I type back. You'll see.

I'm still up when Bash gets home, barking something about cast drama. I'm also up when my mom gets home, though I've very cleverly blocked out the glow from my laptop screen with a towel rolled up against my bedroom door. I eventually go to sleep only to be woken in the morning by a text message, which I half-consciously reply to, and then knock out again until almost noon.

Then I open my eyes to Bash standing over me and startle awake.

"Oi," he says. "Olivia's here."

I respond with something like "mlmph?" and he shrugs.

"She's downstairs but Mom's working. Should I send her up here?"

"Why?"

"Because our mother is *working*," Bash enunciates (shouts) in my ear.

"I meant why is she *here*, idiot," I reply, shoving him away. "Did she say?"

He shrugs again. "You're supposed to be working on your project, I gather."

"What?"

"PRO-JECT," he says.

This is going nowhere. "Look, just . . . stall," I say, stumbling to my feet to kick a pile of dirty clothes into my closet. "I'll, um—"

"Brush your teeth," Bash advises sagely.

"Right. Yeah. So just—"

"Bring the charm? You got it." Then he's out the door.

According to my phone, the message I stupidly replied to was me agreeing to work on our scene this morning instead of tomorrow afternoon, since apparently Olivia has something-something Popular Girl Activities to do. I brush my teeth and throw on a bra under my T-shirt; everything else she can deal with.

"—and here is the dragon's lair," Bash says loudly, presumably to indicate that I should have myself pulled together by now, which I have. "Here we go. One maiden, safely delivered. No promises as to what happens after this."

Olivia laughs and shrugs her backpack off her shoulder, giving me a small wave that's almost shy, if I could suspect her of any shyness. "Thanks for being flexible," she says.

"No problem." I kick a mismatched shoe under my desk. "You can just set stuff on my bed if you want. My desk is . . ." Covered in fabric swatches, books, my laptop. Weekend Vi is a whole other beast. "Sort of otherwise occupied."

"No worries." She swings a leg beneath her and perches on my bed like a fawn. "What'd you do last night?"

"Oh, you know me, lots of plans," I tell her. "The same thing I do every night."

"Try to take over the world?" she prompts, and I laugh.

"Wait, did you just—"

"*Pinky and the Brain*," she confirms while I dig through my school bag for my copy of the script. "It's my cousin's favorite way to annoy me when I ask her what we're doing."

"Cousin?" I echo.

"Yeah, older. Her family lives in Jordan but she's at Columbia now."

"Oh, that's cool. That's on my list of dream schools," I admit, gesturing to a postcard of New York that I keep tacked up above my desk.

"Mine too." Olivia looks dreamily away. "I love New York. It's so . . . vibrant, you know? There's this—"

"Don't say energy!" I groan.

She laughs. "There *is*, though. There's a *flow*."

"Wow," I say, shaking my head. "Wooooow. You sound like a New Yorker already."

"Oof. I wish I were interesting enough." She glances around my room, eyeing the books on my shelves. "What exactly is Con-Quest?" she asks me before I can conjure up something polite and uninformed about how I'm sure she's plenty interesting. "Like, I know what it is," she adds, "I just don't really *get it*, you know?"

Part of me braces for the conversation getting weird. I tried to explain the concept of ConQuest to my grandma once, but she thought it sounded like witchcraft. (Once Lola thinks a thing is witchcraft it's hard to convince her that it isn't.)

"It's a role-playing game," I say. "You design a character and then . . . be them, basically."

"Just . . . *be* them?" she echoes.

"Well, there's an adventure of some kind. A task, or a quest. But you make decisions that you think your character would make."

"Sort of like a choose-your-own-adventure thing?"

"Yeah, sort of, except there's no prompts or anything. You can just do whatever you want." I flop onto my bed. "No rules. Anything you want to do, you can do. Within the constraints of the game, anyway."

"That's cool." She gets up and peers at the spines, then runs her finger along one of the bindings. I thought she just brought it up to be nice, but then she says something again, surprising me while I'm fumbling through my scene annotations. "I think I'd be afraid to just . . . let go like that," Olivia admits, more to my bookshelf than to me. "It's almost easier to just do whatever people want me to do."

"Is it?" I ask, and she looks at me, a little startled.

"Well . . . maybe not," she admits, looking sheepish. "But I think I'd be embarrassed to do something wrong. Or say something dumb."

"Why? Boys never worry about all the dumb things *they* say and do, trust me," I mutter, and she laughs.

"Maybe you could teach me sometime." She sits gingerly next to me. "If you wanted."

"It's kind of better in a group." At the very least, you need another player and a QuestMaster, which I obviously don't have.

"Oh. Yeah, I guess I can see that." Olivia plays with a loose thread on my duvet, quiet for a minute, and I realize that maybe she wasn't just being polite.

"We could try a sample game to start with," I offer, and she looks up, brightening a little. "You'd just have to pick a character."

"And my character can be . . . anyone?" Olivia asks.

"Anyone. Any*thing*," I add. "Any mythological creature, any lore, as long as you define their skills and weaknesses."

"So I could be like . . ." She considers it. "A shark-headed gnome?"

I burst out laughing. "Okay, *not* what my guess would have been," I admit when she grins, "but yeah, you technically *could*—"

"What's your character?" she asks me.

Oh. Hm. I know she seems genuine, but it's still kind of geeky to admit. "I've had a few over the years."

"Who's your favorite?"

"My current character, probably. Astrea Starscream." I walk over to my desk and hold up the costume, or the parts of it that are finished. "She's an assassin seeking revenge. The usual stuff."

"Ooh, jealous." She skips to her feet to touch the fabric. "Did you make this?"

"Yeah." I clear my throat. "It's not done."

"It's so cool. You can sew?"

"I learned for this, specifically," I admit with a laugh. "Same reason I learned to fight."

"Fight?"

"Muay Thai. Not seriously, just for fun. But with sewing I have an actual skill in the event of a zombie apocalypse."

"Oh my god, you're right." Olivia groans. "I should start learning to weave, stat."

"Maybe spin?" I suggest. "Though I don't know where we'll get the wool once manufacturing is no longer on the table."

"See, *these* are the real concerns! You know Volio, on the football team?" I obviously don't, but I nod anyway. "He was trying to talk to me about the apocalypse the other day," she says, making a face. "Thinks he's got it figured out."

"Let me guess, he thinks you need a big strong man to protect you?"

"Guns," she says simply.

"What's with boys and guns? So phallic," I point out, and she laughs.

"I know, right? He's been . . . a lot, recently." She sits back on my bed with a sigh. "Apparently some of the guys on the team have decided that 'on a break' is just a one-way street to single."

It crosses my mind that this is a good time to get some information for Jack, but I'm not in a hurry. I kind of need him to stay on the hook for long enough that Kayla permanently redirects her pestering, and anyway, this isn't about him.

"That sucks," I say, resuming my seat next to Olivia, who glances at me with an intense look of . . . something.

"You know what? It *does* suck," she says firmly. "And I can't really talk about it because everyone just thinks I'm bragging or something."

"Why, because boys like you? That's not a secret," I assure her. "I *did* have to rescue you from the clutches of a thousand pubescent Romeos."

"It was hardly a thousand," she says with a roll of her eyes. "And that's the thing—they don't *know* me. Jack did. Does," she corrects herself quickly. Too quickly. She's got a real talent for watching what she says out loud. "But the rest of them just see a cheerleading uniform and some, I don't know, expertly applied mascara—"

"Couple of other things, too," I remark with an arched brow, but rather than blush, she blurts out a laugh.

"Right, yeah, even better. Why do boys even *like* boobs? They're pointless."

"Not for the apocalypse babies. Or the dying man at the end of *Grapes of Wrath*."

"You're really cynical," she observes.

"What? I brought up babies!"

"No, I mean . . . first the romance thing, then you instantly leapt to the apocalypse." She's smiling. "Is it super dark inside your head?"

"I consider other outcomes, too. It's just best to be prepared for every possible scenario," I assure her.

"Ah," she says. "Makes sense."

There's a lull in conversation, so I turn my attention back to the script.

"Maybe that's it," Olivia says unexpectedly. "The thing I can't do."

"Hm?" I look up with a frown.

"You're . . . imaginative. Creative." She looks over at my Con-Quest books again. "I just keep thinking how I'd need to watch someone else play, to find out what another person would do first. I can't really imagine myself doing something on my own, you know? Figuring it out for myself like that."

"There's nothing wrong with that. And there's plenty of ways to watch other people play first. There's videos on YouTube, or—" Just then, a thought occurs to me. "Or you could watch the live game at MagiCon."

"What?" She blinks.

"MagiCon. It's a sci-fi and fantasy convention. I go every year with—" Not important. "I volunteer every year. I could probably get you a spot." Particularly since I happen to know that one's available. "Won't cost you any money, and we could probably slip out to watch parts of the game if you wanted."

"Oh, I've always wanted to see what those conventions are like." She considers it. "Would I need a costume?"

"It's more fun with a costume, yeah. But if you don't want to—"

"No, I want to. I *love* dressing up."

"I could lend you one of my old ones, if you wanted," I offer. "Or I have the costume I usually wear to RenFaire—"

"Oh my god, you mean like a dress with a corset?"

"Yeah," I say, laughing at the wide-eyed expression on her face. "We can look for one later, if you want. After we, you know"—I hold up my script—"run lines."

"Oh, right." She sighs. "Sorry, I got all worked up thinking about corsets."

"You know, you can't possibly be bad at ConQuest," I inform her. "You're perfectly good at being Juliet, and she's not you, right? She's basically just a horny teen who doesn't care what anyone thinks so long as she can bang Romeo."

"Okay, I know you're baiting me on purpose," she sighs, to which I provide her an innocent shrug, "but you're not wrong, I guess. She genuinely does *not* care what her family thinks, so I guess that's worth keeping in mind."

Part of me perks up at this tiny sliver of new information: her family? I'm guessing that little slip has something to do with her break with Jack. Before I can ask her about it, though, she's nudging me.

"Come on. Your line," she reminds me. "The sooner we have this memorized, the sooner we can do costumes."

"Okay, fair enough," I say quickly, because we may not agree about romance, but we're definitely on the same page about that.

Jack

It was mostly by luck that I happened to be signed on last night when Cesario showed up.

(There's no way I'm calling Bash Reyes by his username. Or by his real name, for that matter. Too weird, even in my own head.)

I had initially planned to be out with my teammates after the away game, but something . . . didn't feel right. Maybe it was the fact that Curio's now being lauded for his arm, or that Andrews is a surprisingly proficient receiver. Or that we're now 5–0 without my help.

"Coach Orsino might never have known to take advantage of his passing game if his son hadn't taken such a hard injury to his right knee," declared the local sports broadcaster at the away game on Friday. "What might have been a struggle for the season has proven a surprise success, making Jack Orsino's torn ACL a blessing in disguise for the Messaline offense."

Yeah. A blessing. That's what I was thinking, too.

I have to give Curio credit for still trying to include me in all team decisions at practice, even though we both know that watching me hobble around is a hell of a bummer for everyone else. Volio's not quite so gracious; whenever someone talks to me, he glances at me with a little divot of confusion on his face, like I'm some kind of plant growing in the background. Funny how easily he thinks he can just slip into my place like I never existed, until I remember that oh yeah, *he can.* He's in my position now, literally, and he doesn't owe me anything. What doesn't get thrown in by Curio has Volio's name on it now, not mine. So yeah, if I were him I'd probably consider me a ghost, too. I've seen him watching Olivia like she's his for the taking, and maybe she is.

I have no idea anymore, so I made my excuses and stayed home. "How's your PT going?" is Dad's idea of casual small talk.

"Fine." It's still mostly stretches.

"You'll be back on the field soon, kid. Promise."

"Yeah." That's what I told Illyria, too, when I disclosed my ACL tear. It's what I tell my mom before she gives me that sad little look of "sure, honey" that I know she doesn't actually mean. I've seen her cover her face with her hands when my brother Cam takes a hard sack and I know, resentfully, that she's grateful I can't treat my body like a punching bag anymore. Not because I don't want to, but because it won't let me. Because for the first time, I'm fragile and vulnerable; because if I try it, I might break.

The truth is my knee, my leg, all of it . . . nothing feels like it used to. I feel trapped in my body, watching parts of me shrink down or swell up while I wait for things to hurt less, or work better. I know it's only been a few weeks, but I'm not used to having to think about the way my knee bends or how to put weight on it. All of that used to come naturally. Not anymore.

Which is why this so-called Camelot Quest is the perfect distraction. It may not be the state championship I was promised, but it makes the game feel way more real, which is fun. Or an escape. And who cares about the difference anymore.

C354R10: okay so the first realm is orkney, as in gawain

C354R10: and there's a trick to this realm

DUKEORSINO12: aside from not getting killed by the black knight??

C354R10: right yeah aside from that, which is true of all realms

C354R10: according to legend gawain's power triples by noon but fades as the sun sets

DUKEORSINO12: meaning . . . ?

C354R10: you have to take advantage of your character's strengths. and watch out for mages or sorcerers who can conjure an artificial night. or knights who have casting skills

This is stupid, right? Part of me feels like I should point out that this is stupid.

But I get it, having rules. Only a certain number of players on the field. Only some eligible receivers. Football's like chess, where each piece has a role, and it makes sense to me that magic—even weird computer game magic—has rules, too.

> **C354R10:** the usual rules still apply to casting, fyi. it takes a lot to summon an eclipse like that but strategically it could be worth it
> **C354R10:** magic has a cost, blah blah
> **DUKEORSINO12:** oh, so it's like the centauri on WoT

This is quite possibly the dorkiest thing I've ever said, but watching *War of Thorns* has made physics seem a lot easier. "Magic has a cost" is always being thrown around on the show, and put within context, all of Newton's laws suddenly seemed a lot less random.

> **C354R10:** yeah except unlike the centauri you just die
> **DUKEORSINO12:** lol bummer

I'm about to type in another question about Orkney when Cesario rapidly cuts in.

> **C354R10:** I forgot you're watching WoT. are you caught up yet?
> **DUKEORSINO12:** almost. I've got one more episode to go

I'm totally not going to be one of those freaks who's obsessed with this show, but . . .

> **DUKEORSINO12:** is it just me or is it total bullshit that the ice queen got overthrown

Cesario types back, stops, then types.

> **C354R10:** I can't believe I'm saying this but
> **C354R10:** you've never been more right

I stifle a laugh.

DUKEORSINO12: at first I really didn't think I was going to like her
DUKEORSINO12: but by the end I thought she was metal as hell
DUKEORSINO12: it totally sucks that that other dude betrayed her
C354R10: do you ever call any of the characters by their names
DUKEORSINO12: general punchy face
C354R10: he really does have a punchable face doesn't he
DUKEORSINO12: 100000%
C354R10: you wouldn't believe how many people think calliope deserved to get overthrown
DUKEORSINO12: what?!
C354R10: oh yeah, it's wild
C354R10: apparently siding with her is the same as condoning genocide
DUKEORSINO12: what?? it's just a show
C354R10: tell that to the rodrigo-worshipping fanboys
DUKEORSINO12: ugh speaking of rodrigo is he ever going to tell star tattoo girl how he feels about her or what
C354R10: you REALLY need to learn their names
DUKEORSINO12: I'll add it to my busy schedule
C354R10: and you also really need to catch up
C354R10: because I can't even begin to list the rodrigo-liliana problems this season
C354R10: top of the list would be: they're boring
DUKEORSINO12: lol
DUKEORSINO12: "ya basic"
C354R10: !! for real though !!
C354R10: he's always trying to make her be "moral" and it's exhausting
DUKEORSINO12: tbh my question is why she'd even want to be with rodrigo when cesario's right there

Once again Cesario says something, then hesitates.

C354R10: I mean, not that I'm biased but ya

Not very chatty, Cesario.

DUKEORSINO12: so, orkney?????
C354R10: right
C354R10: yes
C354R10: orkney

The entrance to Orkney is a tiny, quaint village, beyond which turns out to be a pretty cool forest. I don't know much about how game design works, but this one seems impressive. And you can actually interact with the setting in the game, which makes it better. And, I assume, harder to execute.

Once again: whatever nerd designed this game is really good at what they do.

Before I have a chance to ask Cesario what we're looking for, the sun suddenly dims. The scenery swirls around us, the trees becoming gothic, haunted versions of themselves as a message displays on the screen.

AN ENEMY ATTACKS!

From the creepy haunted trees emerges some kind of sorcerer, which isn't a dopey Magician's Assistant type of avatar or an old dude with a long beard, but instead a chiseled, muscular character with a symbol like a bolt of lightning. I draw my sword, but the sorcerer turns directly to Cesario.

ATTACK! the screen shrieks at us again, which is . . . honestly? Kind of unhelpful. I've never had to wonder if I was under attack and I certainly think I can figure it out now.

Cesario's health bar dims to a golden, mustardy yellow, and so does mine. This must be that power-diminishing spell he was telling me about, which explains the darkness.

Cesario pulls out a normal broadsword, beginning to fight head-on. I've run plays like this before, where there's two people facing one off. It's best to force your opponent into the middle, so I hit the sorcerer from the side, hoping to shift him. From there, Cesario and I can both try to attack from either side of his periphery, catching him off guard.

Luckily Cesario is quick to notice what I'm doing. He repositions himself and fakes high at the same time I go low. I manage a critical hit to the sorcerer, whose green bar wavers and dims. I'm about to turn outside when Cesario beats me to it—again—and manages another critical hit, this time bringing the green bar to yellow. He must determine that to be effective enough for a riskier gamble, because he uses his limited powers to cast something; it's a skill I don't have yet. Somehow a patch of light opens up, and despite a momentary dip into red for Cesario, our power bars glow brightly, unmistakably green.

We pull the same move again, both attacking the sorcerer, who retreats.

ENEMY RETREATS! the screen informs us. (Duh, we noticed.)

DUKEORSINO12: was that the game?
DUKEORSINO12: the environment or whatever?
C354R10: no
C354R10: that was

But before he can finish telling me what just happened, the screen opens up on a long, elaborate scroll.

BRAVE KNIGHT, YOUR VALOUR PRECEDES YOU!
WOULD YOU LIKE TO BEGIN THE CAMELOT QUEST?

Is it weird that I'm excited? I hit Yes, and my knight avatar bends one knee. Cesario's does the same.

VERY WELL, says the scroll, rolling itself up and contributing two more icons over our avatars' heads: a castle and a sword, both glowing, which I'm guessing will be visible to everyone else in the game.

THEN MAY YOU FIND THE TREASURE YOU SEEK.

DO NOT DROP YOUR WEAPON

𝔍𝔞𝔠𝔨

Over the next few nights I proceed to almost die about five dozen times, a few of which take place in the Orkney woods before we make our way to Dumnonia, a seafaring kingdom weakened by a plague of the Black Knight's evil sorcerer's invention. ("For the last time, the sorcerer's name is Mordred," Cesario tells me. "Do you ever learn anyone's names?") There I manage not to die a few more times, despite being targeted by other players who show up out of nowhere to attack us, sometimes one directly after another. Under other circumstances I would call this alarming, but Cesario doesn't get alarmed by much.

> **C354R10:** you get that the relics we have are live, right?
> **C354R10:** we're walking around with stuff other people want, and they're gonna come for us because of it

Oh sure, because I've never had things other people wanted. Popularity, a school record, a hot girlfriend . . .

> **DUKEORSINO12:** uh, I'm kind of a big deal? I'm used to it

I'm joking, but Cesario's reply is scathing.

> **C354R10:** used to be
> **C354R10:** not everything is football, brah

I make a face.

> **DUKEORSINO12:** don't "brah" me

DUKEORSINO12: and I'll be back to it soon. this is all just temporary

Cesario says nothing for a couple of seconds.

C354R10: maybe you should consider the possibility that there's more to life than football.
DUKEORSINO12: duh
DUKEORSINO12: there's also knights
C354R10: I'm serious
C354R10: injuries like yours take a long time to heal
DUKEORSINO12: you're an expert in ACL tears now?
C354R10: it happens sometimes in muay thai
DUKEORSINO12: muay thai??

That's intense. No wonder he loves combat games.

C354R10: the point is you should probably start thinking about what you're going to do if you're not eligible to play this year. or next.

Wow. That stings.

DUKEORSINO12: I thought we were leaving real life out of this????
C354R10: true

But he doesn't apologize.

C354R10: just a thought

I've never thought of Social Committee Kayla as a chill person, but damn. I had no idea someone could get so worked up about a homecoming ticket.

"I don't think hiring a graphic designer is a very, uh. Good use of funds," I tell her, which is exactly the sort of thing I try not to say, because it makes Kayla's smile warp into something extremely less than pleased.

I mean honestly, it should be obvious to anyone that most of the things involved in planning a dance are pointless wastes of money. But I can't *say* that, out loud, ever. The secret to not being hated is to just never tell someone they can't have what they want, which is exactly why I've always considered this task better left to someone else.

Like, say, Vi Reyes, who is currently sitting at her usual lab table typing some report to the admins.

"The ticket is everyone's first impression," Kayla tells me with a sharpness I've been hearing from her more and more often these days. "Doesn't that matter to you?"

"Of course it matters." (It doesn't.)

"Okay, then I don't see why we wouldn't be able t—"

"It's not like anyone saves them to wallpaper their bedroom with," I say helplessly, and Kayla draws upright like I just insulted her mother.

"Excuse me?" she demands, though before she can launch into her forthcoming rant, someone else interrupts.

"We don't use paper tickets," Vi says, apparently to me but also to no one, and she does it without looking up from something that looks even more mind-numbing than the conversation I'm having. "Waste of paper. Student Carbon Footprint Initiative," she adds, as if this is something I should care about.

Okay, so this isn't even a real ticket? It's basically an Instagram post. Aren't there about twenty aspiring influencers who could easily throw something together? And don't even get me started on whatever that "initiative" is. All I know is it's yet another example of kids at this school caring more about being vegan than talking about police shootings. I'm never more aware of what color my skin is than when people are suddenly asking me how they can be a better ally. Uh, don't call me an Oreo or tell me I sound white like it's impressive? Everyone wants racism to be this bomb they can disarm rather than what it is, which is . . . fluid. Usually it's so small it's not even worth explaining. And even if I could, I wouldn't, because nobody wants to listen to the ways they failed, period, much less how they might have failed *me*.

It's all about smiles and compromise, baby.

"I'm sure there's someone who can design it. Mackenzie," I say, startling her from where she's struggling with posters for the game on Friday. "You can sketch something out, can't you?"

Her eyes widen, which I think is probably a yes. Given her position as Kayla's lieutenant, I'm guessing she already tried and got shot down. "Oh," she says, flushing. "Sure. I mean, I could definitely try to—"

"Ugh. *Ugh*," Kayla says, emphasizing her scorn for good measure before stomping away, leaving me alone with a conspicuously inattentive Vi.

"This," I inform her in an undertone, "is the worst job ever."

She says nothing, apathetically clicking her mouse.

"I hope you have some news for me," I add, referencing our deal.

"Nope," Vi replies with another mouse click.

"Seriously?"

"Rome wasn't built in a day, Orsino." Two clicks.

"Well, this sucks," I tell her. She's had at least two weeks to get something out of Olivia. Don't girls talk about this sort of thing while they travel in packs to the bathroom? "I'm not sure this is turning out to be an equal bargain."

"Okay." She glances at me. "Then call it off."

She is such a thorn in my side, I swear. I glare at her, and she simpers snidely back.

"You're in a pleasant mood," she observes, resuming whatever she's typing.

"I'm always in a pleasant mood," I retort with a growl, which only makes her inattentive smile twitch. "Just . . . give me *something*, okay? Please, I just—"

Nope, no way. This isn't the time or place to talk about how much it drives me crazy not to know what Olivia's thinking. And Vi Reyes is certainly not the person to care how my knee feels today. (It's irking me, like an itchy tag.)

"Forget it," I exhale, and turn away on my crutches only to trip on a chair, banging my injured knee into the edge of a desk.

A few choice expletives escape me. Vi doesn't notice, which is kind of a weird, mixed blessing. I don't need her to look at me like I'm less than I was before the way everyone else does, though I *would* like her to acknowledge that just because she thinks my life is easy doesn't mean it is. Hard to say whether I'm more frustrated with her or just . . . everything.

"I'm doing what you wanted," I remind her.

"Yes. Your job," she replies.

"No, I mean—"

"I know what you meant." She flicks her gaze up to mine from the screen. "You really want me to feel bad about this, don't you? Sorry. I don't." She purses her lips. "When you've held up your end of the bargain, it'll just revert back to me doing everything anyway, so why am I supposed to care? You and Olivia will work things out, you'll win your little sportball game—"

"Oh, nice, Viola," I say with a groan. "That's *definitely* what the state championship is called—"

"—and when *I'm* the one dealing with Miss Society Pages again," she continues, unfazed, "where will you be? Not here. Not listening to me, or even remotely giving me the time of day. So no," she informs me, clicking again and whirring the printer to life. "I do not feel sorry for you."

I open my mouth to point out that I've never been nearly as much of a dick to her as she is to me, but instead what comes out is, "What makes you so sure things will ever go back to normal for me? Maybe I'll just be miserable forever," I point out bitterly, "and then you'll get your wish."

The room falls silent, like a record scratch, and she pauses with her finger poised on the mouse. Part of me wants to shrivel up in horror. The other part of me thinks it serves her right. A *third* part of me, quiet and small, hopes she doesn't try to apologize. Her pity would only make this worse.

But eventually she shrugs. "You're not *dead*, Orsino. Maybe tomorrow you'll be cult leader for the jock squad once again."

God, she is impossible.

"Okay, first of all, stop calling me that," I say, which she ignores, "and you know what else?" She's still not listening. "It kinda seems like a scam to worry about our carbon footprint considering that none of us are billionaires with private jets," I half-heartedly snap, furiously shoving the desk out of my way with the edge of my crutch.

From the corner of my eye I see Vi's mouth quirk when I turn away, though she doesn't bother replying.

Impossible. Unbearable.

But at least she didn't make things worse.

While Vi's lack of intel about Olivia continues to be very Vi of her, I do find it increasingly stressful. By the end of the week, the first elaborate homecoming invitation has been delivered: one of the ASB newscasters asks his girlfriend over the morning announcements, and just like that the season of bizarre flash mobs, bad scavenger hunts, and painful songwriting has begun.

If Olivia and I were still . . . Olivia and me, I'd do something flashy. Last year I had every member of the freshman team deliver a rose to her throughout the day, ending with them spelling out her name on their bare chests as I swanned in with a full bouquet. This is the kind of thing that's expected of me, and I know she loves it.

Olivia's a romantic at heart; she tears up at the end of every sappy romance. Part of me wants to text her every time I'm watching *War of Thorns*—she'd love the Liliana and Cesario plot. It's right up her alley: forbidden love on opposite sides, like Romeo and Juliet.

Which is why I fall prey to desperation and attempt, unwisely and certainly without chill, to talk to her again, despite my promises to give her space. I manage to catch her alone at lunch, by some miracle. Volio's been spending a lot of time around her lately, though she never looks like she's enjoying it.

"Hey," I say, struggling to sit down at the tiny outdoor tables without wrenching my knee in two separate directions. Before I lose my nerve, I offer, "What do you think about having an us day on Saturday?"

"Oh, Jack." She softens, and for a second she looks at me like she used to. "We haven't had one of those in ages."

An "us day" is what we used to do when we first started dating. We took turns planning out a day where we both put our phones away and just spent some time hanging out, though they got less frequent over time. I had football, then she had the SATs, then she was gone for most of summer . . . But I'm hoping she'll feel nostalgic enough to say yes.

"I'll plan it out," I promise her, thinking maybe I was right that she was feeling neglected. "We can do a marathon of those movies you love, or—"

"I actually can't Saturday," she tells me, looking apologetic the way Olivia does, where you're not sure if she's actually sorry about what she's saying or just sorry that she has to say it. Unlike, say, Vi Reyes, Olivia is a nice person who tends to feel bad about disappointing people, which . . . does make her harder to read.

"I have plans," she explains.

"All day?" I ask, ignoring the little divot of disappointment in my chest.

"Yeah." She grimaces. "I'm so sorry."

"What are you up to?" I ask, hoping to sound casually interested. After all, this is the closest thing we've had to real conversation in almost a month.

"Oh, you'll laugh," she says. "Seriously."

"Try me," I insist.

"It's just . . . I'm volunteering at MagiCon? You know, the fantasy convention in the city," she says, as I blink, extremely taken aback.

"Isn't that for, like . . . comic book geeks? Gamers?" Oh god, like all the other people who play *Twelfth Knight*. Which I guess includes me now, but she doesn't need to know that.

"The way I hear it, it's for everyone," Olivia says with a sudden coolness, and just like that there's distance between us again. "A friend asked me if I wanted to go volunteer for the day, so yeah. Other plans."

"Well—" I rack my brain for a way to save this. "I've always wanted to go to one of those. I mean, they seem so interesting, right?" I say, which seems to be the right track, because she doesn't immediately try to exit the conversation. "What if I got a ticket?"

She frowns. "I'm pretty sure I'll be busy with volunteer work for most of the day—"

"Just to see what it's like, I mean," I say hastily. "I've been kind of getting into that *War of Thorns* show—"

"Really?" she asks, looking at me like I took a hard blow to the head.

"Well, just a normal amount. I'm not obsessed with it or anything." This is getting worse, isn't it? "And then maybe we could get something to eat? Or something." Someone save me. A storm, a bolt of lightning. A casual sorcerer plague. "Or I could bring you something to eat, in case you're not supposed to leave your post. Or whatever. Maybe we could drive up together!" God, it's like I lost all of my cool when I tore my ACL. "Just a thought. I mean, who knows if I can even get tickets," I finish with an awkward gulp of laughter.

"I hear they're hard to get," she agrees, and glances at my knee. "And it might be a lot of walking," she adds, sounding . . . concerned? That's promising, at least. She still cares about whether I can move around in public, which is . . . something.

"Oh, it's fine," I lie. "I barely even feel it. So I'll just let you know, if that's cool?" I ask, noticing that other people are about to join us. I don't think I can live down a public conversation about MagiCon right now.

"Yeah, that's fine. That works." She nods, slowly and then quicker. "Yeah, that sounds good, Jack. We can do that."

"Cool. Well, I'll leave you to it," I say, bolstered by the presence of a plan. The goal line's back in sight, thank god, and it doesn't even matter that the table's flooded with people before I can fully get up. "I'll text you."

She nods, looking a little dazed, and I struggle to get out my phone before sitting at the adjacent table, ignoring Curio's worried flash of a glance.

yo, please help me get tickets to magicon, I text to Nick. *seriously, this is urgent.*

uhhhhh I'm not a wizard, he says. *don't you know those things sell out way in advance??*

can I get one on ebay or something? I ask desperately.

unlikely. they're registered to the specific user and you have to get one that's legit

Wait a minute. *have you been to one???*

look, my sister loves it okay? he says, and then follows up with, *oh hang on*

I wait a few minutes, jiggling my left knee while trying not to think about my right one.

good news. ant's not going this year so you can go in her place. it's a volunteer pass though so you'll have to help out and stuff

With Olivia? I pause for a second to count my lucky stars.

even better, I type back with relief. *dude thank you, you're saving my life*

don't forget to take breaks from twelfth knight my guy, he says. *I know it's addictive but I never thought you'd go this far*

oh, come on. it's not like I'll be one of those weirdos in costumes. And anyway it's not about me. It's for Olivia, which is legit. Romantic, even.

bro, Nick says with one of those forehead-smacking emojis. *trust me. you have NO idea what you're in for.*

𝔙𝔦

"Weird thing happened today," Bash says in the car after school.

"Weird things happen to you every day," I remind him, flicking on the turn signal.

"True," he agrees. "Aren't you going to ask me about it?"

"I assume you're going to tell me."

"It's more fun if you ask me."

I hum along to my usual alt-pop, saying nothing.

"Fine," Bash says, caving within seconds as I knew he would. "Jack Orsino nodded to me."

I freeze for a second, nearly choking. "What?"

"You can stop pretending, I know you can hear me—"

I manage to elbow him without removing my hands from the wheel. "Shut up. What do you mean he *nodded* at you?"

"He nodded *to* me," Bash corrects me. "Like, you know—" He mimics the universal sportzboi gesture for *'sup*. "Like that."

Oh god. What part of "keep real life out of it" doesn't Jack understand? Though I guess the last violation of that agreement was technically mine.

Despite how it might look, my feelings on Jack haven't changed. I still don't care what's going on with him or his life, but when I'm Cesario and he's Duke Orsino, I can enjoy myself in a way that I can't with anyone else. Somehow, despite pretending to be somebody different, I'm exactly as me as I want to be.

Which, as far as I can tell, he seems to need just as badly as I do.

But that's not the point. "I'm sure you imagined it," I say breezily. Bash is very imaginative, so that's not a stretch, even for someone who already knows that Jack Orsino thinks he's playing *Twelfth Knight* with Bash every night.

"Vi, please. Not even *my* inner life is that creative," Bash assures me, fiddling with the vents. "By the way, how'd your scene go with Olivia?"

"As expected." Meehan was *thrilled* with us, which I figured he would be. He told Olivia she had a "natural presence" and insisted she consider the spring musical. To me he said I made a very convincing pining gentleman, which was somewhat less flattering.

"I'm assuming she and Jack are still off," Bash says thoughtfully, and at my sidelong glance, he shrugs. "Hello? She's hanging out with *you*," he points out, which might be rude coming from someone else (and is technically rude coming from him), but is also probably true. "Until she inevitably annoys you or something," he adds in a very loaded tone.

He obviously means my falling-out with Antonia, but once again, Antonia and I are merely having a disagreement of conviction: she's convinced that I suck, and I disagree.

"Olivia's coming with me to MagiCon tomorrow," I tell him. As in, see? I'm not incapable of human interaction.

Bash explodes in a snort of something incoherent. "She's *what*?"

"What's so funny? It's a very popular event," I remind him. He used to come with me before I started going with Antonia, but Ren-Faire is more his speed. He likes his pop culture to be centuries-old with fake accents. (Though there is plenty of that at MagiCon. For some reason—cough, imperialism—a person is free to dream up a world with mythical creatures and magical powers so long as it's still mostly British.)

"Have you *seen* Olivia Hadid?" Bash asks rhetorically, and I shrug. "Though I suppose she does have period face," he concedes.

"Ew, what?"

"Period face. Like Keira Knightley. And that other guy." He gestures to his own face, which doesn't help.

"Like she belongs in period dramas, you mean?"

"Yeah. Oh," he adds with a snap of his fingers. "Rufus."

"Rufus?"

"Rufus." He nods, and I give up on trying to make any of this make sense.

"Why do you care about me hanging out with Olivia, anyway? Or whether or not Jack Orsino nods at you, for that matter," I add, because for better or worse, Jack seems to be at the root of every conversation I have lately.

"He nodded *to* me," Bash insists again, "and I don't *care,* really. I just find it kind of funny."

"Funny ha-ha?"

"No, funny odd." He shrugs. "Olivia seems way too cool for you."

"Why, because I'm not a cheerleader?"

"No. Because you hate everything and she willingly chooses to be positive in public several times a week." He glances at me. "Go, fight, win! Et cetera."

I grimace. "I do not *hate* everything. I like plenty of stuff."

"Said like a robot trying to pass for a human. Or an alien anthropologist. Or a narc."

"I have hobbies, Bash," I remind him. "And interests." Like my costume, which I rushed to finish the moment I realized that someone aside from me might pay attention. It came out even better than I'd hoped, though I'm trying to manage my expectations.

"You like fictional characters more than actual people," Bash accuses.

"Why shouldn't I? Real people harass me while I'm trying to drive."

"And what's the deal with you and Mom?" he asks tangentially. He seems to be getting at something, though I cannot imagine what. (I can. I'm simply choosing not to.)

"The deal? We've known each other about seventeen years, give or take—"

"Come on." He nudges me. "I know all's not well in the Viola-verse. You've been . . . mercurial."

By "mercurial" he probably means bitchy, in that ever since our militantly feminist mother tried to give me a TED Talk about the value of human connection, I keep brushing her off.

It's not that I don't want to talk to her. I just feel like with this new guy in her life, I can't quite trust her. There's something about Mom's sudden urgency to fix me that makes me feel like she's forgotten who I am. No—who *we* are. After all, she's supposed to be the one to tell me not to give some dumb boy an unnecessary chance and never to back down from something I believe in. My mom's supposed to be the one who understands me best. If I were in the business of talking about my feelings, I might admit that what I'm feeling is lonely.

Which I don't expect Bash, a consummately lovable person, to understand.

"Nothing. No deal. And remember what I said about harassing me?" I point out.

"Only faintly. And anyway, you love me."

"Only because it's genetic."

"Cool. I figured." He hesitates for a moment like he might say something else, but then reaches over and tugs my ponytail. "For the record, I think you're weird, which is better than being cool. Anyone can be cool."

"I disagree," I reply drily.

"Well, maybe if we had more money. Or if you wore better clothes."

"This," I inform him, "is a great shirt." It says *Village Witch*.

"Sure it is," Bash says happily, making me circle the block twice until the song ends.

I'm about to transition from messing around on Tumblr to my nightly game of *Twelfth Knight* (next up is Galles, which is full of enchantress magic that we'll need to recharge all our relics for) when I get an email from Stacey, one of the MagiCon volunteers.

Hey Viola! So excited to see you again tomorrow—can't believe it's been a year already! Unfortunately, we somehow got our wires crossed on our end. I know I promised you Olivia Hadid could take Antonia's spot on our volunteer list, but it looks like Megha already gave it to someone else at Antonia's request. I'm SOOOOO sorry about the mix-up! We can put Olivia down for next year, but unfortunately our list is full for this weekend. :(Hope it's not too inconvenient.

Um, what? They double-booked Antonia's spot? Is that a joke?
I inhale, then exhale.
Telling people they're incompetent usually doesn't end well.
Inhale, exhale.
After a brief email exchange (forcibly polite) during which we come to the conclusion that there's nothing Stacey can do, I have no choice but to accept that I have to tell Olivia she can't come. I glance over at my costume, disappointed all over again, which is probably stupid. Not that Olivia and I are actually friends, but at least show-ing her the ropes would have been a decent distraction from the reminder that I won't be there with Antonia. I don't mind going alone—easier that way, honestly, than worrying about if someone else is hungry or thirsty or if their feet hurt—but I feel bad. Olivia seemed like she really wanted to come.

I send her a text that I hope expresses how sorry I am, but she doesn't reply.

Well, that's probably another friendship over.

I sign in to the *Twelfth Knight* game client, soothed again by the picture filling the screen. It's probably a bad sign that I like it here so much. Oh well. That's for my future self to work out in therapy.

I've been on for about five seconds before my chat window blinks with a message.

> **DUKEORSINO12:** is it just me or are some days just really good days to kill monsters

Speaking of people who need therapy.

> **C354R10:** what happened? did the pep squad run out of pep
> **DUKEORSINO12:** HILARIOUS
> **DUKEORSINO12:** no
> **DUKEORSINO12:** kind of
> **DUKEORSINO12:** but no
> **C354R10:** you know we don't actually have a pep squad right
> **DUKEORSINO12:** I am aware

Well, at least there's that.

> **DUKEORSINO12:** everything just sucks
> **DUKEORSINO12:** I know that's not strictly within the rules of leaving reality out of it but
> **C354R10:** no
> **C354R10:** it counts

Not sure why I said that. Or why I raced to say it before he finished typing.

> **C354R10:** what happens in the game stays in the game
> **C354R10:** which includes whatever the mascot did to you today
> **C354R10:** which I assume was some kind of hostile takeover
> **DUKEORSINO12:** the kid in the mascot has about 8 different kinds of asthma
> **C354R10:** medically unlikely
> **DUKEORSINO12:** aren't we all

Ah. Okay. Sounds like "medical" hit close to home.

C354R10: is this about . . . you know
C354R10: the events of black friday
DUKEORSINO12: if that means the day I got hurt then yes

I feel like I probably shouldn't push this.
I shouldn't, right?

C354R10: are you ok?
DUKEORSINO12: not really

Of course he's not okay, what a stupid question. And it's not like he's going to tell me, because pretty much all boys are programmed not to have feelings, so basically there's no point in—

DUKEORSINO12: I feel like my power bar is red
DUKEORSINO12: or at least yellow
DUKEORSINO12: I haven't been green in ages

That's actually a pretty good metaphor.

DUKEORSINO12: I've got no relics
DUKEORSINO12: people keep coming for me and it keeps getting worse
DUKEORSINO12: I saw my PT again today and

He stops.

DUKEORSINO12: you might have been right
DUKEORSINO12: what you said the other day

I swallow.

DUKEORSINO12: idk if I can come back
DUKEORSINO12: I also don't know what I'll do if I can't

Whoa.

DUKEORSINO12: sorry, I just
DUKEORSINO12: I don't know who else I can talk to about this
DUKEORSINO12: my mom wants me to focus on school but I just took whatever I had to because I thought I was going to illyria
DUKEORSINO12: my dad and my brother think I've given up
DUKEORSINO12: my girlfriend is barely my girlfriend
DUKEORSINO12: my team doesn't even need me

He stops, and suddenly I remember the look on his face when he was complaining to me about Kayla. He seemed genuinely frustrated, even a little confused, like he didn't know how to handle all the anger he was feeling at the world. Which is definitely something I can relate to.

DUKEORSINO12: you don't have to respond to any of this
DUKEORSINO12: and anyway we have other stuff to talk about
DUKEORSINO12: enchantresses and also last week's WoT
DUKEORSINO12: bc I need cesario to kill rodrigo, like, yesterday

Okay, this is true, but—

C354R10: we can talk about it
C354R10: if you want to

I chew my lip, then try for a joke.

C354R10: undress to your comfort level
C354R10: (metaphorically)
DUKEORSINO12: lol

I wonder if I actually made him laugh.

DUKEORSINO12: there's not much to tell really
DUKEORSINO12: I'm working on the girlfriend thing

He means his deal with me, presumably. Me-Vi, not me-Cesario. (Weird thought.)

DUKEORSINO12: as for the other stuff, I think you might be right about that too
DUKEORSINO12: focusing on stuff that isn't football
C354R10: if it helps you're not terrible at this game
C354R10: you're like pretty decent
DUKEORSINO12: "pretty decent"?
C354R10: mm
C354R10: fairly adequate
C354R10: marginally competent
DUKEORSINO12: stop, I'm blushing

Ugh, and I'm smiling. I shake it away because ew, no.

C354R10: the point is there's other stuff out there
C354R10: maybe this is a good thing
C354R10: your life's not over. you just have space now for other stuff
DUKEORSINO12: becoming toxically addicted to a computer game was not high on my list of achievements for the year
C354R10: stop whining
C354R10: make a new list

He types back in fits and starts.

DUKEORSINO12: I think secretly I might have really needed to hear that
DUKEORSINO12: not that you care obviously
C354R10: definitely not
C354R10: I just can't have you moping around on a quest
DUKEORSINO12: obviously
C354R10: obviously
DUKEORSINO12: so. go time?

C354R10: you mean should we stop standing perfectly still on top of this weird fairy mole hill? ya
DUKEORSINO12: is that what this is??

It turns out this realm isn't so bad. It kind of looks like the Shire. Also, enchantresses are usually really good, so the combat portions are intricate and fun. Their castings create a radius you have to work around to avoid falling under their control, so it's all about tactical positioning, which Jack's gotten much better at since I taught him how to use keybindings.

Oops, not Jack. Duke. DukeOrsino12.

DUKEORSINO12: oh btw not sure when I'll be free tomorrow
DUKEORSINO12: doing something all day
C354R10: me too actually
C354R10: probably won't be on til late
DUKEORSINO12: cool see you then

He signs off first, and I lean back in my chair, exhaling.

Even though there's all that weird stuff with Olivia and no Antonia tomorrow, I feel . . . strangely okay.

It's a really fun game, I remind myself, and fall into bed with a yawn.

I wake up to my phone ringing and answer it groggily. "Hello?"

"Hey." The voice on the other end is scratchy and almost unintelligible. "It's Olivia."

"Oh. *Oh.*" I rub my eyes. "Are you okay? You sound—"

"Sick," she confirms in a mournful tone. "I'm sorry I missed your message. I passed out around six last night."

"Oof, that sucks."

"I know. It's not great. But I guess it's good news? The ticket isn't being wasted."

"Oh." I'd forgotten about that. "Yeah, true."

"I was feeling really guilty about bailing," she admits. "I was hoping to sleep it off so that I could still go—"

"Oh, that's—"

"What?"

"No, nothing, you finish."

"Well, it's kind of a short story." She laughs, which sounds like a hacking cough. "But actually I was hoping to ask a favor. Someone else who's going needs a ride and now I obviously can't help, so . . . think you can take them instead?"

"Oh . . . yeah, sure. Sure, no problem." It's about an hour drive, so actually that sounds awful, but whatever. (Olivia's not an easy person to say no to. I assume it's all that niceness.) "Do I need to pick them up?"

"Yeah, but they live close to you. It's Jack, actually."

I choke on something I think is my own saliva. "What?"

My costume all but winks at me from where it's hanging off the edge of my closet.

"You okay?" Olivia says while I cough. "You're not sick too, are you? I didn't have any symptoms until yesterday, but—"

"No, no, I'm—" I manage to catch my breath. "You want me to take *Jack Orsino* to MagiCon?"

Honestly, this might as well happen.

"Yeah, he's volunteering, too. Funny coincidence, right?" Oh, hysterical. Somehow I have a guess who might have gotten Antonia's ticket instead of Olivia. "Anyway yeah, if you don't mind. I hope it's not too inconvenient, but he can't drive himself, so . . ."

Lola always says God laughs at our plans, and somewhere, distantly, I can hear it.

"I'll make it up to you," Olivia adds. "Movie night, your pick, my treat. Or, you know, whatever you like to do. Manicures?"

"Ha." Oops. "I mean—"

"No, I get it. Bad guess." She laughs. "Something else."

"Food? I like food."

"Oh my god, I *love* food," she jokes, and coughs again. "Sorry, sorry—"

"No, you should drink some water. Get some sleep. Sounds like a battlefield over there."

"Yeah," she coughs. "It's—I don't—"

"Just text me Jack's address, okay? I'll try not to drive him directly into the bay or anything," I offer generously.

She coughs some more in response.

"I'm going to assume that was a goodbye, so bye!" I say into the phone, hanging up to save her the effort of responding. Within seconds, she's sent me Jack's address.

I click to open a new message, half holding my breath to brace for dread.

But oddly, the intensity I expect to feel isn't there. Maybe being repeatedly forced into the orbit of Jack's life is starting to numb me? Sounds dangerous. Maybe I'm getting used to him? Sounds worse. Or maybe I don't *hate* this idea so much as . . . feel strange about it. Surprised by it, the same way I've been consistently surprised by him in the world of *Twelfth Knight*.

Then again, whatever tenuous friendship Duke Orsino has with Cesario doesn't remotely exist for Jack and Viola, and for all Jack knows, that's all there is. My cautious optimism vanishes without a trace, and the guard I might have let down lurches safely back up as a message hovers at the top of my screen.

hey. apparently you're my ride.

Damn. Could I pretend not to get the message? New phone, who dis? Maybe I'll be doing us both a favor if I just ignore Olivia's request altogether.

(Sigh.)

I'll be there at 8, I tell him. *don't be late.*

good morning to you too, he replies. I roll my eyes, God laughs.

It's about to be a very weird day.

HEAD SWAP

Jack

The person at my front door is *not* Viola Reyes.

"Close your mouth," she says. "You look ridiculous."

(Okay, maybe it's Vi after all.)

"*What*," I begin somewhat belligerently, "are you *wearing?*"

It's something that at first glance I can only describe as . . . glittery black armor. Well, there's definitely some sort of iron breastplate involved, like what the knights wear in *Twelfth Knight*, only her chain mail is tiny and delicate, more like jewelry, with little stars blinking and catching the light. The actual armor portion cuts off around her ribs and then there's some sheer paneling that skims the waistline of black leather leggings; on her feet are a pair of black combat boots embellished with studs, rhinestones, and more stars. She's also wearing a lot more makeup—thick black eyeliner and dark lipstick with silver drawn on beside the corners of her eyes— and her black hair is pulled up high on her head, braided like a crown.

Just when I'm thinking she looks like she could pull a knife on me, she shifts, revealing the leather-wrapped handles of two daggers strapped to her legs: one to her left thigh, the other to her right ankle, sticking just out of her boot.

"Jesus," I say, unable to manage much of anything else, and her eyes narrow.

"You can't go like that," she says.

I blink. "What?"

"You're not in costume."

"So?"

She gives me a sharp glance.

"Come on," she says, and walks away.

There's a moment—while I'm caught in a battle between my crutches and the keys to the door—where the glimpse of her lingers in my periphery, and as annoyed as I want to be about this situation, there's something else I haven't put into words yet. Obviously I don't spend a lot of time thinking about Vi Reyes (not *that* much, anyway), but there's a fraction of a second when the possibility flutters across my brain that I might actually respect her more than I dislike her. Sure, she's a dick most of the time and she's a headache to work with, but in a strange way, this outfit suits her.

No, not the outfit. The power, I guess. It's broad daylight on my pristinely suburban street, but that doesn't seem to bother her in the slightest. She walks like nobody's going to stop her. Even I don't walk like that, like I make no apologies for existing. My swagger is built on a foundation of adoration and envy. Hers is a flat-out refusal to let anyone tell her who to be.

I guess she must have figured out that bending to other people's opinions didn't do much for her, which is the opposite of my approach. I wonder which of us is better off for that.

"Stop gaping, Orsino," she says over her shoulder, unlocking her car and dropping into the driver's seat while I linger helplessly at the edge of the curb.

Before Olivia called me this morning, I'd been really looking forward to today. An hour-long car ride with Olivia was not only sixty times longer than any conversation I've had with her in weeks, it was also the convenient brokerage of an entire day's worth of progress. The fact that I was still on crutches? Unimportant. The fact that it was *MagiCon*, which is by all accounts a festive gathering for dweebs? Irrelevant. I thought it was my chance to regain a little of what I've lost—right up until Olivia coughed at me that not only was she no longer going (gutting enough on its own), I was on the hook for a full day's volunteer hours, per the contract that Past Me very optimistically signed, and thanks to my still-injured knee, I *also* had to catch a ride with someone else.

A wide-awake nightmare of a person, it turns out. And embarrassingly, it's occurring to me that I can't figure out how to get into the car without asking said nightmare for help.

I reach carefully for the passenger door, trying to maintain my balance without toppling into the gutter, but then, quick as a flash, Vi is out of the car and at my elbow. "I'm fine," I grunt to her, which she ignores. She puts her shoulder under my arm, firmly but not forcefully, and I take it because why not? This day is already slipping out from under me. Why not my legs, too?

When I'm seated, she takes the crutches and slides them into her back seat.

"We're going to my house first," she says when she resumes her place in the driver's seat. "We'll still make it as long as we get on the road in twenty minutes."

"What? But you said—"

"Yes, I know what I said. But the point of making sure you were on time was to allow for any necessary delays."

"And is this necessary?" I demand.

She looks at me for a second, then purses her lips.

"Yes," she says, and starts the car, dutifully tapping her turn signal despite the street being empty. (So much for neighborhood watch, right? It's a wasteland on an early Saturday morning as a fully weaponized villainess steals me away.)

We drive for about two seconds before my confusion outweighs my preference for silence. "What are you?"

"Who," she corrects me. "Who am I."

"Fine. *Who* are you?"

"Astrea Starscream. Assassin."

"From . . . a comic book, or . . . ?"

"Original character."

"Wait," I say, and she glances at me, a flicker of something—annoyance? Dread?—appearing briefly on her face. "You *made* this? From nothing? Like, no copying a character or anything, you just . . . made this up? Originally?"

She opens her mouth.

Closes it.

"I obviously have an idea what the character looks like," she says in a hard-toned voice. "She has a full backstory. And her wardrobe is part of who she is."

"Are those real knives?"

Her mouth twists. "No." She pauses. "Seriously?" she adds, but it doesn't sound vicious, like usual. She sounds like she's making fun of me.

"It's not like I know the rules," I grumble.

"You think the convention center is going to be cool with me taking *actual* weapons inside?" she asks, using her are-you-literally-the-dumbest-boy-in-school voice, which is totally undeserved.

"I've never been! How am I supposed to know?"

"What made you want to go to this, anyway?" she demands—and *aha*, do I detect a hint of curiosity in her voice? I think she's been wanting to ask me that all morning.

"Can't a guy be curious how the geekier half lives?" I reply musically, knowing it'll irritate her not to get a real answer.

She shoots a glare at me. "I assume this is about Olivia—"

"Well, you know what they say about assumptions—"

"—which means you must be *miserable* about this outcome," she comments over me.

"No more miserable than you," I reply.

"Me? I'm thrilled. I *love* MagiCon."

Ha. Liar. "That may be true, but you don't want to spend the day with me any more than I want to spend it with you."

"I *won't* spend the day with you, Orsino. I'll dump you on some volunteer coordinator and have a wonderful time by myself."

I know this is my opening to say something clever, or something about how I, too, would rather be surgically attached to a complete stranger than spend the entire day with her, but instead there's a tiny lump in my throat. A whole day alone, with no one I know?

I'm not good at being alone. And contrary to whatever Vi thinks, being charming takes a lot of energy that I don't currently have. Wish I'd just stayed home.

By the time I realize I haven't snarked back, Vi's talking again.

"It's for ConQuest," she says. "This character. She's my Con-Quest character."

I nod silently.

"I kind of assumed you were going to make fun of me for that," she adds.

I'm not surprised she thinks so. She always thinks the worst of me, but if she paid any attention at all, she'd realize that I can't afford to make people hate me. And that includes making fun of them, even if I do secretly think ConQuest sounds like an extremely weird way to spend your time. Isn't it essentially make-believe?

Which, a small voice in my head reminds me, *is what computer games are, too.*

"There's still a whole day left," I say casually. "Can't just waste all my heckling in the car. Have to warm up to it."

"Thanks," she mutters, but I think she knows I'm not going to. Somehow, the stiffness between us melts just a little.

Just a bit.

"Are you sure I don't look stupid?" I ask, shifting to get a better look at myself in her bathroom mirror.

"Of course you look stupid. But there's no changing that," she replies, adjusting my . . . tunic. It's her brother's Renaissance Faire costume, which is interesting. And weird. I feel more than a moment's awkwardness about being in Cesario's house, given how insistent he is about privacy, but apparently Bash is busy with some band-related thing. It's very strange to think that this is where he plays *Twelfth Knight,* because nothing about his room seems like the kind of place for someone who loves fantasy TV shows or combat games. There's just scripts and sheet music littering the desk, to the point where I don't even see a laptop.

Anyway, I'm wearing "hose" and a "tunic" and I have a "shield" and it's all extremely dumb, but Vi insists she's not letting me back in her car unless I wear a costume.

"Do they seriously not let you in if you don't have one?" I demand.

"Oh, they'll let you in. But the ride isn't free."

"Ah," I realized glumly. "You're trying to embarrass me."

"Embarrass you? No." Liar. Her starry eyes are laughing. "But if you're going to experience this, you've got to do the whole thing. Costume included."

Everything's a little short on me, so she bends down and lets out some of the seams, adjusting so it fits. It's amazing how quickly she can do this.

"Hm?" she asks, pins in her mouth, and I realize I said it aloud.

"Nothing."

"Mm." She stands up, scrutinizing her work. "Want a sword?"

"Seriously?"

"Fake sword. Sheathed." She rolls her eyes.

"No, I mean—" *Duh* I want a sword. What's the point of a costume like this if it doesn't involve a sword? "Yeah, sure, sword works."

"One sec." She disappears, and though I expect her to go back into Bash's room, she opens a door farther down the hall and slips inside, shutting it hastily behind her. I peer into the hallway, leaning as far as I can on one leg to see if I can catch a glimpse.

I'm assuming it's her bedroom.

She reemerges in a whirl of black leather and shuts the door so quickly that I don't see anything but a darkened cavern. "Here," she says, strapping the sword around my waist so perfunctorily that I don't think either of us notices she's manhandling my hips. "Now you'll at least pass as a knight or something, so—"

"Arthur," I say.

"What?" She blinks up at me.

"Arthur. He's a king. Better than a knight."

"Oh. True." She clears her throat. "But that's not really, you know, *con*-related . . . unless you count the game."

"Game?" I echo. I guess part of me is curious whether she knows what her brother is up to at night, or if Cesario (Bash) keeps a secret from his own twin.

Her reply is a shrug. "*Twelfth Knight.* It's kind of a big deal at the con."

Oh. That's something I might want to see. "Is it?" I ask casually.

"I'm not a gamer," she says evasively, which I figured. In my experience, girls aren't fans of violent video games; Olivia would probably be repulsed if she knew how I spent my free time these days.

"Right, yeah." I cough. "Does your brother have a crown, or . . . ?"

"God." She rolls her eyes. "He's been like four different Shakespearean kings. He's got a museum of crowns."

"Should we go look, or—?"

"No, I'll grab one. You get started down the stairs."

Ah, I was hoping to look around for more evidence of Bash's secret life. "But—"

"We're going to be late, Orsino!" she barks like a drill sergeant. "Move it or lose it."

Good ol' Vi Reyes. "Good talk, chief," I reply with a salute.

"Oh my *god*," she informs me, pivoting away while I hide a laugh.

I didn't believe Nick when he said this thing was huge. I mean, I *believed* him—I've seen the stuff on the news about it—but even before we reach the convention center there are people wandering the streets of San Francisco in every costume you could possibly think of. Superman is standing in line at Starbucks behind someone with a press badge and a pair of Yoda ears. Three Zelda-looking dudes walk over from one of the parking garages. It feels like every other person is holding a lightsaber. I thought people would stare at me—certainly at Vi—but there's no staring going on at all. People are *looking*, but they're doing it appreciatively, or waving to us like we're friends. Initially I assume Vi knows them, since she seems to know her way around the area, but then someone comes up to her that's clearly a stranger.

"I hope this isn't weird, but can you tell me who you're dressed as?" asks a twenty-something girl dressed as some kind of haunted Victorian doll. "I *love* those boots."

"Oh, I'm an OC," says Vi, "and thanks, they took ages."

"I bet," the girl gushes. "Can I take a picture with you?"

"Oh sure, yes." Vi's cheeks flush a little and I realize she's . . . excited. Which is fair, because if that outfit took as long as it looks like it did, I'm sure she's happy someone noticed.

Which makes me realize that I don't see Vi looking happy very often.

Which *also* makes me realize that I don't see Vi getting noticed very much.

"Want me to take it?" I offer, startling Vi into remembering I'm standing next to her.

"Oh, sure, that's—"

"I'd love one as well," comes another voice. "Original character, you said? ConQuest?"

"Yeah," Vi exhales, looking giddy and trying to hide it. "Astrea Starscream."

"*Great* name," says the first girl. The other, I realize, is wearing a press badge that says the name of some website: MonstressMag.com.

"Can you both sign this release?" asks the photographer, and I realize with a little thrill of secondhand excitement that Vi's going to end up in a blog or a magazine or something.

Vi and the other girl scribble their signatures electronically and then pose. Neither of them smile; instead they assume different stances that must represent their characters. I'm impressed, and also elated that I'm not part of this.

"Thanks, girls! Check out our coverage this afternoon." The journalist or photographer smiles and is gone, ready to snap pictures of other people, and the haunted doll blows Vi a kiss.

"Have fun today! You guys are adorable together," she tells us, and though Vi and I both start to protest, she's already gone.

"Well." Vi falls into step beside me again. "That was weird."

Oh, she's glowing. It's hilarious and kind of cute, though I don't know where to put that observation. It's not a thought I've ever had about Vi, or that anyone in history has ever had about Vi, to my knowledge. "Have you ever been stopped like that before?"

"A couple times, yeah. But usually only when I'm dressed as a recognizable character." She's pink-cheeked and winded. "That was weird."

"It was awesome," I tell her, because it was. "That was really, really cool. Was that a blog?"

"Monstress Mag? Yeah, it's a pop culture blog." She's practically skipping with joy. "I love it, I read it all the time. I've tried submitting things before—"

"Yeah?"

"Just a review of—" She clears her throat. "This show. And a blog post. Like, an opinion post about . . ." She trails off and swallows. "Anyway, it's not a big deal."

"Kind of seems like it is," I observe, and she breaks out in a broad smile.

"It *totally* is," she half shouts, and I can't help a laugh. "God, that felt great. I'm sure you think it's stupid, but—"

"Not stupid." I shake my head, but then I can't resist the opportunity to tease her. "You know, unlike you," I add loftily, "*I* don't make fun of other people's hobbies."

"Whose hobbies do I make fun of?" she demands.

"Uh, I believe your exact words were 'jock cult'?"

She rolls her eyes. "Oh come on, the sportballs are asking for it."

"Would you *stop*—"

We argue until we have to flash our volunteer badges, and then Vi herds me over to the central station. "We're the second shift. Kind of a prime spot," she informs me, "so you're welcome. Setup isn't nearly as fun."

"Why didn't Antonia want to come to this?" I ask, and Vi falters. "What?"

"Well, I just assumed that since I took her spot—"

"Assuming again," she says, a little more snippily than our earlier tone of banter. "I'm not in charge of her. I have no idea what she's doing instead."

"Oh, I just thought—" I shake my head. "Sorry. Never mind."

She opens her mouth, maybe to retort again, but softens.

Softens? No way. Vi Reyes doesn't soften. But she doesn't say anything back, instead leading me over to one of the volunteers in her typical bossy way, parting the crowd so easily I have to be grateful. Dressed like this and acting like that, she certainly knows how to get people to make room for a guy on crutches, even if she's not doing it specifically for me. Or even on purpose.

"Hey, Megha," she says to the person who must be in charge. She's dressed as something I sense I should recognize but don't. "Got something for me?"

Megha directs her to another person, much younger, and because I don't know what else to do, I follow.

"Can you put us somewhere central?" Vi's asking when I reach her side. "It's his first time."

Us. So she's not going to leave me.

I let out a small, internal sigh of relief.

"Aw, I love a virgin," says the other volunteer, Stacey, who I think is dressed as the princess from the movie *Empire Lost.* (I've only seen it once, at my mom's insistence. My dad was kind of interested when they cast a Black actor as the lead for one of the spin-offs, but as usual, that storyline got tossed aside for the two white leads.) "Sure, as long as you're up for the usual?"

"Law and order?" Vi guesses with a smirk.

"You bet." Stacey glances at me. "Sorry about the mix-up, by the way."

I don't know what she's talking about, but Vi waves her concern away. "It's nothing."

"Better he's not a runner anyway," Stacey adds. "Bum knee?" she asks me.

"Yeah." Sure, let's go with that.

"Oof, been there. We'll make sure you're somewhere easy. Though—" She leans in. "If you want me to move you, just let me know. Xavier's here."

Vi's eyes blow wide. "What? You're joking."

"Who's Xavier?" I ask.

Apparently this is such a big deal that Vi doesn't waste time with disdain at my ignorance. "Jeremy Xavier. He wrote *War of Thorns.*"

"Oh, no way," I say, and the next words fall out of my mouth unbidden: "I love that show."

"Me too." Luckily Vi's too enthralled to notice. "God, that's tempting."

"I can move you," Stacey sings, teasingly hovering her pen tip over the page, but Vi looks at me, then shakes her head.

"It's okay. I'll have time to wait in line later."

"You sure?"

She nods. "Just put us in the middle of the floor so he can see."

"You got it, babe. Mwah," says Stacey, air-kissing Vi until she leads me again to our new location.

"You didn't have to do that," I say, trying to keep up with her. She walks fast, purposefully, though she slows down once I catch her.

"You'd be useless as a runner. I'd end up doing your job for you, like always."

"Ha, ha," I drawl. "But really, you could've done it without me. He seems like he's a big deal."

"Nah. Never meet your heroes."

"Seriously?"

"People are always disappointing in real life." She shrugs. "They never live up to what you want them to be. This way, he'll always be interesting."

At first I think she's making excuses, but then I realize she really believes that. I don't have time to say anything, though, because she's pointing things out to me.

"Those are the rooms where they have guest speakers and stuff. There's some really cool ones this afternoon—there's one with a graphic novel editor who publishes all the best stuff out there. She's amazing." It's a tiny room with a long line. "That's the room where the ConQuest exhibition will be, if you want to catch a live game." A larger room with a longer line. "That's the artist alley, and over there's the gallery." That's massive, easily the biggest room here, nearly the size of a stadium with bright lights and a wave of sound. "That's where the gamers are." She glances at me. "We can check it out, if you want. Just to see. Pointless not to go look, right?"

"Right." The gallery does look exciting; it seems like all the film companies and game companies have enormous stalls, each one transformed from a basic cubicle-style area to manufactured versions of their movie sets and game worlds.

"Well," I say, "listen, I appreciate . . . this."

"Hm?"

"You showing me around and stuff, I appreciate it." It's loud, so I don't think she hears me, but by then we've reached whatever it was Vi was aiming for, which seems to be the head of yet another extremely long line.

"Hey," Vi says, tapping the person taking tickets at the front of the line. "We're here to relieve you."

"Oh, thank god," says the other volunteer, a small dude dressed as Ironman who looks more frantic than Ironman probably should.

"That bad?" Vi asks playfully, and Ironman's gaze flicks to someone in line before hastily returning.

"Well, I wouldn't say *bad*—"

"You never do," Vi assures him, adding with a nod to me, "Can we get a chair?"

"Sure, have this one," offers someone, setting it up for me without needing to be asked. (There's something about being here that's so bizarrely welcoming.)

"Oh," I attempt, "you don't have t—"

"Shut up and sit down," Vi advises, taking an eagle-eyed spot next to me. "Okay, next?" she barks to the line.

An older guy, possibly in his thirties, wearing a bow and arrow and elf ears, storms up to her in a way that immediately explains Ironman's twitchiness. "I have been waiting here for three hours," he says without preamble, "unlike *those* girls—" He jerks his head to a few neon-haired con attendees, most of whom look as giddy as I felt when I first arrived. Before we can brace for whatever inevitably comes next, Vi interrupts him.

"I see," she says. "Is there a problem with your ticket?"

The lanyard around his neck is littered with pins from previous cons, so I take it he expects to be treated a certain way for being a *real* fan, not unlike some NFL attendees. "No, but—"

"This is ticket support," Vi says, pointing over her head to a sign that I'm assuming says *Ticket Support*. "So, do you have a ticket-related question?"

"Listen, I know my way around this con, okay? And if *that's* the kind of group who gets priority in the queuing system—"

"Sounds to me like an issue for queuing support," Vi says coolly. "But your displeasure is noted."

The man (elf) stares at her.

"Bitch," he says, and turns away. Part of me wonders if I should say something, but the word just bounces off Vi, or seems to.

"What?" she says, catching me looking at her. "Gonna tell me to be nicer?"

I know I shouldn't, but . . . "It might help."

"Ha." The sound is hollow. "Yeah. I bet."

On further consideration, I think maybe I should just shut up. Something tells me that guy would have felt he had a right to call Vi a bitch whether she'd been nice to him or not.

"Your way does seem a lot more efficient," I admit.

She slides a glance to me, surprised. Her eyes get Disney Princess big, and all of a sudden she looks younger. Grateful.

"Well, it's not always like that," she informs me gruffly. "Most people are friendly. It's just . . . the occasional tantrum." Which, by the looks of the much calmer conversations around us, people are more than willing to hand off to her.

"And this is a *good* job?"

"Centrally located," she reminds me, gesturing to our view of the convention center. "And someone will relieve us soon." She glances at me. "Gonna have trouble with people hating you?"

There's a whole subset of people who do that on sight. But I know what she means.

"Trouble? Nah," I say, gesturing to some dude in a barbarian cloak who's almost definitely going to yell at me. "Come on, Viola, you know that's not my style."

Vi

In a lot of ways, conventions are like Disneyland: the happiest place on earth. By and large, everyone is friendly, accepting, and smiling, including me. But lest you forget that the antis on Reddit are also likely to attend a con, there's the support line. It's a nice reminder that while the internet allows a convenient cover of anonymity, it doesn't change the fact that some people just are what they are.

When it comes to that special genre of buzzkills, Antonia and I made a great team. I played bad cop, of course, reminding the bully in question that he's not actually king of the world, and then Antonia brought it home with an apology so impossibly earnest he'd wind up flustered, torn between glaring at me and staring at her in confusion.

Jack Orsino has a slightly different approach.

"I don't understand why you can't just make this go faster," says someone in a ConQuest T-shirt. It says *CHOOSE YOUR WEAPON*, followed by the images of several different dice, and I loathe that I want it. "You people are exactly the problem," the dice guy adds under his breath, which is funny, because I was just thinking *he's* the exact kind of con-goer who thinks that Jack and I are here to steal something that rightfully belongs to him.

Never mind that I've been in fandom for, oh, only my *whole life* or whatever. And even if Jack is new to it, that doesn't mean he should get shut out.

"Wait, is the line slow?" asks Jack, with a look so incredibly vacuous I have to actively work at not laughing.

Don't get me wrong—most people I'm happy to help. But others . . .

"Yes," says Dice Guy, getting red-faced. "We've been waiting for over an hour!"

"Oh my god, an hour?" Jack echoes, again with palpable concern.

"Listen," Dice Guy says angrily, "that's not funny—"

"I agree," Jack cuts in, turning to me. "Do you think it's funny, Vi?"

"Did he say he's been waiting for *forty-five minutes*, Jack?" I reply.

"No, Vi. An hour," Jack tells me solemnly.

"An hour?"

"An *hour*," Jack repeats.

"A *whole hour*?" I say, aghast.

"This is seriously messed up," Dice Guy interrupts with a growl.

"I agree," I reply. I'm not sure what our approach technically is—it's not good cop/bad cop so much as *let's see who can be more annoying*—but it's certainly making the time go faster.

"I'd like to speak to your manager," Dice Guy informs me.

"Me too," says Jack with his usual sport-star grin. "I'm thirsty."

"When you speak to our manager, please inform them that Jack would like a Pellegrino," I tell Dice Guy, whose cheeks flare again.

"Listen, you little—"

"I am not especially picky," I assure him. "Tap water will be fine."

"Show-off," says Jack, sending Dice Guy off in a huff before the universe rewards us with the sweetest seventy-two-year-old Empire Lost fan the world's ever seen. (Her barcode got messed up by her new baby grandson, named after the hero of the franchise.)

After pledging my life to my new idol, Maura, who started a fanzine at her high school back before social media fandom was a twinkle in Mark Zuckerberg's eye, there's only a handful of difficult cases, and then it's finally our turn to venture out into the con.

"So, what do we do now?" Jack says, reaching for his crutches. I can see on his face how much he hates using them; I don't blame him. I do a lot of waiting around for him, which I try not to make obvious. People think I walk too fast, but in my defense, I have to. My mom says the best way to avoid being a convenient target for anyone with nefarious intent is to always seem like I have somewhere to be. (Super fun how she had to teach *me* that, but not Bash.)

"Well, I'd like to pop in on the ConQuest game," I say. "And I told you we could check out the gaming expo."

"Right," Jack says. I can tell he's dying to see the *Twelfth Knight* booth, which makes sense because I am, too. Not that I can let him know that.

"If you're hungry—"

But then I cut myself off, noticing someone in the crowd.

"Honestly, I think I ate about ten of those mini-bags of Doritos," Jack answers, and frowns at me. "What?"

"It's Cesario," I say without thinking, and Jack immediately looks in the wrong direction.

"*Actual* Cesario?"

"What? No, Jack—" Honestly. "No, of course not. But it's a really good costume," I say, aiming him in the direction of the oncoming Cesario cosplayer just before he passes by. It's an astonishingly good replica of Cesario's winter clothing, complete with multiple kinds of fake fur and all the leather armor and everything. It would have taken *forever*, and it has to be from scratch.

I'm openly staring when I realize Jack is saying something again. "Can we get a picture? I mean—is that, like, allowed?"

I glance at his face in time to catch it faltering. "Because if you want one," Jack clarifies, "I can take one for you—"

Oh my god. It'd almost be cute how excited he's trying not to be. If he weren't Jack Orsino, that is, and therefore not cute at all. "Come on," I say, darting into the aisle to catch Cesario before he walks by.

"So sorry," I say, a little breathless when I reach him. I know I'm fangirling, but come on. I know from experience that the whole point of putting in this much effort is so that other people will appreciate it. "Would you mind taking a picture with me and my friend?"

Fake-Cesario is good-natured, a total himbo. "Sure! What are you?"

"I'm my ConQuest OC, Astrea Starscream, and he's—"

"Oh, no way? King Arthur," Cesario says to Jack, bowing before him. "My liege. Sorry to see you took a war wound."

Jack smiles back, composed and no longer hilariously starstruck. I forgot how easily he takes to being the center of attention, though today is the first time I realized the extent of how his Duke Orsino persona is less real than I thought. "That costume looks awesome."

"Are you both fans of *War of Thorns*?" Cesario asks. I hand my phone off to someone else in his group that offers to take it, but then another photographer—this one a MagiCon media person—hops in to grab a shot.

"Yeah, we love it," I say, blithely forgetting whether this version of me knows that or not. There's a bustle of activity, though, so nobody's paying attention; we pose for the shot, Cesario's hand very carefully hovering over my waist without touching it, and then Cesario's friend hands me back my phone.

"Check out our official blog!" chirps the MagiCon guy before disappearing.

"Enjoy the con," Cesario adds, nodding to Jack and me before continuing on his way.

"Damn," Jack says, sidling up to me as I glance down at my screen to look at the picture. "He even *walks* like Cesario, it's uncanny—"

"Oh hey, you posed," I say, noticing that rather than smile, Jack put a hand on his fake sword, looking cool as a cucumber next to Cesario himself. I didn't realize how close in height the two of them would be, but Jack looks almost as impressive. Minus the impromptu costume, but at least he got into character.

"Well, duh. Even I know smiling would be the dorky thing to do." He glances at me, and I think for a second that it's incredible how quickly Jack can figure out the right move in any situation. No wonder this whole injury-plus-Olivia thing threw him for an existential loop.

Which is *definitely* something I shouldn't know. For a moment I feel a wave of guilt, like I've done something awful. It occurs to me that Jack's an actual person who deserves better than a lie, which is ultimately what I'm doing, even if it's a harmless one. Or meant to be harmless, before he confessed his life and problems to someone he thought was a friend but was actually just me, a person he doesn't even like.

Shame curdles temporarily on my tongue, but it's not like telling him the truth would do either of us any good. Besides, it won't happen again. He had a bad day, that's all, and so did I. It's not worth jeopardizing my identity over.

(A small voice reminds me that Jack probably wouldn't tell anyone my secret if I told him the truth, but that's easily silenced when I remember everything that Antonia chose over me. I thought I could trust her and I was wrong. What do I really know about Jack?)

"Congratulations on not embarrassing me," I tell him, safely recovered from my momentary crisis of conscience. "Much appreciated."

"Hey, I do what I can, Viola." His gaze drifts hungrily out to the expo. "So, should we . . . ?"

"Oh my god, just admit it," I groan. "You're dying to see the game demos, aren't you?"

"Wait, they demo it? In front of everyone?" He looks awestruck.

"Uh, yeah, of course. That's how they sell it."

"They get people to play it? Like, good players?"

"Again, that's how they *sell it*, Jack—"

He's already rocketing off on his crutches, and I have to fight a laugh.

"Okay, okay," I sigh to myself, before realizing I'm smiling.

So obviously I wipe it off my face before reminding him not to look like such a noob.

By the time we get back in my car, we're both exhausted. I have to sit there for a couple of minutes just to relieve the pressure on my feet. (The first rule of MagiCon is to wear comfortable shoes, but even that only goes so far after a whole day of wandering around.)

"So everyone who plays ConQuest makes up their own characters?" Jack says. He's been asking me questions like that all day.

"There are specific game characters you can get assigned," I reply, massaging out my neck, "but yeah, mostly everyone makes their own."

"It's so wild how talented people are," Jack says. "The voices and stuff."

He means the QuestMaster who organized the live game. "Yeah, that guy's awesome."

Jack nods, adding tangentially, "Jeremy Xavier isn't what I expected, though."

"Hm?" I'm fiddling with my phone, trying to pick out a playlist.

"Jeremy Xavier, the *War of Thorns* author." We managed to listen to him when he was a surprise guest on a panel about worldbuilding, which Jack did not want to go to. By the end, though, I think he was more into it than I was.

"Well, he's, like, a millionaire now," I remind him. "Even if he used to be a dork playing ConQuest in his mom's basement, he probably doesn't look like that anymore."

"No, I know." Jack laughs. "I just thought he was surprising."

"You should really read the books."

"Yeah, I think I might." He clears his throat. "If I have time, I mean," he says quickly, without looking at me. "I'll be off crutches soon and probably ready to play again, so I'll be going back to practice and stuff in a few weeks."

Cesario knows that what Jack just said is a lie, and *Jack* seems to know that, too, but I'm not Cesario in this situation. I'm just me, and Vi Reyes isn't exactly the kind of person Jack Orsino wants to have an honest conversation with.

Still, it doesn't seem right to just blindly agree with him. That's not very Vi Reyes, either.

"You know," I attempt slowly, "you're good at stuff besides football."

"Yeah?" He cuts me an arrogant smirk. "Glad you finally noticed."

"Seriously?" How quickly good intentions backfire. "Shut up or I won't drive you home."

"You'd just *leave* me here?" he says, feigning devastation.

"Stop. I'm just trying to tell you that maybe you shouldn't hang your whole future on football, okay? I'm no anatomy expert," I add, "but it seems like you don't screw up your knee and get right back on the field. Didn't you have surgery?"

Of course he deflects. "Keeping up with the rumor mill, Viola?"

"Don't make me tell you to shut up again. And it's none of my business what you do or don't do," I point out, turning the car on. "I'm just saying that maybe you need to accept that some things are out of your control. Like the fact that your knee hurts."

"It doesn't hurt."

I glance skeptically at him before checking over my shoulder to reverse.

"Well, whatever," Jack sighs. "But greatness is pain, right?"

"No. Pain is just pain, and it's there for a reason." I back up, then put the car in drive. "Personally, I don't think there's only one outcome for life," I add, and when he says nothing, I continue, "I mean, I don't think there's a predestined fate or anything. You're not *born* to play football. There's a version of your life where you do other things. Infinite versions. And when you make a choice, you cast off one possible outcome, but then, I don't know—*ten more* pop up in its place. And you just keep going like that, choosing a path and watching new paths branch off in front of you. Even if the old ones disappear behind you, it doesn't have to be sad," I say with a shrug, though of course I feel a little pang in my chest, like it's Antonia I can see in my rearview.

Jack is quiet for a few more minutes, so I get us from the parking garage to the street, turning on my GPS to lead us to the freeway.

Eventually I assume he's asleep, but then he interrupts the sound of Elvis Costello crooning to Veronica. "What if I don't see any other paths?"

I sigh. "It's just a metaphor, Orsino. We're teenagers. We don't know what comes next."

"I know, but—" He stops. "What if I just see nothing?"

Somehow I can tell that what he's really asking is what if *he* is nothing, but the idea that Jack Orsino—*Duke Orsino,* who so many people like and respect—would think he doesn't matter is so painfully unfunny I want to laugh until my throat falls out.

Or maybe cry.

"Then make something." I think my voice is harder than it needs to be. "Don't you understand how good you are at just, like, existing?"

"What?" He looks amused, which makes me want to shake him. Or to make him swap places with me so he can see what I see and quit whining.

"I know you think I'm a bitch, Jack," I say irritably, "but it's because I already understand that most people aren't going to like me. I already *get* that I'm not for everyone, but—"

"I don't think you're a bitch."

I shake him off. "Whatever, of course you do. I'm just saying—"

"Viola, you are not a bitch." He looks at me. "Or, like, you are," he corrects himself, and I roll my eyes. "But it doesn't mean what other people think it means."

"Pretty sure the whole world is clear on what it means, Orsino." I'm the kind of girl that other people want to make suffer because I refuse to be as small as they want me to be. I know that, and I don't

take it personally. If other people think I'm a bitch, that's fine. I
don't need to be loved. I don't need to be liked. I don't *need* anyone,
and that's the gospel truth.

I don't know why I'm not saying any of that out loud, but after
a couple of minutes Jack twists in his seat, staring at me from the
passenger side before shifting his attention to his injured knee.

"If you were me," he says, "you'd have come up with a million
other solutions by now. You wouldn't just sit around waiting for life
to happen to you."

"And if *you* were *me*," I retort gruffly, "you'd be going to MagiCon
with your best friend instead of driving back with someone who can
barely stand you."

We sit in silence a few minutes longer, the lights of the freeway
rushing by. In the wordless quiet, Jack's phone screen lights up, and
he glances down.

"I texted my brother the picture we took with Cesario," he says,
"and he asked me if I have a concussion."

It's such a random comment that I snort in response, which
snowballs into something that's a full-on uproar of giggles, and I
can tell that Jack is laughing just as hard. We're sitting there, driving, not talking, trying our best not to howl hysterically at something that's not even very funny—except, somehow, *it is*. Because
the idea that I just went to MagiCon with Jack Orsino and took a
picture with some dude dressed up as a fantasy outlaw prince can't
possibly be funny, but it is. It really, really is.

My stomach hurts by the time I regain my sanity, wiping away
moisture from the corners of my eyes while Jack pulls at his smile,
shaking his head.

"You're all right, Viola," he says eventually.

"Yeah," I manage, sniffling like I just had a four-hour sob. "Yeah,
Orsino. You're okay, too."

10

MIRROR-MATCH

Jack

Cesario and I make it out of Galles, the land of a thousand enchant-resses, around three in the morning. The next crusade, Gaunnes, is pure combat—so, nothing new, except for the tournament-style PvP arena. (Player versus player. See? I'm starting to get this.) Cesario grunts at me in the chat to remember to work on hotkeys and then eventually I pass out in my now-permanent dent in the sofa.

how was MagiCon? says Olivia, the buzz of my phone waking me sometime late morning.

It's the first time she's initiated a conversation in almost two months. *I actually had a great time,* I reply through my sleep-deprived haze. *missed you though*

yeah, bummed I couldn't make it, Olivia says back. *vi says she had fun!*

One loud starburst of reality suggests I should laugh at that, be-cause the idea that my maybe-girlfriend Olivia is telling me that my definitely-nemesis Vi Reyes had fun with me is so ridiculous it's like we've all fallen into a black hole.

But another part of me feels a smaller, sharper bleed of memory, like a tiny puncture that leaks out in my chest. The moment I had with Vi in the car . . . that was more honest than I expected. More real, too, than anything I've felt in a long time.

yeah, it was fun, I say, because that's the simplest response.

Just then, my dad raps on the end of the sofa. "Knock, knock."

"You rang?" I ask him, contemplating a way to express some-thing devilishly romantic to Olivia while also being thoughtful and understanding about her need for space. A real mind-twister.

"Ready for PT?" my dad prompts, and ah yes, he's filling in for my mom today. "Maybe if all goes well you'll be able to put weight on that knee again."

God, and wouldn't that be a miracle. It's been my goal to be off crutches by homecoming, because I've got a feeling that if I can just get back to normal, Olivia will see that nothing's really changed between us. That I'm still me, and we're still *us*.

Briefly, the image of Vi's profile floats through my head at that; not the usual scowl that says I'm an idiot, but the way she looked last night. *Infinite versions,* she said, the little fading stars beside her eyes mixing with the glints from passing streetlights.

I blink it away, because the important thing is being off crutches. "How soon would I be able to practice?"

Dad looks like he has to bite down on one possible answer, choosing instead the sensible and Mom-approved "One thing at a time. Let's make sure that leg's load-bearing first." Then he offers me half a smile. "But it'd be a good first step to coming back for the postseason."

For the first time in days, all thoughts of knights disappear. "Then let's go get my life back," I say, and my dad gives me a thump on the back.

It's time to get back to normal.

"Whoa, slow down," Eric tells me. "Last thing we need is that knee buckling on you. Remember, this is about balance and stability. We gotta strengthen that quad first, and then—"

"I got it." I tore my knee, not my quad, and everything feels fine. "I got this."

"Hey, kid, relax. It's my job to keep you playing for the next five years, not the next five weeks." He crouches down, eye level with my surgery scar. "How's that feel?"

Fine. Perfect. "Great."

"How's it going with the team?"

"Just waiting on you," I remind him, and he glances up at me with an arched look of *Chill.*

"There's still a long way to go, kid." He stands up. "Timeline hasn't changed. You're still looking at close to a year for a full repair."

"I don't have a year," I grumble, frustrated.

His glance at me is serious. "Either you will give yourself the time you need, Jack, or your knee will do it for you. The risk of reinjuring yourself if you go back to practice too soon is incredibly high."

"But you said—"

"I said you'd be weight-bearing, but football puts your body through hell, Jack. Trust me, I would know." He flashes me his own knee scars. "How'd you think I ended up here?"

When I say nothing, he sighs. "Look. All that time in training facilities helped me realize I wanted to be able to do that—heal people. Take something broken and make it work again." A shrug. "Sometimes life happens the way it does for a reason."

A more bitter part of me wants to point out that a physical therapy job wouldn't make up for having a pro career stolen out from under me. (Vi would probably say it, but it's for the best there's only one of her.)

"Just something to think about," Eric adds, standing up to make some notes.

My chest sinks. "So does that mean I'm not approved?"

"Nah, we can eighty-six the crutches." He tosses them symbolically aside, and the sunken piece of me resurrects just slightly. "But you're still coming in here every week. More often, if you and your parents can work it out."

"Yeah, yeah, I know—"

"We can get you running in another month or so. Maybe practicing with your team in time for the end of the season. As for playing—"

I grimace. "We'll cross that bridge when we get to it?"

He points at me. "Bingo. Smart kid."

I walk a few steps, just to do it.

"Take it easy," Eric reminds me.

I bristle a little. "It's just walking. Been an expert my whole life, give or take."

"Hey." He pauses me, reaching into the empty space between us like he'd prefer to take me by the shoulder. "Listen, I know you're pissed about all this—"

"I'm not."

"You are."

He actually has no idea how angry I *haven't* gotten about all this, but fine. I say nothing.

"Anyone can take a bad hit," he tells me. "The end of a career is never totally out of sight. You're young and healthy," he assures me, "and you'll heal. But you can't rush this."

"I know."

"And it doesn't hurt to consider other possibilities," he says again.

"Oh, are there other possibilities?" I joke without thinking, slipping back into my double act with Vi, but since she's not here to play along, Eric just shakes his head at me.

"All right, smart guy," he says. "See you back here on Tuesday."

For the first few days after MagiCon, Vi conspicuously avoids me—probably so I won't accidentally think we're friends or something—but by mid-week, I can't avoid seeking her out. When it comes to homecoming stuff, she really does know more than the rest of ASB combined, so I shoot her a text just after school. She curtly replies that she's still on campus; specifically the small gym, though weird as that answer is, it's nothing compared to what I walk in to find.

"Whoa," I say, spotting her alone in the corner, pacing tensely around one of the wrestling team's heavy punching bags. She doesn't hear me come in and launches into a series of kicks; I count ten quick ones in a row before she spots me and removes her headphones. "What is this, fight club?"

"First rule of fight club," she replies, breathing hard, then purses her lips at me, more puzzled than rude. "What exactly did you need?" she asks, shoving her headphones into the inner pocket of what I'm shocked to see are athletic shorts. (She's also wearing a tank top, loose-fitted, but conspicuously lacking any satanic feminist slogans. Oddly, I almost miss them.) "Your text was mystifying."

"Oh, sorry, um." I dig through my bag for my notes. "You know that index of forms in the leadership room?"

"Uh-huh." She slides me a tiny smirk and I sigh, pausing my attempt to organize myself.

"You made it, didn't you?"

She shrugs in tacit confirmation, glancing at the weighted bag like she longs to kick it again, but turns back to me instead. "You needed a form?"

"Yeah, for financial approval, but one of the binders is missing, so—"

"Ah, got it, sorry." She turns away, walking over to her own back-pack, which is on the floor. She's obviously dressed for a workout, her wrists and hands done up in black wraps that look extremely complicated, and it's . . . hard not to notice that it suits her. This, whatever it is.

Briefly, it occurs to me that I might enjoy stumbling on these weird little pieces of who she is. It makes the sum of her less puzzling—or more surprising. I'm not technically sure which.

"Is this, like, stress relief or something?" I ask her, and she looks up, startled.

"What?"

"This." I gesture over my shoulder to the bag she was just pummeling. "Something wrong?"

"No." *Yes,* I interpret clearly, though she obviously doesn't want to talk about it.

"Is this . . . Tae Kwon Do? Or something?"

She digs out what is apparently the wrong binder, frowns, and reaches in for a different one, answering absent-mindedly, "No, Muay Thai."

"Oh, that's—" I blink. "Wait, do you do that with your brother?"

She looks up sharply and I realize: *Shit. Oops.*

"Yes," she says, her voice wary. "We train together."

Amazing that Bash can do all that. Vi's the only person I know with that kind of superhuman time management, but I guess it makes sense. They *are* twins.

"I didn't know you knew that about Bash," Vi adds in a voice that's carefully measured.

"Yeah, I just . . . heard it somewhere, I think. It's not like it's that common, so yeah. Anyway, why are you here?" I ask, trying to play this off like it's a normal thing to know. I crouch beside her, waiting, and she freezes a little, visibly going tense.

"My studio is closed for the week, and—" She glances at me and swallows, suddenly awkward. "Bowen let me in. He's the girls' volleyball coach, so—" Another break. "Anyway. Is this the form you need?" she asks brusquely.

"Oh." I glance down at my notes, relieved for an excuse to look away. "Yeah, it's this one, for administrative approval . . . ?"

"Right. Here you go." She hands it to me, and I notice that the binder in her hands is labeled *ASB TREASURER*.

"You know, I asked Ryan if there was something like this. He said no," I comment, and she gives me a bark of a laugh.

"Figures. Luckily, now that I'm no longer so concerned with *your* job, I have time to do his unencumbered." I can see there's some festering agitation there, which makes sense—I've never actually seen Ryan do anything.

"I always thought his job was just signing checks."

She rolls her eyes. "He's *supposed* to manage all the club budgets, plus our ASB budget. This is for senior gift," she explains, showing me the binder page with her notes on it.

"Ah."

We both start to rise at the same time and then stop, like we might accidentally collide.

"Sorry." She takes a deep breath. I'm not sure what she's apologizing for, but I think I would have said it too, if she hadn't. Something does feel distinctly . . . present between us. "Anything else?"

"Not unless you want to teach me some Muay Thai," I say, half-jokingly.

She, meanwhile, reaches for her water bottle, glancing at my knee. "Not sure that's a good idea, champ. You've been off crutches for what, five minutes?"

"Three days, but thanks for noticing." I scrutinize the punching bag, since that seems safer than meeting her eye at the moment. "Can't say I've got the instincts for it, anyway."

"Never been in a fight?" She looks amused.

"You know, funnily enough, I don't really have enemies."

"God, how boring for you." She reaches one arm over, stretching, and I notice the definition in her shoulders before abruptly reminding myself that's not for me to notice. "Could teach you some other time, though, if you actually wanted."

"How to have enemies?" I joke.

"Nah, that's just a natural talent."

If I didn't know better, I'd say she was teasing me. "I'm honestly not sure I could hit you."

"Why?" Instantly, her amusement falters. "Don't tell me you're one of those guys who refuses to hit girls. Even the ones who are"— she pauses, turning to kick high on the bag—"*trained* for this."

That undercurrent of frustration I noticed in her earlier is back. She might be lying about it, but she clearly *is* stressed. There's something else here that bothers her, which I hope isn't me.

"No. I just couldn't hit *you*," I clarify, and though she's been gearing up for some kind of change-up between her feet, she pauses midstep. "Pretty sure you'd do some serious damage to my pretty face."

I watch her fight a laugh. "Scared, Orsino?"

"Of you? Absolutely," I assure her. "Terrified. I consider it a massive relief that you're not a linebacker."

"Not yet, at least." She permits half a smirk before hiding it to glance at me. "So, got everything you need?"

"Hm?" Ah, she wants me to leave. Part of me flinches at the dismissal, but in fairness, I *did* interrupt her. "Oh, yeah, definitely. Thanks again." I hold up the page before tucking it into my notebook, and then I stop. "Hey, are you . . . okay?" I ask, hesitating.

It's not like I expect her to open up to me. Part of me thinks she might, given the last conversation we had, and an even stranger part of me wants overwhelmingly, for just a moment, to be given a reason to stay.

Still, it doesn't surprise me when she shrugs me off. "Don't worry about me, Duke Orsino," she says, gearing up to go another round against whatever she doesn't want me to see. "You've got your old life to get back to," she says, putting her headphones in and glancing at my knee before tuning me out altogether.

Unfortunately, within days it becomes very clear that being off crutches doesn't actually return me to my old life. I'm still nowhere near being allowed to run at practice, plus Olivia stays out sick from school all week, declining my offers to bring her soup (or some other boyfriend-y thing). *Better you just stay home where it's safe,* she says. At this point, I think her concept of my priorities is pretty off. I'd gladly catch her cold if it meant winning back some of that precious space she's so intent on keeping between us.

But, since that's not happening, it's back to knights.

DUKEORSINO12: this sucks
C354R10: hello sunshine
DUKEORSINO12: when do we get to move on
DUKEORSINO12: we've been on this level forever
C354R10: we literally just got here
DUKEORSINO12: I can't remember a time before Iambourc
C354R10: excuse me, we're about to fight thirty knights at the same time
C354R10: spare me the hysterics

Oddly enough, this *does* make me feel better, though it's hard to believe Cesario is actually this way in real life. When I walked by Bash Reyes the other day, he was with Vi, talking animatedly with his hands. She didn't see me, but he did. He frowned when I nodded to him, so I guess he really takes this whole separation of identities thing very seriously.

DUKEORSINO12: don't you ever have shit to complain about
DUKEORSINO12: I feel like all I do is rant
C354R10: correct
C354R10: you do
DUKEORSINO12: well it'd be a lot more fun if it was mutual
DUKEORSINO12: personally I love a good rant
DUKEORSINO12: and considering you're also awake at 2:30 am, I'm thinking your life isn't all sunshine and rainbows either

Cesario pauses for a second before typing.

C354R10: would it make you stop whining if I told you one (1) problem
DUKEORSINO12: !! yes
DUKEORSINO12: this is the basis of friendship, fyi
DUKEORSINO12: mutual give and take, supportive comments like "spare me the hysterics," etc etc
C354R10: we're not friends
DUKEORSINO12: true, add that to my list of problems
C354R10: ugh

I wait, and he types some more.

C354R10: my mom is dating someone, ok?

Oof, been there. The first time my mom went on a date I was pretty messed up about it, but my brother Cam forced me to go to the gym with him, so I ended up sweating out of my eyeballs and forgetting the whole thing.

C354R10: and now she thinks I need to be more "forgiving"
C354R10: or something
C354R10: he's infecting her brain

I wonder if this is what's been bothering Vi, too.
(Not that I care.)

DUKEORSINO12: I did not anticipate zombie boyfriend being on the list of possible problems, but tbh I'm not mad
C354R10: hey, you asked for this
C354R10: you get what you get
DUKEORSINO12: is he some kind of health guru? a therapist?
C354R10: worse
C354R10: a youth pastor

I burst out laughing, which thankfully is fine, since I'm back in my bedroom and no longer occupying a common space in the living room.

DUKEORSINO12: your mom is dating a man of the cloth??? is that even allowed??
C354R10: it shouldn't be
C354R10: for my sanity
DUKEORSINO12: right
C354R10: we're not even protestant
C354R10: I mean sure, the vatican has its problems OBVIOUSLY but martin luther was paid off by german princes to rewrite the bible so like institutionally the whole foundation is cracked
DUKEORSINO12: no idea what you're talking about but go off king
C354R10: ugh

He sends me an eye roll emoji.

C354R10: you're enjoying this aren't you
C354R10: the devolution of my psyche
DUKEORSINO12: kinda yeah
DUKEORSINO12: wish I had some useful advice, but you already know "spare me the hysterics," so . . .
C354R10: you're very helpful
DUKEORSINO12: I know right it's a curse

He doesn't say anything, so I decide it's safe to change the subject.

DUKEORSINO12: on another note

DUKEORSINO12: this new girl cesario's working with on WoT

C354R10: her name is crescentia

DUKEORSINO12: I am literally never going to learn her name

DUKEORSINO12: she's just a stopover to liliana anyway

C354R10: omg are you a crescentia anti

DUKEORSINO12: I have no idea what you're talking about but I am not a fan

C354R10: omg

DUKEORSINO12: she's wasting our time

DUKEORSINO12: she and rodrigo should just go mushroom hunting together or something idk

DUKEORSINO12: go be boring somewhere else

C354R10: wowwwwwww

C354R10: you REALLY ship cesario and liliana huh

DUKEORSINO12: ???

C354R10: they're totally your otp

DUKEORSINO12: ??????????

C354R10: it means "one true pairing"

C354R10: dumb phrase but basically if you go on tumblr right now there'll be edits all over the place

C354R10: google "cesario x liliana"

I open a new window and am instantly flooded with YouTube videos set to sad pop songs and a bunch of lengthy Twitter rants.

DUKEORSINO12: WELL THANK GOD NOT EVERYONE'S AN IDIOT

C354R10: omg lol forever

C354R10: I can't believe it

C354R10: baby's first non-canon ship

DUKEORSINO12: idk what that means

C354R10: don't worry about it

C354R10: the point is I had no idea you were such a *~rOmAnTiC~*

DUKEORSINO12: dude yes this is my whole thing

DUKEORSINO12: I'm actively trying to get my girlfriend back

DUKEORSINO12: hello

DUKEORSINO12: I am a romance king

C354R10: you should hang out with my mom's zombie boyfriend pastor isaac

DUKEORSINO12: oh hey that's my pastor

C354R10: OMG YOU'RE JOKING

DUKEORSINO12: yes lol definitely joking my pastor is sixty and loves dad jokes and motown

C354R10: I would honestly take that over "love thy neighbor" ike

DUKEORSINO12: well you're welcome to hate on ike anytime

DUKEORSINO12: this is a safe space

He goes quiet again for a second.

C354R10: can we please just kill some knights now

I stifle another laugh.

DUKEORSINO12: what a healthy outlook

DUKEORSINO12: in fairness I didn't mean to hate on lambourc so much

DUKEORSINO12: it is cool how each of the levels are so different. keeps it interesting

C354R10: yeah that's why I like it

C354R10: the lore is good and the gameplay is good too

They were talking about this at the MagiCon gaming expo. I hadn't really thought about what made *Twelfth Knight* good since I obviously don't have a lot of experience playing these types of games—nor do I discuss them with anyone—but I think the goal is to have an interesting story and a world that builds on itself. There was also a bunch of technical stuff about how the players move, though I don't know anything about that. It was only after I heard people say things like "dynamic lighting" and "ray-traced reflections" that I realized oh yeah, they're saying things I already noticed about how cool and realistic it looks—the way that water reflects back or lights that go on and off, or stuff about the non-player characters' animation—but I didn't know how to put all that into words.

> **DUKEORSINO12:** must be a fun job
> **DUKEORSINO12:** more fun than what my PT does

I don't see how watching someone slowly walk on a treadmill could ever be as cool as bringing something to life from nothing. A few zeroes and ones. Wild.

> **C354R10:** well
> **C354R10:** fyi
> **C354R10:** there are more jobs in the world than physical therapist and football player
> **C354R10:** so I've heard anyway
> **DUKEORSINO12:** my turn for the eyeroll emoji
> **C354R10:** well listen, if you're going to say something dumb idk what you want me to do about it
> **DUKEORSINO12:** fair enough
> **DUKEORSINO12:** what's your plan

He types something, then deletes it. Then types again.

> **C354R10:** do we need to have a plan? I have interests and hobbies and passions. Isn't that enough?
> **C354R10:** feels like kind of a scam tbh
> **C354R10:** we have like fifty years to do nothing but make money, so I don't see why I'd need to know right now what kind of job I want to work until I die
> **DUKEORSINO12:** I like how you instantly take things to the darkest possible place
> **C354R10:** thank you it's a gift

But honestly, I can't stop thinking about this. Interests? Hobbies? Passions?? Before now I thought football was a passion, but ever since I started playing *Twelfth Knight*, I guess I've realized it's more than that. I love the sport, sure, but what I like about it isn't the mechanics of how I move. It's not the motion or the physics.

It's the *game*.

Not that I know what to do with that information.

I don't think I can go to the dance on Saturday, Olivia texts me the next day. *I'm so sorry, Jack.*

I won't lie, it dampens things for me, though it's not like I can hold it against her. Instead, I focus on all the mind-numbing minutiae I can find to fill my afternoon. I help Mackenzie hold up things she can't reach. I sign things, paint things, and move things. When Kayla complains that we don't have enough people working refreshments or taking tickets, I tell her I'll do it.

"Seriously?" I hear from behind me, and turn to find Vi Reyes watching me.

We haven't spoken since our encounter in the gym the other day. I wouldn't mind talking to her now—weird as that is to admit—but I get the feeling our new friendly-ish dynamic isn't ready to test-drive for an audience.

I turn back to Kayla. "Not like I'll really be gettin' down on the dance floor," I joke with a reference to my knee, adding my name to her sheet below Vi's. "Just let me know whatever you need me to do."

"Thanks, Jack." Kayla flashes me what has become a fairly rare smile before turning to bark orders at someone else; something about not abandoning the "gravitas" of the theme.

Behind me, though, Vi hasn't moved.

"Actually attending a school event, I see," I observe aloud.

"And apparently I'll see you there," she replies.

If she was trying for cold, it doesn't hit that way.

It hits, though. Somewhere.

"Guess so," I exhale, clearing my throat before we both turn quickly away.

𝔙i

On Friday afternoon I find myself knocking on the door of the biggest house I've ever personally been to. Which isn't to say there aren't enormous houses in Messaline Hills, but I usually don't know the people who live inside them.

"Hey," Olivia says when she opens the door. She's wearing a blanket like a cape, her hair piled high on her head. "Thanks so much for doing this."

"No problem. Should I . . . ?" I gesture to my shoes, but she shakes her head.

"Up to you. Kick 'em off if you're more comfortable."

I can't imagine feeling comfortable here, a place that gleams with things I'd probably break. But, since Olivia's not wearing any shoes and I'm also terrified of tracking dirt inside, I slip out of my sneakers and leave them by the door.

"How are you feeling?" I ask when she gestures for me to follow.

"Better, thanks. Not contagious anymore, but let's sit outside just in case."

"It's a nice day," I contribute in agreement, looking at the family portraits on the wall. Olivia and her sisters make a clan of clean-cut princesses standing beside her regal-looking mother and father.

"My family's out, by the way," Olivia says, catching my glance around. The foyer leads to a corridor that gives way to an open-plan living area, the back half of which reveals an expansive lawn, pool, hot tub, and charmingly unexpected gazebo. "So no need to worry about running into anyone."

I follow her as she takes a few steps outside, barefoot. I tiptoe in my socks until we reach a sunken fire pit that I hadn't seen from the living area of the house.

"This is . . ." *Nice* won't cut it.

Olivia laughs. "I know."

"I wasn't expecting—"

"Nobody does. But the more impressive the house, the more

people are inclined to think we're 'nice neighbors' instead of, I don't know, terrorists." She says this like it's nothing.

"Has that ever . . . been an issue?"

She smiles thinly. "Sometimes. But my dad's a very good oncologist, and you'd be surprised how much nicer people can be when they're scared of a slow, painful death."

Oof, I bet. "What about your mom?"

"Mm, she's kind of like a Middle Eastern socialite."

"Really?"

"Yep. Beauty queen and all that. She and my aunties spend most of their time together at the spa."

"Are your cousins mostly on her side?" I feel dwarfed by grandeur, hence the superficial chatter.

"Both sides have big families, but I prefer the ones on her side, yes. My dad's cousins are more conservative, less . . . cosmopolitan. I have a portion of my closet dedicated to when we see them." She sits down snuggled in the blanket, shading her eyes. "Lots of turtlenecks," she explains. "And long skirts."

"Gotcha." I settle on the opposite side of the fire pit's corner, digging through my backpack for my notebook. "Same with my grandma." Who, coincidentally, I just saw, as every now and then Lola fears for our heathen souls and insists we attend church events with her. Normally these are not noteworthy occasions, as I'm sorry to report there's been no sign of any Pentecostal tongues of fire, but she's now convinced I have a secret boyfriend, having caught me smiling at the MagiCon blog on my phone. (She thinks I'm swooning over sentimental texts when really, I was just remembering something that . . . well, never mind.)

"Not that my wardrobe ever gets terribly exciting," I add to Olivia, clearing my throat and hoping to change the subject.

Olivia arches a brow, gesturing to my T-shirt. It's one of those retro designs with a bunch of cartoon children holding daggers that says *LET'S SACRIFICE TOBY!*

"Okay, this one's mildly exciting," I acknowledge, "but my usual nerd apparel was dirty. And for the record, I don't harbor vengeful fantasies against any Tobys. Bash got it for me because it was, quote, *so random*."

"It is. I like it." Olivia smiles at me, then turns her attention to the notes in my hands. "Thanks again for doing all this."

"Oh, it's no problem. You can keep them," I add, handing her the notes. "I made copies."

"Wow, these are thorough." She sifts through them. "I mean, I knew you took good notes, but these . . . are these annotated outlines? For each lesson?"

I shrug. "Easier to study with come test time."

"Yeah, tell me about it." She looks up, still smiling. "Thank you."

"No problem. I also brought you something else," I add, sliding a page out of my notebook. "It's kind of dumb, though—just warning you."

"Perfect." She dimples with pleasure. "I love dumb."

"You say that now . . ."

"Just show me!"

I pull out the page and scoot a little closer. "I was thinking while I was watching the live ConQuest game at MagiCon that I could simplify the process for you," I tell her, handing her the worksheet I put together. "I basically turned it into a questionnaire."

"For my character?" Her voice quickens with excitement. "What kinds of questions?"

"Well, basic stuff. How old are they, who raised them, do they have siblings—"

"What kind of *music* do they like?" she reads off the page with surprise.

"I mean—" I can feel my cheeks flush. "It's relevant to the whole character development process, so—"

"Wait, can we do this? Like, right now?" She looks up at me hopefully.

"Oh, yeah. Sure." I told my mom I'd be home right after school, but I don't think she'll mind if I stay out of the house. We're not exactly on the same page at the moment. "I thought maybe you'd want to do it alone, but yeah. Honestly, I love this part," I admit.

"I can see why." She scans the page. "This is going to be *way* better than getting my hair done for the dance," she comments idly.

"So you're really not going to homecoming?" I figured not, given that Jack offered to volunteer instead of wandering around like a golden god, which is what I expected him to do.

(Okay, maybe it's not fair of me to keep saying things like that, but I didn't know this version of Jack Orsino existed. I'm still not accustomed to the idea that maybe he isn't the person I imagined him to be, which is a strange thing to try to trust.)

(About anyone, I mean. Not him specifically.)

(Although yes, him.)

"Just seems kind of pointless, you know? And I'm sick," Olivia adds, though it sounds . . . convenient.

Once again, I grudgingly understand why Jack wanted me to find out what was going through Olivia's head. I don't condone it, but she isn't very forthcoming with the truth.

"Well, here. I'll write if you want," I say, taking a pen out of my school bag. "You can just give me rapid-fire answers."

"But what if I need to think about them?" she demands.

"Then we'll be here all day," I say. "You can make changes later."

"Fine." She relinquishes the page with a sigh, leaning back so that her legs are curled beneath her. "You're not cold, are you?" she asks, offering me the spare corner of her blanket. "Or I can grab another one—"

"I'm good, actually. It's nice out." I click the pen, then sit with the tip poised above the page. "So. Name?"

"Ohmygod," says Olivia, panicked.

"You're right, we'll come back to that. Let's see . . . gender, age?"

"She's a girl. Maybe, like, twenty? Far from home."

I scribble that down. "Did someone force her out?"

"No, she chose to go. Oh!" She blinks. "She's in exile."

"Ooh, nice. So her family is powerful?"

"Yes, very. But she's in disguise."

"I love disguises." I write some more before asking, "Does your character have enemies?"

"Yes. Definitely." She nods firmly, like she's pleased I asked.

"Who?"

"Um . . . an uncle. He wanted to marry her off to some noble for the good of the family but instead she ran, and now he's hell-bent on finding her. Plus she has her own enemies now."

"Love that. What does she do now?"

"She's . . . a thief. A really good thief. No, a smuggler. A traitor to her country!"

"Whoa, slow down," I say with a laugh. "Okay, a smuggler—"

"She's famous, in a black-market scenario. Like Robin Hood."

"So it's about money?"

"No." She shakes her head. "She rescues people."

"People?"

"Times are bad in her kingdom. Women often run away."

I pause, wondering if I should say something, and then nod. "Okay."

"She and her mother and sisters used to help them. Sneak them in and out of the palace."

"But then her uncle tried to marry her off . . . Oh," I realize, "was he on to what she was doing?"

"Yes! Definitely. He was marrying her off to keep her quiet, and now he's going to do the same thing to her sisters."

"Oh shit," I say.

"I know. So they're the first people she smuggles out."

"So she doesn't work alone?"

"No, she would never."

"But then she's got a problem, doesn't she?"

"Yes, her mother's held captive, which is why she can't leave the capital city. She's right under her uncle's nose."

"What about her father?" I ask with a frown.

"Dead. No, *presumed* dead! She's looking for him." Olivia's expression flames.

"This is so exciting," I say, scribbling rapidly. "I'd totally watch this movie."

"I know, right?" Olivia's cheeks are pink, her eyes molten and alight, and it's a weird time to notice how pretty she is, but I do. When she's like this, it's unavoidable. Inescapable, even. "This is so fun."

I nudge aside an unproductive ray of warmth. "So, what are her strengths?"

"Ooh, um. She forced her father's captain of the guards to teach her to fight. And she's obviously very light-fingered."

"Obviously. Anything witchy, magical, stuff like that?"

"She's immune to some magic. Oh—she can see through illusions and stuff! That's why she knows when her uncle is lying about her mother and father."

"Ooh, nice, perfect—"

"She knows all the military moves. People think she's ex-military."

"Any personal items?"

"A locket. With a picture of her sisters. Oh, and she has an army of people she smuggles to safety who have nowhere else to go. She teaches them to fight."

I give a low whistle. "Damn, she's cool."

"I know." She pauses. "But sometimes people go back."

I frown. "Go back?"

"Yeah. Some people can't live like outlaws and they go back to their old lives, to being powerless. Her best friend, her cousin, goes back and marries the man she was supposed to."

"No way," I exhale, and Olivia nods.

"It breaks her heart. She's always in danger because she trusts too easily."

"That would suck." I write it in. "Any other weaknesses?"

"She's reckless. Brave, but it makes her careless sometimes."

"Anything else?"

"She hates the cold. And—"

Olivia stops, though I'm still writing.

"She likes pretty girls," Olivia says in a different voice. "Especially the ones who try to protect her. Even though she doesn't need protecting."

I blink, pausing.

Then, slowly, I look up.

"Sorry," Olivia says, watching me like she's waiting for my reaction. "Probably a weird way to say that."

I'm not quite sure how to react. It's hard not to read into that comment, but I'm also not sure if I'm supposed to.

"It doesn't have to be you if you don't want it to be," I remind her. "It's . . . just your character. Not real life."

She exhales. "I appreciate the out, but I don't need to be rescued." She smiles a little faintly. "Ironically, that's what I like about you."

"Me?" I blink.

"You were Romeo to save me."

"I—"

"You did all this for me. More than I asked."

"Olivia—"

"This," she says softly. "This is why . . . with Jack, it's not . . ."

She trails off, swallowing hard, and I realize I'm finding out something really personal.

Specifically, the truth that Olivia Hadid has been keeping to herself all year.

"There was a girl, this summer. In New York," she says, and then adds quickly, "Nothing happened. Nothing . . . physical. But I'd never felt anything like that. It was . . . so *right*, you know? And I knew it wasn't just friendship—it was her smile, her laugh. The way she'd drag me into a bodega for some water if I looked even *remotely* dehydrated—"

She stops.

"And it was other things," she admits, glancing at her hands. "And I think about her a lot. All the time."

"Do you still talk," I ask, "or . . . ?"

"No, no, nothing like that. On my last night I told her I had a boyfriend, that I had to think about things. She's . . . her family is like mine. Strict, and much more religious than mine. The risk for her was way bigger. But she—" Olivia hugs the blanket tighter around her. "She said what I felt. She made me feel like it wasn't just my feeling. But I didn't say anything back." She swallows hard. "I . . . couldn't. Not at the time."

"Oh." The wind escapes me, because I know how private this

is, how vulnerable. I've never really considered myself the kind of person people open up to, and I don't want to do it wrong.

"It must be lonely," I say. "Not being able to tell anyone."

"It is." She blinks. "It *is*."

"I'm sorry—"

"No, it's . . ." She shakes her head. "It's not like I don't have support, or that I couldn't if I wanted. It's not like I *can't*. It's . . ."

"I wouldn't blame you if you couldn't."

"I just want to be sure." She exhales swiftly. "I have a really good thing with Jack. *Had*." She winces, and turns to me. "It's not the same between us now that I'm keeping all these secrets. And whatever he feels for me—"

"You don't feel the same way?"

"Not anymore. Not after I realized I could feel what I felt for Razia." She exhales heavily, like air deflating from a balloon. "But I'm afraid that I'm, like, too different now, you know? And as long as I'm with him, I'm still . . . safe." She grimaces. "God. And to think I told you I didn't need to be rescued."

"I don't blame you." I shake my head. "It must feel scary."

She winces. "I don't know how my friends would take it if they knew."

Understandable. I'm not sure I'd want a pack of cheerleaders knowing something that private about me either, though I hope they're better friends to her than that.

"And with you . . ." She gives me an apologetic look. "You remind me of her."

Oh. Hm.

"Not that I'm expecting you to say anything," Olivia adds in a rush. "I'm not . . . I don't even know how you . . . whether you . . ."

"Me? For . . . you?" Is she saying what I think she's saying?

I think she is.

Her cheeks are flushed now. "You don't have to say anything. In fact, don't."

On that, I'm happy to oblige her. Although the question does linger in my head: Why me?

"I guess I just wanted to tell you," Olivia admits in a soft voice, "because . . . I don't know. You make me feel safe."

I inhale. Exhale. I conserve my expressions, my concerns.

And then, about an hour later, I burst into Bash's bedroom and let it all explode.

"HELP ME," I shout at his back, and he jumps, removing his headphones.

"Yeesh, about time," he comments when he recovers from the surprise, patting the spot next to him on his bed. "You've been weird for weeks now—I'd nearly given up hope that you'd remember I exist. So, did you finally want to talk about Antonia?" he prompts knowingly. "Something you'd like to tell me about why you're picking fights with Mom every chance you get and refusing to have any friends?"

"What? No." I haven't the faintest idea what he's talking about and I'm too busy with a far more pressing crisis to try to sort it out.

God. Where to start?

Regrettably, and with alarming ease, my mind leaps—once again—to Jack.

"Jack Orsino thinks I'm you," I blurt out in a panic.

Bash blinks.

Blinks again.

Blink, blink, blink, until it's clear he's not understanding this. At all.

"Okay," Bash exhales while I collapse backward beside him. "Clearly this is going to be even weirder than I thought."

PRESS X TO NOT DIE

𝔙𝔦

"You did WHAT?" Bash barks at me, launching to his feet. "You could have named literally any human man that *wasn't* me!"

"Okay, I think we can both agree that *human man* is a stretch," I scoff, which Bash ignores in favor of rapidly melting through the floors.

"This explains the nods, Viola! The nods!"

"Oh my god, *stop it* with the nods—"

"Do you realize how weird this could have gotten if he'd ever tried to *speak* to me?"

"I panicked!" I shout back.

"IDENTITY THEFT IS A CRIME, VI!"

"CALM DOWN!"

"*YOU* CALM DOWN!"

"Kids?" calls our mom, poking her head in. "I'm heading out, okay, babes? Play nice."

"HAVE A GOOD TIME," Bash and I retort in unison.

Mom frowns, but shrugs. "Text me when you finish whatever this is," she says, leaving Bash and me to stare at each other from our battle positions across the room.

"You're the dumbest girl in school," Bash informs me.

"I know that. And shut up," I remind him. "The Cesario thing's not even part of this."

"How is it not *the most important part*?"

"Because he *doesn't* talk to you, does he? He talks to *me*. And Olivia told *me* something about their relationship that Jack probably needs to know." Among the other things she told me, not that I've had time to take the temperature of whether I might return her feelings. (I mean really, where on the sexual spectrum do you have to fall in order to consider a smart, gorgeous, and delightfully low-key nerdy girl to be smart, gorgeous, and delightfully low-key nerdy? Truly, the mind reels.) "But—"

"But it's not your information to tell!" Bash growls.

"Exactly!" I retort. "Hello, it's a moral quandary!"

"It's the dumbest moral quandary I've ever seen!"

"*You're* the dumbest moral quandary I've ever seen—"

"You should come clean," Bash says firmly. "To everyone. Now."

"Sure," I scoff, "and tell Olivia that Jack asked me to spy on her and I said yes because I had no idea what he was asking of me? Tell Jack that Olivia's issue is serious and private and he needs to talk to her, not me?" Okay, it sounds a lot more logical when I say it out loud.

"Yes, exactly," grumps Bash, who unfortunately gets the high ground for this one (1) conversation only. "*And* you need to tell Jack who you really are."

"No," I say instantly. "No way. The other stuff maybe, but—"

"There's no chance this doesn't come back to bite you somehow," Bash warns in a snotty, know-it-all voice that must be the main reason people don't like me.

"How? Nobody knows about that, so unless *you* plan to tell him—"

"Absolutely not." Bash looks aghast. "*I'm* clearly going to be busy pretending I had no idea that Jack Orsino thinks he's been talking to me when instead he's been pouring his secrets out to my *sister*—"

"He's not pouring out his secrets," I mutter with a grimace, because I have compelling reasons for the deceit. I'm pretty sure I have reasons. Last I checked, I definitely had a defense. "He's just, I don't know. Talking."

"About his life? And feelings?"

Everything sounds much worse from Bash's perspective. But let's be honest, has Jack actually told Cesario anything he couldn't have said in real life? (*Yes*, a small voice reminds me, *and you know it, because you've told him things online that you never would have said to him out loud.*) "I—"

"YOUR HOUSE OF LIES IS GOING TO CRUMBLE, VIOLA!" Bash says vitriolically.

"Oh my god, calm down." I take my own calming breath or two. Or four, or six. "It's fine," I manage to say. (It's not fine.)

"It's not fine! And what does this have to do with Mom?" Bash demands.

"It doesn't. I just . . ." I swallow, looking away. "I may have told Jack about how much Pastor Ike sucks." I left most of the details out—like how my mom is basically a Stepfordian pile of goo since meeting him—but weirdly, Jack seemed to understand. Even weirder, I felt better after talking about it, which I almost never do.

"His name is Isaac?!" Bash informs me hysterically.

"Literally *who cares*, Bash—"

"HE'S NICE," Bash bellows. "And what about Antonia?"

"Oh, she hates me, what else is new—"

"Viola, why are you like this?"

"DADDY PROBLEMS, PROBABLY," I reply, to which Bash rolls his eyes.

"Apologize to Antonia," he says.

"Uh, no? I'm not sorry."

"Shut up. Fine. Whatever." He rubs his temples. "I thought this conversation was going to be completely different. I thought you'd finally—" He gives me a look I'd describe as hurt if I thought there was anything rational to derive from that conclusion. "Never mind. It doesn't matter what I thought." Before I can ponder the significance of *that* tone, Bash hurtles onward. "But you *do* need to come clean to Olivia and Jack."

"But—"

"NO BUTS," Bash hurls at me.

"FINE," I roar back.

"AND BE NICE TO MOM'S BOYFRIEND! SHE DE-SERVES TO BE HAPPY!"

"I KNOW THAT, BASH!"

"Stop yelling!"

"*You* stop yelling—"

"You know, I like you most of the time," Bash cuts in, now irritable at a normal volume. "And contrary to whatever goes on in your twisted fantasy life, people *do* care about you."

I bristle. "So?"

"So! Stop acting like you're this weird plague of a person and just accept that people have feelings and you do, too! YOU'RE NOT IMMUNE TO HUMAN FRAILTY, VIOLA," he bellows as a final note, or what I choose to interpret as a final note, because I can't follow the thread of this conversation at all.

Bash seems genuinely angry with me, which isn't unreasonable, though I don't think it's the so-called identity theft. True, it wasn't my best moment as a sister or a citizen of the world, but the Bash I know would have no trouble laughing that off at my expense.

It definitely doesn't explain him looking at me like I've let him down.

"Well, you're . . ." I stop, frustrated. "Someday *you're* going to do something dumb, you know that, Sebastian? It's not just me."

"Of course not. I do dumb things all the time."

"Exactly."

"Today's your day, though," he says, and turns away. "Shut the door on your way out."

Well, that's unusually cold for him, though his attention span does have its limits. I walk out of his room and exhale, groaning quietly to myself because he's right.

It doesn't matter which part upset him. The point is I can fix this. Just tell the truth. Easy, right?

I can do that, starting tonight at homecoming.

Okay, but here's the thing—I can't do it. From the moment I set foot on campus, I can feel my impending doom pulsing in the air like a ticking clock. Jack, in an apparent attempt by the universe to haunt me like some kind of demonic poltergeist, is already here, helpfully setting up the table outside the gym to take tickets as people start to arrive.

"You look profoundly weird," Jack tells me, waking me from yet another unsolicited thought spiral. "You okay?"

Of course not. I'm trapped somewhere in ethical limbo, tugged this way and that by my conscience and the two unfairly attractive people situated at either end. Jack, of course, makes a nebulous situation immediately worse. Either he's finally getting some sleep or that outrageous slim-fit ombre blazer is doing way more work than any garment has a right to. Gone are the violent shadows, the faint but unmistakable hint of malaise. He looks exactly like someone who's got homecoming king on lock, and I'm 78 percent sure I hate him for it.

"What? I'm fine. Here's the petty cash." I practically throw it at him. "And it's not polite to tell someone they look weird when they put on a dumb dress for this crap."

It's not a dumb dress. Actually, my mom picked it out for me, since she knows I have no patience to sift through stuff at the mall. Which isn't to say I don't like shopping, but after three homecomings vying for a dress that someone else will inevitably be wearing as well, I've kind of given up. The one she picked out is, I have to say, very me, as in it's not very formal. It's almost like a simplified Renaissance dress, actually. Short, with peasant sleeves and a corset-y top, in a chiffon pale pink that's more like blush. Girly, I'll admit. But at least I can be pretty confident that nobody else will be wearing it.

"Peace offering?" Mom said when she set it on my bed.

"We're not fighting." Am I betrayed by her sudden, cringey devotion to romance, which feels like aliens have abducted my actual mother? Yes. But we're not fighting.

"Could've fooled me."

She had a point, as did Bash when he told me I was being "mercurial." I have not handled meeting her new boyfriend very well, though that has less to do with Pastor Ike than with the fact that my mom becoming abruptly unrecognizable makes me worry I might be susceptible as well.

"I mean, it's not armor," Jack points out, startling me into recalling we're still talking about my dress, "so obviously I've seen better."

He's got this grin on his face that's so uncalled for it makes me want to shriek at him to be less nice, specifically to me.

"Wanna stick around?" he says, patting the chair next to him. "We're good at this now."

"What?" I say, alarmed.

"We make a good team."

"No we don't."

He gives me a look like he finds me distinctly amusing. "Okay fine, we don't, you're awful. Sit down, Viola."

"*You* sit down," I tell him, and promptly turn to leave.

Unfortunately, I smack directly into someone else, because of course I do.

"Oh, sorry—"

"Vi," says Antonia, and blinks, adjusting her dress. It looks like a version of her Larissa Highbrow costume, which only I would know. "Sorry," she adds, reddening.

"Sorry, I wasn't—" I stop, noticing her date.

It's Matt Das. You know, as in "just go out with him, he's nice" Matt Das. "I've been nice to you, so you owe me something" Matt Das. The Matt Das that Antonia picked over being friends with me. *That* Matt Das.

I think he says my name when we accidentally make eye contact, but all I can hear out of his mouth is "bitch."

As in, *You really are a bitch, Vi Reyes.*

Any hope I had of apologizing to Antonia, or of talking to her at all, escapes me like a collapsed lung.

"Right. Have fun." I turn around and gruffly take the seat next to Jack, trying to look like that was my intention all along.

To my relief, Jack doesn't say anything.

For a while, anyway.

"So," he says, after at least fifty people check in with their tickets. "You and Antonia."

"Please don't." I already have Bash in my head yelling at me, but I can't talk to Antonia now. Not here. Not if it means pulling her away from Matt Das on the gossamer, insubstantial hope that she doesn't go back and snicker with him about how desperate I was to be her friend again.

"Fair enough," says Jack.

More students show up. A whole train of them. At this point anyone who arrives is late, but whatever, we're in high school. Such is life.

Jack reaches for his phone. I assume he's going to scroll through his social media or something, but instead he holds it out for me.

"Look."

I glance down and it's the shot of us with Cesario, which I already saw featured on the MagiCon blog. "Did you just see this now?"

"Yeah," he says, too insistently, so I think it's a lie. "It's not like I check this blog regularly."

Except he totally does now. "*Le fame*, am I right?"

"I know, exactly. Finally, my moment."

"You have moments all the time." I gesture up to the banner with his name on it in the gym's foyer. It hangs below his father's banner, next to his brother's banner. The royal line of Orsino. "Your life is full of moments."

"All lives are full of moments, Viola," he says with an obnoxious gravity, just before another group of people shows up to have their tickets scanned.

I lift a hand to rub my eyes before remembering that my mom talked me into a full face of makeup. She insisted, saying it had been a long time since we'd played makeover like we used to. It's why Bash is so good at his own stage makeup; he's somewhere on the dance floor now, which is where he'll be for the rest of the night. I let him drag me off to his multiple pre-dance picture-taking extravaganzas where I did most of the photography, so hopefully he's forgiven me for my offenses. Personally, I'd call my penance made.

"So anyway," Jack says. "About you looking weird—"

I groan. "Okay, that's enough from you."

He slides me a sidelong, slanted grin and I fiddle with my phone, opening and closing apps for no reason. "How long are you supposed to just sit here?" I ask him.

"Dunno. Until someone relieves me, I guess." He shrugs, sinking farther down into his chair.

"I can do it. You can go—" I wave a hand. "Socialize."

"Socialize?"

"Survey your kingdom."

"Nah," he says. "Not my kingdom anymore."

I drum my fingers absently on the table as more people show up. They're trickling in now: giggling dates with their lipstick smeared off, trying (not very hard) to hide things they're bringing in their jacket pockets. I have a system for this—I call it the stumble system. Anyone who stumbles up the stairs gets stopped, but nobody's that far gone. And anyway, I'm careful, not a narc.

"You know," Jack says, "we don't have to just sit here all night."

"I'll probably check out the bathrooms later."

"For what?"

I shrug. "Shenanigans."

"Shenanigans, Viola?"

"Hijinks."

"We're all much too mature for hijinks," Jack says solemnly.

"Stop."

"I imagine we've elevated."

"What comes after hijinks? Crimes?"

"Always the darkest possible outcome." He tuts at me. "Terrible."

"I have a calamitous imagination."

"What?"

"Calamitous. Calamity."

"Bad? Sounds bad."

"Yes, bad," I confirm with an irritable sigh.

"So if I asked you to dance or something instead of haunting the bathrooms, you'd probably say no," Jack muses aloud.

Something locks in my throat.

"Yeah, probably," I manage. "I'd just assume one of us would get shot. Or kidnapped."

"That *is* catastrophic."

"Calamitous."

"Same thing. It *is* the same thing, right?"

The thing in my throat won't go away and I don't know why. "Yeah."

He looks at me, grinning like I'm being funny.

Viola, you are not a bitch.

Or, like, you are, but it doesn't mean what they think it means.

Oh, I think through the sudden pain in my chest. Oh.

Oh, *no.*

"I'm gonna go," I say, shooting upright. The chair falls behind me with a clatter.

"You okay?" Jack says with—*ugh*—concern.

"Fine. I'm fine." I can't tell him the truth about Bash. I have to, I know, for both their sakes, but not right now. "I'm . . . yeah." Ruin his night? No way.

Maybe later.

Yeah, later.

"You sure?"

I blink, realizing he's staring at me in obvious bemusement while I'm still lingering next to my overturned chair.

"Bye," I blurt out, fumbling away. Someone, anyone else, can have his attention. I don't need it. I don't want it.

And I definitely don't deserve it, I think, exhaling as I walk swiftly away.

I'm almost relieved when, as usual, no one wants to stay to clean up at the end of the dance. Half the volunteers conveniently vanish. I'm able to wave off a conciliatory Bash—who, at the peak of his dance-enthused extroversion, tries to persuade me that what my life really needs is an evening at IHOP with the rest of the band kids (half of which are aggressively making out)—and Kayla, who is making a responsible but perfunctory effort. I'm positive she'd rather bask in the success of her evening than stay behind, so I shoo her away and prowl the gym, picking up decorations that wound up on the floor and making sure the DJ got paid. You know, things that relax me.

"Need help?"

I jump when I realize Jack's behind me. "What?"

He bends to pick up a garbage bag, motioning like he'll follow while I finish picking things up.

"Oh. You don't have t—"

He lifts a brow. "It's my job, isn't it?"

"No, it's—"

"If you're doing it, then it's probably *someone's* job," he jokes.

"I—" Fine. Whatever, fine. "Okay, let's get this over with."

It goes quickly, so much so that our leadership teacher is already motioning us out the doors, assuring us the weekend custodial staff will take care of the rest.

Before I know it, I'm outside the gym alone with Jack. There's a small parking lot back here, which is where I parked when I arrived. Certain perks to being ASB vice president, I guess. Good parking.

"You don't need a ride, do you?" I say, forcing conversation.

He looks at me, one brow lifted. "Is that an offer?"

"Is *that* a request?" He's tormenting me on purpose, I know it.

"Paranoid much, Viola?"

Honestly. "Just get in the car, Orsino."

But he doesn't move. He just stares at me, half smiling.

"What?" I grumble.

"You're funny."

This time, I'm indignant. *"What?"*

"You're so prickly all the time, but you're thoughtful, aren't you? You"—he leans closer, dropping his voice—"*care.*"

"Okay, shut *up*," I say violently, and he smirks.

"Why? Worried I'll tell people?"

"Nobody would believe you," I mutter, and I move for the driver door, but he catches my wrist.

Well, *tries* to catch my wrist. Instead, his fingers inadvertently brush my palm.

Even he looks surprised; maybe even startled, like a jolt of static shock just passed from me to him.

But then he looks at me and says, "I believe you."

My chest punctures. "What?"

"Whatever happened with you and Antonia. I believe you."

I bristle. "I never said—"

"You didn't have to." He's not joking now. Not smiling his usual king-of-campus smile, and still, somehow, it's unfair. How good he looks. How much better, actually, when the spark in his eyes is real. When the look on his face is true.

"Orsino," I sigh, "you don't know what you're talking about."

"No, you're right, I don't. But if you ever want to tell me—"

He steps closer to me and my heart drums, battering itself in answer to a question he hasn't asked. Finishing his sentence for him.

"You can't convince me that you're heartless, Viola," he says, and it's low and soft, close to my ear, a little rustle through my hair like a breeze. "I hate to tell you this, but you're not as cleverly disguised as you think."

My eyes flutter shut from the irony. "You don't actually know me." It's almost a confession.

"No, but I could," he says, and my pulse stutters again, recklessly, until he takes a step back. "But you're right," he adds, "not now. Not like this."

I feel the loss of him like a splintering in space. "Not like what?"

He tilts his head, opening his mouth like he'll answer, but then he just smiles at me.

He smiles, and I ache.

"My car's over there," he says, pointing to it. "My knee's operational now, so I don't need any more rides." He gestures and I look down.

"Oh." Cool. I feel like an idiot. "Okay, then."

He nods, uncertain. "Get home safe?"

I roll my eyes, looking up again. "Do I have another option?"

"No." He shakes his head, surer this time, then reaches for my door. I swat his hand away before he can open it for me.

"I've *got* it—"

"Of course you do." He looks amused again while I shove myself into the driver's seat, reaching for my seat belt.

Now is when I'd reach out to close the door, but I don't.

And he . . . *lingers.*

Like someone who has no idea who or what I really am.

"You're an idiot," I sigh, and I think I'm relieved when he merely smirks at me.

"I know. It's how I lead such a blissfully non-calamitous life." He reaches out, giving my seat belt a snap to irritate me, which it does. "For what it's worth," he adds, still smirking, "you almost looked passably normal tonight. Probably just a trick of the light, though."

From my vantage point, he looks infuriating. And perfect.

"You," I inform him, "are the bane of my existence, Jack Orsino."

"As you are mine," he assures me, and shuts my door for me.

He takes a few backward strides in retreat, eyes locked on mine before turning away, and the moment slips out from under me. It's drawn out and fleeting at the same time, acute like a throbbing pain, and then my headlights are momentarily blinding, the outline of his face still there when I blink.

Jack

DUKEORSINO12: something weird happened tonight

I jiggle my foot, then my entire leg. I'm relieved Cesario's online; not sure who else to talk to.

C354R10: it was a school dance what did you expect

Typical Cesario answer.

C354R10: I assume you're going to tell me about it so you might as well do it quickly
C354R10: I'd like to make it out of celyddon without getting burned alive

Celyddon, the ancestral realm of Kay, is the most mythical part of the quest so far. There are dragons here, and spellcasting, and people continuously trying to rob us of our most valuable relic aside from the Ring of Dispell: the Shield of Maccabee, which coincidentally protects the wearer from dragon flame.

DUKEORSINO12: I think I had a moment
DUKEORSINO12: with someone

I fidget again, unsure if I should say more.

The whole night was kind of strange. Once Vi darted off from the ticket booth, I wound up with some of the guys on the team, including Curio.

"Been a long time," he pointed out. "You don't come around much aside from practice."

"Just busy." That was a lie, of course. I can't exactly admit to him how much I feel like an outsider. He deserves to enjoy his success; with seven consecutive wins, this is definitely Curio's season.

But it was supposed to be mine.

"Gotcha." He didn't push me. "How's PT going?"

"Pretty good. Should be able to run soon." Couple weeks if I'm lucky.

"Oh, no way, that's great. Feeling good?"

"Yeah, almost back to normal." I feel like I'm relearning how to walk.

"Well, the guys miss you."

Not Volio, that's for sure. He's making the most of his time in the sun. "Yeah, I miss them, too."

"You should come out with us after this," Curio suggested.

"Afterparty?"

A shrug. "Volio's parents are out of town."

"Ah." I glanced around the room. "I'll have to do some cleanup for ASB, but maybe."

"Really? No shit."

"Yeah, well, I'm told I have to pull my weight around here." That part was true, at least.

"Well, if you change your mind."

Fast-forward a couple of hours and all of a sudden I'm standing in the doorway telling Curio I'm not gonna make it, I've got somewhere else to be. Fast-forward a few more minutes to the harsh bright lights on Vi Reyes's dark hair, and the look of concentration on her face while she ordered around some adults.

She didn't need my help—she never does—but I stayed.

Why did I stay?

Cesario points out the obvious.

C354R10: I thought you were still trying to get back with olivia

I am. I was. No, I am. But in some ways it does feel like she steps further and further into my rearview with every day she actively avoids me. It was only recently that I realized how long it's been since she and I had an actual conversation. Not just since she asked for a break, but before then.

DUKEORSINO12: I'm still with olivia, yeah

DUKEORSINO12: but I don't know if it still feels . . . right

DUKEORSINO12: I mean is it supposed to be this complicated?

I feel like all my relationships are fraught right now. My mom wants me to take this knee injury as some kind of sign from above that I should move on and give up football. My dad wants me to come back stronger and faster than ever. My friends want me to move backward but I can't, I can only move forward, which is going a lot slower than I thought.

But things are weirdly easy with Vi. For someone so harsh, she's not actually judgmental. She's a lot more sensitive than she lets on, and still, I've never known a person to be so unafraid of who they are. As much as she's constantly pushing me, she also makes it easier for me to be who *I* am—whoever that is at any given time. I don't have a relationship like that with anyone else.

Well, except Cesario.

C354R10: well

He types, then deletes.

Types again, then stops.

Types. Stops.

Types.

Stops.
A minute goes by.
Typing.
More typing.
Stops.

C354R10: what kind of moment was it

I sit back in my chair, thinking about it. It was when I realized Vi was offering me a ride home just because she thought I needed it.

No. No, it was before that.

It was when I noticed Vi shrinking up for the first time when she saw Antonia with that dude, the kid who was Olivia's first kiss. When Olivia told me about it, she said it didn't count because she hadn't been ready for it; they went out for a week in middle school and then he just grabbed her and took it. "Stole it" were her words for it. She broke up with him later and he told everyone she was a snob.

No, but it wasn't that moment, either. It was when I realized that if I'm the kind of person who is never allowed to get angry, then Vi is never allowed to be sad. And something about that made me feel like the girl standing next to me was braver and bolder than anyone I'd ever met. And that she was lonelier, too.

Like me.

DUKEORSINO12: synchronicity I guess
C354R10: gonna go out on a limb and suggest you not have any moments with anyone until after you talk to your girlfriend

Sensible advice.

DUKEORSINO12: assuming I can get my girlfriend to talk to me
C354R10: maybe you need to do the talking
C354R10: you've either got to tell her that you're in this no matter what
C354R10: or . . .

I wait, but Cesario doesn't finish his sentence. Not that he needs to—point made.

DUKEORSINO12: it's probably too soon to say if anything would ever happen with vi anyway

Oh shit. Whoops. Man, it is way too easy to say things online.

DUKEORSINO12: sorry dude I know that's your sister
DUKEORSINO12: didn't mean to just throw that one at you
C354R10: why would it matter what I think? she's her own person
C354R10: but either way I don't think she wants to be your second choice
DUKEORSINO12: she's not
DUKEORSINO12: I mean . . .
DUKEORSINO12: I don't know what I mean

I sigh, shaking my head.

DUKEORSINO12: I guess I'm just trying to say that you're right, I need to talk to olivia, whether or not I feel something for vi

Cesario types, then stops. A repeat of his earlier halting pause.

C354R10: DO you feel something for vi?

Part of me thinks it's impossible not to feel *something* about Vi. It's hard to feel neutral about someone as brash and relentless and generally unconcerned with feelings as she is.

But there's also part of me that thinks that maybe it's a good thing that she isn't for everyone. It feels like maybe being someone who gets to actually know her, even in a small way, is something I've earned.

DUKEORSINO12: doesn't matter, right?
DUKEORSINO12: not until I clear things up with olivia

Which is going to be hard. Or maybe I just haven't tried hard enough. Or tried correctly.

> **C354R10:** okay well whatever
> **C354R10:** can we play now

Typical.

> **DUKEORSINO12:** you know, you and your sister are weirdly alike
> **C354R10:** shows what you know

It's a good thing he never lets me get too sentimental, because right around then a pack of mages shows up to challenge us to a round of combat.

It's funny that earlier today I got a text from Nick asking me if I'd gotten bored of *Twelfth Knight* yet. According to him it was a good use of a couple of weeks, maybe a month. But I'm getting close to two months now and honestly, I'm increasingly uninterested in whether or not what I'm doing is cool. Again, it's nowhere near the state championship I was prophesied to win, but one football title being all I am or was or ever will be suddenly feels like an unacceptable position, even if some people might believe it's true.

Besides, maybe Vi's commitment to nerddom has rubbed off on me in a socially reckless way, but I kind of wish more people knew about this game. I've been watching some technical reviews of it online and it's kind of staggering how much better it is than other MMORPGs like it. I find it so fascinating to know that everything I'm seeing is, like, millions of triangles in a few blocks of code.

dude, Nick said when I accidentally went off on a ramble. *you know you could study this, right?*

what, the psychology of getting unhealthily obsessed with video games??

no, genius. computer science. the CS kids at my school are always doing hackathons and shit, maybe you'd be into that

I mean, maybe, but still. *I'm pretty sure everyone wants to make video games no. EVERYONE wants to play football at Illyria. so if you can do one of those things, why not both?*

I told him he was reading a little too much into my interest in this one thing, which he was. But it's hard not to admire again how cool it is that I can move as an avatar better than I can in real life. There's something freeing about the fact that there's an entire world out there where my imagination is my only constraint. Or that it could even be *this* world, if I could just learn to imagine something like this. It makes the future seem limitless and vast—just like Vi said.

Infinite versions. Endless possibilities.

C354R10: a little help, please?

Right. Back to work.

LEVEL-UP AT INTIMACY 5

Vi

After Duke Orsino signs off, I can't sleep. I try, tossing and turning, but every time I do, I see the same thing: *whether or not I have feelings for Vi—*

The snap of my seat belt. His voice in my ear. I felt . . . oh god, don't say it.

(Butterflies.)

Olivia's bright smile flickers behind my eyes, as does Bash's look of disappointment, and eventually I give up on sleeping. Restless, I get up to comb through the archives of my mom's old advice columns. I'm not sure what I'm looking for until it finds me in the early morning, and then a sound downstairs startles me awake from where I passed out on my laptop keyboard, drool crusting on my wrist.

"Mom?" I snatch up the laptop and stumble downstairs, finding her in the kitchen.

"Yeah?" she says, voice muffled from where it's buried in a cabinet.

"Can I ask you about something? One of your old columns."

"Hm? Yeah, of course, just . . ." She sighs heavily, then pokes her head out to frown at me. "Is there coffee in the house?"

"Well, Mother, if it's not at the back of the cupboard we never use, I just can't think where else it would be," I reply, and she groans, withdrawing to find her keys.

"No snark this early, hija. Can we drive and talk? I've got a deadline that'll take either excessive caffeine or a miracle," she grumbles, gesturing for me to follow as she kicks off her slippers and shoves her feet into the Birkenstocks beside the door. "Naturally you're more important but, you know. We do have to eat."

"Yeah, that's—" I hunt around for the first shoes I find, which are rainboots, and follow her as she heads out the door. "It's going to be weird, though—"

"Good." She yawns while she shuffles to the car, pulling the door open and falling into the driver's seat. "Inspire me."

I climb into the passenger seat, fidgeting while she puts the car in reverse.

Where to start?

I guess I might as well just say it.

"How did you know you were bi?" I ask my mother.

She stops with her hand on the gearshift.

"I mean, was there, like . . . a specific moment? Or something? I don't know," I hastily equivocate, feeling very, very stupid. "But I read that column you wrote for the girl who was questioning her sexuality, and the way you answered her, I thought maybe it might be helpful if you could . . ."

I trail off, not sure what exactly I'm confessing to, and she nods, thinking.

"I doubt I'm going to be able to make this the kind of neatly packaged answer you seem to be looking for," she manages after a second. "There wasn't a specific moment, no. More like a series of moments that only made sense to me once I realized there were a lot of ways that love could look, and some that sounded like the way I felt. But I've always told you kids that it's more about the person for me, not the, um. Package." She glances over at me. "Is that confusing for you?"

"No." She's always been more open-minded about sexuality than any parent I've ever known, so we've definitely had the safety part of this talk. "Theoretically it sounds very straightforward," I observe, and she starts to say something, then shrugs.

"Theoretically," she agrees, waiting for me to make my point.

"Right." I clear my throat. "Well, I guess my question is, um. Does liking women feel . . . different?" I ask her, watching her frown a little at the steering wheel as she idles in the driveway.

"Different from liking men, you mean?"

"Yeah. Well—" I laugh shakily. "More like . . . uh. Say there's a girl who's really, really cool," I offer in ambiguous explanation of Olivia. "And she's pretty, and you really like her."

"Sounds pretty simple so far," Mom says carefully. She's probably starting to wish she had coffee for this conversation, but here we are.

"Right, but . . ." I make a face, struggling. There's a reason we don't talk about this, and it has a lot more to do with my comfort than my mom's. "But what if there's someone else, too? Someone who makes you feel . . ." It's deeply uninspiring to keep coming back to the same word, but there really only seems to be one. "Someone who makes you feel different."

Someone who keeps colliding with you, over and over. In everything you love, he's there, too, and real or not, you can exist in every universe with ease because of him. Because for every version of him, there is a corresponding one of you.

"Ah." Mom rests her head against the back of her seat. "Well, I hate to tell you this, but I don't think this is a sexuality question so much as a conflict of emotions."

"Ugh." I sink down in my seat, grim. "I hate emotions."

"I know." She smiles tiredly at me. "But I think you already know this isn't about anatomy. There's a person here, hija. Two people, obviously—but one of them really got under your skin, didn't they?"

"I wouldn't go *that* far," I say with repulsion, and she laughs.

"Okay, well, look—I know you don't want to hear about my love life. You've made that plenty clear." I glance down at my hands, guilty, and she continues, "But the thing is, Vi, wanting someone in your life doesn't have to mean you're weak. It doesn't mean you're soft. It just means there's someone in this world who makes you like everything just a little bit more when they're with you, and in the end, isn't that something?" She looks at me again, half smiling. "Life is hard enough without depriving yourself of joy."

"It's not that simple," I sigh, glancing away.

"Yeah, babe, I know. It never is."

"And I'm not saying I have *feelings*," I argue, "I just—"

"I know." She nods. "Maybe you do, maybe you don't. Maybe this is something big, or maybe not. Maybe someday you'll meet a girl and feel something that answers all your questions, or maybe not. Maybe the world is big and life is long." She shrugs, then chews her lip. "Does that . . . help?"

Not really. But at the same time, yes. "I think so. Pretty much, yeah."

"Good." She breathes out swiftly, with relief. "So . . . can we get coffee now, or would that be violating this, um, consecrated mother-daughter moment?"

"Oh, no, I for *sure* need coffee," I tell her. "Are you kidding? I need to think."

She laughs at me, finally turning to reverse down the driveway.

"Darling Viola, my clever, brilliant girl. The last thing you need is more thinking," Mom assures me, tugging my hair before pulling into our street.

Mom's deadline keeps her busy all day, which is fine, since I have homework and some stuff to do for ASB. We typically arrange a schoolwide activity for the end of the semester—something for the students to do after finals before heading off for winter break. Unfortunately, there isn't much left in the budget, so I have to spend a couple of hours researching ideas online.

I emerge from my room with an urgent craving for gummy bears when Bash materializes from the stairs, greeting me with, "VIOLA!"

"SEBASTIAN," I reply as usual, and then freeze when Olivia suddenly appears behind him, each of us startling the other.

"Oh, hi," Olivia says when she sees me, cheeks flushing. "Bash said you were up here, so—"

"Oh, right, yeah—"

"Hey," Bash interrupts with a gesture from me to Olivia, "can you tell her she'd be great for the musical?"

"What musical?" I ask, because I am suddenly adrift in space and time.

"The spring musical. I'm trying to convince her to audition." He nudges Olivia. "I almost have her convinced, I think."

"I've only been here for, like, two seconds," Olivia assures me, though no one would know better than me that two seconds is plenty of time to get sucked in by Bash. "He brought it up and I said I'd think about it."

"So *think* about it," Bash purrs, then disappears down the stairs.

I stand there for a second, still a little shocked by Olivia being in my house, until I remember that oh, yeah, I probably have some idea what she wants to talk about.

I gesture to my bedroom. "So, do you—?"

"Yeah, if that's—?"

"No, yeah, come in." I'm not sure what the protocol is here, so I walk inside to take a seat at my desk while Olivia perches on the edge of my bed.

"Feeling better?" I ask.

"Much." She clears her throat. "Though, um, I wanted to apologize about—"

"Actually," I say. "Do you mind if I . . . ?"

"Oh. Yeah, sure. Of course." She blinks and nods, letting me go first, though I wish I knew what I wanted to say. Almost as much as I wish I'd told Jack who I really was before he confided in Cesario. Sometimes it feels like there's a cliff-edge, the right moment for the truth, and you either pull yourself back from it or you sail headfirst into a crevasse.

But this is not about Jack. This is a different cliff, and I have to fix it.

"I should have said a lot of things to you before," I confess. "Some bad, some worse."

"Worst news first?" Olivia suggests with a thin smile, and I take a deep breath.

"Jack knew we were partners for AP Lit, so he asked me to try to find out why you wanted a break. I didn't tell him anything," I assure her, though she doesn't react, "and I promise, I won't say a word to anyone. But I did initially agree to try to find out."

"I see," she says slowly. "And the other bad things?"

"Well—" I hesitate. "So, I asked myself whether there was maybe something . . . here. With us. Like you said."

She doesn't move. "And?"

"And . . ." She is never going to want to speak to me again. This is going to be like Antonia, which you'd think I'd be numb to by now, but I'm not. My mom is right—it never gets easier to be hurt. As much as I try to be thick-skinned, I am sad to know that Olivia Hadid will walk out of this room and probably not be my friend anymore.

But still, it needs to be said.

"I don't think I have the same feelings you do," I say, and swallow. "Which is dumb, because I wish I did?" Truly, if I could make myself fall for Olivia instead of . . .

It doesn't matter who else. "You're smart and funny and, like, generally amazing, and I wish I'd said that sooner. I wish I'd told you that it's really brave of you, I mean," I clarify awkwardly, "to be so honest about how you feel. I don't think I could do it. I know I couldn't, actually." Not that this is about me. "I just want you to know that I'll be here for you, for anything, whatever you need. I know it might not be in the way you wanted, but—" A sigh. "I just think you should know that I think you're brave and strong, and—"

A secret, fragile portion of my chest cracks.

"And I really would like to be your friend," I admit. "I know what it's like to feel alone. And misunderstood, I guess. Or sad, but nobody can know. So yeah. That's all." I fix my gaze at my chewed-up cuticles. "So if you need a friend, or want one . . ."

God, what a self-important speech. I end it with a mumbled, "I'm here."

I keep staring at my hands.

Then, eventually, Olivia shifts slightly.

"I do want a friend," she says. "I actually came here to tell you that."

I look up, surprised. "Really?"

"Of course," she says. "I mean, you're giving me *way* too much credit, first of all. I'm pretty sure I'm not ready to be in a relationship with anyone until I can be completely honest about who I am. So as much as I do think you're, like, *very* cool—"

"Stop," I groan.

"You are. But I could be a lot braver than how I left things with Razia. Or Jack." Olivia makes a face. "So can we be friends? I'd really, really like to be friends."

"Yeah. Yeah, of course. Yes." I feel like I'm about to faint with relief.

"Great." She looks equally relieved, then glances at her lap. "Wow, I was so nervous. I'm, like, shaking."

"Oh my god, me too!" I thought it was just me.

"I'm sweating, it's so gross—"

"It's like a cold sweat, right? Like, cold sweat of terror," I confess, and she laughs so hard she almost tears up.

"Why are feelings so brutal?" she wails. "Everyone makes friendship seem like garden parties and sleepovers when really it's *Jurassic Park* for emotions."

"I think my teeth are kind of chattering?"

"Oh my god, same." She laughs again. "Wow. Embarrassing."

"Very."

"But at least it's mutual."

"This is true."

There's a brief lull as we both manage to settle back into normalcy.

"So, uh—what do you think about Bash?" Olivia says, changing the subject.

"Dunno. He looks kind of weird." She snorts a laugh and I ask, slightly more seriously, "So is it not *just* girls, then, or . . . ?"

"What? Oh my god, no, not like that." She rolls her eyes at me. "No, I meant what do you think about what Bash suggested—the musical," she explains, and oh, right—*totally* forgot about that. "Would it be weird if he helped me come up with an audition piece and stuff?"

"Weird for who? You, definitely. He's kind of a maniac, just FYI."

"No." She barks a laugh. "For you."

"Me? No way. I think it makes sense." I pause. "Though, if what you actually want is to be yourself, isn't it kind of backwards to pick up acting?"

"I . . . don't think I'm ready yet to be completely me," she admits. "I think soon. Maybe college. Hopefully college. But for now . . ."

She trails off again. "I just want to escape into something else for a while."

"I get that." Boy, do I ever; the memory of my false life as Cesario returns to me, and with it, thoughts of the other person I have yet to come clean with. "But—"

I hesitate.

"Yeah?" Olivia says, tilting her head.

"I do think you need to be honest with Jack," I admit, and Olivia gives me a look like, *Ah*. "I think he deserves to know the truth. Actually," I correct myself, "he *does* deserve the truth, and more importantly, he can handle it. I can see how it'd be scary, but I think . . ." Another heavy exhale. "I think you could trust him with your real self if you wanted to."

His face flashes in my head: *I believe you, Viola*. Oddly enough, he's the only person I can think of to ever side with me with no conditions—just acceptance. "I really think he won't let you down," I say, which is kind of like saying I don't think he'll let *me* down, which is a terrifying thought. Because with few exceptions, everyone lets me down. And anyway, I'll let *him* down once he finds out about me—whenever that will be.

In response Olivia gives me an odd look, then tilts her head.

"You've really changed your tune on him, haven't you?" she observes. "Interesting."

"Well, apparently he kept part of his personality in his ACL or whatever," I mutter, because that's the only excuse I have for it. Either that or computer games are better for your personal growth than people are ready to admit.

She laughs. "Well, it's funny you bring him up, actually."

"It is?" He said he was going to talk to her last night, though at the time I was busy thinking about other things.

A moment, he said. A stupid way to put it—I would never be so trite. But if what happened between us *was* a moment—and more importantly, if we both felt it—what does that mean?

But now's not the time to wonder. The way Olivia brings it up makes me feel like I'm missing something, and as it turns out, I am.

Jack

"So," Mom says after I get home from physical therapy; she brought a bunch of meals for Dad and me this morning, and now it looks like the impulse has struck to laboriously clean the kitchen. "How's it going?"

"Slow." I shrug. "Very slow." Eric has me focusing on stability right now, which feels easy. Unfortunately, things that feel easy always make me want to push more, go faster.

"Yeah, well, everything's too slow when you're young." Mom lingers behind the kitchen counter, looking like she's waiting for something to say. "How'd things go with Olivia?"

Hm. How to sum up for your mother the conversation you and your girlfriend had this morning? Or, for that matter, how to honor the secrets she told you about herself?

"We broke up," I admit.

Mom's face instantly warps. "Oh, honey—"

"No, Mom, it's fine. It's more than fine, actually." It was a relief to finally understand, then a smack upside the head to realize I wasn't remotely the center of her narrative, then comforting to know we could still be friends. "Can I just run upstairs for a sec? Something I have to do for school."

"Sure, of course—"

"Are you staying for dinner?"

She blinks. "Yeah. Yeah, if you want me to—"

"Stay. Please. It'll be nice." I give her my most encouraging smile and then gesture upstairs. "I'll just be a few minutes, okay?"

"Okay." She nods, and I take myself up the stairs, testing my range of motion for each step. Eric says this will be the first step to beginning my run program, and I admit, I'm itching for it. Patience, he says. The better I heal now, the better I'll be in the future. Time, it's all about time. The time I give and the time I take.

But with only a handful of weeks left before the postseason starts, time isn't on my side.

I pull my desk chair out and sit, flipping open my laptop.

DUKEORSINO12: you there? I've got something to ask you

For the first time, though, there's no answer on Cesario's end.

Monday afternoon I find Vi sitting with a laptop at her lab table, as usual. Looks like she's mocking something up for our social media, which typically the ASB secretary would do, or one of the social chairs. For whatever reason, all the overhead lights in the leadership room are off; I move to turn them on but she waves me away.

"Don't bother," she says. "Bowen's doing presentations in here later."

"So you're just going to sit in the dark?"

She shrugs. "It's fine. Just leave it."

I do. She can have whatever weird work habits she wants.

"What?" she says expressionlessly. "You're lingering."

"Hi to you, too, Viola." I walk over to her lab table, pulling out the stool next to hers. "You want help?"

She turns a bracing glance at me. "The way I hear it, our deal's over."

"What?"

"Our deal. Intel in exchange for—"

"Right." She must have already heard that Olivia and I broke up. "Well, homecoming's over."

"True."

"And honestly, you were no help with Olivia at all."

The corners of her mouth flicker with the threat of a smile.

"Yeah," she says. "True."

"But I can still do . . . whatever this is." I gesture to her screen. "If you want."

"Do you have access to the ASB Instagram?"

"No."

"Twitter?"

"No."

"Website?"

"Nope."

"So then what's this mystical 'help' you're offering me?"

"Pleasant as always," I murmur, and she glances at me, a small divot of hesitation appearing between her brows.

"I meant—" She stops. "I just meant you're not that useful for this specific task, that's all."

"True." I lean onto my forearms and she jerks away, abruptly skittish. "You all right there, Viola?"

"Fine." She shifts over. "You're in my space."

"Right, sorry."

She clears her throat. "So . . . everything with Olivia . . . ?"

I shrug. "She told me the truth."

"And?"

And it made me realize just how little truth we'd ever really told each other over the course of our relationship. It was our first actual, real talk in a long time. I brought up my fears about my knee, my future. She told me she wasn't sure who to be anymore. That, I said, was relatable.

"But I'm still your biggest fan," Olivia promised me. "I know I haven't seemed like it lately, but I promise, Jack. Always and forever."

She proved it today, finally chatting with me on our way to class instead of ducking me in the halls like she's been doing all semester. At lunch we joked about her AP Lit teacher, Mr. Meehan, who's apparently been tipped off about her budding interest in theater.

"Who told him?" I asked.

Olivia shrugged. "Bash Reyes, probably."

"Huh." I've been wondering since then why Cesario never mentioned anything to me. Actually, it's occurring to me that I don't know how Bash Reyes could be in so many places at once. Band, drama, *and* an ongoing video game quest? Which, as I suddenly recall, is what I wanted to discuss with Vi, who's still waiting for an answer.

"We're good now" is my belated reply to her question about Olivia.

"That's it?" She arches a brow. "You're good?"

"Well, it's been over for a while." I clear my throat. "And anyway,

I was asking a favor? Which," I add pointedly, "you owe me, since your end of the deal remains unfulfilled."

I wait for her to argue with me; I look forward to it, I think. Sparring with Vi is the most exciting thing that happens in a day filled with the monotony of slow, underwhelming stability exercises. Well, and knights.

But she doesn't argue. "I guess that's true" is all she says.

Under the table her leg jiggles apprehensively.

"Am I making you nervous?" I say, and she shoots me a glare.

"What do you want?"

"I need your support for something."

"Fine, go team." She turns away and I nudge her elbow with mine.

"So, every year we do something, right? For students, after finals."

"I obviously know that." She types an ironically sunny caption under some pictures on the ASB blog. "I've been trying to think of something, I just—"

"Remember that game at MagiCon?" I cut in. "*Twelfth Knight*?"

She stops typing, so I guess I have her attention.

"I know it sounds dorky, but it's a fun game," I admit to her. "So I was thinking maybe we could set up some of the library's laptops and do a tournament or something. Shouldn't cost much—I already made a list of all the equipment I know we have." I pull the page out of my binder, sliding it across the table to her. In the very low light below the shelving by the lab tables, she can see I've actually put thought into this: projected costs and possible student organizations we can collaborate with. "Plus a small budget for snacks and drinks."

She looks down at my notes, her hands still poised and glowing above the laptop keyboard.

"The thing is, this game's really helped me a lot this year," I confess. "Primarily because it's a distraction, but also because it's really cool. Fun to watch. The graphics are amazing, too."

"I know." She doesn't sound sold.

"Plus we could show a movie after," I add, "since I assume not everyone will want to play. We could make a night of it, like a lock-in or something . . . I don't know. Depends what's in the budget." I stop, and she says nothing. "Are you listening?"

She's staring straight ahead, but then blinks. "Of course I'm listening."

"And?"

"And what? Like you said, depends what's in the budget."

"But you're on board?"

"What?"

"Okay, seriously, are you just—?"

"Does it matter?" she asks, and it's as blunt as it always is when Vi Reyes asks me anything, but there's . . . something else there. Normally she's combative and impatient, brusque and rushed, but now she seems seriously wary, like she thinks I'm trying to trick her.

"Yeah, it matters," I say, bewildered. "Your opinion matters. It's basically social suicide to admit I like this game," I point out, to which she rolls her eyes, "so it'd be cool to have an ally. Plus I'd probably screw it up on my own."

"It's not like it's rocket science." Her mouth twitches. "Or football."

"Hilaaaaaaarious. So, are you in?"

She looks at me, the heart shape of her face suddenly softer, nearer. It takes hold of me, hard, until the screen of her laptop goes black.

"Yeah, sure, why not," she says disinterestedly, clearing her throat. "Sounds fun, I guess."

"You guess? Don't hurt yourself with that enthusiasm."

"Is everyone supposed to automatically love the things you love, Orsino?" she sighs.

"I don't see why not. I've got good taste." This, after all, is the crux of my social gamble. It might be geeky, but not when I do it— even if my social qualifications *are* contingent on how fast I run.

She flashes me a skeptical glare.

"What? I do," I insist, and gamble again by angling toward her.

"Mm," she offers noncommittally, though she doesn't turn away.

"Anyway, I'm glad you're in." It feels like we're having two different conversations; one in words, one in movements, but we seem to agree in both. "You're the only one who matters. Not like Ryan will care."

She rolls her eyes. "No, he will not."

"So it's basically a done deal, then." I lean closer.

"Guess so." So does she.

"You'll like it. The game."

"If you say so."

"I usually play with someone," I add, close enough now to brush the tips of her fingers with mine. "I'm hoping I can convince him to do the tournament, too."

"You—what?" She looks startled. Maybe it's the idea that I really do spend my time playing a computer game, which I admit is an unlikely revelation.

"Yeah, it's a long story, but—"

All of a sudden the overhead lights flick on, fluorescence buzzing to life. Immediately, it becomes apparent not just how dark the room was, but also how close together we're sitting; below the lab table my foot is resting on her stool, and her leg is crossed toward mine.

"What are you two doing in the dark?" Kayla asks, frowning with her hand on the light switch. Vi and I instantly shift apart, Vi jamming the laptop's keyboard awake while I fumble to return my budget page to my notebook.

"Nothing," we say in unison.

Then I sneak a glance at her. She catches my eye and turns quickly away. Is it guilt? Maybe.

Or maybe it's something else.

"Whatever," Kayla informs us ambivalently, flipping her hair over her shoulder before she struts away.

DUAL-WORLD GAMEPLAY

𝔙i

DUKEORSINO12: okay so don't be mad but I signed you up for the asb tournament
DUKEORSINO12: I know for a fact you're free that day
DUKEORSINO12: and listen, I get that you're Secretive about all this, but like . . .
DUKEORSINO12: can I be honest?
DUKEORSINO12: I kind of need this
DUKEORSINO12: okay no, I REALLY need this
DUKEORSINO12: I know that's lame but look, it's been a tough year
DUKEORSINO12: I just really need a win, you know?
DUKEORSINO12: and it won't be the same if you're not there, so . . .
DUKEORSINO12: please?

Oh *great*. Because I can definitely say no to that.

"I told you to come clean" is Bash's annoying but predictable first response. He's not actively angry at me, probably because without me he'd have no method of getting to school, but in the realm of fraternal fealty, my debts are seriously racking up. (Luckily I've been solidly in the lead for about seventeen years—I'm coasting on a lifetime's worth of responsible behavior and free rides.) "Didn't I say this would all come around and bite you eventually?"

"*Helpful*, Sebastian, thank you—"

"Tell him now," Bash urges me. "Just tell him that you're the real Cesario, and that you were only—"

"Only what? Only lying to him this whole time?" I flop backward onto my bed, groaning. "I shouldn't have agreed to this tournament. And I never should have agreed to do the quest with him. And—"

"Uh, okay, stop," Bash says, kicking at my ankles until I kick him swiftly back. "*Ouch*, Viola—"

"I should just change my mind and say no, right? I'll just say no." You'd think I'd have figured out a solution before now, given that Jack told me (Vi, girl, apparent idiot) in advance of asking Cesario (boy, virtual knight guru, also me). By the time he informed me that he'd already signed me up, though, it was a little too late to share what I actually think, which is: OH GOD NO, PLEASE DON'T.

"If you change your mind, he'll just try to persuade the person he thinks is the real Cesario, which is *me*," Bash reminds me, as if any part of this has somehow escaped my notice. "And if he's as persistent as you say he is—"

"He is." Newly so, which is probably my fault. Would the old Jack Orsino have thought to put together a *budget*? Or an *itemized list* of the school's available equipment? I should have just been satisfied with doing everyone's jobs for them. It was a simpler time when I could look around at all the incompetence and decide for myself how things should be done. "You're right, he'd probably try to persuade you in person." As DukeOrsino12, he's already all but begged. Something about wanting to move forward with things outside of football, which, damn it, is *also* my fault. (Could I kindly just shut up?!)

"So," Bash says, "your options are to come clean—"

"Or. *Or.*" I sit upright so abruptly I knock into Bash's shoulder. "Or . . . ?"

"There's no *or*," Bash corrects me. "I didn't mean to phrase it like there would be multiple options. There's *one* option, and it's—"

"You." Suddenly, it's obvious. "I'll just teach you to play the game like you're me."

"What?" Bash squawks, but oh my god, *of course*.

"You can play for me in the tournament!" I can't believe I didn't think of it sooner. "Jack and I will be almost done with the quest by then anyway, so—"

But Bash's eyes are bulging out of his face with disbelief. Or something way weirder.

"MOM," he shouts, rising to his feet and bursting from my bedroom.

"Hey! *Bash*—" That little dick. I wind up chasing him down the stairs, both of us descending to the bottom with a clatter. "I swear to god, if you make a big thing of this—"

Bash comes to a sudden halt, leaving me to crash into his back. I nearly trip over the hallway sideboard, smacking my shin into its wooden leg and letting out a stream of thoughtless curses.

"Oh," says Bash. "Sorry."

"You'd better be sorry," I growl, since I can feel a bruise the size of Pluto forming on my leg. "Have you lost your mind? You can't just go running to Mommy every time you . . ."

But then I trail off, because Bash isn't talking to me. Or to Mom.

"Hey, kids," says Pastor Ike, half smiling. "Something wrong?"

When I first met Pastor Ike, I thought, okay. All right, fine, so I see the appeal. He's not my mom's usual type—i.e., handsome the way television detectives are handsome—but I can see why an unspecified person would like him. He's got a boyish look to him, a slight slouch and the appearance of someone whose hands touch musical instruments all day, plus a tendency to give a sheepish laugh and a thoughtful pause before he answers most questions. He's got that dirty blond, gray mixing-in, thoughtlessly half-styled hair that makes him seem approachable and blithely distracted, and obviously I hate him.

Okay, I don't hate him. I hate the *idea* of him, though, for obvious reasons. For one thing, he's currently sitting at the dining table we never use in the chair across from me that nobody ever sits in, totally oblivious to the fact that hosting outsiders for dinner is not something we do in general. (All three of us are somewhere on a spectrum of "unfit for company," with any attempts at matching silverware or polite niceties hopeless before they've begun.)

Also, my mom is much more cheerful these days and it's incredibly annoying. Not because I want her to be miserable, obviously.

It's just fundamentally weird that whoever she is because of Pastor Ike—okay, *Isaac*—is someone, um—

"Vi, how's the pasta? It's her favorite," Mom chatters in the same breath, leaning over to Pastor Ike. He gives me a polite smile and then turns a much fonder one to my mom, who is once again babbling.

This would be very cute, obviously, if my mom were the kind of woman who habitually got nervous. But *my* mother is an ice-cold feminist who thinks most people are stupid and all men are useless. She's a barely adequate cook and this pasta is essentially baked macaroni and cheese, which Bash and I have at least once a week because Mom has deadlines and can't slave away inventing new stuff all the time. If having Pastor Ike around means that suddenly our household is beholden to the opinions of a man (Bash doesn't count), then I don't think I want it.

"It's great. I can practically taste the centuries of unpaid domestic labor," I say, and my mom barks a laugh that says she's deeply uncomfortable. Pastor Ike gives me a funny look.

"So, anyway," Bash announces, "Vi and I are having an ethical dilemma."

"No we're not," I say at once, because even if this *were* open to discussion with someone liable to weaponize psalms, we already have Lola. "Don't mind him," I tell Pastor Ike. "He's deeply imaginative. Borderline delusional."

"What's going on?" my mom asks, meticulously arranging a forkful of pasta.

"Nothing," I say at the same time Bash says, "Vi's a con artist."

"I am not a *con artist*—"

"True, you're not actually very successful—"

"Does this mean you're going to tell us why you've been staying up half the night every night?" my mom asks, finally dropping her chipper housewife energy and giving me a look that's pure *I have a master's in journalism, Viola, don't try me.* "Don't think that just because I haven't said anything means I haven't noticed."

I bristle, because once again, I do not need Pastor Ike to gang up on me along with my mother and brother. "What happened to being trusted to make my own choices?" I demand. "Practicing for an independent adulthood?"

"That's why I'm not interfering. But I'd like to think that trusting your choices means you'd consider making some healthy ones." My mom shoots me a warning glance.

"It's really nothing," I tell her irritably. "I'm just . . . I need Bash's help with something and he doesn't want to."

"Help with what?" Mom asks.

"Nothing," I say when Bash says, "Criminal conspiracy."

"It's not *conspiracy*—"

"At very least I'm an appendage," he insists over my loud groan.

"I think you mean *accomplice*—"

"So you admit it!" he trumpets.

"*Ahem,*" my mom interrupts loudly, at which point we all simultaneously notice that Pastor Ike has his head bent, obscuring a laugh. "Is something funny?" she asks him, sounding . . . Well. Sounding very brisk and Mom-like.

He coughs. "Yes. Sorry. A bit."

I'd love to continue being annoyed with him, but he looks properly chagrined, like he really had hoped not to be noticed.

"Please," my mother grunts. "Enlighten us."

"It's just very charming," Pastor Ike says. "How well you all know each other."

"We live together," I point out. Mom gives me a look like *Tone, please.*

"Well, that doesn't necessarily mean anything," says Pastor Ike. "I meet with plenty of families who sit through dinner without speaking. It's just very clear that you like each other very much, I suppose."

"Vi called me an imbecilic clown this morning," Bash volunteers.

"It's true," I confirm. "I did and he is."

"By choice," Bash insists.

"You're both clowns," says my mother.

Pastor Ike smiles again.

"Stop it," we say to him in unison.

"See? Cute." He shrugs, and my mom backhands his arm.

"Don't call us *cute*—"

"We're not cute," I agree.

"Aesthetically it's more of a fond antagonism," contributes Bash.

"Mm," says Pastor Ike. "Well, in that case, my apologies."

"Do you have any advice for my sinful children?" asks my mom. "Professionally speaking. As a man of the cloth."

"Try not to quote a dead white man," I add. My mom kicks me under the table. *"What?"*

"Well," Pastor Ike says, wiping his mouth on his napkin and leaning back in his chair. "Honesty is usually the best policy—"

"Ha," says Bash, brandishing a fork at me.

"—but," Pastor Ike continues, "as a society, there is a definite anthropological value assigned to lies. Particularly to avoid pain or insult."

"Ha-*ha*," I inform Bash, adding to Pastor Ike, "Now tell him that loving thy sister involves occasionally doing her one tiny favor."

"To avoid pain or insult?" Pastor Ike guesses mildly.

"Sure, why not." I lift another bite of pasta to my mouth while across the table, my mom's brow furrows.

"Well, ultimately you have no control over anyone but yourself," Pastor Ike says. "And as a personal doctrine, I tend to believe that you get in this life what you give."

"You reap what you sow? Very biblical," I point out.

"It's fairly ancient wisdom," Pastor Ike counters. "I don't think you always get it back right away. Sometimes it takes a long time, a lifetime, to get back what you give to others. In the best case that is love." He glances at my mom and looks quickly, guiltily, away. "In other cases it is decency, friendship, kindness—"

"Then how do you explain what happened to Jesus?" I ask. (My mom kicks me again.)

"He's an anomaly," says Pastor Ike.

"So you're saying this is a matter of karma?"

"Karma is much more complex than that." Pastor Ike takes a sip of water, then returns his attention to me. "But ideologically, the concept is there. Nature shows a reliance on balance. For every action, an equal and opposite reaction."

"What if not everything is just good or bad, decent or indecent, kind or unkind?" I counter. "Ultimately what I want Bash to do is for someone else's benefit, not mine."

"Nothing is black and white," acknowledges Pastor Ike slowly.

"Not even good and evil?"

"No. Most of religion's flaws are rooted in a false dichotomy."

"Isn't that blasphemous?"

"Is it?" he replies. "Does faith have to be blind?"

"As far as I can tell, institutional religion strongly suggests yes."

"Institutional religion is not faith. We are equipped with consciences, but also free will. We make choices. It's not unlike your mother," he says, "teaching you right from wrong, but then leaving you to decide what bedtime is appropriate."

"Don't drag me into this," my mother says instantly.

"So, is every choice purely good or purely evil? No," continues Pastor Ike. "In complex situations there will be pain in goodness, kindness in selfishness."

"Okay." I set down my fork. "So what's your call, then? Should Bash help me even though it involves a lie that will spare someone else's pain?"

"Sounds like a question for Bash's free will," says Pastor Ike.

"Boooooooo," announces Bash, who's been unusually quiet.

"Well. Whatever you two are up to, it had better not be anything illegal," my mom says. "If either of you get arrested, you'll have to call Lola and deal with her wrath. That's the deal."

"Very effective," Bash says hastily.

"I look forward to meeting your grandmother," Pastor Ike remarks, adding to me, "Any advice?"

I shrug. "Don't ask me. Bash is the nice one."

"No. Vi's Lola's favorite," Bash says with a vigorous shake of his head.

"Lola loves you both equally," Mom chides us.

"She yells at me more," I retort, to which Bash shrugs, because nobody ever yells at him. He's too naturally delightful. "And she bugs me to smile. And consistently asks about boyfriends I don't have. But you're, like, a human man that my mom's actually dating,"

I point out to Pastor Ike, "so that's already a step in the right direction. Just praise her cooking and you're golden."

I don't realize I've given Pastor Ike an honest answer until after I notice him exchanging a look with my mom. The look, whatever it's intended to mean, is kind of tender. It's like an entire conversation passes between them in less than a blink. Like a heartbeat of symmetry.

You'd think it might make me feel lonely to know that someone understands something sacred about my mother, but I don't. I feel profoundly *un*-empty. Satiated, I guess. Full.

Later, Bash sneaks into my room like we're still five years old and failing at falling asleep.

"I'll help you," he says, getting under the covers while shoving me over to make room. "But only because you were nice to Pastor Ike."

"Aha!" I shout-whisper triumphantly, "I *knew* you called him that, too—"

"But you have to promise me it ends here," Bash adds. "As soon as this tournament is over, you have to stop."

"First of all, I'm nice to people when I want to be nice," I say.

"Yes, I'm familiar. You're like a terrible house cat."

"And secondly, I know." I sigh. "I really do mean it, Bash. Just this one thing and then I promise, I'll tell Jack the truth."

"The *whole* truth?" Bash asks, arching a brow.

"What's that supposed to mean? Yes, I'll tell him that I'm Cesario and you're just my useless pawn."

"Not that." He tugs my hair. "The other thing."

"What, about Olivia?"

"*No.*"

"Okay good, because duh, he already knows—"

He looks at me for a second like he wants to say more, but then doesn't.

"What else is there?" I demand.

"You're impossible," Bash mutters unhelpfully, and steals my pillow. "And why's your bed comfier than mine?"

"Probably because I actually wash my sheets."

"Be quiet, I'm sleeping."

I roll my eyes and then close them, exhausted. It was a long day, not only because I've been roped into Jack's tournament project, but also because we were in the Red Lands today on the latest leg of the quest. This realm partially inspired my ConQuest idea: there *is* a fairy market and it's *extremely* cool, regardless of what the rest of my dumb former group thinks. You have to find the portal and enter a realm filled with tricksy fae magic. After that is Lyonesse, a sea voyage over an ocean of monsters. Every realm gets cooler and more challenging, more exciting, and Jack is more and more intuitive as the days go by. Yesterday, we were attacked by yet another person trying to steal one of our relics (Tristan's Fail-Not Bow this time, which we'll need in order to kill the questing beast in Brittany) and Jack didn't even have to ask what I wanted him to do. And not in the usual obnoxious way, like he no longer thinks he needs any help or that he's god's gift to gaming, but because he's actually thinking about what I need.

People don't really think about me. I'm not complaining—it's just a fact. I'm used to being the one responsible for what comes next, what needs to be done, and it's not very often that people bother taking things off my plate. When I want things, I need to ask for them, which I do, and sure, not always all that nicely, because I know that most people are busy thinking about themselves. Only one person has ever changed their behavior without me having to force them to do it, and to my surprise, it was the duke himself: Jack Orsino.

So this thing he wants, this tournament? I can't explain it, but I can't not give it to him.

"Just tell him you like him," Bash murmurs to me.

Maturely, I pretend to be asleep.

Jack

"Orsino." Dad's in Coach mode, jaw hinging rapidly around the usual Big Red. "Think you can work with Andrews?"

"Sure." I rise to my feet, testing a light jog over to the sideline while the defense takes the field. Andrews is pacing, apprehensive.

He dropped the last two passes in practice and now he's in his head. "Catch," I tell him, throwing a languid spiral.

The ball hits his palms easily, like it was made to rest there. Nothing about this is meant to be strenuous; it's just a reminder that not everything has the stakes of a fourth down with one minute to go. Sometimes, the best way to build someone back up is to remind them it's a game.

I test my knee, feeling the usual urge to take off until everything turns to dust behind me.

Yeah, just a game.

"Still feels weird on the field without you," Andrews comments, tossing the ball back.

I don't say anything at first. "You're having a hell of a season," I remind him eventually.

He shrugs. "So did you when you were my year."

This is true—I had a better year, statistically speaking—but the implication still stings. I'm proof that one good sophomore year does not a pro career make, which is a depressing reminder that even the quickest knees can take a hit. I'm probably saving his ego.

Can't say being a cautionary tale feels all that great.

He catches a few more. "I heard one of the other Illyria prospects is out. Suspended for partying or something."

"Mm." I can tell he thinks that's good for me; that even a player recovering from a major injury in their senior year is better than one who's sure to screw around in college. I feel differently. If Illyria is going to hold up their end of my signing, it doesn't matter who else disqualifies themselves from my position. I wanted—I *still* want—to be their choice because I'm the best. Even if that means asking them to gamble on how well I can build myself back up. Even if it means proving something about myself that I'm not entirely sure about.

"Heard from them?" Andrews asks.

No, actually. Not in a long time. "I'm sure they'll be in touch before the season's over."

"Oh, sweet. You'll be on the field by State, right?"

Eric says no. It'll be three more weeks of pure stability before I could do football-specific workouts. Mom says no because Eric says no. Dad says we'll see, I've always been special, I practically ran before I could walk.

Frank's watching me. Waiting for me to do something dumb, I'd guess.

"Yeah, probably." A lie, but a white one.

"Awesome. Wouldn't be the same without you."

I throw another spiral. "You'd be fine."

He grins. "Sure I would."

His next throw goes a little to the side, a little low. He's a receiver—his job is to catch the ball, meaning a certain lack of throwing proficiency is to be expected—so it's not a big deal, but it occurs to me I'd have to cut low and sideways to catch it. Instead I wave him away, letting the ball go out of bounds. "You're warm now. Go stretch."

"Aye aye, Captain." Andrews jogs away and I pick up the ball again, squinting a little. "Hey, Andrews? Put this away."

The ball soars and is caught, and I hear a faint but memorable ringing in my ears.

(*DUKE, DUKE, DUKE—*)

"Good thing you never wanted my position," says a voice behind me, and I turn to spot Curio approaching from where he's just been running drills with special teams.

"Nah. My arm's nothing special." Not compared to my legs, anyway.

"Doubt that." Curio sidles up next to me and we both turn to face the field. "Last game of the season, huh?"

"Yeah." The sun's going down over the far sideline, behind the hills, which is one of my favorite sights. I know it's weird, but I really do love the smell of turf; the plastic-y taste of the water from the Gatorade coolers. I love the energizing buzz of the stadium lights turning on, and the incredible, crisp solitude of hearing them shut off.

"You'll be back," Curio says. "It doesn't end here for you."

His voice sounds a little strange. "You okay?" I ask.

"Hm? Yeah, oh yeah." His mouth twists in a wistful smile. "Just gonna miss it, that's all."

"Could still play in college, right?"

"Not the same way. Not like this."

"But you got an offer, didn't you?" From a small school down south, but still.

"Yeah, but I know it's over."

"Hey, don't say that—"

"No, I'm not . . . I'm not being mopey or anything." Curio shrugs. "I don't have an arm to compete at that level. It just happens to be good enough for high school football, and I'm cool with that, honestly I am." He glances sideways at me. "I've been trying to figure out how to thank you."

"For what? Getting hurt?" I laugh, and he does, too.

"Yeah, that."

"My pleasure. Happy to fall on that sword for you."

"No seriously, seriously." He sobers a little. "Thanks for . . . I don't know. Showing me what it looks like to step up, I guess." He shrugs. "I had three seasons to watch you and Valentine, and I don't know, it just matters."

That means a lot, but there's no way to acknowledge that without making us both uncomfortable.

"You're right," I say. "You can't be a college quarterback. You're way too nice."

"Yeah, yeah." He rolls his eyes, knocking his shoulder pads against my arm. "Anyway, you're more than just your yardage, you know? Just thought someone should tell you that."

I open my mouth to say something—what that something will be, I have no idea—but then Coach is blowing the whistle, summoning everyone back to the field. Curio kicks off to jog over, but I catch his arm.

"Just enjoy it, okay?" I say in a low tone. "Every second. You guys are good enough to win State, but even if you don't . . . don't waste it."

What I mean is that you never know how many more seconds you get on that field before someone takes it all away from you. A torn meniscus or a Hail Mary that knocks you out in the last five seconds. A tornado or a flood. Nothing is guaranteed except for now, right now.

"Yeah. Thanks, man." Curio nods to me and I follow behind him to the team huddle, picking up speed. Eric would say no. Mom would say no. Frank's not looking.

I run and it feels . . .

Fine.

"Hands in!" shouts Coach, and nobody even noticed. Nobody saw me. No lightning bolts descended from the sky. No divine smitings. I'm completely unharmed.

I exhale, thinking for the first time: maybe it's worth it. Maybe right now is worth everything. Maybe it's worth more than next year or the next four years or a career.

Are you literally an idiot? asks a voice in my head that I'm 95 percent sure belongs to Vi Reyes, but I shake it off, joining the huddle for Coach's dismissal.

I wait for my dad to go to sleep before slipping outside again, shoes laced.

I just want to see what happens.

I stretch my calves carefully, meticulously. Stretch my quads, do my usual stability exercises, activate my glutes. I take a full twenty minutes to work on everything, warm it all up, my run playlist blaring in my headphones.

I turn and face the end of my street. It's a cool night—cold enough that I can see my breath—and the swish of my shorts feels insubstantial. Freeing.

The song cuts out briefly to a chime in my ears. A text message.

"From Viola Reyes," my chipper Siri says before announcing in her monotonous chanting, "Orsino-do-you-have-the-signed-permission-forms-yet-or-are-you-planning-to-wait-until-everyone's-already-graduated."

I roll my eyes, ignoring it.

The phone chimes again.

"Also from Viola Reyes," Siri chirps. "By-the-way-I'm-sorry."

Hm. Interesting.

"Also from Viola Reyes: Not-about-this-because-you-do-have-a-job."

Another eye roll. I bounce a little, back and forth on the balls of my feet.

"Also from Viola Reyes: I'm-just-sorry. About-a-lot-of-things."

That puzzles me. I exhale another foggy breath, then dig my phone out of my pocket. I'm about to text Vi back to ask what the hell she's talking about when I see a starred message on my phone: an email from Illyria.

Dear Jack,

Hope all is well! Congratulations to Messaline High and Coach Orsino on a perfect season. Best of luck at the East Bay finals next week!

Wanted to check in about your progress. Hoping that we can schedule a time to chat about your readiness on the field in advance of next season. I'm sure you've got a lot going on, but possibly sometime before the holidays? Hoping we'll get a chance to see you at State.

Wait. See me at State?

See me *play* at State?

I look out over the empty suburban street, a rush of adrenaline in my veins.

It's not cutting it *that* close. Besides, Eric's just being overly cautious. It's his job.

I could run. I *could*. If I just had good blockers . . .

Even one play could be enough to prove a miraculous recovery.

Dad would do it. He'd put me in.

If he could just *put me in*, I could—

I blink, the beat heavy in my ears.

My heart stutters and pounds.

"Come on," I whisper to whoever's listening. The universe, God, whoever.

And then, slowly at first, like something gradually catching flame, I take off down the street.

DUKEORSINO12: okay I know we're doing corbenic tonight but I really need help with something
DUKEORSINO12: I went for a run, right?
DUKEORSINO12: and it was fine
DUKEORSINO12: not just fine. great
DUKEORSINO12: I feel fucking great
DUKEORSINO12: I'm icing now
DUKEORSINO12: I'm not an idiot
DUKEORSINO12: but I might still have a shot with illyria
DUKEORSINO12: I might still play next year and like
DUKEORSINO12: this changes everything
DUKEORSINO12: EVERYTHING
DUKEORSINO12: if I can get in for even a minute during the postseason
DUKEORSINO12: I could have it all back
DUKEORSINO12: everything I lost, I could have it back and I just
DUKEORSINO12: I sound like a maniac I know but I just really need

I sit back in my chair, exhaling with my hands on my head.

What *do* I need? I'm not sure how to finish the sentence. Am I looking for someone to stop me? To encourage me? To validate me, set me straight, enable me, what? I already screwed this up once, so do I want someone to tell me no or tell me yes? I know who to go to for one or the other, but neither answer feels completely right.

What do I need?

Someone I trust. Right or wrong, yes or no. Someone who'll be honest with me, be real with me, whether it's what I want to hear or not.

And I know exactly who that is.

DUKEORSINO12: sorry hang on there's something I gotta do

Cesario says something back (uhhhh???) but it's too late, I'm already dialing.

"Hello?"

"Hi." I exhale, relieved beyond measure to hear her voice. "Can we . . . Can we go somewhere? Can I talk to you?"

Vi pauses a second.

Two seconds.

"Yeah," she says eventually. "Yeah, sure."

AND NOW FOR SOMEONE
COMPLETELY DIFFERENT

Vi

I sat there, frozen, while all of Jack's messages poured in. Elation over being able to run. I can't even imagine what that must feel like. Then pressure, frustration, fear. How am I supposed to help with this? Part of me thought okay, this is good. Perfect. He'll go back to football, the little blip with you will be easily forgotten, and it won't even matter that you lied. He won't have time for gaming or for ASB tournaments or for any of it. Maybe he won't even have to find out.

But then I hear his voice on the phone and it changes something. Maybe everything.

"Is the park on Main okay?" he asks. He sounds urgent. "I don't want you to get in trouble or anything. It's walkable."

Given the handful of things I have gathered about the world, walking alone this late at night seems like a dumb idea for both of us. Ugh, maybe Jack is dumb. Maybe I'm dumb. No, I'm definitely dumb. He hasn't even addressed the stupid apology text I compulsively sent him, which was about . . . nothing. But also everything. "I'll pick you up."

"You sure?"

"Don't test me, Orsino." I hang up and suffer some jitters, closing my laptop without even bothering to wonder if he'll say more to Cesario. At least for the time being, it's me he wants to talk to.

The real me.

I slip downstairs and into the car, starting it with the headlights off and pulling out into the street. The suburbs are so uncanny at night; the way lights flash over neat hedges and oversized sidewalks, glinting off custom mailboxes and manicured lawns.

I pull up to his house and flip off the headlights again, texting

him, and he immediately slips out the front door like he was waiting for me just inside. He shivers and pulls open the passenger side,
still in his running gear.

"Do you want to go somewhere specific?" I ask him.

He jiggles his knee. "I don't know."

"You're killing me."

"It doesn't matter, I just—" He fidgets, rubs his hand over his
head, stares at the road. Then he turns to look at me.

"I can run," he says, and I know him well enough to know there's
more, so I listen. "I *can* run, I know I can. Which means I could do
this—keep my spot at Illyria, make it work. Take things into my own
hands. Or I could do nothing and see if they'll miraculously want me
anyway." He scoffs, like he doesn't believe that's actually possible.
"But if it's just a choice between gambles, why shouldn't I pick the
one that wins big? No risk, no reward, right?" He slumps down in his
seat. "Which also means a big loss if I lose."

I nod. It's not like this is my choice to make, but—

"What do you think?" he asks me, and I blink.

"Who cares what I think?"

"I do. Obviously." He gives me an unnervingly long look.

"I'm not an expert on knee injuries," I remind him.

"So? I know plenty of experts and they're not helping."

"How are they not helping?"

He bounces his leg up and down again, then shakes his head.
"Come on," he says, throwing the door open. "Let's walk."

I step grudgingly out of the car. "Where are we going?"

"Nowhere, Viola. There's nowhere *to* go." He shoves his hands in
his pockets and glances at me. "You cold?"

"No." Kind of—my stupid brain notes that it's interesting, in
an ultimately dismissible way, that he's concerned about me in this
moment of severe personal crisis—but that's not important. "Okay,
so, I take it the experts say . . . ?"

"Four weeks until I can play."

I frown. "But you ran today anyway."

"Yes."

"Because you're . . . superhuman?"

"Maybe." He flashes me a glance that's pure Duke Orsino.

So, naturally, I pause to smack him in the arm. "Seriously?"

"What?" he says, and then sighs. "Fine, I know what."

"Yeah, you'd better. You really think your ability to regenerate exceeds basic anatomy?"

"So you think no, then." He continues down the sidewalk, brow furrowed in thought. "Is that your vote?"

"I didn't say that."

"But you think I'm being irresponsible."

I shrug. "What else is new?"

The expression on his face morphs from concentration to something else. "I kinda thought you'd cut me a little more slack," he says tonelessly. "You know. After everything."

"You oversaw *one dance,* Orsino," I sigh. "This is what the gods call hubris."

This time he stops, turning to face me when we reach the corner.

"Viola," he says.

"Jackary," I reply.

"You get that this is serious, right?"

"I mean, it's football. So, no, I don't."

"It's not just football, though. It's my life. And I know you're disparaging of the sports industry but honestly, it seems a little childish. We're talking millions here, billions."

He's rationalizing, so I rationalize right back. "I've always thought the economy was ridiculous. It's just fake. We don't even have a gold standard anymore. Paper money is worthless enough, and now what? Bitcoin? Please."

His eyes dance with the laugh he's too focused to give me.

"You're seriously off topic," he replies, suddenly breathless.

"Maybe what you really need is perspective."

He squares his shoulders, which has the effect (unintended?) of shifting him toward me. "Okay, then give me yours."

Oh sure, put this on me. I'm used to being the bad guy, but even so, these stakes are higher than I'm used to. (When did Jack Orsino's happiness become so important to me? A blistering thought, easily reduced to annoyance.)

"I'm not going to make up your mind for you," I reply testily, lifting my chin.

He's standing close, like he's been doing lately. He smells clean, a little salty.

I wait for him to argue. To push back, or to leave.

"I wish I had your certainty," he says.

Too close. Too much. My breath catches, and I'm in very real danger of doing something I'll regret, like reaching for his hand. Or being honest.

So I turn and keep walking.

"I'm opinionated, not certain," I correct him, crossing the street to get some distance from whoever I almost was for a second there. "I'm not sure of anything."

"So what's your plan, then?" His tone is bouncy, like he's amused.

"I don't have one. I don't need one. I know what I like, what I care about, what I'm good at, and that's enough. I'm allowed to want things, Jack. To change my mind. And," I add, whirling to face him, "don't make this into some kind of manic dream girl situation, okay? I'm not here to inspire your life choices with my generosity of spirit or whatever."

"I'd have to be crazy to dream up you," he replies without hesitation, facing me again.

He glances down. I look up. The effect of meeting in the middle undoes me, and I'm nearly positive he's looking at my lips. Or I'm looking at his.

Nope, nope, nope.

I turn and walk again, faster this time. "You know what your problem is?" I snap.

"Yes, Viola, now we're on to something!" Jack exhales, trailing me in a mockery of relief. "*Please* tell me what my problem is. I already know you know."

I turn away, annoyed. "If you're just going to be obnoxious about it—"

"No, I'm serious." He catches my elbow, rooting me in place.

We're in front of someone's house. I think I went here once, maybe in fourth grade, for a class pool party or something with someone I'm no longer friends with. God, I hate the suburbs. Or maybe I just hate feeling like this, like I'm teetering on the edge of something that could so easily be destroyed.

"I just think," I say, my voice more brittle than even I expect it to be, "that you don't know *what* you want, Jack, because there must be part of you that already knows the right choice, but for whatever reason, you don't like the answer. You say you want to move forward," I remind him, launching myself into the empty street to cross over to the park. "And you *say* you want to be more than just football, but the truth is you're afraid, aren't you? You're afraid to admit that you don't know who you are without it. And you know what's honestly *hilarious* about that?" I demand, whipping around to face him.

He's standing in the middle of the road with me, hands in his pockets, waiting.

"It took you getting hurt and almost losing everything for you to actually let someone *see* you," I tell him bitterly, my breath a thin fog in the night air as the truth—part of it—suddenly comes pouring out. "But whoever Duke Orsino was, whatever he becomes, whatever trophies he wins or championships he earns or whatever legacy he came from, he will never be to me what you are—"

"Which is?"

I stop, almost choking, before I go too far. "Nothing. Never mind. The point is—"

"What am I, Viola?" he presses me, taking a step closer.

I glance at my shoes, the manicured roundabout, the empty road. "I'm just saying, it's a complete waste of time," I mumble over the morbid grossness of my near-confession, "trying to gamble your entire life on your fear of starting over. What if you get hurt again, Jack? What if it's worse the next time? Is it really worth throwing away your mobility at seventeen?"

"Vi," he says. His eyes are soft, and I am wretched.

"You were more than that knee before you tore it, Jack, and you still are." I'm staring at something behind him, at nothing. The glint of a hubcap, I don't know. Anything but his face. "You're—you're more than just a collection of working or non-working parts, you're—"

"Vi."

"I just think," I say, and realize I'm sniffling; the air is cold, and given everything that's coming out of my mouth, I'm obviously violently ill. "I just think that it's your decision. And honestly, it's very rude of you to ask me to make your choices for you."

I turn away, furious or feverish or something else altogether, but he reaches out and touches my cheek, like he cares. "Yeah, true."

And maybe I want him to.

"You should do what feels right." My voice is softer than I planned. "You're smart enough to know the costs."

"Yeah." His fingers track the edge of my jaw, finding the back of my neck and toying with my ponytail until a sigh parts my lips.

"I can't tell you what to do, Jack." He leans in and my traitorous eyes fall shut. His cheek is warm against mine, reassuring.

"No, you can't," he says in my ear.

"Besides, I barely know you."

"Oh now, Viola." I can feel the motion of his throat when he swallows. "That's just not true."

I'm not sure how or when I reach for him. How my fingers become coiled in his sweatshirt, my forearms braced against his chest. Why I breathe when he breathes, almost like we practiced this. Like every contact until now was just a rehearsal for what we might one day do, for what we'd maybe feel. For how close we could one day get.

"This is stupid," I exhale. I'm not sure if I mean standing in the middle of the street or any of the other stupid circumstances.

"Yes," he says gravely. "Very."

"Did you know when you called me . . . ?"

"I had a feeling. A lot of feelings. Wasn't sure about yours, though."

"What are yours?"

He tilts my chin up; leans halfway down.

"Well," he says, his lips floating above mine. "You had me almost right, Viola. It's just that I'm not as afraid of starting over as you think I am."

"Funny." I swallow. "I'm a little petrified."

"You?" He shakes his head. "You're not scared of anything. Of anyone."

"You mean I'm not nice to anyone."

"You don't try to please anyone. There's a difference."

His nose brushes mine. My lips part, then snap shut.

"You're waiting," I observe aloud, noticing he hasn't moved. He's just standing there, frozen, me in his arms and half on his lips but not completely. Not quite.

He shrugs. "I don't think you're where I am yet."

"And where exactly is that?"

"Meet me halfway and find out."

I inhale sharply, the distance between us crackling like static. He doesn't know about Cesario. Doesn't know who he's really been talking to.

Just say it, Bash's voice tells me. *Just tell him before it's too late.*

"What are you going to do?" I ask, attempting to be rational. "About . . . your knee. About Illyria."

He shrugs. "Meditate on it."

"Seriously?"

"Nah. But it's my call, you're right." He tilts toward me, half swaying like the pull of a tide, then thinks better of it.

"You're not ready," he says, leaning away.

I nearly follow, pulled into his orbit.

"But I'll be here," he adds. "If and when you are. This isn't a one-time offer or anything."

"Gonna recruit someone else to try and see inside my head?" I joke, incensed by him, enraged by me.

"No. I know what's in your head. What I want is something else."

It bruises me. Cracks me open. *Jack, there's something I have to tell you—*

"Jack," I attempt, but he shakes his head. He untangles his fingers from my hair, his thumb stroking my shoulder before dropping to brush the knuckles of my hand, and the motion is so thoughtful, so fundamentally patient, it makes my chest ache.

"I appreciate you helping me," he says. "I think maybe you've already let me in more than you usually do, and that means something to me. But—" He touches the edge of my palm, then shrugs. "I don't want to push you into something you can't give me."

I don't know how to explain this, but I know he means me, the real me. Not me-Cesario or ASB-me. Not me on a good day, when I'm tamed or when I'm smiling. Not fractions of me.

He means all of me. Every version.

"Jack," I say desperately, "you know I'm like . . . a bitch, right?"

He snorts a little. "Sure, Vi, if that means you never give up. Never accept defeat. Never bend just because someone expects you to." His hand still dances near mine. "If that makes you a bitch, Vi, then fine, I hope you never change. In fact, I hope you change me. I like to think you already have."

That, more than anything, hits me like a blow.

"But look," he says, about to release me. "Let's just get out of the road, and then—"

I tighten my hand in his and tug him back.

He crashes into me, nearly stumbling. "Vi, are you—"

It's graceless, I know. I circle my arms around his neck and practically bruise his lips with mine—and the things I do, the motions I attempt, it's all a mess. For all I have to say about romance narratives or morality arcs, I don't actually know how to kiss someone, not like this. Not the way I want to kiss Jack Orsino, which happens to be with my entire self, my whole heart.

The laugh that escapes from his mouth to mine almost crushes me with sweetness. It's tender and sharp, authentic and free. He cradles the back of my head, relieved and amused and helplessly fond, and I feel it, emanating from him to me: joy.

"Just so you know," I say, pulling away for a second to scold him, "this doesn't mean that I—"

"Yes it does," he cuts me off, and kisses me again.

This time it's slow and honest, like he knows exactly what it means to kiss me and he's planning to do it right. He touches my cheeks, my jaw, my hair, the side of my neck, and it's only when headlights flash from afar that I jolt back to myself, up from oblivion and down to reality, tugging him to the sidewalk just in time to stumble out of the road.

I'm out of breath, choking out a gasp when Jack's laugh rips through the night.

"Come on." He bundles me under his arm. "I'll walk you back to your car."

"What? But—"

"We've got tomorrow. And the day after. And the day after." We trip our way forward and he kisses me between words, trying hopelessly to word between kisses.

"Jack, I should tell you . . ."

But the words die on my tongue. I can't do this to him.

I can't be the person who tells him none of this was real. Not now.

"I know," he says, and he doesn't. He couldn't possibly. There's no way he can feel the mix of things inside my chest, ugly and garish and bright. But then he opens my car door, jokingly straps my seat belt for me, and draws into the moisture of my window: I LIKE YOU VI REYES.

I know it'll be there in the morning, and for as long as I never wipe it clean. For as long as I never screw it up—which of course I will eventually.

Because I'm going to tell him. I have to tell him.

But not before he kisses me through the window one last time, and I think *Okay, Mom.*

Okay, so maybe you were just a tiny bit right.

Jack

"Oh shit, I'm dead," says Curio, frowning as his knight (which I have already cleverly told him *not* to name after himself) gets stabbed in the chest by a mage staff. "Damn, that looks brutal."

"I told you," I sigh, "if you just use the mouse to turn—"

"You didn't tell me shit, Orsino—"

I look up and spot Vi watching me from where she's sitting at her usual lab table. I wink, and she groans silently from afar, though I catch a trace of a smile on her lips.

"I'm shocked this isn't banned on school computers," Curio says mundanely, unaware that the entire universe has shifted since I kissed Vi Reyes two nights ago. "So we can't get on Twitter, but computer games are no problem?"

"It's educational," I say. "Practically intro to computer science."

"You do know that we *have* an intro to computer science class, right?"

"Oh shit, we do?" Damn, probably worth paying attention to our elective options. "Whatever, it's not rocket science, Curio."

"Maybe not for you." He kicks out his legs, turning to face me. "Not really what I had in mind, by the way."

"Well, you said you wanted to be out of the quad." He caught me as I was on my way into the leadership room with a mock-up of our tournament posters. "Besides," I add, pointing to where Curio's avatar winds up right back in Camelot, "I can't have you embarrassing me like this during the tournament."

"I am definitely going to embarrass myself," Curio assures me, "but I guess if it's for a good cause."

"My ego? Definitely."

He laughs. "I'm just glad to see you relax a little bit. I take it you've worked something out with Illyria?"

I'm aware from afar that Vi's feverishly clackety presence on the laptop has paused.

"Honestly? Probably not." I force a cheerful tone, which isn't quite as hard as I expected. "I guess we'll see what they get back to me with."

"What'd you tell them?"

"The truth." I try to make it sound easy, although it wasn't. My reply was essentially that while my rehab is going well, it's also going slowly, and I don't think I'll be ready to play for any portion of the postseason. I attached a letter from Eric and Dr. Barnes about the likelihood that I'd be back to playing strength within eighteen months and added that if that was too long for them, well, I understood and wished them luck.

Illyria is my dream school, I said. *Nothing about that has changed, but I've learned I can't make promises about things I can't control. I will be sticking to the training plan assigned to me by my doctors and I will continue to treat my physical therapy regimen with the same dedication and effort I gave my four seasons of Messaline Varsity. I can promise that if Jack Orsino is the player you want, I will still be him in every way that matters come the fall. But if you prefer to judge me by the health of my knee or by the risks I'm willing to take, I understand if you choose to go a different direction.*

I guess you could say I gave them an out. One I'm hoping they won't take, obviously. But the possibility doesn't seem as terrifying as it did before.

"Huh," says Curio. Not rudely, just thoughtfully. "Well, I'm here for you. If you need it."

"Eh, I might." My dad took it with silence. My brother was a little bit angrier. He demanded to know what I was thinking, adding that in college there was real money on the line, real stakes, and it wasn't about being a Boy Scout. I figure that has something to do with him being knocked out of contention for the NCAA playoffs and left off the final list of Heisman candidates, but it still hurts a little. More than I thought it would.

Nick's supportive, though he's finally gotten the hang of college and isn't available as much. He's busy studying for finals and trying to get into the architecture program, which as far as I can tell is a real drain on his time. He spends more hours in the design lab than he ever used to spend on the field—which is maybe a good thing, since he says it doesn't feel exhausting. It just feels exciting and new.

As for Vi . . . I'm giving her a breather. No point making her life revolve around mine; I learned that lesson from Olivia. Instead I'm waiting to see if she'll tell me what *she* wants from this, if anything. After we kissed, I texted her that the ball was in her court, and she didn't answer. Well, she said this: *a sports metaphor, really?*

Since then we've been sort of orbiting each other. I think she's making excuses to be near me, but I also want to see what happens when she's ready to do it on purpose. When she's ready to tell me something real, I'll be here.

Until then, let's just say I've learned a lot about patience this year.

"Wanna play again?" I ask Curio.

"I think I've taken enough of a beating for now. Let's see you play." He rises from the desk, swapping places with me, and I sign in. "You said Valentine got you hooked on this?"

"Apparently it's, like, *the* thing to do when you're injured."

"I'll keep that in mind." Curio drums his fingers on the seat. "Hey, just so you know, I'm not like . . . I don't really approve of Volio or anything."

"Hm?" I'm barely paying attention.

"Volio, with Olivia, I'm not . . . Oh shit, that's you? You've got hella jewels."

"Relics," I correct him. "And look, Volio's got his own problems." If I've learned anything about Olivia, it's that she's not a damsel who needs rescuing. I don't know what befriending Vi Reyes did to her, but I don't think she'll have any trouble shutting him down.

"Sure, but I'm just . . . Whoa," Curio says, leaning forward. "And you've only been playing for, like, a few months?"

"Oh, here and there," I lie, as if I haven't been sacrificing the majority of my sleep to the Camelot Quest. We're almost done with it—only two realms are left, including our current crusade for the Holy Grail, which I was surprised to learn wasn't the final relic in the game *or* the solution to the mystery of the so-called Black Knight. I asked Cesario if he knew anything about how to actually beat the game but he said no, it's apparently a huge secret. So who knows what happens after we make it to Avalon.

"Who do you play with?" Curio asks.

"Hm?"

"I mean, do you play alone, or . . . ?"

"Oh." Hm, how to explain this. "I've got a partner, sort of."

"Someone you know?"

I notice that Vi is listening again, which makes me want to laugh. For all that she pretends she doesn't care . . .

"Hey, sorry, I actually just remembered I've got to finish something for Bowen," I tell Curio, shutting the laptop. "Mind if we do this another time?"

"Oh yeah, sure. I should get going anyway." Curio slings his backpack over one shoulder, then offers me a salute. "See you at practice?"

"You know it."

When he's gone I meander over to Vi, who pointedly keeps her eyes fixed on the screen of her laptop.

"Busy?" I ask, pausing behind her lab stool. If she leaned back even a fraction of an inch her spine would meet my chest, so to make sure she knows it, I rest my arms on either side of hers, pretending to linger there casually.

"Obviously," she says.

"What's this? English paper?"

"Mm."

"Looks finished to me."

"Well," she begins snottily, "obviously to the untrained eye—"

I lean closer for further pretend inspection, my chin brushing the line of her shoulder, and she inhales so sharply I think she scares herself.

"Nervous?" I ask in her ear, and she elbows me.

"All this just to get out of admitting your secret gaming life?" she grumbles when I double over, ironically forcing me to curl around her so she's more securely in my arms.

"Nope. Just figured it had been a while since I last antagonized you."

"What happened to the ball being in my end zone?"

"Court, but you know that. You're being difficult on purpose."

"Nah, it just comes naturally."

I wonder if she feels the way she gives in to me, vertebra by vertebra, breath by breath. It's like she's calculating each degree she relaxes against me, slowly, and I relish it.

Temporarily. Then I step away and she catches herself. "Dickhead," she mutters.

"As a reminder," I point out, "you could have me if you wanted."

She lifts a brow. "Aren't there some kind of Neanderthal sportzboi rules about admitting things like that?"

"Probably." I tip her chin up and mirror the face she makes, a little scrunched-up look of irritation. "Cute."

"Don't you have work to do?" she sighs.

"Yes." I lean forward like I'm going to kiss her, then stop, waiting for the telltale stutter of her breath that says she wants me to. "See you later," I say, releasing her in the same motion as I step away, pivoting to grab my bag and returning the borrowed laptop to its charging port.

"Dickhead," she calls after me again, and I hide a smile.

DUKEORSINO12: everything good with you?
C354R10: it'd be better if we had the friggin grail

The Grail is allegedly somewhere inside this massive castle, for which I thought the Ring of Dispell relic Cesario used before would be helpful. It isn't, because of course that would be too easy. There's a bunch of magical traps lying around, for which our only source of light is the Corbenic Sword with a glowing red hilt; a relic of this realm that we had to win off a particularly nasty sorcerer.

This is not why I asked how Cesario was doing, of course, though I feel weird about bringing up things I notice in real life. I caught Bash and Vi Reyes arguing in the parking lot from inside their car; I don't know what it is, but I'm much more attuned to whatever Vi is doing these days. It's like my brain zeroes in on her if I so much as catch her profile out of the corner of my eye.

DUKEORSINO12: I'm serious
C354R10: I'm seriously fine
C354R10: a little pissed about this week's WoT but fine

It's the second-to-last episode before the season finale, which is supposed to be epic. Nick's going to be home for winter break by then, so he asked me if I wanted to come over and watch it at his house. I haven't decided if I'm going to go; I want to, but I also kind of want to watch it with Vi. I haven't brought it up to her yet, but I have a feeling she doesn't want to be at Antonia's house.

> **DUKEORSINO12:** still mad the writers sent cesario on that random side quest?
> **C354R10:** pissed about liliana this time actually
> **C354R10:** sucks whenever they take the only interesting female character and make her ~eViL~
> **C354R10:** you know what I mean
> **C354R10:** they made her suffer for so long and now I bet they're going to kill her off for rodrigo's story
> **C354R10:** or maybe even cesario's
> **DUKEORSINO12:** no way, they can't just kill her off
> **DUKEORSINO12:** she's way too important
> **C354R10:** yeah well writers always think killing off a female character is "new" and "edgy"
> **C354R10:** since that way she never actually becomes anything
> **DUKEORSINO12:** you have a lot of feelings on this
> **C354R10:** I have a normal amount of feelings on this
> **C354R10:** it's bad storytelling
> **DUKEORSINO12:** it hasn't happened yet!
> **C354R10:** k but it will
> **C354R10:** just watch
> **DUKEORSINO12:** if it does vi is going to lose her shit
> **C354R10:** for sure

The thought of it, Vi getting angry at something that isn't me for once, nearly makes me smile. I dig out my phone and text her: *what do you think about watching the WoT finale with me?*

It'll be the weekend after the tournament. Which is the week after State. So I guess by then, I'll know whether or not Illyria is planning to cut me loose.

Before I can think about it too much, her answer comes in: *k*

A woman of many words. I roll my eyes, adding, *nick asked me if we wanted to watch at his house but I'm guessing . . . no?*

She answers just as succinctly: *no*
are you ever going to tell me what happened with you and antonia?
She types for a second.
it was my fault
I don't believe that, I reply.
I'm not actually that great of a person, Orsino, she says.

again, doubtful, I tell her, because as mean as she wants to think
she is, I don't believe she's capable of hurting anyone. I've already
seen her in action—she's impatient, she's prickly, she's rude, but she's
never cruel. I'm about to remind her that I actually *do* know her, but
then my computer screen flashes, a red invading the dull tones of
shadowy blacks, and I look up, startled.

C354R10: uh, hello?? quest??

"Shit," I say aloud, realizing it's an ambush; not combat, from
another player, but an environmental challenge from a non-player
character, built into the quest. The *game* is attacking us, which, on
the plus side, must mean we're getting close to the Grail.

It's a sorcerer, someone who looks very much like a jacked and
possibly possessed Merlin. Are we supposed to kill him? Not if he
knows something.

DUKEORSINO12: don't we have a relic for this?
DUKEORSINO12: something that can get him to talk

It hits me that the Ring of Dispell would probably work at the
exact moment Cesario decides to use it. The shroud of sorcery lifts,
and then, like a bolt of lightning, the sorcerer's appearance changes;
the game shifts to tell us he's been freed from a curse. Would we
like to ask him anything?

Uh, hello? Yes.

where is the Holy Grail? I type in.

The sorcerer steps aside, revealing a stone passageway we might
never have found.

C354R10: well, check you out orsino

C354R10: you're not nearly as useless as you look

It's funny, but I almost hear it in Vi's voice. I guess she's just on my mind, though right now I'm focused on getting the hell out of this castle.

EVERYTHING TRYING TO KILL YOU

Jack

Everyone's abuzz at school leading up to State. It's been promised to us since I was a freshman—*Jack Orsino is the best running back in the state, mark our words, Messaline High is the team to beat*, every single year for the last four years—and now, finally, it's here. It's hard at first, knowing how little I can really make an impact on the outcome of this game, but I do manage to put my ego aside, helping my dad run drills with the team and prepping Curio for the biggest game of his life.

"I don't see how this is helping," he says over the shouts of a diss track I'm playing on the speakers.

"Crowd's going to be huge," I yell back. "Might as well get used to not being able to concentrate."

"Are you helping me or torturing me?"

"Both," I assure him, as he shakes his head and goes long to connect with Andrews.

It's the first time I can't really lose myself in *Twelfth Knight*, or in wooing Vi. Helpfully, though, Vi isn't the kind of person who needs wooing.

"Coming to the game on Saturday?" I ask her while we sort through projector cables, vaguely wondering if her answer will disappoint me.

"Ha," she says, which does disappoint me, a little. But I always knew Vi wasn't the cheerleader Olivia is, and it still doesn't really change anything. Certainly not the way she makes me feel, or the time I'm willing to wait.

I also get an email back from Illyria, because of course when it rains it pours. The offensive coach, Williams, doesn't say much aside from telling me he'd like to chat in person at State. It's NorCal's year to host the state championships, so we'll be playing for the title at Illyria's stadium. I wonder if he's going to try to talk me out of something, or into something. I'm getting more comfortable with my decision, though—a little more so every day.

Illyria's stands are packed with people, the energy in the air humming like stadium lights. I'm absolutely freezing and it's awesome.

"Orsino!" Dad shouts, and yep, he's Coach again, only I'm happy to be part of the team in whatever way I can today. I expect him to ask me to keep Curio's arm warm, or play catch with the receivers or something before the game starts, but instead he waves someone in my direction.

Ah. So we're doing this now, I guess.

"Coach Williams," I say, greeting the Illyrian offensive coordinator with a deferential hand extended.

"Mr. Orsino," he replies. "How's that knee?"

Starting right off with a loaded question. "Coming along, sir. Ready to dig into my run regimen next week."

He nods. "Feeling good?"

"Feeling really good." I've been itching for it. "I'm ready."

"Are you planning to stick with the same PT in the spring?"

I nod. "I believe so. My orthopedist has a lot of football-specific plans, so—"

"Otherwise, you're welcome to transition to an Illyrian training plan," Williams cuts in, which surprises me.

"Sorry, I . . . am?"

"Well, we like to think we have the best," Williams jokes. "Here at our humble multi-million-dollar training facility."

"Oh, that's—" This is confusing, right? "Thank you, I just . . . I didn't think—"

"Jack, there's a place waiting for you at Illyria," Williams says, looking surprised by my hesitation. "Were you not aware?"

"I . . . well, no, not really—"

"We respect your honesty and dedication to your training, Jack. Not every high school student is able to advocate so well for their long-term needs."

I frown. "But if I do take the full eighteen months of recovery—"

"Redshirt your freshman season," Williams says simply, meaning I can have academic standing, but not as an active player on the roster—a full year of college training with the team, but without putting my injured knee at risk. "Come back the following season ready to run for us, if that's still what you want."

It's a solution so neatly, unimaginably perfect that I can barely believe it exists. I mean, I knew redshirting existed in theory, but for him to offer it to me now, after all the torment of wondering—

"Yes, absolutely, yes," I blurt out, totally losing my chill for a second. "That's . . . that's an incredible offer, thank you—"

"Listen, a great player is more than a set of knees. We know you're going to do big things when the time is right, or we wouldn't have signed you," Williams says. "But anyway, I'll let you get back to the game. I'm sure you want to be there with your teammates."

I can still hardly believe it. "Thanks! I mean—" I clear my throat, aiming for professional or at the very least calm. "Thank you, I really do appreciate it—"

He nods to me, giving my dad a nod from afar, and slips away in time for me to catch Olivia's eye. Hard not to—she and the other cheerleaders have glitter all over them, like human disco balls, and she darts over to wave a shiny pom-pom in my face.

"That looked like good news," she says, practically vibrating. "You still in?"

"I'm still in." I could scream it, or sob it. "He said everything is fine. I can't believe it. It's, like, too easy."

"No way, Jack. None of this was ever easy for you." She smooshes the pom-pom into my face until I duck it, laughing. "Go, fight, win!" she bellows at me, and it's nice, seeing Olivia this happy. It's been a long time since I've seen her let loose.

"How are you doing?" I ask her. "Audition prep going well?"

"Oh, Bash Reyes is a total drill sergeant," she says with a roll of her eyes. "He had me rehearsing the same line in my monologue until, like, midnight. Oh, there he is!" she says, waving at the band section in the stands. "Speak of the devil."

"Midnight?" Weird. Cesario and I were both online at midnight last night. I'm not really sure how someone goes around battling mages while also rehearsing monologues . . . though, I guess I'm also not entirely sure what that entails.

"Yeah, well . . . Oh my god, look who's here! Vi—VIOLA," Olivia calls, both hands around her mouth like a megaphone, and I whip around in surprise.

There she is.

She looks ridiculous. She's bundled up in a woolen hat and a scarf and she's grimacing next to someone I assume is her mom, and then a man who's wearing a sweatshirt I've seen Andrews wear before—a youth group or something, so I take it that's Pastor Ike. Olivia waves wildly, and Vi makes a face, sort of half *oh my god stop* and half *ugh, fine* as she grudgingly waves back.

I lift a hand, and Vi's already pink cheeks redden.

So I wink, and she hurriedly turns away.

"You know what? I love this," comments Olivia when I turn back to her, a note of amusement in her voice. "You couldn't have picked someone more different from me, could you?"

Oops. "You're not mad, are you?" I ask cautiously.

"No, god no." She gives me a very Vi-like eye roll. "I think she makes way more sense."

"You think *Vi Reyes* and I make sense?"

Just then one of the other cheerleaders barks for Olivia, who turns with a sigh, giving Vi one last pom-pom wave and me another omniscient glance.

"What?" I demand.

"You know what." She jogs away backward. "Or-si-no, Or-si-no!" she chants, and for whatever reason—insanity, probably—the waiting crowd picks up my old cheer the way that only a crowd can.

"Duke, Duke, Duke, Duke—!"

I turn and lift a hand in the air as the cheer dissolves into shouts. My mom is screaming, because of course she is. I look over at my dad, who nods (he's in the zone), and then I focus my attention on the person in the audience I'm happiest to see.

She catches my eye, smiling faintly, and I think she's proud of me. I'm proud of me, too, and for a second of perfect freedom, I don't need the winning TD, I don't need the records, I don't need a ring or a trophy to prove to me exactly who I am. It's enough to be here, to take part; it's enough that she sees me. It means everything to have come this far.

I hope you change me—I like to think you already have. That's what I said to her.

What a relief to know that I was right.

The game is brutal from the first whistle. I know none of us wanted a start that ugly, but a fumbled punt return puts us at a disadvantage and Arden, an Orange County private school known for churning out celebrity quarterbacks, is a relentless opponent. The first half of the game is messy, and I would go so far as to say a mess. Curio's head is everywhere, Andrews drops multiple passes, Volio can't get more than a single yard before being pummeled by the Arden defense. We manage to hold them to a slim 10–0 lead, but morale filing into the locker room at halftime is bleak. Despite our perfect season, it's clear right away that we're suffering from underdog syndrome—nobody expects us to win, and the tide isn't in our favor.

I wait for my dad's usual Coach-isms. See it, make it happen. That kind of thing. *Visualize the game turning around, turn it yourself. Big outcomes take big moves.* But instead he stands up, tells everyone he's proud of them, that this is a long way to come, that life doesn't begin or end with a single football game. That sure, second place isn't what they wanted for the season, but the best thing they can do is leave it all on the field. No regrets.

Then he looks at me, and before I know it, words are falling out of my mouth.

"Actually," I say, "speaking as someone who *really* didn't get to have the season they wanted, I'd like to say a few words. If Coach doesn't mind."

I don't really know what comes over me until I'm already standing, but my dad waves me in like he figured I'd have something to say. Or maybe trusted that I did.

"Look, we've all seen the movies," I tell my team. "We know that sometimes the best team doesn't win, or the best-laid plans don't work out. I happen to know that one wrong move can tear open a knee that's perfectly healthy. We're all a little f-*messed up* like that," I correct myself quickly. "We're always walking some line between triumph and disaster. And you can play this in your minds over and over—what if I'd done this, should I have done that?—but in the end, it doesn't matter what you could have done. It matters what you do, and more importantly, it matters who you do it with."

I pause, a little worked up now. "This team did the unthinkable!" I remind them. "We pivoted our offense for a *perfect season*. Our defense is a well-oiled machine that's currently keeping this game from being a blowout. This isn't about who's the better team!" I add with a thump of my fist to my chest. "The team who wins is the team that has a good day, that's all. But we make our good days. We choose how we are remembered. A mistake does not define us. An injury does not define us. A loss *will not* define us, but how we make our fate? That does. It doesn't matter what kind of day Curio has, or Volio or Andrews or Aguecheek, it matters what day we make as a team, for each other. It matters how we choose to take the field. It matters what we see when we look at our possibilities. What we see determines what we are."

See it, make it happen. It doesn't apply to making your girlfriend love you again, but it sure as hell means something when it comes to yourself.

"The only thing you can control on that field is you," I tell them. "So don't give up on you."

I step down from the bench, a little winded, and Curio stands up.

"Messaline on three," he says, and I can see it already, the way his shoulders are a little squarer. *This is your last chance,* I think to him, strong enough that hopefully he can feel it. *This is your last dance.*

"One-two-three-MESSALINE!"

We break and jog back out, though Coach catches my arm.

"Jack," he says.

When I'm on the field, I'm just another member of the team. But this time, when he looks at me like I did something good, I don't need to be told. I understand.

"Thanks, Dad," I tell him. "Really. For everything."

"Yeah?"

"Yeah." I shrug, and then to lighten the mood, I offer in my smuggest voice, "Think I've got a future as a motivational speaker?"

He gives me the usual look of *Calm down, kid.*

"Get on the field with your team, Duke," he says.

"Yes, Coach," I say with my eat-shit grin, and make my way back to the bench.

Curio throws deep, then Andrews runs for almost sixty yards. Touchdown, 10–7.

Arden is held to a field goal. 13–7.

It stays like that, stagnant, until the final thirty seconds.

"You sure you don't want in?" my dad says. "One run play?"

I know he's just nervous. "They've got this, Coach."

Sure enough, Volio makes it through to the end zone after a clever call from Curio—a play almost identical to the one that tore my ACL. Thankfully, though, they're both unharmed.

13–13. Special teams wastes no time securing the critical extra point, and with one second remaining, the scoreboard flashes:

14–13. Messaline wins over Arden.

From then on, the whole stadium is one big stream of chaos. The band rushes the field. The rest of the school follows. Curio gets handed the State Champion trophy and he gestures me over, the two of us holding it up above the crowd.

The same chant starts up again, only this time, it comes from my team.

"Duke, Duke, Duke—!"

I look up to find Vi's eyes on mine, and in that moment, I make a decision. I'm gonna kiss her. Right now.

So I push through the crowd and I do.

𝔙i

"I knew you had a boyfriend," Lola says smugly when we come over for dinner that week.

"Oh my *god*, Lola—"

"Your mother tells me it was very romantic, like a movie."

It was, and I spent the whole car ride home reliving the shock of Jack launching himself into the stands just to kiss me, but that's hardly the point. The way people suddenly started whispering is also not the point. The quality of the kiss? Epic, but irrelevant.

What was I saying? The point is—"Mom did *not* say that."

I read one of her most recent columns, curious to see if her relationship with Pastor Ike (he does not take offense to this nickname, which makes it a little less fun) has changed anything about her usual feminist overtones. Turns out she still thinks we should eat the rich and that women of color will ultimately save the world. So yeah, she may be in love, but not much else about her use of language has changed. She's not suddenly Snow White or something.

"I can read between the lines," Lola sniffs, which is confirmation that she made it up.

"And Jack's not my boyfriend, he's just—"

"The guy she's currently lying to," mutters Bash in an unusually derisive tone from where he's sitting at Lola's dining table.

There's a loud sound and a burst of light from his laptop, and he grimaces.

"Okay, seriously?" I walk over to look at the screen, which he tries to hide from me. "You see how you just got killed again? *That* does not happen to Cesario. Like, ever." I take the screen from him, frowning. "You're still in the trial combat rounds? Bash!"

"First of all, of course I am," Bash informs me at a mutter, "and secondly, this is pointless."

"I don't like these computer games of yours," comments Lola from where she's stirring the arroz caldo, a chicken soup that she's insisting we need because she thought she heard Bash sniffle. "Too violent."

"Lola, there's people stoned to death in the Bible," I remind her, and then to Bash I point out, "There's no way Jack is going to believe this is you."

"Uh, spoiler? I KNOW," snaps Bash, flashing me a look of accusation.

A wave of frustration sweeps through me; Bash is on my case again today. I thought I'd already won him over on doing me this particular favor, but apparently there are limits to Bash's philanthropy. "You said you'd help me, did you not?"

"I *am* helping you! That doesn't mean I'm magically good at this," he grumbles. "The last video game I played was, like, Pac-Man."

"Okay, that's—" I press a hand to my forehead. "*Twelfth Knight* is an RPG. Pac-Man is, like, a friggin' arcade game—"

"LOLA," explodes Bash, storming to his feet. "Tell Vi to go pray the rosary or something. She looks all devilish again."

"You need to stop getting so overexcited, anak," Lola calls to me, which is incredibly unhelpful. "Not good for your heart."

"Lola, I'm seventeen, I don't have heart problems—and as for *you*, Sebastian—"

I shove him back into his chair and start a new combat round. "Okay, so I feel like this is obvious, but try to make sure the other knight doesn't stab you this time."

"Has anyone ever told you that you're an incredibly gifted teacher?" Bash mutters.

"Just focus, please?"

"I want to meet this boy," Lola announces.

"No," Bash and I say in unison, which surprises me until he adds, "It's not going to last, anyway. Vi is lying to him."

"Some lies are healthy," says Lola. "Keeps the peace."

"She's catfishing him on the internet," Bash clarifies with a pointed glance at me.

"Bash, *focus*—"

"Vi's a pretty girl, Sebas," Lola says. "Don't call your sister a catfish."

"*Thank* you, Lola," I tell her, watching Bash's health drop to yellow. "What did I say about not getting stabbed? And I'm not *catfishing* him, I'm just—"

"Pretending to be someone you're not?"

"Bash, pay attention, you're going to—!"

Boom, he's dead. The screen flashes with his latest defeat and I sink into the chair beside him with a grimace. "Are you being this bad on purpose?" I ask with a sigh. "Like, because you want to teach me a lesson or something?"

Bash gives me the closest thing to a glare that Bash is capable of producing. "Do you think I *enjoy* being bad at this, Viola? Believe me, I do not. And might I remind you that I agreed to do this as a *favor to you*—"

"Okay, sorry, sorry," I say quickly, before he launches into some *Hamlet*-inspired soliloquy. "I'm sorry, I'm just . . . I'm nervous, that's all."

"*You're* nervous?" he bleats. "You're not the one who's going to look stupid in front of the entire school—"

"It's not the entire school, it's just—" I hesitate, knowing that with all the effort Jack put into hyping people, this tournament is about to sell more tickets than the homecoming dance. "Okay, it's sort of well attended so far, but that's only because Jack is promoting the hell out of it—"

"Heaven," Lola corrects me from the kitchen.

"Not really the vibe I was going for, Lola," I call back.

"Vi," Bash says twitchily, "you're really not helping—"

"All right." I exhale, taking a deep, conflict-resolving breath. "Okay, I'm sorry. It's fine. It's *fine*, okay? We just have to work on a few things. Some tactics. We just have t—"

"Vi." Bash cuts me off with a wearied look. "Can I take a break?"

"I mean, I feel like we'd be more productive if—" The expression on his face stops me in my tracks. "Yeah. Yeah, oh yeah, of course," I say in a forcefully positive voice that I never use except for when Bash looks like he's going to kill me. "After dinner we can try again?"

"Yeah, fine." He pushes the laptop away. "And I'm really not trying to screw this up for you, Vi. I mean it." He gives me a long look—one that I can't quite interpret. "You get that, right? That I'm trying to help you?"

"Oh, Bash, I'm . . ." I trail off, because yeah, he's right. Bash would never do that, ever. He's a better person than me, times a million, and as hard as it is to puncture Bash, I get why he doesn't want to do this, like, at all. He's used to praise, to being naturally talented at things, and this is just not in his wheelhouse.

"Bash," I offer in plaintive reconciliation, "I really am grateful to you."

"You'd better be," he mumbles.

"I *am*, I promise—"

"Because it would be way easier if you'd just—"

"I know. I know." But I'm practically breaking a sweat just thinking about it.

The truth is that yes, contrary to how it might appear, I *do* care that I'm lying to Jack. I care a lot; more than I expected. I know he's going to be angry because I would be, too. He thinks he knows who I am, that I'm the kind of person who wouldn't keep secrets from him, who would only do things if they were right . . .

And I wish I didn't have to prove him wrong.

Jack: *you ready to prep the gym tomorrow??*
Jack: *I know you must be pretty sick of being impressed by me*
Vi: *please*
Vi: *don't hurt yourself on all this humility*
Jack: *there's that classic viola charm*
Jack: *so glad finals aren't draining that cheery wit*
Jack: *(no but seriously, can't wait to see you)*

He's going to hate me. When he finds out exactly who I am, he's going to absolutely hate me. I just need to get through the tournament that means so much to him, and then . . .

I don't know.

"Everything okay?" Bash asks, arching a brow, and I hurry to put my phone away. The last thing I need is for Bash to know that I think he's right. He'll get completely insufferable.

"It will be once I can get you to stop embarrassing yourself," I assure him, and we bicker until Lola tells us to start eating before the soup gets cold.

Finals week is a disaster.

Not because of finals. Those are fine. I've had my notes prepped all semester and Olivia makes a great study partner. But unfortunately, one of Bash's weaknesses is that he . . . doesn't deal with stress all that well. And his ineptitude at *Twelfth Knight*?

VERY stressful.

"Are you even listening to me? I said use your sword and don't—Oh my god, Bash, do *not* do that—"

"STOP TELLING ME WHAT TO DO!" he bellows.

"Okay, but if I don't *tell* you what to do, you don't know what you're *doing*—"

"YOU CAN STOP REMINDING ME," he says, "I AM AWARE."

"Hey, kids?" says my mom, poking her head in. "You're not actively killing each other, are you?"

"Not yet," we shout in unison.

"Delightful," she replies. "Snacks downstairs when you're ready!"

It continues like that until the day of the tournament, which is a Thursday. I'm in the gym setting up the stage (we thought it'd be fun to display the chairs with usernames on the backs so spectators know who is who on the screen) when Bash comes in looking for me.

"Vi," he says fretfully. "Vi, I'm . . . I don't know if I can do this."

I adjust the sign with Cesario's username, trying to figure out how to play this. "Sebastian, you're fine. Everything's fine. You just have to play one round and then if it goes badly—" (Oh, it's *for sure* going to go badly.) "We'll just tell everyone you have food poisoning or something."

In fairness, he *does* look extremely ill.

"Oh my god, I'm sweating," he babbles to me, pulling out his phone. "Like, *really* sweating. It's bad sweat, Vi. It's *stress* sweat—"

"What are you doing?"

"I'm texting Olivia. I need her to run her scene with me so I don't spontaneously implode—"

"What?"

"Shakespeare relaxes me, Viola!" he bellows at me, to which I obviously cannot argue. As usual, he looks like he might say something else, but again—frustratingly—he doesn't. Instead he turns away, but I reach for his arm.

"Bash, listen." I let out a sigh. "I know you hate this—and I get that, really. I know you're not happy with me about any of this—"

"You do?" He squints at me.

"Well, I mean . . . it's not like you've made it a secret," I mumble. He's been on the verge of yelling at me for what feels like weeks, maybe longer. "And look, I *know* I messed up," I add, more adamantly this time. "I lied to you about Jack—"

"Mm-hmm," Bash says profoundly, in something of a sung chorus.

"—and I was mean to Mom, and weird about Pastor Ike—"

"Correct," he confirms, ticking off his invisible ledger.

"—and now I'm forcing you to do something embarrassing or whatever," I say with a roll of my eyes, "but I really just—"

"Hang on." Bash jerks so unexpectedly out of my grip that it startles me into silence. "That's what you think this is about? You think I'm worried about being *embarrassed*?"

"I—" I stop, considering where on the ledger I might have gotten tripped up. "I mean," I attempt at levity, "I think my alleged crimes against your hummus are kind of overblown—"

"No. No, hang on a second." He turns to face me, squaring off like we're in the ring. "Do you really not know why I'm upset?"

Okay, I sigh internally, *here we go.* I thought Bash had already come to terms with what I did—you know, because he's Bash, and he sincerely did seem to think it was funny—but I guess I always sort of wondered whether I was due for a bigger reckoning. "Bash, I know it was wrong to say I was you," I say, guiltily inspecting my feet, "but I swear, I was honestly just—"

"Oh, screw *that*, Vi." I blink, shocked into meeting Bash's eye again. "You think I care that you used my name? That you pretended to be me? Come on," Bash scoffs, visibly repulsed that I could be so wildly off base. "That's nothing."

I gape at him, completely incapable of following the thread of this conversation. "If that's nothing, then *what*—"

"Are you serious?" He folds his arms across his chest, his brow now furrowed so deeply I'm concerned he'll give himself a migraine. "Is it really *this hard* for you to figure it out?"

Apparently so, which is doing nothing for my temperament. "Bash," I grit through my teeth, "would you stop being so cryptic and *just tell me*—"

"All I wanted," Bash suddenly explodes at me, "was for you to come to me. That's *all*."

"What?" At first I assume I misheard him. Then I'm just confused. "Wait, come to you for what?"

"For *anything*." He gives me a plaintive glance. "Viola, come on. Don't you get it?"

I know he's my brother and for obvious (genetic) reasons I know his face like it's my own, but sometimes he manages a look that's so open, so impossibly honest, that I can't believe we're even remotely related.

"You were hurting," he says, his hands falling to his sides in helpless surrender. "You're hurting, and you could have told me. I would have been there for you. I *tried* to be there for you, Viola, so many times!"

"I—"

I don't know what to say to that, because my mind suddenly treats me to an unsolicited flashback reel—a moody key change, followed by a montage of the past three months.

(Bash cheering me up about the ConQuest group.)

(Bash asking me if I'm okay after RenFaire. After Antonia.)

(Bash trying to get me to talk about my feelings.)

(Bash forgiving me for my mistakes without a moment's hesitation.)

(Bash being there for me, even when I push him away.)

(Bash accepting me. Bash believing in me. Bash dreaming up

adventures with me. Bash making me laugh when I don't even want to smile.)

(Bash sitting in the car with me, telling me I'm worth loving, that I'm worth liking. That I'm something better than cool.)

"And you know what the worst part is?" Bash asks me, punctuating my internal revelation with a pained look of frustration and disappointment. "I know you think people suck, Vi, but that wasn't supposed to include me. You know?" Bash shakes his head, and my stomach roils with pain. "You act like you're alone, but you're not. You've never been alone. You just didn't want to choose what I had to give you."

I swallow, something hot pricking dangerously behind my eyes.

"But *this*—" Bash swings a hand to reference the *Twelfth Knight* stage, as if he's suddenly remembered the more pressing issue of me and my tyrannical schemes. "This is using me, Vi. You're just *using* me, and I—"

He shakes his head again, defeated. And then, as if there's nothing left worth saying, he turns resignedly away.

"Bash, wait." I struggle to find my voice as Bash strides off toward the gym doors. "Just . . . Bash!" I call after him helplessly.

My feeble attempts to pause him fail, obviously. And what would I say to him, even if he did stay to listen? He must know that whatever the right response is, I don't have it.

"Damn," I whisper to myself, wincing a little through my guilt.

Because he's right, of course. Of course he's right. I've literally never been alone. Bash used to routinely crow ". . . and we were wombmates!" in my face to the point of utter madness (mine), so why did I feel I had to take everything on by myself? Even if Bash couldn't fix my problems, he's still always been there for me, and I've always taken him for granted.

For a moment, my own selfishness stings. Because I used his identity, and him, without ever acknowledging the truth: that he would have just given it to me—given anything to me—if only I'd asked.

Just before Bash disappears from view, I officially become the worst person in the world by noticing the definite wet spot on his back. It's totally stress sweat, but what am I supposed to do now?

Inwardly, I sigh. I'm just relieved I had the foresight to send Jack to deal with the pizzas. Whatever needs to be fixed, I can do it. I've always done it.

"Everything okay?" I hear behind me, and instantly wince.

Spoke too soon.

It's not Jack, so you'd think that would mean it's not the worst case. But it's Antonia, so the pinprick of hurt in my chest tells me it's not *not* the worst case, either.

Looks like she's been brought in to help with the projectors, which makes sense. We used to do this sort of thing together, once upon a time.

"I'm fine. Everything's fine." I turn away, ready to push past her and pretend to be doing literally anything else, but she pauses me.

"Vi, I just—"

She stops, chewing her lip.

"Can we talk?" she asks, looking troubled. No, looking sad. Looking like she really does need me, which is the SOS I would have known in a past life not to ignore.

Part of me is desperate to say no. Part of me? Ha, no. All of me.

But I also know that I dip my french fries in chocolate milk-shakes and mix my candy corn with pretzels because Antonia loves sweet with salty. She might have started listening to '70s pop because of me, but I love the Studio Ghibli films because of her. I went to MagiCon for the first time because Antonia convinced me to go with her, and I auditioned for the Renaissance Faire because she told me she'd do it if I did. I've never been afraid to wear outland-ish costumes or even run for ASB office because Antonia always told me I could do it. Everything I love or have loved has traces of Antonia all over it, and even if I've had to spend most of this se-mester without her, she's still there with me. She's this fingerprint on who I am and what I do and where I go, and as much as I wish I could burn this bridge and stop suffering the ways she made me feel small, I don't actually want to be someone who causes her pain.

"Yeah, sure." I gesture. She nods, and we walk around the perimeter of the gym.

"So, um." She folds her hands together. "This weird thing happened with Matt."

"Matt Das?"

"Yeah. He, uh. He was kind of like . . . pushing me. Like—" She looks askance guiltily. "Pressuring me."

"You mean, for like . . . ?" I brace myself. I think I already know how this story ends; it's a version of the same story I tried to tell her a few months ago. But as vindicating as it might seem, I really hope it goes differently for her.

"Yeah," she confirms uncomfortably. "And, like, not that I wasn't . . . It wasn't *that*. I mean, it almost was. But it was more how he reacted, when I . . ."

She falters, cheeks flushing red.

"Said no?" I offer, because unfortunately, I do know a version of this story.

"Yes." She exhales it out in a rush. "He just got really mean, like I wasn't giving him something he—"

Another pause.

"Deserved?" I guess.

"*Yes.*" She's adamant now. "Like he thought because he'd been nice to me—"

"You owed him?"

"Yes! And then he said—" Her cheeks turn slightly pink. "He said that maybe I was a bitch like you, and I said—"

This time, I don't fill in the blanks for her.

"I said I wished that were true, because you knew a lot sooner than I did what kind of guy he really was," she finishes abruptly, and then she stops, like she's waiting for my reaction.

People are starting to filter into the gym, trickling in gradually for the event, so I gesture her to the door and we step outside for some quiet, both a little chilly as the wind whips by.

"I guess what I'm trying to say is that I'm sorry," she says.

I wait for something to happen. The earth to shift, I guess. I wait for triumph or validation or something, for the cosmic synchronicity of confirming I was always in the right, but even against the shameful backdrop of Bash's confession, all I can feel in this moment is . . . relief.

Not just relief. Catharsis. As if suddenly—finally—I can set the pain down and breathe.

"I'm sorry, too," I say, and I am.

She gives me a grateful half smile. "Things are probably different now, though. Aren't they?"

"I guess so." I tuck my hands into my jacket pockets.

"Right." She stares into one of the many Messaline campus planters while I inspect my shoes.

"But different doesn't have to mean bad, right?" I ask quietly.

From the corner of my eye, I watch her shift a glance to me.

"Larissa Highbrow casts a friendship healing spell," she says.

My smile twitches.

"Astrea Starscream takes a critical hit," I reply.

We turn to face each other.

"So. What's wrong with Bash?" she says.

"Oh, god. Uh. It's a long story." I could easily lie and say it's just Bash being Bash, but this secret has burned through enough of my conscience already. "There's, um. There's maybe . . . something going on. With me and Jack Orsino."

"I'm pretty sure the whole school knows that," she says, and I roll my eyes.

"Yeah, but . . . you know how I play *Twelfth Knight*?"

"Of course."

"I guess I never mentioned I play as a boy. Like, as a male knight. Named Cesario."

"Oh." She tilts her head. "I mean, makes sense."

"Right. Well." Deep breath. "Jack plays too, *with* Cesario." I clear my throat. "Which is me. But also not me."

"Oh my god." Her eyes widen. "He doesn't know it's you? At all?"

"No, he has no idea. But then he signed Cesario up for this tournament, so . . ."

She looks at me blankly, waiting, and I sigh. "Well, I had to do *something*, right? I had to find a boy who could conceivably be Cesario in real life, so—"

"Oh my god," she says again, one hand flying to her mouth. "So you're trying to pass off *Bash* as you?"

"Yes." I grimace, and she frowns.

"But Bash is, like, a *disaster* at gaming. He's hopeless."

"Yes."

"Why did you even—?"

"Temporary insanity?"

"Dang," she says, whistling. "You must really like Jack, huh?"

"I don't—" But I stop, because the look she gives me is the one that means *Don't bother, I already know you're lying*. It's annoying, but there's that feeling again: relief.

I really, really missed my friend.

"I don't know what came over me," I admit with a grumble. "Probably a severe head wound."

She shrugs, rolling her eyes at my expense. "I keep telling you he's really hot."

"That's not . . . that has nothing to do with this," I protest.

"Oh, it doesn't?" she says skeptically.

"I mean—"

"HA!"

"Look," I sigh, cutting her off before she can make it worse. "I just need to get Bash through this, and then . . . I don't know." I kick at the sidewalk. "This whole Jack thing was bound to fall apart anyway. I'm, like, very me. And he's very him."

"He seems to like how very 'you' you are," Antonia says drily. "And contrary to things that certain people might have said while they were angry, you are . . . not really so bad." She bumps her shoulder with mine. "In fact, I always liked you."

"Until a boy changed your mind?"

She groans. "Okay, okay, not my finest move, I get it. And it wasn't—"

"I know it wasn't." This wasn't really about a *boy*. Certainly not in the classic sense.

"The thing is, you don't have to always push people away, Vi." Antonia looks at me squarely. "You don't have to assume they'll leave."

"You did."

"You shoved me out. And anyway, I came back, right? People come back."

"He'll be pissed," I sigh.

"Yeah, probably."

"I deserve that."

"You do. But has he ever asked you to be something you're not?" she poses to me. "Because if he has, then he isn't worth it. And if he hasn't, then I don't see the point of not being exactly who you are."

I'm about to answer when someone else calls my name.

"Hey, Vi?"

I turn to find Olivia poking her head out from the gym. "Oh, sorry," she says, noticing that Antonia and I are talking. "Want me to give you a sec, or . . . ?"

I glance at Antonia, who shrugs. "We've got lots of time," she tells me. "Maybe we can meet up over break? The ConQuest group kinda fell apart," she adds sheepishly. "Leon and Danny Kim were getting on everyone's nerves. So if you wanted to play again . . ."

"Sure, yeah. Yeah, maybe." I nod, and she steps back, acknowledging Olivia with a thoughtful half smile before she wanders back to the gym. It's been gradually filling up during the time I've been out here with Antonia, and I can already hear the buzz of the projector, the tinny sound of speakers coming to life with the *Twelfth Knight* theme. I can hear Jack's voice on the mic, too, though instead of being soothing, it's like the start of a countdown in my chest. Seconds ticking before a bomb goes off.

"That seemed promising," Olivia comments, flipping a look over her shoulder at Antonia's retreat. "You guys okay?"

"Getting there. What's going on?"

"Oh god, um. It's Bash." She winces. "It's just . . . he's freaking out."

"I know." I echo her wince with a grimace. "I know."

"He kind of told me the whole story," she adds, and hastily continues, "which, no judgment, right? I've told some lies too, so I get it. But I figure maybe you might want to hear what someone once told me when I was feeling a little . . . not myself."

She gives me a knowing look, and I shrug, resigned. "Why not? Hit me."

"You told me that if I decided to be myself, I wouldn't have to be alone," she says simply. "Neither will you."

But, I think witheringly.

(Plus a thousand flimsy excuses that have been holding me back for weeks.)

"It's a little different when someone else's feelings are on the line," I attempt.

"Yeah, but better a late truth than another timely lie, right?" she prompts me, and I think again how my mom was right about connecting with people. About forgiving people and letting people in. I understand it a little bit more every day, like something slowly taking root.

Because whatever pain love brings me, I wouldn't give it up for a second. Not for a single irrational beat of my ravenous heart, so even if I've made mistakes with Bash, and with Antonia, and especially with Jack, it's not too late to do things differently.

Because Jack Orsino may think I'm helping him, but maybe thanks to him, I can do him one better.

I'll let him help me.

"Okay," I sigh. "Okay."

Olivia smiles her brilliant cheerleader smile, steering me toward the gym.

"That's the Vi Reyes I know," she says, and gives my shoulders a squeeze.

It was Jack's idea to do a practice round before the tournament to let the others orient themselves to the game, and I walk in just in time to see him frowning with confusion at Bash, who's been completely demolished, while Bash refuses to look anywhere but his keyboard.

Ultimately, there's nothing like watching my twin brother look like he's about to pass out to convince me that I absolutely need to intervene. Like, now.

"Hey." Ignoring the voices of confusion around me, I trot up the platform stairs to tap him on the shoulder. "Come on. I'll do it."

Jack's brow is furrowed, but I can't look at him right now.

"What?" Bash croaks.

"Come on, you look like a ghost."

"Remember me," he whimpers, never too vulnerable to skip the theatrics.

"*Hamlet*, really? I knew you'd go tragedy." I nudge him again. "I've got this, Bash. Thank you."

The look that passes between us is one I've known forever. It's a precious, wordless exchange of *I'm sorry* and *I forgive you*. It's equal parts *I love you* and *I know*.

He doesn't need to be told twice. He fumbles out of his chair, stumbling down the platform, and darts right for Olivia. The others in the tournament—all boys—frown at me, beginning to whisper among themselves, but they don't matter. I calmly pull out Bash's chair to take Cesario's seat across from Jack, who is looking at me very strangely.

"What are you doing?" he says.

I reorient the keyboard to suit my preferences, adjusting the chair. My Cesario avatar fills the screen, flashing in wait, and there it is. The truth.

The real me. No more secrets, finally.

"I'm sorry," I tell Jack. "I hope you'll let me explain."

He blinks. His eyes flicker with calculation, then narrow. If he hasn't already figured it out, he will soon. I know his confusion is slowly giving way to betrayal, just like I know that this will be a long, difficult day.

But for once I don't feel like I'm hiding anything, and that feels good. As good as knowing I'm about to lose him can possibly feel, anyway.

"Ready?" I ask.

He looks at me like he's never seen me before.

"Let's play," he says bluntly, hitting Start with the click of a mouse.

LAST CHANCE HIT POINT

𝔍𝔞𝔠𝔨

I remember the first time Cesario and I took a hit from some other players in the game. He'd explained it before, that we had relics people wanted, that they would attack us and it wouldn't be part of the quest, and in fact this was part of what made the quest so impossible. I told him I know, I know, I get it, I'm not stupid, and Cesario said okay prove it, and for a few days I was arrogant; I thought it was obvious that he was just trying to scare me. After all, what was a game? Just that, a game.

I hadn't realized until then that there were massive leagues of people who play this game by policing it internally, carving out their own little social networks within the constraints of an imaginary world. I didn't realize, either, that Cesario had encountered them before. That first time we were attacked, Cesario had recognized the usernames of our attackers. They're bullies, he said. I was busy trying not to die, but Cesario was doing something else. We beat them soundly, mercilessly, with Cesario claiming their points and currency as prizes even when we didn't need them. He was teaching them a lesson, though at first I didn't really understand why.

Later, I asked him how he knew they were bullies. He explained, briskly, that he had a friend who liked the game but didn't feel comfortable in the world anymore. Not the world of the game, but the world of its players. They had harassed her and flooded her chat with derogatory comments and were the same kind of people who'd attacked her on fandom blogs, who left mean comments on her fan fiction, who trashed her blog by sending anonymous hate day after day until she stopped writing, stopped even wanting to write. I said, I think: holy shit, geek-on-geek violence is so intense these days.

yeah was all he said back to me.

Why do I think of this now? Because something felt off when I was watching Bash play. Not just because he was confusingly, unrecognizably awful—which he *was,* and I was *bewildered*—but it was also something like an itch. A sneeze. A moment out of place that needed cosmic rearranging, because something about it just . . . wasn't right.

I want to say it's a shock when Vi Reyes sits across from me in the seat marked for Cesario. I want to say it stuns me, sends my world spinning, throws me for a loop. Which isn't to say that *doesn't* happen to some extent—I do feel like a pincushion, suddenly stuck through with jabs of something brutal. But I don't think it's shock, or at least not as much of a shock as it should be.

I guess when the avatar of an enormous male knight stood in front of me and was decisive and good with a sword, it was easy for me to believe they were exactly who they said they were. I never really asked questions; never wondered why the stranger I've been spending half my time with over the last few months seemed so instantly, intuitively familiar to me.

I think what I feel isn't shock—it's the pieces fitting together.

How could I not have recognized her? No matter what forms she and I take, I know her. I know her because of what she makes me know about myself. I know how it feels to have her in my life.

But I didn't see it before, and now I feel blindsided. Angry.

There's no way it's not her. I'm busy with my own combat rounds, the din of the gym a mix of cheering, booing, and people chatting over the silly computer game filling the screen. From afar, though, I recognize all of Cesario's signature moves. The way he approaches the offensive, the opening moves. The way he controls the center, forcing his opponent to the outside.

Not his opponents. Hers.

Vi's the only girl on the platform. I realize that's probably my fault; the way I sold this tournament to other people, like Kayla and Mackenzie, made it seem like two separate events. There was going to be a movie after this—a "girl movie," I promised—since we were starting off with this rowdy tournament filled with testosterone. I nudged girls into buying tickets because even if they weren't interested, which I assumed they weren't, there'd be lots of other stuff to do. Not once did I wonder if the girls themselves should have been invited to play the way I tried to coax my male friends into it; I never bothered to sell them on how fun it was, how satisfying, how easy to learn, and now I'm sitting very uncomfortably with the idea that maybe I didn't even stop to think it would be.

Did I leave space for Vi to feel like the tournament was as much hers as it was mine? No, I didn't. I wanted her to be there, of course, but I just assumed there was no way she'd pick it up. It just didn't seem like her thing.

She should have told me.

Shame and irritation meet up like conjoined twins in my angry, smarting chest. She's so direct about everything, but she couldn't just tell me?

And in the meantime, how much have I told *her*?

My pulse convulses. God, I told her everything. I told her how I felt about her, how I felt about Olivia. Everything I thought I was confessing to a friend, I was really telling some shadow on the internet. In my frustration I take out Volio, who curses next to me, and feel the increasing heat of my temper. I don't get angry. I can't get angry. She knows this about me. She should know.

I try to focus on the screen. Cesario—Vi—takes down Curio. She's methodical, placid, expression unchanging, exactly the way I thought Cesario would look when he played the game, only I never actually knew who Cesario was. I got close to Vi without knowing she had a window into me that I've never had with her.

I kept saying I knew her. What the hell did I know?

Matt Das is knocked out by Tom Murphy. Murph faces Vi and loses, then she takes out that kid Leon, who talks a big game and complains loudly when he gets knocked out. She doesn't look like it matters much.

Ah. Because she's not here for them. I get it.

Some sophomore who looks like he's never seen the sun is my last victim before Vi and I are the only two players left on the platform. People are interested now; not in the game, but in the way Vi and I aren't looking at each other, aren't speaking. There's an awkwardness radiating from us and I can practically feel the whispers. *First Olivia Hadid, now Vi Reyes?* I'm sure they think I'm getting somehow unmanned by the entirety of this brutal semester, but I'm glad, I'm glad it's her. She's the only one here worth beating.

She and I face each other on the screen. Cesario versus The Duke. I don't ask if she's ready, because I don't need to. She launches forward and so do I.

A bunch of Coach-isms come to me, like always. See it, make it happen. Do I want to beat her? Yes, yes I do, and not for my ego. Okay, kind of for my ego. I like winning and I'm not going to pretend I don't. But do I feel like she owes me something? Yeah, right now I do, I definitely do. I don't want her to walk away from this like it was easy. I want to put her through her paces and I want her to see the look on my face, the proof that she broke this. That it ends here, with one of us walking away a champion and the other just walking away.

"You lied to me," I say in a low voice. It's the first time we've spoken aloud since she sat down, and it might very well be the last time.

"I know," she says, and pulls out a sword to stab me in the chest.

Cesario—Vi—has always been handy with combo moves. He—she—moves quickly, easily, dexterously. She feints, sprints, conceals moves with stealth, takes blind shots she knows by instinct. But she taught me how to do all those things, so I do them, too.

Not everyone has the efficiency of her calculation; Cesario, the avatar she built, is a tactician with assassin-level skills. I remember suddenly that her ConQuest character is an assassin, too, and how did I not see it? Was I blind? Yes, I was blind. She made sure I was.

I position myself for attack and she takes a hit, albeit not critically, because she never stays still for very long. She knows how to defend herself, to make sure she never gets hurt. I never learned that. I never learned to protect myself, to keep things close, to play them safe, so I feint and attack, which she parries and counters. There's a whoop from the crowd, and I realize people are rooting for me. They think I'm the better player, and there it is again, the stab to my chest—the little fissure of understanding why she had to hide the truth. But why from me?

She shouldn't have hid from me.

Someone riles up the Duke Orsino chant when I manage a stealth combo that normally wouldn't work on Cesario, but she must be rattled. We've only ever played alone, staying up too late, escaping into the game. The only audience we've ever had has been the game's environment; the battlefields, ruins and castles, razed-down villages; the enchanted forests and monster-filled seas. She's not like me, comfortable with an audience, and since she's not Bash, she's not like him, either. I can see on her face that she isn't having fun, and I feel it again, another wash of too-much feeling: anger, that she took this simple little joy from us. Sadness that now I'm taking it from her.

I resolve to get this over with. Be brutal. I gear up for another combo, this one with a finishing move that's almost impossible to defend. I gauge how much life she has left and time it precisely, expending close to what's left of my own health bar, and then I—

Get killed.

I blink.

The entire room starts booing.

DUKEORSINO12 IS ELIMINATED! says my screen.

"I'm sorry," Vi breathes.

Ah. So she was never really rattled. I thought I knew her, but I don't. She told me that, *you don't know me*, a thousand times, but I never actually listened, did I? She showed me the truth and I chose the lie.

I try to relive the last ten seconds, maybe twenty by now. What did she do, how did she do it so quickly? She took advantage of my miscalculation; I thought she had less in her. I made a mistake because I underestimated her and she knew it, she knew I would, because she has known me this whole time, but I have never really known her.

Shame, pain, fury. She always, always turns my world upside down.

"You should be sorry," I tell her.

Then I step away from the platform and walk out.

𝔙𝔦

Olivia and Bash are sympathetic. Even Antonia gives me a small half grimace from afar, like she's apologizing all over again, even though this has nothing to do with her. Ultimately, though, I don't want to be comforted.

I find Jack on the field, standing on the track like he plans to take off running.

"It's freezing," I point out.

He glances at me and looks away. "I'm fine."

I try to be . . . I don't know. Light, I guess. "I thought you were going to take care of your knee?"

"Do you see me doing anything?" he snaps.

Normally it's my job to say things in a mean voice. I find I really don't want to be mean to him, though. Clearly I've already been mean enough.

"Jack," I start to say, but he looks up at the sky, kicking something on the ground.

"We should finish the quest." His voice is perfunctory. "I don't want all that work to go to waste."

"I . . . sure, yeah." I was actually wondering if he'd want to. "Does that mean—?"

"When we're done, we're done," he says. "I'm done."

"Right." I shiver unintentionally. It's cold. "Well, there's the laptops we used for the tournament. Could do it right now."

"Yeah, let's do it." He turns sharply and walks past me, so quickly he clips my shoulder, and okay, I get it. I amble after him, reminding myself: I get it. He doesn't want to talk to me. This is . . . not news to me. I'm not surprised.

I'm fine.

I'm fine.

I'm—

"Here." He hands me the laptop while I'm still following numbly after him, not realizing he outpaced me by what seems like eons. He already went into the gym, grabbed two laptops, and came back out. Inside there's the sound of laughter from some comedy that Kayla and Mackenzie picked. Everyone else is cozied up in there, too cold outside by California standards for even the most anarchistic teens to revolt out here in the courtyard.

Jack kicks the door shut behind him and sits on top of one of the planters. I follow his lead, hissing a little at how chilly the cement is beneath my woefully thin jeans.

Wordlessly, he takes off his jacket and hands it to me.

I hesitate. "Jack, I don't—"

"Just take it."

"Won't you be cold?"

"I'm fine." Sounds familiar.

He's already signed in. I accept the jacket because it's freezing (I've got island blood, I'm not built for this) and wrap it around my shoulders. I shiver a little at the way it smells like him, like a different cold night—a sharp laugh, a shared kiss.

I sign in as Cesario, resuming our quest. "So, listen, as far as—"

"Vi," Jack says, looking up from his screen briefly. "Whatever reason you had for lying to me, whatever it is you want to say now—"

I grimace. "I just want to tell you I'm sorry—"

"Yeah, I heard you." He fidgets, tapping his thumb against the keyboard. "It's fine. Whatever your reasons are, I don't care. I just want to be done with this, okay? Let's just be done."

For a second there's a part of me that wants to argue. It's the exact part of me that I couldn't conjure up before when I was fighting with Antonia. The part of me that Bash has always said was missing; the piece that wants to stay and fight.

I *never* want to do that. I always want to cut people out of my life, suck the poison out, feel nothing. I want to stop feeling squishy and small as soon as possible—immediately, or even sooner than that. And even though another part of me is saying in a tiny, hopeful voice that Jack isn't like me, that he doesn't do that and he doesn't have to, because if he wants me to, I'll stay, I'll stay, I'll stay . . .

It's small. So it's easy to squash.

"Right. Yeah." I focus on my screen. "Let's do this."

The very last realm is Avalon. According to legend, this is the fairy isle where Arthur was taken after he was killed, and where he's now being preserved to return at some future time. The whole point of the game is to get Arthur back, so now that we've revived the magic of eleven knights in eleven realms, we're supposed to make ourselves the twelfth knight. The final piece in the puzzle before we can resurrect Arthur.

The thing is: nobody actually knows what happens from here. People pass around theories or make fan videos about it all the time, but because this is one of the areas of the game that can only be unlocked by reaching this point in the Camelot Quest, not many people have done it. We're near the end, but also, we have no idea exactly how to reach it.

It's dark here, full of mist, so that we can only see what's directly in front of us. We can hear the sounds of our avatars breathing, but that's it. It's easy to imagine being there while we're sitting out here alone, the dull roar from the gym accounting for almost nothing. My breath escapes me and it's like the Avalonian fog, drifting outward in translucent mists. I can see myself as Cesario walking in silence beside Duke Orsino, who has decisively taken the lead.

Rather than speak aloud, I type into the chat.

we have to find excalibur. that has to be the last relic, the one that brings arthur back.

He types back without looking up. how?

I pause to consider what I know of the legend. I guess we have t

But before I can finish typing, the screen goes dark. Eerily black.

I blink, then tap my keyboard. "Is your—?"

"Yeah." He does the same. "Could the school network have shut down, or . . . ?"

Then the screen lights up again in a burst that's almost blinding. From over the top of my screen, I watch the sudden illumination reflect on Jack's frowning face.

The full island of Avalon is in view now, as if someone simply turned on the lights. There's a forest, distant mountains, a palace, all of it beautiful and ancient and still as the dead. The fog that was obscuring our view is lifted now while the rest of the island stretches up around us, enveloping us in a valley of mountain peaks and open sky.

Within sight—but not within reach—an inlet of sea stretches into a glassy, placid lake, and I know instantly what's inside it.

Excalibur.

Standing between us and the relic, though, is a knight. Not a normal knight; not another player. This knight is an NPC generated by the game. He's wearing full black armor, head to toe, and beneath the visor of his helmet is a glint of red eyes.

Across the screen, the game flashes with a message:

THE BLACK KNIGHT HAS CHALLENGED YOU TO A DUEL.

"Oh," I say dully, putting it together aloud. "I guess in order to reach the lake, we're supposed—"

"To kill the Black Knight, yeah." Jack's shoulder twitches with an unspoken *duh*.

"Right, well—"

Before I can try to figure out a strategy, the game has launched into a full-scale environmental war. There are bursts of sorcery, a line of enchantresses, all of whom stand behind the Black Knight, and there's almost nothing I can say before it's time for one of the biggest battle sequences we've seen in the game so far.

Scratch that, *the* biggest. An enchantress comes my way, and judging by the appearance of a variety of creatures, there are mages here as well. I pull out Tristan's Fail-Not Bow and aim as much as I can overhead, trying to control the upper levels while the Duke—Jack—takes the valley floor, dousing a fire and taking on the Black Knight alone.

"Wait, Jack—"

He ignores me. Not that he's not good at combat, but this can't be a normal fight, right? I dispatch an enchantress, knock a flying dragon out of the sky, and then replace the bow in my hand with my usual sword instead. Jack, I notice, is using Galahad's red sword, which requires more lifeline points to operate than a normal one. But it's worth it if he can land a lethal hit.

I try to work my way in, triangulating so that I can land a hit on the Black Knight from somewhere behind. I could use a render like the one Jack used on me earlier, but they're tricky.

"A little help?" mutters Jack, who gets struck in the chest so hard he knocks from orange-yellow to pulsing, troubling red.

"Sorry." I target the Black Knight and attack.

"You keep saying that," Jack mutters.

My attack does very little. "I actually mean it."

"As opposed to the first time? Or the second?"

Another attack. Unsurprisingly, the Black Knight does *not* have a lot of weaknesses.

"I'm sorry for all of it."

"Sorry doesn't do much for me, though, does it?"

Exasperated, I give up on the Black Knight and select the Holy Grail. Let's see if it has any healing power . . . and ah, look at that. It does. With my help, Jack reverts back to yellow just in time to land a critical hit on the Black Knight, who swipes in a blind arc that narrowly misses me.

Irritated, I point out, "If I could do something about it—"

"Like what? Undo it?" The Black Knight aims for Duke, but he slips it, which pins me in a bad position I have to scramble to get out of.

"Yeah." Wait, did he ask me if I'd undo it? "No—*no*, not that—"

"No? You're cool with what you did?"

"What? No, I'm—" I slam down on the Black Knight with one of my better assassin skills, which successfully . . . dents him. Great. "Of course not. I wish it had been different, but like . . . how?"

"How could you not have lied to me?" he answers gruffly.

"No, I—" I take a hit that knocks me down to a very pale yellow. "I never *planned* to lie to you, Jack—this was never about *tricking* you—"

"But you did."

"I know, I know." I swallow, trying to fight and survive the fight at the same time. "I was already too far in to come clean, and eventually I just couldn't do it, I couldn't, because I was—"

I stop.

"You were what?" he says blandly.

"Happy" comes out of my mouth in a weird, disemboweling blurt. My eyes are stinging suddenly, and for a second, it's hard to see where exactly I'm aiming. I pivot behind the Black Knight, striking from the back while Duke attacks from the front.

"Is that an excuse?" he asks.

"No, it's an explanation. I never thought you'd . . ." I swallow around a knot in my throat. "I just didn't think—"

"You didn't think I'd fall for you?"

It ruptures me to hear it that way. So plainly.

"Or," he continues, "did you not think you'd fall for me?"

"Who says I did?" I rumble in frustration.

"Right." Jack's voice is hard-edged again, and honestly, *what* is wrong with me?

The Black Knight knocks me down to red. I have to step back and heal myself.

"I didn't mean that. Jack, I—"

"What." It's lifeless, not even a question. Totally uninterested.

But he deserves to hear it, even if he no longer wants it. Even if it no longer counts.

"Of course I fell for you, I'm . . ." I sound ridiculous. "Honestly, I'm sorry—"

"There it is again," he mutters.

"I can't help it!" I growl. "I just got to be someone different, someone *else*, and—"

"It was you I wanted. The real you, not the mask. I thought you understood that."

The use of past tense hurts. "Of course I know that *now*, but at the time—"

Jack manages another critical hit.

He barely needs me. If he even does.

"You were my friend," I say in a small voice. "You were my friend when I needed one, when I had *no one*, and maybe if I were a better person—"

"Stop saying you're a bad person, Viola." He sounds annoyed.

"Well, obviously I'm—"

"You're not a bad person. You're just a weirdly difficult one."

"Okay—"

"And you're scared, Vi. You're so scared of everything."

I want to argue.

I *should* argue.

"I know," I exhale. "I'm terrified. It's hard."

"I would have made it easy for you." Jack's voice sounds more strained than angry. "I would have at least tried."

You did, I think. You did. "I didn't want to hurt you."

"Yeah? Well, I'm hurt. I'm embarrassed, I'm exposed and upset—"

"I know—"

"No. No, you don't know." He gives the Black Knight another critical hit, and I think, Jack can win this. I think he can win, and soon. I think he'll be gone from my life in a matter of minutes.

"I was more myself with you than I've ever been with anyone," Jack says tonelessly. "And I wish that it had been the same for you. I hate that I felt something you didn't."

"But I did." My eyes feel swollen. My throat aches. "I *do*, Jack—"

He doesn't say anything. The Black Knight swings and Jack blocks. He has the warrior skillset, all precision and direct hits. He goes and goes and goes and I think of all the things I'd never known that he could do until he did them, the yards I never cared that he could run until he ran them, the pressures I'd never understood he carried around until he chose to share them. All the parts of himself that he gave to me, and I couldn't even give him back the smallest fraction of myself.

"I think that I'm just lonely," I say. "I'm not tough, I'm just *fragile*, and every time anyone hurts me, it stays with me like a bruise that never fully heals." I inhale shakily, cutting it with a swallow. "I don't know how to change, how to be an easier person. I don't know how to be nice to anyone, not even me. And you trusted me and I didn't know how to trust you back, I didn't know how t—"

"Viola," Jack says.

"I just—"

"A little help, please?" he cuts in bluntly.

I refocus on the game, shaking myself to realize he has the Black Knight in a final, combat-ending blow. The Black Knight should be in pieces by now, but he isn't. Why not?

"Oh." Because one person can't win this quest alone.

I take my sword and slice it through the Black Knight's chest, his lifeline flashing bright like a bolt of lightning before dropping perilously to red.

The view shifts. The fog lifts.

The Black Knight plummets to the ground, bleeding out, and suddenly we're closer to the lake than we imagined, as if this battle was always going to lead us here. The surface of the water parts, and an enchantress comes out of the lake carrying a sword.

Excalibur.

THE ONCE AND FUTURE KING AWAITS YOU, the game screen says.

I exhale. "Is that . . . is this it?"

Jack doesn't say anything, and from the lake, a man in a crown appears.

It's obvious that these are the end titles. This is the animation meant to end the quest and therefore the game, but it's . . . not over. Not yet. Rather than come toward us, King Arthur takes the sword Excalibur from the enchantress and bends over the Black Knight.

He leans down and removes the knight's helmet, and—

I can't help it. I inhale sharply.

IT IS QUEEN GUINEVERE, says the screen.

She is dying, says Arthur to the enchantress. *Help me heal her.*

She betrayed you, says the enchantress. *She deserves her fate.*

She has been cursed. This is not the woman I love.

She betrayed you, the enchantress repeats. *For that she must pay.*

I know this is probably very cheesy, but I for one am riveted. So there's a twist? This whole time the actual twelfth knight wasn't us. It was always Guinevere.

No, says Arthur. *Love and loyalty are what rules this kingdom. If I am to return, I will only do so with her at my side.*

But Your Majesty—

It is not Camelot without her, Arthur says.

He bends his head toward hers. A tear falls from his cheek and into her wounds.

Then, slowly, what remains of the fog is gone.

The island vanishes. The lake disappears. The enchantress fades. The armor of the Black Knight falls away, revealing the truth of the woman beneath, and now we've returned to Camelot, the castle gleaming brightly from the sun shining overhead. The market is filled with colors and noise, and the heraldic Pendragon flag waves once again from the parapets.

King Arthur stands and holds out a hand to a now-conscious Guinevere, which she takes, slowly and with confusion.

It is time to take back Camelot, Arthur says. *Will you stand by me again?*

She stares at him searchingly, in wonder.

I will.

The castle gates burst open, and King Arthur and Queen Guinevere return. The Round Table is filled, one by one, with the knights from every realm of the game.

Then the credits roll, starting with two names.

Narrative Director *Nayeli Brown*
Art Director *Sara Chan*

"They're women," I say aloud, a little flabbergasted. I never thought for even a second that they would be, but of course. I always felt like I especially enjoyed the way the game was designed, the way the story was so cohesive, almost exactly what I would have done if I'd written it—

"I could forgive you if you asked me to," Jack says.

It's so out of the blue that I have no idea what he's talking about. "What?"

"We could fight, you know." He shuts his laptop and looks at me squarely. "We could argue about it. We've got time," he says, gesturing to the gym full of our peers, all of whom prefer him to me except for . . . well, him. "You could tell me I'm being harsh," he says, "and I could tell you I'm really pissed off, and eventually we can acknowledge that we both have a point. And then we can get over it."

It's a lot. It's so much my chest fills up with it.

Hope, that damn deadly thing.

"Wow." I clear my throat, trying to cling to some sense of the familiar. "This game really got to you, huh, Orsino?"

He takes the laptop from my hands.

Closes it. Sets it aside.

"I will forgive you if you ask me to," he says. "I don't need you to say you're sorry. I know you are. What I want to know is if you can ask me to stay instead of letting me leave."

I swallow. "You're way too perceptive for a sportzboi."

"Whereas you're just a marshmallow with spikes."

I look down at my hands. "What if you can't forgive me?"

"You haven't asked."

"Yeah, but what if—?"

"You haven't even tried."

"I just—"

"You lied to me. It sucked." He lifts my chin with one hand. "That's enough to make me pissed at you. Not enough to make me hate you."

I fidget beneath his touch. "I don't want you to hate me."

"Good. That's a good start."

"I want you to like me."

"Like you?"

"Yes." I can feel my cheeks burn. "I want you to . . . want me."

"You need me to need you?" he quotes smirkily.

"Stop." I turn away and he lets me go, but he doesn't let me off the hook.

"Because . . . ?" he prompts.

"Because what?"

"You want me to want you *because* . . . ?"

"Because—"

All right, Mom. Okay, Pastor Ike. Let's try it your way.

"BecauseIwanttobewithyou," I exhale in a burst, looking pitifully up at him.

"What's that?" Jack cups one hand around his ear.

"Because," I mutter, "I want . . . tobewithyou."

He leans in. "Sorry, one more time?"

"I want you, okay?" I burst out in annoyance. "I want you to con-fide in me, I want you to wink at me, I want your dumb smirks and your stupid jokes, I want you to *love me,* and I—"

He cuts me off with a real mindblower of a kiss. Honestly, I hesitate to even call it a kiss, because it's about ten things rolled into one—*you're an idiot* and *oh my god* and also some fireworks, plus the victory of winning a fake quest for fake knights. His teeth bump into mine and I laugh and he grins and kisses me again and his hands are freezing, so I pull them inside of his jacket, winding his arms around my waist.

"I couldn't even hate you enough to let you keep shivering," he admits in my ear.

I groan. "I *told* you you'd be cold—"

"Oh, I'm absolutely freezing," he says in his usual I'm A Beloved Football Star voice.

In response, I hold him tightly, gratefully, and so, so painfully fond that it feels like my poor aching heart is bursting from my chest.

But I give in to it, this feeling, soft as it is. As tender and as terrifying.

"You're a menace, Viola," Jack says, tucking his face into my neck and burying the words there.

"Are we still going to fight about it?"

I'm not really afraid of it, the fight, like I was before. I kind of look forward to it, actually.

"Um, yeah? Definitely." He kisses my cheek, then my lips, then comes back for another tight bear hug. "Just as soon as I get warm."

ENDGAME+

Three days later

Jack

When the *War of Thorns* finale credits roll, Vi lets out a loud groan. "Seriously?"

(Sorry to spoil if you haven't seen it, but FYI: Liliana just died.)

"I don't even know what to do with that," Nick says from my other side.

"I feel . . . bad," I acknowledge aloud, frowning. "Right? Like, I don't . . . I didn't like it."

Vi groans again, louder, and buries her face in my shoulder. I give her a squeeze, but distractedly. "Am I too dumb to get it or something?" I ask her. "Is this, like, art?"

"No," she barks, launching upright. "It's totally fridging!"

"What?"

"Fridging," Antonia repeats from the armchair to our left. "It's when you kill off a female character in order to give a male character motivation."

"I know that I am only seeing this show for the first time and therefore understand nothing," says Bash from the floor, "but I have to say, I do not get the hype."

"It used to be good," Vi says furiously. "Now it's stupid. I mean, why did Liliana have to die? Like, literally, for what?"

"Maybe she's not dead," says Nick optimistically. "In weird magic shows like this—"

"Stop calling them 'weird magic shows' when everyone knows you love them," Antonia cuts in, throwing popcorn at him.

"As I was saying, *in weird magic shows like this,* people are never actually dead," Nick finishes, reaching out to kick his sister's foot. "And shut up."

"No, she's gone," Vi says, scrolling her phone. Her eyes are narrow slits of wrath, which I try not to find completely amusing. "The actress is doing a bunch of interviews about how she's not coming back."

"Have the writers said anything yet?" asks Antonia, leaning over. Vi disentangles from me to show her the screen.

"Not yet. Oh, but here's an interview with Jeremy Xavier—"

"Ugh. He *loves* killing off his women," grumbles Antonia. "Apparently the best kind of woman is one who dies."

"Right?!" Vi gasps.

"I saw Jeremy Xavier from afar once," I offer whimsically, which nobody acknowledges.

"I feel like people keep confusing character death with actual meaning, like it's deep or something," Vi says, still aggressively scrolling her phone. "People are going nuts on Tumblr. Oh wait, some people think it's beautiful. Ugh," she retches, "gross."

"No way." Antonia reaches for the screen and the two of them bend over it like a two-headed pop culture machine. "Seriously? They're calling this 'brave'? '*Subversion*'? They didn't *invent* redemption by death—"

"I feel like people should be more okay with happy endings," I say.

"That," Vi says, ungluing to look at me, "is actually a very controversial take."

"Controversial in that you disagree?" I muse.

"No, I agree profoundly. But it's considered very feminine," she qualifies, making a face. "Like only women want to see happy endings. It's deplorable."

"But just wait," Antonia says conspiratorially. "Tomorrow the fanboys are going to be all over Reddit about how Jeremy Xavier is a *genius* who understands stakes."

"Again, I don't understand why people like this show," comments Bash. "Also, it seems like maybe you two hate it."

"We're a critical audience, Sebastian," says Antonia.

"Yeah," adds Vi, who's scrolling again. "I hope someone posts a fix-it fic, like, immediately."

"You should," I tell her. "The ending you made up yesterday would have been way better."

"What ending?" asks Nick.

"Oh, I was just"—Vi waves a hand—"postulating."

"She said Liliana and Cesario should have to be unwilling enemies," I say, because Vi might choose to make light of it, but I thought she really had a good concept. I would have watched it. "They're natural rivals, right? And Liliana dying for Rodrigo doesn't make sense. Wasn't her whole thing about being duty-bound for her family? And then she just . . . sacrifices herself for some guy?"

"Oh my god, you totally get it," Vi says, gripping my arm with her usual intensity. "That's such a good point. I'm telling the internet you said that."

"Okay," I agree, because I have not worked out the details of stan Twitter, if that's even what she's talking about. "I mean, I am usually very right, so . . ."

"Tell the internet that I am also here," Bash tells Vi, who nudges his face away with her foot.

WORST, MOST PANDERING FINALE EVER! THREAD, 1/??, she types into her phone, her actual expression placid with purpose, and a wave of affection comes over me.

"You're a maniac," I tell her when she gets to her fourth post.

"I'm aware," she replies without looking up.

I tuck an arm around her and kiss her cheek, settling in to watch her type the most blistering, incisive criticism that will ever get written about this show and its themes, which includes a discussion about the role of women and the limited perspectives of imperialist narratives in Eurocentric fantasy worlds. (I told her she should start a blog and she elbowed me and said she already had one, duh, I didn't invent content creation on the internet, which was disappointing news because I 100 percent assumed that I had. Technically my idea was something like ESPN for books, and then she showed me "BookTube.")

"Jeremy Xavier who?" I murmur in her ear. She's on tweet twelve. She won't admit it, but I know she cracks a smile.

Needless to say, our fight after the tournament didn't last long.

Which isn't to say we didn't fight, because we did. I did, after all, feel shocked and betrayed and angry about everything she kept from me, and I told her so, without leaving anything out. But I also told her that being angry didn't mean I didn't care about her, or that I would rather let that anger undo the things between us that I knew were real. "I just want to know who you are," I said. "I just want you to let me see you, good and bad."

"Okay," she said, and even though I know she didn't really believe me, it meant a lot that she was willing to try. "Well, get ready," she said with a grimace, "because it's going to be gross."

I won't lie, it's definitely been weird. She showed me all of her costumes ("cosplay") and sat me down to explain ConQuest ("It's an RPG, basically a forerunner to online ones like *Twelfth Knight*") and told me she'd have a hard time dating someone who hadn't at least *seen* all the Empire Lost films (though I had a valid point about the white storylines). I hung out with Bash (for real) and scrolled through her mom's blog. It was basically boot camp for everything Vi loves, but like I told her, none of it was "gross." It was all new and interesting and proof of what I'd always guessed about her, which is that being something Vi Reyes cares about is worth the effort. When she loves something, she loves deeply, thoughtfully, and generously, and she gives back what she gets, tenfold.

Physical therapy is going well. I go for jogs now, which I enjoy. With football season over, things have settled down at home. My dad even got honored at a banquet for his win at State, which Mom and I attended with my brother Cam, during one of his rare visits home.

My dad likes Vi, for the record. "That's the kind of player who starts," he said when he met her. "She's got vision."

"Please don't try to train her, okay? Vi only likes sports that deal blows." That's a direct quote from her, by the way.

"The girl has perfect calf attachments" was Dad's protest in response, though thankfully he didn't tell her to lace up or anything. He just thought her center of gravity would make her a great sprinter and he told her so, which she seemed to recognize as a good thing coming from him.

As for my mom, she was won over when I told her that partially thanks to Vi, I was thinking about taking an intro to computer science class next fall at Illyria. "To see if I like it," I said quickly, because she was doing the thing where she looked a little too excited for what I was telling her. I think it was always difficult for my mom, both her sons having something in common with Dad and not with her. In that sense, I think she's a little relieved about Vi giving me other things in life to look forward to, which is something I often feel myself. (Though don't tell Vi she's motivating my storyline or who knows what kind of media commentary might come out of it.)

Olivia's been held equally captive since becoming Bash's protégée. You'd think it'd be awkward running into my ex-girlfriend unexpectedly while I'm sitting on the couch with my new one, but Olivia and Bash are too busy with their preparations for the spring musical to stop and chat for long. I'm happy for Olivia—it's clear she's found something worth her energy, for which her former hobby of being supportive in our relationship was a very poor use of her time. She'll make a much better Hodel, not that I know who that is.

"Wait, you don't know who Hodel is? Oh my god, Jack. We're watching it. It's like three hours long but it's worth it, I promise," says Vi.

(Which is how I got roped into watching *Fiddler on the Roof.*)

It's funny to think this year started with what felt like huge ambitions: perfect girlfriend, perfect season, school record, immortality and fame. Illyria, too, not for what it was, but for what it represented. I think there's an argument to be made that my contentedness is a small thing by comparison; that instead of waking up for a grueling practice I'm going to stretch carefully and run slowly, or that I've been sifting through the Illyria catalog to see what electives I might want to consider (a far cry from the "see it, make it happen" drive my father instilled in me). Taken in those terms, it might seem like I've accomplished less than I planned.

But because of this year, the world got bigger. The universe expanded for me. I can see beyond football practice, beyond the need to be faster and stronger, beyond running just to prove that I can. For the first time, I am realizing how vast my edges are, how many things I have yet to experience. It's a discovery that makes me feel brave.

So brave, in fact, that I happened to find a *Twelfth Knight* club on Illyria's campus and reached out to see what exactly that entails. Because I kind of have to know, right? Plus it turns out that one of the game designers is an alum who lectures sometimes on campus, so—

"You ready?"

Vi looks up at me with all sorts of hope. It's a different version of her, the kind who wants to share things with me, who's ready to be seen for everything she is. It's a private version of her, and as grateful as I am that she's as tough as she is, this is a rare glimpse of Vi Reyes that I feel lucky to be allowed to experience from time to time.

"You realize we're going to watch the whole NCAA playoffs, right?" I ask. "Only fair."

"Yes, and I'm totally counting the days," she replies.

"No you're not."

"No," she agrees, "I'm not."

"You'll like it."

"Will I?"

"Come on, you love a little barbarity."

"Yes, but when it's just about carrying around a *toy*—"

She makes a face when I kiss her, but melts.

"Okay," she says, eyes still closed.

"Okay what?"

"Okay, football is very important to me."

"I didn't ask you to go that far, but thank you for referring to it by its proper name."

"It's not rocket science, Orsino."

"Viola," I warn.

"Yes, Your Grace?" she says drily, and only protests a little when I kiss her again.

Vi

The energy in the room tonight is stiff, but not with tension. It's the buzz of excitement before battle, a vibration of camaraderie and nerves that binds us all together. (It's also hunger, because Lola is in the kitchen frying lumpia and we've been able to smell it for the past half hour, which is driving all of us to various acts of desperation.)

"Okay, so," says Olivia, who has taken detailed notes on her character the same way she broke down our *Romeo and Juliet* scene. "Do we get, like, character intros?"

Everyone turns to me, including Antonia. "Um, hello? You know how this works," I remind her.

"Not since you've been QuestMaster." She smiles at me. (We're doing better. Yesterday she came by spontaneously, like she used to, and ended up staying for dinner.)

"Well, it's *our* game, not just mine," I remind her.

"I helped write it," Bash contributes.

"We know," everyone reminds him in unison.

On my right, Nick and Jack exchange a glance of *What did we get ourselves into?*

"Hey," I remind them. "You volunteered."

Olivia's friend Marta, the wild card of the group in that she's also a popular, homecoming court–caliber cheerleader but has apparently been in a ConQuest league with her former Girl Scout troop for the last four years, reaches for Olivia's character sheet. "I think we should do intros."

"But what if we have no showmanship?" Nick says.

"Then you lose," trumpets Bash.

"You don't have to," I tell Nick.

"No, I want to," he assures me. "I was referring to Orsino."

"Excuse me? I'm, like, a hundred percent showmanship," says Jack, which is true.

"Bash can do mine," says Mark Curio, handing his page to my brother.

"Oh, *with pleasure*," says Bash, reaching for it until Olivia swats him down.

"I think we should definitely do our own," she scolds him. "You know, in order to really *inhabit* the characters, right? It would be the best way to feel like we're all fully taking part."

"That's a good point," I say. "So, shall we? Olivia, you can start."

Olivia's character is the same one we designed together a couple of months ago: the former princess with skills in hand-to-hand combat. Bash's character is a smuggler ("And a rake," he announces louchely) who speaks several languages and is a gifted thief. Antonia and Marta are their usual OCs: the healer Larissa Highbrow and a half-elf witch, respectively (this is very cool, as it means Marta can manipulate time; very handy). Jack is, of course, a Robin Hood–type nobleman ("duke of skullduggery," as he puts it), Nick is a seasoned warrior, and Curio, surprisingly, decides to be an astronomer. (We ask why and he says he just likes stars, and anyway, isn't that useful for navigating? Which is a valid point.)

I'm QuestMaster, though if I weren't, I'd probably be debuting a new character for this game. Maybe a lone-wolf type who chooses to disguise herself as a man (or a crone) for safety, only to learn that she can do a lot more when she reveals who she is.

Tactically, of course. Within reason. Not every space is safe.

But some definitely are.

I gather my notes, some of which are peppered with Bash's annotations, and begin reading the opening monologue for the game he and I wrote over the summer.

"Among the capitalist ports of Karagatan d'Oro is a thriving black market for exotic goods," I begin. "Under the corrupt rule of the Shadow King, cargo ships dock each day filled with hundreds of thousands of priceless trinkets. The port is infamous for its security, yet each year there are certain invaluable items that never reach their destination."

"Who wants lumpia?" yells Lola.

"Shhh," Bash calls back to her, but then rethinks it. "Actually, I'll get it."

"Keep going," Jack urges me, nudging my hand. (And he claims he's not a geek.)

"Rumor has it that the Night Market of the Sea of Gold is an actual place," I continue. "Located somewhere within the Shadow King's city, it can only be reached by someone who knows how. Almost everyone has an item, a lost thing, that can be found in the Night Market, but just to find it is so dangerous that most people either disappear forever or turn up months, years later, raving nonsensically about the atrocities they've survived."

"Does anyone else have shivers?" Marta whispers. Olivia shushes her.

"Each of you has something you need to find within the Market," I tell them. "You hold that secret close." As the game goes on, some will reveal it to each other in order to gain their trust or form an alliance. Some will probably lie, though that will be dependent on their character's skills, weaknesses, and motivations. (Bash and I agreed that human nature makes for the best kind of mystery.) "First, though, you need to find a way in."

"We have to find one of the survivors," Curio says immediately, and with that, the discourse begins.

"What if they lie?"

"That's our job to figure out, isn't it?"

"How are we going to find one?"

"It's a *port*, someone has to have connections—"

"We can do it, we're the criminals—"

"We need someone to bribe the guards!"

I can't help but sit back and smile for a moment. I always hoped the game would be played this way: collaboratively, among people who actually listen to each other, and who are busy trying to solve a puzzle instead of just mindlessly fight. But it's more than that, I think. It's the satisfaction of creating a world that other people want to exist in. It's the . . . togetherness of it all.

My mom's advice column had an interesting subject last week.

The question was from someone very focused and ambitious who admitted that relationships, or even *wanting* a relationship, often felt like a waste of time.

My mom asked me what I thought before she wrote up her answer. "It just seems like your area," she said.

"Why," I sighed, "because I'm so cold and devoid of human connection?"

"No, hija, the opposite." She laughed at me. "You don't really think that about yourself, do you?"

"You're the one who said I had to be more open to things," I reminded her.

"Open, yes. I never said you were cold."

"But it's hard to be open," I admitted. "Once you open the door, you have no idea what's getting in."

"So then is it worth it?"

I thought about it. "Probably not all the time."

She laughed again. "Is that your final answer?"

"No." I drummed my fingers on the desk before asking her something hard. "Do you think I'm too sensitive?"

She arched a brow. "Do you think that?"

I hated to admit it, but I was trying to be honest. (For research purposes.) "Maybe."

"Is that bad?"

"Sometimes. Means my protective shell is a lot tougher."

"Harder to get through?" she guessed.

"Yeah."

She didn't say anything, so I added, "I think it's lonely."

"What is?"

"Life."

"You're lonely?"

"No, I think *we're* lonely. Like, as a species."

"So what does that mean?"

"That we can like who we are and like being alone and still want to feel connected."

"So what would you respond, then? If you were me?"

Mom pointed to her empty document.

A lot of things came to my head; Jack, of course. Antonia, Olivia. King Arthur. The two game developers I put up on my wall. Pastor Ike, who didn't *change* my mother's voice, but nourished it. Helped it grow.

"I think the best thing we can do in this life is take care of each other," I said. "Which doesn't have to mean marriage or babies," I added quickly. "I just think maybe happiness isn't crossing a finish line, or finally meeting the right person or getting the right job or finding the right life. It's the little things." Like finally seeing your contributions valued at a tabletop game of ConQuest. "It's the thing that happens to you while you're wide awake and dreaming."

She printed it, word for word.

"Viola," says Jack, nudging me. "You with us?"

I blink, realizing they're waiting on me to determine their next move. For the first time, I'm content to discover what it will be without controlling the outcome.

It makes perfect sense just then, that little lightning bolt of understanding that I can spot in moments of clarity. It's not just about the endgame, you know what I mean?

The game isn't the dice. It's who's with you at the table.

"All right," I say with satisfaction, picking one up to give it a roll. Let the adventure begin.

CREDITS

The book you've just read would not have been possible without the effort and expertise devoted by every member of my unparalleled publishing teams. I am honored to have worked with each one of them, and they all deserve proper recognition for the time and talent they brought to this book.

Executive Editor Lindsey Hall
Assistant Editor Aislyn Fredsall
Agent Amelia Appel
President and Publisher Devi Pillai
Senior Vice President, Associate Publisher Lucille Rettino
Editorial Director Claire Eddy
Editorial Director Will Hinton
Publicity Manager Desirae Friesen
Senior Publicity Manager Saraciea J. Fennell
Vice President, Executive Director of Publicity Sarah Reidy
Assistant Marketing Director Isa Caban
Senior Associate Director of Marketing Anthony Parisi
Vice President, Executive Director of Marketing Eileen Lawrence
Ad/Promo Senior Designer Amy Sefton
Cover Illustrator Jacquelyn Li
End Page Illustrator Little Chmura
Associate Art Director Lesley Worrell
Interior Designer Heather Saunders
Senior Managing Editor Rafal Gibek
Production Manager Jim Kapp
Sensitivity Reader Basil Wright
Associate Director of Publishing Operations Michelle Foytek
Publishing Operations Assistant Erin Robinson

Associate Director of Publishing Strategy   Alex Cameron
Publishing Strategy Coordinator   Rebecca Naimon
Publishing Strategy Assistant   Lizzy Hosty
Assistant Director, Subsidiary Rights   Chris Scheina
Senior Director, Trade Sales   Christine Jaeger
Senior Producer, Macmillan Audio   Steve Wagner
Senior Publicity Manager, Macmillan Audio   Drew Kilman
Voice Talent   Alexandra Palting and Kevin R. Free
Associate Marketing Manager, Macmillan Audio   Claire Beyette

Macmillan Children's

Publishing Director   Emma Jones
Editor   Charlie Castelletti
Publisher   Samantha Smith
Desk Editor   Amy Boxshall
Senior Production Controller   Farzana Adlington
Marketing Manager   Cheyney Smith
Senior Publicity Manager   Louisa Sheridan
Senior Press Officer   Bethan Thoma
Video Marketing Manager   Emma Oulton
Content Marketing Executive   Carol-Anne Royer
Art Director   Rachel Vale
Sales Director   Sarah Ramsey
International Sales Director   Rachel Graves

ACKNOWLEDGMENTS

Reader, you hold in your hands my combination Pregnancy-Pandemic Novel™, which I wrote a few months before my other books (namely *The Atlas Six*, written under my adult pseudonym, Olivie Blake) went viral and my son was born. In these pages lives my anxiety from the long months of fear and isolation, the physical pain of two trimesters with debilitating sciatica and carpal tunnel (and a frankly ungodly consumption of potatoes), and the small, sustaining glimpses of optimism I clung to whilst healing my inner child, reliving the nostalgic camp of early 2000s high school Shakespeare retellings, and paying homage to the fandom communities that gave me my creative start. Writing this book was like passing a kidney stone. As the poet James Acaster once said: started making it, had a breakdown. Bon appétit!

Huge amounts of gratitude to my agent, Amelia Appel, who was such a champion for this story during its somewhat arduous search for a home, and to my editorial team at Tor Teen and Macmillan Children's, Lindsey Hall and Aislyn Fredsall in the US and Emma Jones and Charlie Castelletti in the UK, who cared so unfailingly about the impetus of a story that often defied marketable narrative structures. When I told them (lightly paraphrased), "Okay, so I know that romance novels are supposed to have defined action beats and I'm taking too long with each character, it's just that this story is *really* about anger and who is allowed to feel it, so ultimately the romance is the cherry on top of two characters' coming of age rather than being, you know, The Whole Point—hahaha that's fine, right?" Lindsey, Emma, Aislyn, and Charlie were not only amenable, they were compassionately supportive. I could not have asked for a better team.

Long before I was lucky enough to be embraced by the communities of BookTwt, Bookstagram, and BookTok, there was Tumblr, FFN, and AO3. The communities of fandom offered me so much, from close friendship to creative support to genuine connection. I was a fan fiction writer before I was any sort of conventional novelist, and I will eternally credit fanfic with my understanding of character work and emotional arcs. Aside from my gratitude to the medium itself, I am also undyingly thankful to the women who have read my work so enthusiastically over the years, many of whom also contributed to this book's research—in this case, anecdotes about gendered behaviors in gaming and RPGs (some of the microaggressions Vi faces are way too real!).

And, of course, I cannot understate the significance of fandom bringing me Little Chmura, my artistic collaborator and friend. Chmura, thank you always for your presence (and your beautiful end pages), without which I sincerely do not think I would be sitting here saying any of this.

While I am on the subject of art, thank you to my cover illustrator, the spectacular Jacqueline Li, and cover designer Lesley Worrell. Make some noise for the blade to the throat! What a perfect cover.

I had a few different muses and consultants for this book. Thank you to Dillon Follmuth for your expertise regarding Jack's physical therapy regimen. (The injury itself was actually based on my husband's tenure as an All-State running back, but in Mr. Nine Knee Surgeries' case, not much happened in the realm of actual healing.) Thank you to Krishna and James Farol-Schenck for keeping me as accurate as possible in my made-up versions of DnD and MMORPGs. Thank you to Zac Drake for the finer programming details when it came to gaming. Thank you to my sisters, Kayla Barnett and Mackenzie Nelson (lol, I love you both), and to Marta Miguelena, for the use of their names in what is very much, I promise, total fiction.

Thank you to David Howard, my very best friend. While David and I have always been completely platonic, many of the moments Jack and Vi share in this book are based on conversations David and I had while attending our (then) very white, upper-middle-class high school. I often riff on my memories of David in fiction, but this particular set of character qualities was definitely an homage to one of the kindest men I've ever known. David, much of what I know about love comes from loving and being loved by you. I'm so grateful I get to be alive at the same time as you, and I'm honored to be of your species.

Everything else I know about love comes from Garrett, my eternal muse. I won't make too much of a fuss—you've heard it all before and you'll hear it again (threat!). Thank you to my family; to my mom; to everyone in my life who is so unendingly supportive. Thank you to Stacie, this book's first reader and most ardent supporter. One of the very finest things I ever got from fandom was the honor of calling you my friend. Thank you to my ever-supportive friends Angela, Nacho and Ana, Lauren Schrey, Lauren Myerscough-Mueller, and the wee babes I hope will get some use out of this story someday—Theo, Eli, Harry, Miles, Eve, and Andi. Thank you to talented authors Arya Shahi, an early reader, and Tracy Deonn, friends who generally help keep me sane (or whatever). Thank you to Henry, my squishiest boy, the light of my life. Doing my best to write down everything I know about life for you. (The secret is Mommy's making it up as she goes!)

And finally, to you, Reader, for being here. If you're the kind of person who feels angry all the time but you don't feel like you're allowed to be, I see you. If all the wrongs committed against you are too small and too infinite to be properly put into words, I believe you. Be kind to yourself, be good to your mind, be gentle with your heart. As always, it's an honor to put down these words for you, and I hope you've enjoyed the story.

xx Alexene

ABOUT THE AUTHOR

Aᴸᴇxᴇɴᴇ Fᴀʀᴏʟ Fᴏʟʟᴍᴜᴛʜ is the author of the young adult rom-coms *My Mechanical Romance* and *Twelfth Knight.* As Olivie Blake, she is the *New York Times* bestselling author of *The Atlas Six, Alone with You in the Ether, One for My Enemy,* and *Masters of Death.* She lives in Los Angeles with her husband, goblin prince / toddler, and rescue pit bull.